Some Slack

PETER WINDRIDGE-SMITH

(& Tina J)

Published 2019 by pdsIdeas

ISBN: 978-0-9928881-2-1

http://peterwindridgesmith.net

CHAPTER 1

A fickle breeze stirs the acacias at the edge of the firelight, except... there is no breeze. The stillness of the desert air is unchanged. But there, again, the sound of leaf against twig rises above the cricket filled background.

"What's that noise?"

Our guide's leathery face splits into a grin. "That, Holly, is a little friend. You all come stand behind the Land Rover."

As we rise from our deckchairs, a shape looms in the darkness. All breaths are held as our visitor silently navigates a tent, approaches the stand-pipe, and explores with its trunk.

"He hopes we have left it running." Hearing the whisper, the elephant rocks its head from side to side and takes a step forward. I lean towards a warm male shoulder. For a moment animal and humans stare across the automotive barrier. There's a visible decision and with a cursory double check of the tap, he moves off in search of alternative watering holes. We exhale. My eyes flick towards the shoulder and follow upwards to sun streaked hair glittering in the flame light. My cheeks flush as I realise it's Will I've snuggled up to.

"Scary and cool – simultaneously," he says, nudging me away, seemingly without embarrassment.

"Amazing how quietly they move. If he'd not scraped the bushes he could've been on top of us before we noticed," says Anna, locking her fingers into Will's right hand.

"Their feet are wide, soft they place them." Moses' occasional slips into a Yoda-like word order hint at a greater comfort with the German language. That, and his unsettling ability to turn the steering wheel with his knees whilst holding binoculars to his eyes, has led to Ben christening our guide 'The Jedi'.

"Hey guys, come and look at this." Ben is shining his torch at the sand beside our tent. "He stepped right over the corner." Impressions like misshapen dinner plates lie either side of the canvas.

"Imagine if you'd been inside," says Anna. I shudder at the thought of being trampled in my sleeping bag.

"No danger. Elephant thinks tent is big rock. Solid. Always they go round." Moses is a calming influence as ever. 'Africa is quiet, Africa is safe,' is his constant refrain. 'You watch out when you go home, cross those busy roads.' He probably has a point.

"Did you bring the camera, Holls?" Dur Ben... My hands are empty, this shirt has no pockets and where would I fit a camera in a pair of leggings? Actually see when you look at me.

I answer, "It's still in the Land Rover. Don't worry, I'll fetch it. My phone's in there too." Even before I open the door a familiar trill vies with the insect chorus. The curse of this private reserve is all the mod cons, including a whopping great phone mast. I sigh at the caller ID. Who else?

"Hello David."

"Holly, darling, how is darkest Africa?"

"Beautiful, stark, peaceful. Most of the time..."

"Wonderful. And great for the inspiration, I hope? Just a mo..." The muffled hubbub of some Kensington wine bar seeps between David's fingers. I hand the camera to Ben, who has appeared at my side.

'David,' I mouth. He rolls his eyes and retreats.

"Holly, are you still there?"

"Yes, but..."

"Darling, I've been speaking to Rory at the label and, quite frankly, they're getting twitchy. They love what you do, but it's been two years. They need to hear some new material."

"So you keep saying. It's not like I've been sitting around since the album. I've done endless promo and the tour..."

"I know you have, sweetie, I know you have, but..." He doesn't need to say it. Nothing has quite lived up to the buzz of the first single. "Holly, darling, there must be something you're working on that you could fizz over before Friday? Rough as you like. Just to keep them off our backs for a while, hey?"

"David, we have a special self-drive trip arranged for tomorrow..." This is meant to be some slack time – to relax and recharge my creative batteries, not...

"Just a little snippet, give them a hint of the direction you're taking, that sort of thing. I'm loving the new one by that American country girl, aren't you? Anyway, must fly. I'll be watching my inbox. Ciao."

"Da..." I start, but he's already rung off.

The moon hasn't yet risen and the ghost trail of the Milky Way is obvious amongst the blazing southern stars. It ought to be inspiring. I stand, face raised, trying to channel the awe, but nothing comes. Have I lost it?

"What did he want?" says Ben, as I rejoin the heat and incense of the camp-fire worshippers.

"I think he wants me to be Taylor Swift."

"I wish," says Ben in his teasing voice.

"Well, I'm afraid you'll have to put up with your ancient..." I plonk myself down on his knee, provoking an unsettlingly loud creak from the folding chair beneath, "... and seemingly over-weight wife."

"Over-weight, my foot. These chairs aren't made for two."

"But 'ancient' fits better does it?"

"Careful, Ben," laughs Anna, her perfect teeth reflecting a surprising tangerine from the ember glow.

"If twenty-seven is ancient, I must be in my dotage and you're killing this old man's legs," says Ben, boosting me into a standing position.

I decide to break the news whilst he's still on the back foot. "David wants me to send him some new material before Friday."

"But Holls, that only leaves tomorrow."

"I know."

"Won't it wait? This outing is all lined up."

"There's a big strategy meeting at the label. I think he's trying to make sure I'm part of it."

"And David Henry always knows best... The man is a total pain in the arse." He pauses, waiting for my usual defence of David, but I'm not going to give him the satisfaction. "So you're going to spend all tomorrow back at the lodge playing with your laptop?"

"I'm sorry, but I think I have to," I say, flopping into the empty chair.

"For fuck's sake, Holls."

Moses appears from his tent and discreetly adds wood to the fire. He will have heard every word, but makes no comment. The new log nestles amongst the glowing remnants of its forebears. For a couple of minutes it seems unaffected. Then, with a low sigh, flames begin their caress of destruction...

In the dim alley light at the rear of an en vogue London address, Rory proffers a lighter. Stella leans forward, hand still gripping the fire escape door. "David talks her up but I'm beginning to wonder if Holly has lost her desire. You know how it is sometimes."

Stella nods, taking a long slow drag, "The big dream is to 'ave a top ten and once that 'appens it's never quite the same."

"I'm going to need serious convincing before I throw any more money her way."

"She'd better produce the goods on Friday, then..." Stella blows a stinging cloud into the dank air...

The log splits, gushing a small plume in my direction. An upward blow and furious blinking clears smoke from both my real and mind's eyes. What if Rory really is ready to drop me? I glance towards Anna who brushes a couple of stray ringlets from her face and smiles... awkwardly. It's not fair on them either.

"You three go without me. I'm not that bothered if I miss Anna's special rock-hopper thing."

"Damara Rockjumper," says Anna. "Moses says there's a chance of Herero Chat at the riverbed as well... Sorry, I'm sounding like a twitcher. It's just, you can't see them anywhere else except in the Namib... They are quite pretty..."

"...for small brown birds," Will adds. Anna sticks out her tongue.

"You'll miss out on the deep sand driving." This is what Ben has been looking forward to.

"I'm sure I'll survive."

Ben smiles an apology and squeezes my left knee. "Couldn't we re-schedule the drive, Moses?" he asks.

His expression is pained. "I am sorry Ben. I need the Land Rovers for a trip after tomorrow. There is no guest insurance on the Jeeps and..." The unswerving adherence to 'the rules' of Mr Kaura, the Game Reserve owner, goes unspoken.

"You guys go. Really... My work is my problem."

A distant, rhythmic groaning stills our conversation. Moses cups his hands to his ears, searching for the exact direction. "George the Third. A low roar, he has." Every pride alpha male has been named after a different king and Moses seems to know them like old friends. Even though I've experienced this several times already, the feral power of the sound – quite different from the silly snarl you hear in films – causes my arms to prickle with goose bumps.

By the time George has finished asserting his territorial rights, Ben seems in a more reconciliatory mood: "Holls, do you have an idea for a song?"

"Not really, I'm just going to shake a few chords around and hopefully something will fall out. Maybe about here: the desert, the wildlife?"

"What about 'Der-dup'? You haven't played that for years."

I screw up my nose. "It's pretty immature."

"You did say David was asking for girly pop."

"Maybe..." I don't like the idea one bit, but it's not worth arguing.

"What's 'Der-dup'?" asks Will. "I don't remember that one."

"I wrote it years ago. I never recorded it. It's actually called 'Only Ever You' but the nickname stuck... Thanks, darling."

"Glad to be of assistance, sweetie," says Ben.

AN HOUR LATER, Ben is keen to be of assistance once more. We're standing at the centre of domed canvass, Ben with one finger to his lips. Anna's stifled giggles and gasps are clearly audible from the other tent. As gasp turns to moan Ben rolls his eyes, slings his torch onto the bed-roll and pulls me towards him. It feels a bit false, doing it because they're doing it, but his expression is so eager as he reaches upwards for my lips. At one point, we pause whilst Anna lets out a scream that rises well above our own heavy breathing. "Does the woman have no shame?" Ben whispers, nibbling my ear.

"Apparently not," I answer, but afterwards, as we lie spooning in the sleeping bag, I can't help but wonder. It was nice. It's always nice with Ben... but I wasn't screaming like I didn't care if I woke the whole of Africa. What does Will do to her?

George the Third or one of his fellow monarchs begins to roar once more. "Oh, shut up," I murmur.

Ben kisses my shoulder. "You tell him Holls."

CHAPTER 2

I feel about as inspired as a Bruce Forsyth joke. We were back at the lodge for seven and I've been cooped up in the 'guest office' for more than two hours. They're probably all lazing on some dune in the sunshine by now. David-pain-in-the-arse-Henry, you always have to spoil things, don't you? I slip the guitar off my lap. Coffee: it's the only answer.

"Go sit by the pool Miss Woodlove. Moses will bring your drink." I retreat from the lodge kitchen and stroll round to the north side of the building. Two glossy starlings are searching the verdant lawn for insects attracted by the un-naturally high water levels. Beyond its edge the landscape reverts to natural grey-brown.

"Everything's prettier here, isn't it?" A familiar voice emanates from a shaded deckchair. "Even the starlings are bright green."

"Will? I thought you'd all left ages ago?"

He grins sheepishly, "The other two have gone, but… mm… let's just say I'm sitting within twenty yards of the nearest toilet."

"Oh nuts. I thought you were the one with the cast iron stomach?"

"Something got me in the end. Anyway, I'm fully Imodiumed up and it's been half an hour… But I'm sure you don't want to hear about that. How's the song writing?"

"I've come out for a coffee break."

"That bad?"

"Yup." I pull a second deckchair closer, keeping mine clear of the shade and settle into closed eye sun worship.

"Huh-hum, your coffee." Moses has approached with his usual soundlessness. He smiles at my startled expression.

"Thanks," I say, noting one of my favourite biscuits tucked onto the saucer. "So, you let our partners go off on their own..."

"Do not worry. The track is not difficult and if stuck they become they can phone and I will take the bakkie and pull out. Enjoy." He begins to back away.

"Moses," says Will, "Are there any other Land Rovers free this afternoon? If Holly happens to finish early and my stomach behaves could we drive out to meet them?" Moses purses his lips. It's probably inconvenient but he's not about to admit that to a guest. "Not to worry if it messes with your plans," adds Will.

"You could have number three, but I have to refuel and pack for the morning. Back by five…" he raises his eyebrows, "and in the sand Holly drives?" Moses is referring to our relative success levels in his deep sand driving training.

"Always prefer to be chauffeured anyway," shrugs Will as Moses retreats up the lawn. It never ceases to amaze me how such a big, manly bloke like Will can be so laid back. Ben's male ego has been prickling ever since Moses said I was a natural at the smooth throttle control needed for the sand. "Sorry," says Will, "I didn't ask if you were up for it, I just had a sudden thought while Moses was here."

"It is a good idea… I'm just not sure I'm going to be finished any time soon. I've found a couple of chords but I can't seem to hang anything on them."

"No luck with 'Only Ever You' then?"

I screw up my nose. "I know Ben was trying to help, but…"

"But you don't want to try it because he suggested it?"

"No, I…" My hackles start to rise, but Will is raising and lowering his eyebrows above a cheeky grin. The effect is quite disarming. "Well, maybe there is a bit of that…" I concede.

"Is this old song any good?"

"Ben used to say it was one of my best."

"But you don't like it because…"

"…Because it's 'poppy' and the lyrics are cheesy girls' stuff and I was hoping to move in a more serious direction."

Will is silent for a moment. In the distance a pair of boubous duet their 'qui-quip-chiri's. "But just now, to get round this problem, that's actually what your manager wants?"

"Perhaps…"

"Holly, don't you think one of the signs of a talented musician is that they can pull off a great song in any style?" He winks at me. "Even girly pop?"

"I'd forgotten how direct you can be," I say, smiling at my own stubbornness.

"Anna's always complaining I ask questions like an eight year old." He shrugs, pouts and for a moment that's exactly what he does look like – except a six foot five, broad shouldered, rather handsome eight year old.

"Alright, I'll have a crack at the dreaded 'Der-dup song'." I push myself out of the chair and reach for my untouched coffee.

"Can I help or even just watch?" asks Will, still wearing the eight year old's face.

"Actually, it is quite handy to have someone else press the start and stop buttons," I flash him a full toothed smile, "and there's a loo in the reception building… should you need it."

"YOU HAVE TO IMAGINE you're a waitress."

"Okay..." says Will. "How short is my skirt?"

"Will, you're supposed to be helping," I snigger. "Okay, I'll rephrase that. Imagine the video for this song. A girl is waiting on tables and her dream guy is a regular customer... except he's always there with other dates. The waitress is wishing she could be one of those girls."

"Sounds like she needs to get out more."

"I told you: it's girly pop… I'm ready."

"Okay, 'Only Ever You' – take one – Mrs Woodlove has the mic." Will clicks record before I have a chance to reply verbally. Strangely, the preparation for my first chord position seems to involve flexing the middle finger of my left hand.

Only Ever You (The Der-Dup song)

You're always here with different dates,
As I am handing out the plates,
I watch you. (watch you)
When you return my menu smile,

my heart does somersaults a while.
It's madness. (madness)

And my heart goes: der-dup, der-dup, der-d-der-der...

But I don't know how... I don't know how to start this, oh no
I don't know how... I just don't know how...

I pass the sauce, our fingers touch.
It maybe shouldn't mean that much:
it's magic. (magic)
I ask you if the meal's okay.
It doesn't matter what you say.
I'm melting. (melting)

And my heart goes: der-dup...

One day, I will sit there facing you.
We'll be deciding if we're one or if we're two.
And I already know what you're gonna say,
cos I've seen it before like the scenes of a play,
and I'll know how to make it turn out the right way...

...but for now I don't know how...
I don't know how to start this, oh no
I don't know how... and I don't know when or what to do
But I know it's only ever you...

But now I feel a little chill:
your date is asking for the bill.
Don't leave me. (don't leave me)
But then like breaking of the dawn
I see you stifling a yawn
's not gone well (oh dear!)

And my heart goes: der-dup...
It's only ever you...

The final chord rings out and as it fades to silence I nod and Will clicks stop.

"When I first wrote it, I imagined that at the end of the video, the waitress would hand the guy a paper napkin. Her phone number's written on it with 'Better luck next time, call me'."

Will's face is lit by a broad smile. He glances round the 'guest office' I've commandeered as a makeshift recording studio and then refocuses on me.

"What?" I ask. "You look like you woke up thinking it was Friday but just realised it's actually the weekend."

"I was counting myself lucky to be on the end of a personal live performance from the amazing Holly Woodlove."

"Yeah, alright." I can feel a little heat coming into my cheeks. "What did you really think? It's even more 'poppy' than 'Fusion', isn't it?"

"I loved it. It's fun and catchy." His enthusiasm is so genuine – maybe I have misjudged this song.

"You don't think I'll get typecast as fluffy?"

"Typecast? No, I mean, this one is obviously aimed at – how would they say – 'the young female market' whereas 'Fusion' was the..." He breaks off like a teenager who's just managed to avoid swearing in front of his parents.

"...Geek's Anthem?" I finish, raising my eyebrows like a school teacher.

"Er, yeah," says Will with a sheepish grin. "I suppose you know they call it that?"

"Of course. Is it even an insult these days?" It does still rankle a little, but I never let it show.

"Anyway," says Will quickly, "I'll be Der-dupping all day now, I bet." He glances towards the laptop. "Is that it then?"

I can't help but snigger at his musical naivety. "No. Now I need to redo it about half a dozen times. Then we'll sit down and pick the best bits from the takes, stitch them together, I'll add a second guitar part, and then we'll mix it. After that we can think about pressing send to Mr Henry and getting out of here."

"And how long will that take?"

"A couple of hours, if we're lucky."

"Right then – take two."

CHAPTER 3

It's almost 1pm by the time Moses holds open the gate and our Defender turns onto the gravel road. It may be 'winter' here but the unremitting glare of the early afternoon sun forces our windows closed and air-conditioning on high. The track meanders beside bleached grasses and stunted thorns, making for a gap in the low rocky ridge which marks the start of the descent down the dry river. We pause to watch a line of Gemsbok trudging round one of the outlying kopjes.

"I think they're my favourite antelope," says Will shifting into neutral and reaching for his camera. He winds down the window and clicks off a few shots.

"I know what you mean. It's like someone's painted black and white highlights all round their edges. That second one's horns are ever so long."

"Moses was saying that means it's a female," says Will, not taking his eye from the viewfinder.

"Really? You'd expect it to be the other way round."

"Supposedly, shorter, thicker horns are better for fighting."

"Everything always seems to come down to males fighting."

"That's evolution for you… or politics as we call it these days."

I catch his eye as he smiles at his own joke and notice his forehead has started to glisten. "Come on, shut the window and let's get going. This air con is trying to cool Africa and Africa's winning."

WE REACH THE END of the simple driving where the rock and gravel river bed levels out and widens. The ground ahead is deeply rutted from previous vehicles ploughing through deep sand. "Here's where you take over, Holly. I'll get the tyres."

Whilst Will goes round with the deflators, I shuffle across to the driver's side and push the small lever to select low ratio. I'm pondering which set of ruts are best to follow when Will climbs back in. "There you are, one set of soft and spongies ready to go."

"Fifteen PSI?" I query.

"Just like the man said."

I turn the key, push the main stick and lift the clutch. The Land Rover moves smoothly forward and I concentrate on entering my chosen track. After that it's pretty easy: let the ruts steer you, don't fight them, keep the speed steady. I don't really know what all the fuss is about.

After a couple of miles I begin to notice a tune only slightly louder than the engine, emanating from my left. Will is Der-dupping just like he predicted. A smile born of artistic pride surfaces but I cover it by asking, "What is that awful thing you're humming?"

"Some girly pop rubbish… Over there." He points towards an area of gently sloping rock which rises out of the sand like a car ferry ramp from the sea. "Isn't that where Moses told them to park?"

"You're the one with the map."

"It looks like it, but…" He shrugs the 'where are they?' question.

"Well, these ruts are taking us straight there so we may as well follow them."

Once on solid ground, we stop and climb out. There's not a breath of wind, it's oven hot and the only sounds are pings and clicks from even hotter metal cooling under the bonnet. Across fifty yards of sand, the whole rocky slope of the escarpment seems to squirm in the haze.

"They probably went to find some shade," says Will flapping the front of his T-shirt. "Or maybe they didn't find the Rockjumper and went to look somewhere else."

"Did Moses tell them about anywhere else?" I ask.

"Not that I heard."

"Surely he'd have said… This is typical Ben. Normally he's about as spontaneous as a Belisha beacon, but away from me for half a day and he decides to go off on a wilderness adventure."

"With Anna…" adds Will. He leans against the car with a shrug. "I'll give 'em a ring." I nod, trying not to feel foolish that I hadn't thought to do the obvious before starting my rant. "Anna's is either off or they've no signal. You try."

I reach into the Land Rover and pull the phone from my bag. It springs to life making me physically jump. I answer Will's inquiring, amused eyes with a shake of the head. It's not Ben, it's the other man in my life.

"David...?" I barely disguise a sigh.

"Holly, darling, is there something in the water out there?"

"Come again?"

"What's behind it? What made you think of it?"

"Think of what?"

"Your new track, sweetie."

"You like it then?" I start to pace along the rock.

"Like it? I'm der-dup loving it, darling. It's fresh without being too… And it's so you. I've already fizzed it over to Rory."

"I thought the meeting was tomorrow?"

"It is, but no harm in a petit preview. I'm sure he'll be over the moon."

"Great. David, I'm sort of in the middle of something…"

"Of course, I wouldn't want to dampen the inspiration, freeze the artistic blood when it's pumping, so to speak."

"David, that's not what…"

"No, no darling you carry on. Ciao." The line goes dead and I turn to find hazel eyes staring at me.

"Der-dup a success then?"

"Well, my manager likes it, but it's the label who really matter," I say, sauntering back towards him. He's still staring. It's like I'm being inspected.

"Why do you do that?" he says.

"Do what?"

"The stooping." I furrow my brow in confusion. "When you're standing or walking, you bend forward like you're ashamed of being tall."

"I… I don't know… Do I?"

"Yes. You're doing it now. Come here." My head is such a whirl of thoughts that it doesn't even occur to me to protest as he gently lifts my chin with a finger and then pushes my shoulders back.

"There, you're an inch taller and way se…" He stops mid-word and draws his hands back. "Shit, sorry, I'm doing it again… the direct thing. Anna's so used to it… I forget. Was I rude?" The school boy grin reappears.

For a second, I'm caught between wanting to slap or kiss him, but the moment passes. "Forget it. Did you try Ben's mobile?"

"Yup, but his is the same."

I ring it myself but also only receive the automatic message.

"So, shall we follow them?" asks Will.

"Too right. We'll probably have to pull them out of wherever they've got stuck."

Hardly any tracks turn downstream off the rock ramp. It's more a case of making your own way rather than following someone else's ruts. Still, they can't have gone in any other direction or we'd have passed them. Ahead the valley walls converge and steepen until we're in a cleft between dark volcanic cliffs.

"We are going to fit through here, aren't we?" I ask.

"If I'm reading this right, in about another mile it'll widen right out into a plain... unless I've got this upside down." He twists the map in his hands for effect.

How can he be so relaxed? I'm already fretting about what we might find. I try to keep my voice as light as possible. "Well, there are a few tracks so these other cars must have gone somewhere."

His map reading is not at fault. The valley opens up into a thorn bush and acacia dotted patchwork of yellow grass, sand and exposed rock. Kopjes push their bare summits above the plain like oversized teenage acne.

"Where now?" I shrug, turning gently towards some harder sand close to the left hand cliff and letting the car coast to a halt. One set of tracks leads forward onto the plain. Another follows the bottom of the right hand cliff where it turns to the north. To the south the left hand cliff quickly shallows into a gentle hillside. Maybe a mile in the distance, the slope curves to a promontory hiding the land beyond.

"As the Jedi would say: 'To find them, use our eyes, we must'," says Will. We jump down from the Land Rover and begin to examine the ground. "Their car is the same as ours, so the tracks will be the same. And they should be the freshest ones." He seems to have hit on a good theory, but at the fork, all the tyre patterns look confusingly similar. The ones heading south appear most likely, but it's far from certain. He scans the map. "These Damara Rockjumpers are supposed to like sloping hillsides next to riverbeds. So if I was Anna, I would go south. Another river bed comes out round the other side of that. He jabs the promontory with his finger. It's not too far."

I let out a sigh and head back to the car. We bounce along for a while in silence. In my peripheral vision I notice Will keeps turning his eyes towards me. Eventually he says, "Are you okay?"

"Yeah, fine." I'm such a bad liar. "It's just lumpier here and the sand in the hollows is softer so I'm having to concentrate more. How about you?"

"Alright... I suppose I'm a bit surprised they came this far, that's all. But if Anna didn't see the Rockjumper at the first place…"

"She does like her birds."

"Oo er Matron," says Will with a Kenneth Williams impression so poor that we both chuckle.

"Don't give up your day job," I tease. I steer round the last in a screen of thorn bushes which mark the end of the promontory. "Oh shit." I slam on the brakes, completely forgetting about sand driving. In front of us is a grisly scene. A black rhino lies on its side, belly open, blood staining the sand. Its face is naked, only a rough stump remaining where the horn should be. Beside the carcass, Ben and Anna's empty Land Rover sits with driver and passenger doors wide open.

CHAPTER 4

Several vultures labour into the air as we leap from our vehicle. Will sprints ahead, glances through the driver's door, turns towards the rhino. "It's been shot," he says, pale faced, and strides off round the corpse.

Poachers... with guns. Please, no... I barely dare to peer inside the vehicle. 'Come on,' says rationality, 'Will would have done more than glance if there was anything awful.' Strange, Anna's shoulder bag is in the passenger footwell. A gentle breeze tickles the back of my legs and the rhino's death stink punches me in the nose. My stomach lurches and bile reaches the back of my throat. All I can think of is to pull the neck of my tee shirt over my nose like a child. I grab Anna's bag and back up in what I hope is an upwind direction.

Will has finished his circumnavigation of the rhino and is disappearing behind a cluster of dense thorns where the flat sand meets the base of the hillside. Where's he going?

It feels stupidly naughty to open Anna's bag, but this is an emergency, right? Purse, make-up bag, wipes, and mobile phone, all seemingly untouched. I press the phone but I just get the PIN keypad. My own phone shows no reception. I drop the bag, take a deep breath and head back to the Land Rover. A cool box sits behind the driver's seat. Inside are the substantial remains of one of the lodge's generous lunches. What else would they have with them? Binoculars... where are the binoculars?

"WILL! Their binoculars aren't here."

"What?" Will appears from the opposite side of the bushes.

"Most of their lunch is here, Anna's bag's still here..." I glance towards the dashboard, "...the key's still in the ignition, but their binoculars are gone. I think they've just gone for a walk."

"I hope you're right," says Will. He cups his hands to his mouth. "ANNA! BEN!" His low yell reverberates around the hillside. After a couple of seconds there's a distant muffled reply. Will blows out his cheeks in relief. I can feel the tightness in my shoulders release. Embarrassed smiles lapse into giggles and soon we are guffawing.

"When you stamped on the brake – that's the first time I've ever heard you swear," he gasps.

"I've trained myself not to," I say, calming my breathing. "David reckoned it wouldn't suit my 'nice girl' image if I accidentally said 'fuck' on prime time TV." This sets us both off again.

"I suppose they just left the doors open to keep it cooler."

"And poachers are hardly going to leave a shiny Defender behind, are they?"

He reaches for Anna's bag. "Looking for clues, were you?"

"Find any bodies?" I counter.

"Just one big one." The laughter fades away. Will nudges the rhino's head with his foot. "I think it's been dead for a day at least. Bastards," he adds with feeling.

I squat, staring into a clouded eye. Flies, disturbed by my shadow, begin to settle back around the lashes. "It makes me so angry. They're so muscular, so much lighter on their feet than you would expect and then the third one I've ever seen has this done to it." Will holds out a hand and I use it to pull myself upright. "Shall we go and find them then?" I ask.

"What's the rush?" says Will. "They're probably pissed off with us for making a racket while they're birdwatching and I'm pissed off with them for scaring us. Maybe we'd better leave it ten minutes. Less agro all round." He's probably right. I just... He wanders back to our car and pulls out his camera.

"Do you think it's only the vultures that have been eating it?" I say. Ribs are visible through the flesh of the rhino's belly.

"Dunno. That's a shoe print, but what is that... or that?" The ground is a muddle of prints, scrapes and impressions, but the sand's so soft that nothing is well defined. "I'll take a couple of photos for Moses. He'll know." Will paces round the carcass, stopping frequently to record likely marks.

A shadow passes across my face and I glance upwards. A massive vulture is circling lower, its white legs gleaming against the dark slab of body and wings. It's a little unnerving. "Can we just go and find them now?" I say in a voice that comes out far more petulant than I mean it. Will lowers his camera to reveal a quizzical frown. I grimace an explanation: "I know Moses says the big cats stay on the eastern side where the game is, but…"

"If there's anything round here, it's going to steer well clear of us. After all humans shoot everything," he says, jerking his head towards the rhino. "Come on, it sounded like they were up there." The second dry river bed splits the ridge in front of us. Will is pointing to the right where large boulders thrust up through scanty thorn bushes.

We pick our way up the slope. Even though the sun is well past vertical, it's hot sweaty work. Ahead, a larger outcrop of rocks forms a natural vantage point.

"Shall we climb up there? See if we can spot them?" asks Will. I nod – the rocks are sand-worn but it would barely rate as a scramble. Even so, Will's long legs take him ahead. I'm following with his ankles at about eye height when he gasps, half jumping, half tumbling back towards me. I try to steady him, grabbing a passing arm, but my right foot gives way, we fall onto our sides and slither downwards a couple of metres half entwined. Will's head snaps anxiously upwards.

"Sorry," he gasps. "A sodding great big snake." My eyes follow sharply after his, but there's nothing following us. We roll onto our backsides and examine the damage. I appear to be dusty but unscathed. Ignoring a grazed elbow, Will wrenches his camera round from behind and holds it across his knees. "Oh, well. It was quite old." The UV filter is cracked and deep gouges score one side of the lens and body. He rotates the power dial, raises the viewfinder to one eye and presses the shutter with a hopeful "You never know." There's the wrong sort of scrunching noise. A second press produces no response. "Oh, yes you do. Insurance job."

I'm mortified. "Sorry, if I hadn't grabbed you…"

"If you hadn't grabbed me I might have landed on my head." He shrugs. "Anna can lend me hers."

"This is bloody ridiculous. Why couldn't they just stay where Moses told them?"

Will shakes his head. "She can't have seen the bird at the first place…"

"And Ben would just love playing the hero." I stand and offer him a hand. He pulls himself up, hitching the broken camera back over his shoulder.

"Let's go round that way," he says, moving one foot forward hesitantly. "Maybe you should go first?" Without thinking I frown, but, hell, I'm all for equality.

"Okay," I say. "Are you like Indiana Jones with snakes?"

"No, it was just a shock, but…" he smiles diffidently, "if you slip, there's half a chance of me catching you. I don't want to be the lumbering idiot blamed for breaking Holly Woodlove's guitar arm."

"Very gallant," I say, glancing at almost six and a half feet of well proportioned male. Does he really think of himself as lumbering? If he has a body image problem, heaven help the rest of us.

The top of the outcrop is flat. If it was anywhere on the beaten track it would probably be yet another 'pulpit rock'. About twenty feet below us, Will's snake is still sunning itself on a wide ledge.

"Is that a puff adder?"

"Looks like it to me," says Will. "I didn't hang around to get a positive ID."

"I don't blame you." I shake my head. If Will had been bitten it would have been Ben's fault… and Anna's. We shield our eyes from the sky's glare, searching for human figures. Where the hell are they? I cup my hands to my mouth, "BEN, WHERE ARE YOU? YOU'D BETTER NOT BE MESSING ABOUT. WE'RE GETTING WORRIED HERE." My shout mixes with its echo making a jumble of the last sentence. Nothing stirs.

Will turns along the hillside and bellows, "ANNA!" A second later an echo answers. His face is a mixture of thought and apprehension. "Come on, let's get back to the car." He doesn't wait for a reply and I'm left to scramble in his wake. "ANNA!" He shouts again but doesn't let up his pace. This time I can definitely hear the panic returning to his voice.

"Will, hang on," I gasp.

He pauses, eyes slightly wild. "I don't think they're this way at all."

"But we heard them."

"Did we? ANNA!"

In the thicket beside us, there's a flutey warble. A thrush-sized bird with a white front and chestnut underside flaps to the uppermost branch, peers at the source of all the racket and disappears as quickly as it came.

"Was that…?"

"The bloody rockjumper, yes."

We reach the valley floor in what seems like seconds compared to the slog going up. Will jogs a few yards onto the sand, turns and yells up the hillside. He cocks his head to one side. After two or three seconds there's some sort of reply. "Holly, you try."

"BEN!" After the same amount of time there's a quieter, higher reply. We've been chasing an echo. I glance towards the two Land Rovers. One of the vultures has landed, but apart from that, nothing has moved. "We need to get back to where there's a mobile signal. Now."

"Yeah," is all that Will can manage.

CHAPTER 5

"Would it be quicker that way?"

We're approaching a fork where a few tracks turn out onto the plain, still a way from the river bed we came down.

"How do you mean?" I say.

"We need a mobile signal and it's quite far back to that sloping rock. The mast is up near the lodge so we're in the shadow of this hillside. If we move away from the slope we should get a signal pretty quickly – like when you drive over the downs and the radio keeps coming and going."

"Okay, we'll try it." I follow the ruts between low shrubs and sun-bleached grasses. They seem to be heading towards the nearest pimple of red-brown rocks. After about half a mile we begin to wind through thickets of taller thorn bushes and trees. All the time Will's eyes are fixed on his phone.

"One bar!" I allow us to coast to a halt. Will is out of the door and onto the roof rack before I've even lifted the handbrake. The reception might be better up there. I open my door, stand on the sill and stare upwards. He's got through straight away, thank goodness.

"…and the doors are wide open. We've shouted and shouted but we can't find them… I don't think they would've gone very far… We're worried they might have been kidnapped… by poachers… Well if there aren't any poachers, how come there's a dead rhino with no horn right next to Anna and Ben's Land Rover… No. It's right down the bottom of the valley. You come out onto the plain, turn left and then there's a part of the hillside that juts out. It's just beyond that… I don't know. We just followed their tracks… No, we had to come out onto the plain to get mobile reception… Okay, we'll see you in a while."

Will removes the phone from his ear. "He wasn't taking it too seriously until I said about the rhino. They'll be about an hour."

"Kidnapped?"

"That was what you were thinking too, wasn't it?" His face suddenly seems gaunt.

I nod. Up till now neither of us has wanted to verbalise it. "No, no, no... nooo..." I can feel my chest constricting. I droop back into the driver's seat. There're a couple of thuds from the roof and Will swings into the passenger side.

"You look like I feel," he says, holding a hand out horizontally. The shaking is clearly visible. He lets out a long sigh, folds his arms onto the dashboard and rests his forehead on them. I close my eyes and concentrate on taking steady breaths, but my overactive imagination rolls a horror film on the screen of my lids.

The other Land Rover pulls up sharply a few yards short of the rhino carcass. Ben and Anna sit in stunned silence until the evidence of their eyes causes anger to overwhelm disbelief. "The absolute bastards," says Ben, jumping to the sand. He steps forward, seemingly hypnotised by the vacant stare. "Why would anyone do that to you?" he whispers and bends to lay a hand on the horn's stump. Behind, the passenger door of the Defender opens, but he doesn't turn, caught in the sombre moment.

Crack! The gun shot is so loud, so unexpected, that Ben overbalances in his haste to twist away and falls to the sand. From his prone position he can see Anna, frozen, a puff of dust rising from the sand between her and the car.

"Next one I aim to hit," calls a squat man in combats crossing the valley towards them. "You," the rifle swings towards Ben, "up." Ben pushes himself upright, heedless of the congealed pachyderm blood sticking to the shoulder of his shirt. "There." A swish of the rifle indicates that Ben should move towards Anna. The poacher whistles a signal. There must be others out there.

As Ben reaches Anna he places his mouth next to her ear with a half-hug: "One chance before the rest come. Faint or something..." She replies with a fearful glance as they turn to face their captor. He stands, legs apart, rifle jammed between arm and body, right hand supporting it under the trigger. This close he doesn't even need to aim properly. Anna's breathing starts to quicken with increasingly audible gasps.

"Easy, calm down," says Ben. The gasping only increases.

The poacher takes a step closer. "What is matter with her?"

"Asthma attack." Anna clutches her chest and falls towards the Defender. The poacher's eyes follow. Ben dives for the rifle, but instead of muzzle his hands grip fresh air and the butt hammers round onto the side of his skull. The poacher takes a couple of sharp sideways steps and lowers the rifle towards Anna's terrified eyes.

"Get up. You think I fool?"

"Holly? I open my eyes. "Are you okay?" There's a red pressure mark across Will's forehead.

"Yes..." I mutter, shaking my head back to the now.

"You looked like you were somewhere else completely."

"I was... I was... oh, never mind." No point in worrying him with my stupid imaginings.

"We should go back to their car. That's where I said we'd be."

I nod, turn the key and swing the Land Rover round in as large an arc as possible. "Can you see that?" I ask. A smudge of smoke is spreading across the base of the distant hillside. "Is there a fire?"

"I think it's dust from a vehicle. Moses must be caning it."

He's right, but whatever's throwing up the cloud is hidden by a line of thorn scrub and… "It's going the wrong way." The dust is spreading towards the main river bed not away from it.

"Mind out." I have to swerve to avoid a bush even though Moses said sharp turns are the last thing you should do. Twigs scrape down the offside wing, the nearside wheels dig into the sand and we come quickly to a halt, leaning at a fairly precarious angle.

"Shit." I colour up with embarrassment.

"Shit indeed," says Will, screwing up his face. I can see how his bluntness winds Anna up. What did Moses say? Always come back out the way you went in. I slam it into reverse and gingerly lift the clutch. Nothing but an odd whining noise. I blip the throttle. The pitch of the whining rises but that's it.

"Will, please could you see what's happening?"

He steps out and ducks round the back of the vehicle. "Your offside rear wheel is spinning like mad but nothing else is moving."

"Have I broken something?"

"Dunno... but if we can get the turning wheel back on the ground that might help." I leave the engine idling and help him push. We manage to rock it a little, but Land Rovers are mighty heavy beasts – we might as well be trying to shift an elephant. "We could dig under the front wheel," suggests Will. "There are spades and mats and all sorts in the back. That was what Moses said to do, if you were really stuck." The mention of Moses must have reminded him about the dust. He reaches inside for binoculars and shins up onto the roof. "You're right, whatever that is, it's going away from us. Maybe it's just a herd of gemsbok? Bloody bushes, they're right in the way."

"Sorry," I repeat, handing him one of the two spades. As we dig beside the offside front wheel the Defender's weight pushes the sand out into our hole and little by little the tilting reduces. After five minutes, sweat has begun to darken the front of Will's T-shirt and even I can feel beads tickling my forehead, but the rear wheel looks like it's taking some weight. "Shall I give it a go then?" Will nods.

The Land Rover moves about a foot backwards as I start to lift the clutch, but then the whining starts again and it rocks from side to side. "Stop!" shouts Will. I push my left foot down and the car slips back to its original position.

Will leans through the passenger window. "Weird, one rear wheel was spinning and then the other. It's like they're not attached."

"They're not, there's a... differential," we say the last word together.

"Come on then Holly, you're Moses' star pupil. I remember him babbling about wheels going round corners at different speeds but I think I was asleep for the rest."

"I don't remember much either, I was trying not to laugh every time your head nodded and Anna poked you." Neither of us smiles. That kind of levity seems eons ago...

"I think it had something to do with the low gear lever." I reach between the seats. "It goes sideways as well as forward and backwards." I shove it to the left. "Stand back." The Defender reverses with hardly any more bother than if I was coming out of a parking space at Sainsbury's. I drive well clear of our hole and wait for Will to throw the spades in the back.

"Should've been listening in that lesson..." shrugs Will as I pull away. I'm not sure if he means him or me – both of us, I suppose. I'm extra careful, but the car feels strange. As we curve round the last set of bushes the ground seems a little firmer and I'm really struggling to steer.

"I can hardly turn the... oh." Will shoves the small lever back towards me and the steering immediately frees up. "Weird."

Now that we have a clear view back to the hillside, all seems just as we left it: empty, desolate, forbidding. No dust cloud or other sign of Moses or anyone else. We retrace our route to the promontory and round the thorn bushes at its point.

"What the..." I scrunch to a halt in virtually the same spot as before. The rhino, in all its gory indignity, is still present, but the Land Rover has vanished. "If this is all just some great wind up Ben's gonna be toast."

"I think Anna just slipped out of my top ten favourite people." We get out to inspect the tracks. Only half the vultures bother to take off. The others just hop round to the other side of the carcass. We're old news.

"Look, this is where they were," says Will. "They reversed, looped round, and went back the way we came."

"It must have been their dust cloud." Will nods. The breeze is strengthening and at the edge of every rut and footprint grains are beginning to move. "I can't see how they think this is funny," I say, scraping a small plume of sand into the air with one foot. It spreads into the distance.

"Maybe they never heard us and it's all just bad timing?"

"But we shouted and shouted..."

Will raises his hands in exasperation. "We might as well go back to the lodge."

We drive in silence. Will seems deep in thought. I sneak a glance every so often, but his eyes remain straight ahead. If the inside of his head is anything like mine, he's veering between anger and embarrassment.

The breeze has become wind and shifting cobwebs of airborne sand play across the tracks in front of the Land Rover. Every so often a stronger gust rocks us. It's a relief to turn into the shelter of the dry river bed.

"You don't think they were…" says Will diffidently.

"Were what?"

"When we arrived, maybe they did hear us, but they didn't answer. Maybe we interrupted them. Maybe..."

"...they were shagging?" I interrupt. It all fits. It bloody well fits. "Bastard." Tears start to well as my imagination goes into overdrive.

A picnic rug is thrown across a flat rock at the summit of a hillside. Anna is naked except for a floral sarong pushed up round her hips. Ben is on top of her. The noise of an approaching vehicle causes Anna to arch her head over Ben's shoulder.

"What's that?"

"Don't stop."

"Ben, someone's coming." She pushes him off, grabs her flip flops and moves to peer through a rocky cleft down into the valley. Tangled black hair flows down to the small of her back. I've always been jealous of that hair. "Holy shit, it's a car from the lodge," she says.

"So what, come here, I haven't finished with you yet."

"Ben, it's Will and Holly."

"They don't know we're up here, we can go down in a few minutes. We're birdwatching... or at least I am." Ben nestles close behind her reaching to cup a breast with one hand whilst lifting her sarong with the other. There's a look of wild passion in his eye that he never has with...

"It's just a theory," says Will. "I didn't mean to upset you."

"Don't you worry. It's Ben that needs to worry."

"I can't see what Ben would see in Anna when he has you, anyway." I force a smile for his clumsy compliment. This is Anna we're talking about – the words 'can't see what Ben would see', in fact, the words 'can't see what anyone would see...' just don't apply when you're talking about Miss Gorgeousness herself.

The sloping rock where Anna and Ben should've been comes back into view, but there're no vehicles on it. We pass straight by, gears whining as the incline of the valley increases.

"There's a phone signal. Should I ring anyone?" says Will.

"No. Let them meet Moses and see what trouble they've caused." Will nods, pocketing his phone.

It's mad. But I'm blind mad with Ben. I glance sideways and grin. "Will, back at the rock, when you were giving me your little deportment lesson. What were you going to say?"

Ha, he almost looks embarrassed. "When?" he hedges.

"You said I was an inch taller and looked… and then you stopped."

"Oh, then. I was going to say you looked much better. Not that you didn't look good before, of course," he adds hurriedly.

"Keep digging…" I widen my eyes at him.

"I just meant you're a tall woman and that's something you should flaunt, not hide."

I have to concentrate on the driving for a moment as we negotiate a water smoothed boulder. "I thought you were going to say it made me way more sexy." I say without turning my head. We reach the edge of the deep sand and I turn the key.

"And I can't imagine what Anna would see in Ben when..." I click off my belt and lean towards him. His lips are warm but there's surprise in his eyes and I start to pull back. My head is stopped by a firm hand which pulls me forward once more. His skin smells of sweat mixed with subtle traces of spiced aftershave. He shifts his body to free up his right arm. Where's his other hand going? I can't see, but right now anywhere would be fine. The backs of his fingers brush tenderly down my left cheek. His tongue is surprisingly rough – not like snogging sandpaper, but... there's more texture than I'm used to. It's... different. I... like it. Oh my life, maybe that's why Anna screams. The desire welling up inside me is so strong I can almost feel it like a vibration, hear it like low rumble...

Will pushes me away, almost forcefully. "Cars." I yank my head round to see a bakkie leading a convoy of two Jeeps round the final curve. I scramble back into the driving seat. Moses is at the wheel of the bakkie. On the passenger side sits a figure in a cream trilby. Serious enough for the owner, himself, to come, then. Will and I hold each other's eyes for a second and I start to blush. "I'll go pump the tyres," he says and swings out of the door. Heck, did they see? I decide it's best to follow Will's lead and act like nothing's happened, so I walk to meet Moses as he coasts to a halt.

"I hope you've given Ben and Anna a telling off for the trouble they've caused," I say leaning on the frame of the open window.

Moses' eyes shift from me to Will, who is attaching the portable compressor to a rear wheel, and back again. His grey flecked eyebrows lower in confusion.

"I thought William said that Benjamin and Anna were lost. You have found them?"

"Haven't you seen them? They should have been ahead of us?"

"Yours is the first car we have met," says Mr Kaura.

"But the Land Rover was gone and we saw their dust... They must have come this way..." Moses shakes his head. "Will!" I call. He drops the pipe instantly and jogs over. He must have heard the fear in my voice.

"They haven't seen them. They're still missing."

CHAPTER 6

Mrs Woodlove, it seems I have already mislaid two guests. I am not going to lose any more. The wind will touch gale force later and there may be armed poachers on my land. You and Mr Mason will be driven back to the lodge."

"But they're our partners..."

"... and if you want us to find them as quickly as possible, we need to give the search our full attention. We're wasting time now." Mr Kaura is one of those annoying people who manages to remain completely polite whilst telling you that you're being stupid. His dark oak eyes glare up at me from beneath the brim of his headgear. Despite his diminutive five feet six, somehow I feel like the small one. I know I'm being stupid. Ben could be out there, lost or worse and I was...

"I think he does have a point, Holly," says Will. Of course he has a bloody point... I just don't want to do nothing. It makes the guilt worse. Hell, I deserve it.

"Okay, I'm sorry. I'm just scared," is what actually comes out of my mouth. I turn away as my eyes start to well.

"Mrs Woodlove, I do not mean to upset you. We will find your husband." His eyes flick towards one of the rangers hanging back from the centre of the argument. "Toivo, please," he says with a wave towards our Defender.

Toivo ushers us into the rear seats, props his rifle in the passenger foot well, turns the key part way and closes the doors. We're left in a cocoon of inactivity as he finishes the tyre inflation job. The air-conditioned draft playing round my knees only adds to the chilly atmosphere. Will is staring at his deck shoes. His face is as pale as his tan will allow. He shakes his head slightly and lets out a sigh.

"I'm sorry, it was all me," I whisper. "I was angry, I..."

"Did I or did I not kiss you back?" says Will keeping his eyes down as if he fears to meet my gaze.

"But I threw myself at you."

"Oh, don't give me that 'men can't help themselves' bullshit," he snaps. "Sorry," he immediately apologises, finally raising his head. "The one time Anna needs me most and I'm being a complete bastard to her." His eyes flick from point to point, I suppose reflecting the internal turmoil. I know exactly how he feels. I'm trying to think of something to say that isn't trite, but Toivo saves me by getting in. The convoy passes us right and left before he starts the engine and we begin the climb back to the plateau.

"Not to worry, Miss Holly, Mr William, Moses will find them." Neither of us responds. Will has his thumb on redial while I try to snooze, but guilt keeps playing on the inside of my eyelids. *'Why Holly?' says Ben, staring up a narrow ravine, his arms grazed, broken legs twisted under him. 'Why Holly?' gasps Ben, his mouth foaming as the snake venom poisons his body. '..y H...y?' grunts Ben, the gag digging into his mouth as he lies, bound hand and foot, in the back of a pickup.*

A larger than usual bump causes my eyes to open. Toivo is peering via the rear view mirror. He's not one of the guides I've spoken to. I suppose I've found his greying Robert Redford moustache and battered black cowboy hat a litle off-putting: too much of a cliché. But maybe small talk would be preferable to listening to a muffled voice saying, 'the number you have called is not responding,' over and over again. "Is there going to be a storm?"

"Not rain but wind strong and sand blows. Can be hard to see."

"We got stuck in some deep sand and only one wheel would turn. We used that to get out." I point towards the low gear lever and motion moving it left.

"That is right. Diff lock get you out... but not to keep using, otherwise on corner like this..." says Toivo, steering to skirt a bed of uneven rock "...bump." He gestures straight on into a large boulder.

"The steering doesn't work?"

"If ground is not soft the car only want to go in straight lines. Only use when stuck." That's pretty much what we found by ourselves. I glance towards Will but he's staring out of the window, phone to ear, as if I don't exist. He's making me feel guilty, like I should be ringing too, but if they had a signal they'd ring us wouldn't they? I call, hear the inevitable message, wait for the tone, gabble, "Ben, where are you? Are you okay? Call me." What more can I do?

Will jabs at his phone's screen harder than is strictly necessary and glances towards the driver's seat, "Toivo, if you turn right out of the bottom of this valley, where does the track go? Where could Ben and Anna be going?"

"After about ten 'k's there is a pan. It is dry this time of year. After that, no track."

"So they couldn't go very far?"

"Not them, no."

"But if someone has kidnapped them?"

Toivo blows down his nose with disgust. "You think we are in Kenya here? There is no kidnapped in Namibia. Your husband, wife they make mistake, something like that. Moses will find, easy."

"There weren't supposed to be poachers either." Will's expression reflects what writers must mean when they say, 'his jaw was set with determination.' He's not going to be fobbed off. "Could someone go further than the pan or not?"

"Land Rover not need track. With skill and diesel you make a route anywhere."

"But they'd have to go north because of the escarpment, yes?"

"North or west. You have a map here, yes?" Toivo reaches into the glove box and passes the map over his shoulder. Will unfolds it and is immediately engrossed. Through the mirror I imagine the faintest trace of a smile cross Toivo's lips – found a way to shut up the overly concerned guest.

I don't know how Will can study it so closely whilst we're moving. A couple of glances and my head already feels woozy. I fix my eyes straight ahead and force air in and out of my lungs. After a mile or so I feel well enough to press redial – still the same automatic voice. Jabbing at the screen without leaving a message I pick Anna from contacts. The phone is at my ear for a second or two before I register what I'm hearing. "Will, it's ringing. Anna's phone is ringing." Will's head turns sharply, confusion in his eyes. "I got Ben's voicemail again so I tried Anna instead and it's ringing! Here."

Will's hand trembles as he takes the phone, but his face turns to puzzlement as he holds it to his ear. "I'm not hearing anything... Anna? ...no, shit, it's voicemail again. How d'you redial on this thing?"

He hands it back, but it's no use. All I get is the stupid network message. I can see doubt forming in his eyes.

"It did ring, honestly, and it was the right number, look." I wave the call log screen at him.

He shrugs, "Maybe it was a glitch."

"Maybe." I let out a sigh that ends with a shudder and close my eyes.

A dusty Defender sits beside a skeletal tree – the only sign that water once flowed here. Silk veils of sand play across the slight depression.

Inside, Ben has pushed the driver's seat back as far as it will go and Anna is sitting on his lap, back against the door, feet resting on the side of a large cool box occupying the passenger seat. She's just about still in her bikini. "Does it seem like this wind's getting stronger?" she says, as the car is buffeted once again.

"I thought you were up for an adventure?" says Ben reaching for a grape and holding it to her mouth.

"I am," she says sucking the fruit from his fingers.

"So... we took a wrong turn, got caught in a storm and thought it was best to wait until morning. It's the perfect excu..." Ben is interrupted by increasingly loud music emanating from Anna's bag in the passenger foot well. "I thought we didn't have a signal." Anna leans forward, but can't quite reach far enough without over-balancing.

"Hold on to me."

"Absolutely no problem," says Ben, grabbing her hips. Anna remains prone as she checks the phone.

"It's Holly. Shall I cancel it?"

"Hell, yeah."

"Aren't you worried that they'll suspect?" She swipes the screen and the ringing stops.

"Holly? I don't think she'd even be bothered. She's probably working out how to get Superfan into bed as we speak."

"Superfan? You mean Will?"

"He dotes on her like it's a privilege to be in the company of musical greatness. I'm surprised he hasn't asked her to autograph his pecks or something."

"You're so rude, Ben... Pull me back up."

"Do I have to, I'm enjoying the view."

A rustling of paper collapses the waking dream. Will is pulling the map from the foot well where it had slipped, forgotten when the phone rang. Does the real Ben think that about me? Would he do that with Anna? He did fancy her first. Bloody hell, I'm worrying about that and he might be kidnapped. What is wrong with me? I try to concentrate on the scenery, but beyond the windscreen the gravel track winds monotonously up the dry river bed.

The driver turns to regard his charges with a wide, gap-toothed smile. "What you two lovebird do in the back there? Move by door... Anna Templeton." He backs up this order with a wave of his hand gun so casual that it seems as likely to go off by accident as on purpose. Anna's eyes widen, she pushes off with her tight bound legs and slams against the side of the Defender in her haste to comply. With hands tied behind her back, she struggles to remain upright. Her hair is thick with sand, face dirt streaked, and the neck of her khaki T-shirt damp with tears and sweat.

The Land Rover lurches and the driver has to concentrate harder on the sand. His eyes flick to Ben's swollen eye and gagged mouth in the rear view mirror. "I know you just touching your girlfriend bottom. I man also. I see she has very nice bottom. If I think you trying to undo rope then I have to tie you to roof."

The Defender, nestled in convoy between two Jeeps, rounds the end of a low reddish dune and makes its way diagonally up a rock-strewn hillside. Almost at the crest, Anna coughs violently but it's not enough to cover the increasingly loud music. The poacher sounds his horn and stamps on the brakes. Unable to hold themselves back, the captives slide forward, Ben taking the impact on his right shoulder whilst Anna ends up in a heap in the footwell. The driver leaps out, heaves open Anna's door and drags her onto the sand.

"You stay there..." he says, pointing the gun towards Ben who is edging along the bench seat. "...or I shoot your girlfriend." The gun transfers to Anna's head.

"Phone, now," he says, prodding the mussel against her temple.

"It...it's d...down my shorts," she stammers, visibly shaking. The poacher grabs a handful of hair and pulls her, screaming, to a standing position. The music is clearly coming from behind. Her hair is released and the hand shoves roughly down the back of her shorts. It reappears almost instantly with the phone. He turns and throws it, still ringing, down the hillside. It hits rock and is silent.

"Tssk..." grumbles the poacher, flicking liquid from his fingers.

A shout from the passenger window of the rear Jeep is followed by loud laughing from the driver's side. Anna is standing in a puddle of her own urine.

"No. No..." I say out loud.

Will's head jerks towards me, his eyebrows raised.

"Are you okay, Miss Holly?" asks Toivo.

"I keep imagining something awful's happened. And I can't look at the map like Will or I feel sick."

"Maybe we talk?" Before I have time to answer, Toivo continues, "You born near Christmas, Miss Holly?"

"No, April. Why?"

"You have a Christmas name."

"I suppose it is. I never really thought about it."

"Never see real holly myself," says Toivo.

I'm not sure how to respond, but he's right, small talk is a distraction, so I play along, "Toivo doesn't sound like an African name."

He grins with neat yellow teeth. "Some Ovambo people take their names as well as their God from missionaries. My grandfather is fine Lutheran – as stiff as his Bible," he adds catching my eye in the mirror. "All my brothers and sisters have missionary names: Martta, Vilho, Usko..."

"German missionaries?"

"No, from Finland."

"Finland? They must have found it hot here."

"They travel to hell to save poor sinners," he grins again.

"Doesn't sound like you're a believer."

"No? Maybe I go to Finland and preach." He raises his voice into what I suppose must be a parody of his grandfather. "Repent from the evil of cell phone. Turn away from godless sport of ice-hockey. Find healing beauty of..." he pauses for effect, "... cricket."

I suppose he's trying to cheer me up but his attempt at humour jars against reality. I lift the corners of my mouth politely. "I can't see that being a very popular message. Have you been to Finland?"

"No, but I Google." The mental picture of this old cowboy silver surfing the world courtesy of the lodge's high speed broadband almost brings a genuine smile to my lips.

We reach the top of the dry river bed and emerge onto the plateau. The Defender bumps and sways gently on the gravel track and for some reason I find myself humming the chorus of 'I'm a believer.' In the distance, a giraffe nibbles at the top of a knob-thorn and I think back to that poor rhino. The tune morphs and my teeth click to add a sort of galloping rhythm.

"Toivo, how far away could a rhino smell a person?" I ask, before I realise what's happening.

"Maybe a kilometre, half a mile, if downwind. Why?"

"Just wondering," I say, weakly. Stop it. Not now, please, I berate myself. Ben's missing, it's hardly the time for song writing. I stare out of the window, trying to distract myself by counting Springbok, but an image keeps intruding: *an old rhino, head held high, is sniffing the air. Somewhere ahead is the poacher who's killed her mate. She paws the ground, shakes her head and begins to move. Like Tennyson's 'Light Brigade' her charge is valour and futility combined.*

CHAPTER 7

With this human I will...

I stop singing abruptly as the door to my make-shift studio opens. Will peers round diffidently. "Sorry, I didn't mean to interrupt. S'pose you can't sleep either?"

"I haven't even tried," I answer, slipping the guitar off my knee. "Any news?"

"Nothing. Toivo says they've probably had to find shelter and sit this out until dawn. Can I come in?"

"Sure." He's either very bleary eyed or he's been crying too. His hair is sticking out at various wild angles. This is all so crap. I grab the tuner and notebook off the only other chair and shove it in his direction with my foot. He pulls it even further from me before slumping down with a frustrated sigh. I receive a grimace but no conversation. The map and phone appear from his cargo trouser pockets, he checks for messages, and then returns to a vegetative state.

The wind is whistling a mournful tune through the thatch above us. I don't want to listen to it. I want to block it all out – lose myself in music. I reach for the guitar and rest it on the floor with the neck vertically upwards. With only the tiniest movement of my fingers it rocks back and forth... back and forth...

The credit card sized park pass swings on its chain from the rear view mirror. Even lying on its side, the gusts are strong enough to make the Land Rover shudder. Every so often the pass clicks against the cracked windscreen. "What's noise?" mumbles Anna. She's lying along the rear side windows which are face down to the sand, a ripped shirt sleeve bandage around her head. Ben is crouching awkwardly beside her.

"Try to keep still," he says. "It's just the green card banging the window. If you move your head too much you'll be sick... At least, that's what happens with dogs who've been hit by cars."

"Ta."

"I didn't mean..."

"I know. Lucky for me you have medical..."

"Shush," whispers Ben, gently. "Talking won't help either." He furtively glances forward, where, in the glow of the courtesy light, sand is relentlessly piling against the windscreen. "Help me Holly," he says, staring into my soul. "Help if you still care; before we get buried ali..."

"You want to..."

"What?" Will is talking and I'm still rocking the guitar.

"You want to play, don't you? How can you play with all this going on?"

"What, you mean, don't I care?" I snap, voicing my dream fears. "Shouldn't I be phoning every five seconds or trying to work out every possible route they might have taken on a bloody map that I can't even read?" All my pent up worry is pouring down my cheeks. "How can she write a song like everything is normal?" I sniff but fail to prevent a drip of liquid snot falling to the floor. As I reach for a tissue from my bag, the heat sputters out into a whispered, "Am I so cold?"

When I look up, Will's eyes are moist. "I didn't mean it like that," he says, slinging the map onto a table. "Anyone can see you're worried. I know it's pointless phoning and phoning... but what the hell can I do? I feel so... so helpless, so... impotent." As he says the last, I have to turn away – I'm sure he didn't mean it, but that word is too loaded, too close to the bone. He continues in a rush, "I suppose what I really meant was: why do you play at a time like now? How does that work – for you?"

I risk a peek. He's leaning forward, elbows on knees, hands gripping opposite biceps and despite the tousled hair, handsome like one of those black and white posters. His face is pure guard-dropping curiosity. "You sound like a journalist."

"I don't mean to pry... It doesn't matter."

I'm silent for a moment, marshalling thoughts. "I have a very vivid imagination. That can be great for song writing but right now it's a curse. Every time I shut my eyes I see Ben with some awful injury or something..."

"Shit..." murmurs Will.

"...and somehow he knows about... in the Land Rover and he's asking 'why?' with his dying breath. I feel so ashamed I can hardly bear it."

"And you feel guilty that you're worrying about being ashamed more than if they're alright?"

"You too?" He nods. Why do I find it surprising that he feels the same? "So anything that keeps me from closing my eyes is good," I continue, "and song writing... song writing is like cliff diving into a sea of sounds and words. You plunge in deep and all around are lyrics, riffs and hooks. You try to grab them, make sense of them. It's hard enough to remember to come up for air, let alone worry about what's happening in the real world. Sometimes I used to find I'd gone all day without eating or drinking."

"Wow," says Will, seemingly with genuine amazement.

"But, recently, I've had to drag myself to the cliff edge... and every time I jump it's been into a paddling pool, not an ocean. And then when Toivo was driving us back it was like, whoosh, I'm drowning in ideas."

"You got your mojo back?"

"Maybe. I mean, if there was anything I could do that would actually help find them then I'd be right on it. But there's nothing is there? Not until morning?" Will shakes his head. "Why do I feel like this is so wrong, then?"

Will shrugs and says with a sigh, "It's a shame, I think we're both in need of a hug but I'm not sure that would be a good idea." He pushes against the chair with both hands as if to lift out of it. "I'm interrupting you, I should go."

"No, stay, you can tell me what you think." I hitch the guitar strap back over my shoulder.

"The new one?"

"Yes, about the rhino." He raises his eyebrows but makes no comment. "It's called...

Right between the Eyes

I know you're out there,
I can smell you from half a mile.
You've got a gun, I know
but I can wait a while.

I could run from you,
I know places a Jeep can't drive.
But here is mine, I'll stand firm.
With this human I will strive...
I will strive...

I can't see why they attack me
but the answer's right between my eyes.
I have heard of the greed of this species,
I suppose it should be no surprise... no surprise.

The man comes closer...
I know that he can see me now
I turn and show my profile
How can you do it, tell me how?

Don't you think it looks better on me, man?
Don't you think it looks better on me? (repeat)

I can't see why they attack me
but the answer's right between my eyes.
I have heard of the greed of this species,
I suppose it should be no surprise, no, no, (first time into repeat)
I suppose it should be no surprise... no surprise. (second time)

You can sculpt it into ornaments,
you can put it in your pills.
It is an aphrodisiac,
but what would you know about that?
You're not my mate, that you killed.

So I'll fight, fight, fight for my life;
I'll fight, fight, fight for my horn;
I'll run, run, run this human down;
I'll knock, knock, knock him to the ground;
and I'll charge... yes, I'll charge
I'll charge, charge, charge, charge, chaaaarge.
Yes, I'll charge, charge, charge, charge, chaaaarge.
Yes, I'll char...

I stop mid-word and simultaneously slap the face of the guitar to simulate the inevitable gunshot.

"Whoa, that's different from the last one," says Will

"I'm not feeling in a very quirky-teen-romance sort of mood at the moment." I wait for more, but he's silent. The window panes rattle with each gust like some manic percussion accompanying the overhead moans. "You don't like it, do you? It's just anthropomorphic drivel, isn't it? Heck, I knew..."

"Why do you say that?" he interrupts, his voice hardly more than a whisper. "I'm kind of a bit stunned. I was expecting... I don't know what I was expecting." He pauses, clearly searching for the right words: "What sort of feelings do you want people to have after they've heard it?"

"I want them to be angry, I want them to go and slap the faces of people who use the horn powder and say, 'Brainless idiots! Use Viagra if you have to. You're killing a majestic creature for no reason.'"

"I'm definitely feeling that."

"I suppose I want people to feel the pain, the futility, as if it were them."

"I think you've done that."

"But do you want to hear it again? I mean, it's all pointless if no one wants to hear it more than once."

"I could listen to you all night."

A wan smile forms on my lips but I can't help wondering what he means by that. He said, 'you' not 'the song'. Oh, stop over analysing... "In that case, will you press the buttons again while I record it?"

MUCH LATER, once the email is winging its way to await the dreaded David Henry opinion, I shuffle past reception en route to the toilet. Toivo is slumped in a padded office chair, Stetson half over his face. I think he's asleep but as I draw level he pushes down on the back of the hat to reveal glittering eyes in the half light.

"Any news?"

"Sorry, sand in the air not good for radio waves. But Moses searches. It will be okay."

I nod and continue past. Maybe the wind's violence has lessened a little but it's still pretty wild out there. I hope Anna and Ben are somewhere sheltered.

"Hear that?" says Anna. The latest gust seems to carry a momentary mechanical growl.

"Maybe," says Ben, threading his way to a hunched standing position between the sideways seats. "I'll take a look". As he winds the window, sand pours onto his face. He shakes his head and thrusts it up through the opening. Needles poke at exposed skin causing him to turn away sharply from the possible sound. Even facing downwind, opening eyes more than a crack is impossible. He pulls his head back inside and reaches forward for the horn giving a couple of blasts. No response. He tries again but it's barely audible above the howl of the open window.

"It's no use while this storm's blowing," he shouts, frantically winding the weather back out of the car.

Fifty yards away, the low gears of Moses' vehicle scream as he ploughs forward. "This is impossible," says Mr Kaura, staring out at two beams of wavering brown light. "I do not know how you even know where we are."

"I feel the ruts. Our own tracks, lead us back they will. Shelter by Mongoose Rock in fifteen minutes."

"I hope you are right. Otherwise they will be sending searchers for us too."

"Ridiculous," I say out loud, reaching for the toilet paper. As if Moses and Kaura would be talking in English. Anna and Ben are probably fast asleep by now in some sheltered camp.

As I pass on the way back, Toivo calls out, "Mr William keep you company?" I snap my head round, but there's no smirk on his lips or anything else to indicate more than an innocent inquiry. Still, I feel the need to defend myself.

"Neither of us can sleep and there's nothing we can do so he's helping me record a song."

"You want to sleep?" He rolls the chair backwards, rummages in one of the desk drawers and produces an old style brown plastic pill bottle. Anything that shortens this interminable waiting seems like a good idea. I reach out. The name and any instructions have long since faded from the yellowing label. As I start to unscrew the lid Toivo says, "You can keep, but only one at a time, yes?"

"Thanks," I nod, continuing on my way. I'm sure Will wouldn't approve, so I stuff one tablet into my mouth before opening the door and gulp it dry. He's peering through window blinds behind the desk where my laptop is set up. "Something out there?" I ask, slipping the bottle into my bag.

"I can't even see the cracks in the shutters."

"Is your digestion okay now?" I ask, my own visit having reminded me about his earlier condition.

"How do you mean?"

"This morning, you were... having trouble." I take the seat Will has vacated.

"Was that only this morning?" He glances at his watch. "Yesterday morning now... Seems like forever ago... I've probably got the opposite problem now." He meets my eyes cautiously, "Holly? Can we try something? Can we talk about Anna and Ben? Is that too weird?"

"I don't want to think about where they might be."

"No, I mean, talk about them, you know, things you love, what their most annoying habit is, stuff like that."

"If you want," I say, unconvinced. One thing's for sure, he's going first. "Go on then, what do you love about Anna."

He yawns, stretching his hands behind his head. How long does this stuff take to work, I wonder? I don't feel the slightest bit tired. He finishes considering: "I love the way she gets so enthusiastic about stuff. I mean, I like to see a cheetah or something else impressive, but these little brown birds that look just like the previous one don't float my boat. But she actually trembles with excitement if it's something new."

"She trembles? Really?"

"Yup, like a little kid with an unopened present. Go on, you now."

Ben – what do I love about Ben? Just recently it's seemed easier to list his faults. No, don't think like that. "He has a funny face." I realise how that may sound before Will reacts and clarify: "funny, ha-ha, not funny peculiar. When he's telling a story he does it with his whole face. Half the time his eyebrow gymnastics have me laughing more than what he's actually saying."

"Ben definitely has the gift of the gab." He sounds almost rueful.

"You again."

"Her hair, it's..."

"Oh, I knew you were going to say the hair. How can it be so perfect for so little effort?"

"Did I touch a nerve there?" Will almost manages a grin.

"Remember I shared a bathroom with her for two years at uni. I'd be in front of the mirror for half an hour trying to make something of... this." I wave in the general direction of my hair. Goodness knows what it looks like at the moment. "...and Anna would stand beside me, run her fingers through those waves, give it a shake and say, 'Oh that'll do,' and it always looked amazing.

"It is like living with a permanently moulting cat, though."

"They get everywhere, don't they? Not just the plug hole, on the chairs, in the carpet, you know just the other day I even found one..." I start to falter as a possible implication hits me, "on... my... pillow..."

Will's tired eyes flick one way and then the other as his mind struggles round the same thoughts as I'm having. He closes them and shakes his head, "No, they just get everywhere – I often pull them out of the fridge."

He's right, we don't want to think down that line again. "Talking of moulting cats, that's another thing I love about Ben: how gentle he is with the animals. Sometimes I'm at the surgery when he does the rounds of the overnight patients. Mostly the nurses do it, but I think he likes to keep a hand in. He hugs them, strokes them and piles on loads of attention. Somewhere in the middle of all the fuss they have a tablet popped in or a wound checked and they don't even seem to notice... Oh heck, I've just thought, the rhino would have made him incandescent with rage. The pain it must have gone through. I hope he didn't do anything stupid."

"He's not stupid though is he? He's a bloody vet. He's got more letters after his name than I've got in mine... Is this helping?" A concerned frown forms on Will's brow.

"It's not as bad as I thought it might be." A yawn interrupts my flow. "What about Anna's cute little faults, then?"

Will paces the length of the wall twice before answering. "She's a terror with sweets. Suppose someone comes round and leaves us a box of chocolates. Next day, she'll suddenly decide to go for a run and later I'll find she was burning off the calories from most of the bottom layer. I'm just left with the nut ones 'cause she doesn't like them."

"Oh, you poor thing."

He grins sheepishly, "I know it's not a big deal, but it can be maddening."

"I'll make a note to only ever bring chocolate brazils, shall I?"

"What about Ben then?"

I've been considering whilst Will has been on his choco-rant so I can dive straight in. "He's always giving people slightly demeaning nicknames. You know, "The Jedi" and I think he calls Toivo "Butch" because of the hat. They're kind of funny but kind of cruel at the same time. He was nearly dumped after we'd been going out for a month when someone let slip that he called me Crazylegs.

"The tall and gawky cartoon bird?"

"The very same."

Will shakes his head and perches on the edge of the desk. "Real cranes are tall and graceful."

"You see, Ben never does compliments like that, but..." I trail off with a feeling like I'm speaking ill of the dead. The dead, no don't think that. "Will, tell me about your latest project." He always has a 'latest project'.

"Really?"

"I'll let you know if it gets too boring." On a normal day I'd add a wink, but Will's mock frown tells me I don't need to.

"The actual latest project is just a fairly standard floor to ceiling bookcase, but there's a really interesting one we've just quoted for. It's a whole turntable between two rooms. On one side there's a grand piano and a bookcase and on the other there's a bar with optics and a drinks rack."

"What, and the piano can be in one room or..." another yawn barges its way into my sentence.

"Yup, the piano, the bar, the bookcase – everything goes right round. But the best bit is they want it operated by secret switches. You know, like pressing a particular book on the third shelf down."

"Like in Scooby..." My brain feels woozy. "Scooby... wotsit..."

Trapped in mind treacle fug, the name fails to surface. "The cartoon thing." I lean back against the seat and regard Will through half closed lids.

"Yeah, like that." His brow furrows quizzically but he continues. "They want the whole thing to blend in so you can't see the joins, so you don't know it's there. The slewing rings under the floor will cost a fortune and then there are the silent motors and the control, before we even get to the furniture. It will be so cool though. Jack says it'll set us up for... real showpiece, like something from a theatre." Did I miss something there? Just resting my eyes for a moment. "They've definitely got the money for a quality job. It'll be won on..." Lids are so heavy, must try to... "These City traders, money's like... bonus bigger than I'll make in... whole different level..."

IT'S DARK, so dark there's no difference between having my eyes open or shut. Yet I know I'm in a bush tent: the firm sleeping mat beneath me, the cool rough touch of a zip against my left foot, the pervading smell of canvas. Away in the night, George the Third or one of his fellow monarchs starts to proclaim his territorial rights. The double sleeping bag pulls at my side as its other occupant stirs. The breathing is wrong, the faint masculine odour is wrong... and yet... The hairs stand up all over my body as I realise I'm naked. My bedfellow turns onto his side and gently slides towards me. I'm paralysed, sensing the approach by the lifting of the bag, fearing, anticipating, that first touch. I let out a shuddering breath as a warm, rough tongue kisses my hip and makes its way across to my belly button.

"Are you awake?" says Will's voice, *strangely muffled by the bag.*

"Will, we can't," I murmur. "Not now, not when..."

Somehow Will's hand is on my shoulder. "Holly, are you alright? I think someone's coming. Holly? Hol-ly!"

Pale light streams through my lids as I wrench them open. "Oh, uhh... Will." His blurry face looms in front of me as I struggle to focus.

"I can see lights in the distance," he says turning towards open shutters. Beyond him, the sky is tobacco coloured.

I'm in the office, slumped on the chair. That doesn't make any sense. "Will?" I croak.

He turns, the corners of his mouth twitching. "You were asleep."

"Wha? I know, there was a lion and you..." My face burns with embarrassment as I finally manage to unscramble reality from dream.

Heck, I hope there's not enough light for him to see. "I didn't say anything did I?"

"What are you on about Holly? Didn't you hear me? A car's coming. Look, there." I blink hard and start to shake the sleep out of my head. A blinding pain runs down my neck, "Aaa..."

"Are you okay?" says Will, brow furrowed.

"Crick... in my neck..." I gasp. I try to stand but lurch sideways. Will throws out a steadying arm and fixes me with concerned eyes.

"Holly, did you take something?"

"Sleeping tablet," I say, meekly. "Toivo."

"Not good. You'll be feeling like shit for hours."

"Sorry, I... I just couldn't stand... It seemed like a good idea at the..." I dissolve into a flood of tears. Even as it's happening, part of me is pissed off with this emotional woman clichéd rubbish. Ben would sweep me up, whispering annoyingly sweet platitudes.

Will just squeezes a shoulder and says, "I know..." He glances over his shoulder, already moving towards the door. "They've nearly reached the gate. Come on."

My head is throbbing as I shuffle out into cool dawn air. I expect Will to be striding down the track, but he's stopped just a few yards from the door, holding a protective hand to the side of his face. As I clear the lee of the lodge, the first gust's gritty bite has me copying his action. I draw next to him, trouser legs and shirt flapping. "What you said about the tablets: sounded like from personal experience?"

"Guilty as charged, m'lud," he answers. "Weird sky." As far as I dare squint against the stinging particles, the western sky remains bluish brown, but in the east the rising sun seems to be setting the sky on fire.

"Sand high in the air," says Toivo, appearing alongside us. For a moment I'm caught in the indecision of which way to look – the approaching Jeep wins. Kaura is driving. I crane my neck to see if he has any passengers in the back. As he draws to a halt, it's clear he's on his own.

"Oh, shit," I hear breathed from between Will's lips.

CHAPTER 8

The dark hollows around Mr Kaura's eyes tell of a sleepless, fruitless night. As he opens the door, his head shakes slowly. "We found nothing, yet."

"Nothing?" The breath hisses out of us in what must be a visible deflation. My legs feel like burst balloon rubber. Instinctively, I clasp Will's hand. He acknowledges my touch with the slightest of squeezes.

In a noticeably lighter tone Kaura adds, "But with the daylight and the wind dropping it will be much easier. Mr Mason, Mrs Woodlove, please follow me."

As we fall in step beside him, Will immediately begins an interrogation. "You didn't find anything at all? Where have you been searching?"

"We checked as many of the driving trails as we could until the conditions became difficult. The search was restarted at first light with a wider radius."

"And you saw the rhino?"

"Yes, we found the carcass. Poachers!" The sudden flare of anger filling Kaura's voice is vented with an over-heavy push of the reception door which bends visibly as the floor-mounted stop brings it to a quivering halt. "One of *my* rhino... When I find these men..." He trails off, perhaps not wanting to actually verbalise the threat. His vehemence is somehow simultaneously scary and comforting.

"So there's no sign of the poachers?" says Will as we cross the lobby area and are ushered into Kaura's inner sanctum. I've never been in here before. Above the wide mahogany desk a huge stuffed lion's head and a gilded certificate for *Southern African Conservation Project of the Year – 2011* make unusual wall fellows.

"No..." says Mr Kaura, a brief expression of confusion creasing his brow. "Searching for your partners has obviously been our priority. Please, take a seat," he adds, rounding the desk and flopping rather heavily into the plush chair beyond. From the patterning, I suspect several crocodiles have contributed to its covering. "The poachers will be long gone, I'm afraid."

"But we thought Anna and Ben had been kidnapped by the poachers..." says Will.

"Ah, no. No, quite impossible." His left hand dabs absently at his hair as if he feels slightly naked without the usual trilby.

"Isn't it a bit strange?" I blurt out. "Anna and Ben go missing just where a rhino is killed? And you're saying there's no connection."

"Mrs Woodlove," says Kaura with a tone of condescension which immediately gets my back up. "I agree that it is a coincidence, but this morning, once the storm was passing we returned to the rhino. It had been dead for two days. Let me explain something about poachers. They are cowards. They arrive in the night. They confuse the animals with spotlights. They do not know how to kill with one clean shot. Moses counted fourteen entry points. Fourteen! And that poor old bull was still alive when they sawed off the horn." Kaura glances towards a large antique hunting rifle on the wall to our left. "Once they have their powdered gold, they run. They do not wait for two days or waste time on kidnaps. They run... because they know what they will get if people like me catch them."

"So what do you think's happened?" says Will, taking the gist if not the exact words out of my mouth. "We're going crazy here with worry."

"And nobody's telling us anything," I add.

"I am sorry, but the weather has made contact with base difficult. I am here now." He pauses for a moment, gazing over our heads, clearly ordering things in his mind. "Mr Mason, in answer to your question, the truth is that we do not know what has happened yet. What I do know is that yesterday two of my guests went missing whilst on a self-drive wilderness experience. What I also know – and, please, I only speak from the facts – is that they drove far beyond the sensible and safe limit set by Moses."

"So it's their fault? Surely this..."

Kaura manages to interrupt before I get up a head of steam, "No, you misunderstand me, Mrs Woodlove. This is no time for blame. I just want to know what made them drive further than the limit. If... ah, Prudence, thank you." One of the almost invisible domestic staff appears from behind us carrying a tray of coffees, croissants, and a box of steaming flannels. As she distributes the cups and plates, Kaura offers each of us a flannel. He immediately sets to work giving his face a vigorous rub but I just pull mine slowly down my forehead until my pores start to open and my nose is filled with refreshing lemon and tea tree vapours. For a moment I pause in the bliss of an almost clear head but as the heat starts to subside, and I wipe my hands, the throbbing fog returns.

"You said, 'If'," I say, carefully reaching for my cup.

Mr Kaura finishes wringing his hands and returns a decidedly brown flannel to the box. "If we understood what Mr Woodlove and Miss Templeton were doing then it might be easier to find them. That is partly why I have returned, that and to update you, and to call for assistance."

"The police?" says Will.

"Possibly, but out here, right now, the National Park survey helicopter will be of much more use. I will make some calls immediately we have finished. Please, eat," he adds, indicating the untouched croissants.

"We think it must have been not seeing the bird, don't we?"

"Sorry, I do not follow?"

"Anna particularly wanted to see a Damara Rock-jumper," says Will. "If they didn't find one where Moses said, we think she might have been keen to look somewhere else."

"And Ben was really into sand driving so he would have been up for it," I add.

Will reaches into his back pocket and produces a now somewhat bent and tatty map. "They had a copy like this – can we just move..." I pull the tray to one side whilst Will spreads the map in front of Mr Kaura. "Rock jumpers are supposed to like hillsides next to dry river beds so if I was here – at the rocky ramp – and I was looking for another likely place..." His finger traces along the edge of the escarpment.

"You might go along to the next riverbed," Kaura finishes.

"We did actually see the bird there whilst we were searching for them."

"After you found the Defender with its doors open next to the carcass?"

"Yes, it was like they'd just got out for a moment," I say. "Their lunch was half eaten, Anna's handbag in the foot well. We were a bit panicky right then, weren't we?" Will sits back and we exchange a glance of mutually recalled fear. Once again our hands slip together in support. "We couldn't decide if they'd been kidnapped or just gone birdwatching."

"And you shouted and searched without finding them?"

"Not a sign."

"But when you returned from phoning, the car was gone. So they must have been close by?"

"It doesn't make any sense, does it?" I sigh. "That's why we thought they must have been kidnapped..."

Kaura sips his coffee, screwing his eyes up in thought. "It is almost like they did not want you to find them." His eyes drop to where Will's and my fingers are still entwined. "There is not, maybe, any personal reason why Miss Templeton and Mr Woodlove would wish to drive off on an adventure... or in anger?" Simultaneously, Will and I reach for plates and croissants.

"No," says Will.

"None," I add, stuffing in a large bite. Kaura sits in silence. The lion stares down from the wall in glassy-eyed accusation. An image forms in my mind *of a Defender parked close under the cliff of a large kopi. Despite being sheltered from the wind, the vehicle is rocking rhythmically on its springs.* "'ee 'underd if 'ey 'ere..." A large swallow is needed. "We wondered if they were messing about. You know... hiding for a joke... but you wouldn't do that and then drive off into the desert, would you?"

"Umm. I would not think... but it seems like that is what they have done," says Kaura with a final shrug.

"Maybe they somehow missed the turn up the river valley and then got lost?" says Will.

I lean forward as a thought occurs: "If the dust cloud we saw was them, then they must have been going quite fast, yes?" I look towards Kaura for agreement. He nods. "So couldn't they have reached the top of the valley before you did?"

Kaura springs to his feet, his chair striking the wall behind. "And then they take a wrong turn up here..." he says with animation. "They would have to be going fast, but maybe not impossible... there is one place where... I will send Toivo." He bustles towards the door, intent on his new purpose, leaving us seemingly forgotten. Will and I share a bemused expression.

"Seems like you had a good idea, Holly," says Will as we scramble from our chairs.

CHAPTER 9

We catch up with Mr Kaura on the eastern side of the lodge where the remaining vehicles are parked in the lee of the workshop. As the wind drops, the world is disappearing under settling dust. Cars, fences, even the leaves on the bushes, smothered with a layer of golden red icing by some fanatical cake decorator. Kaura is perching on the running boards of a Defender, conversing with Toivo as he straps down a jerry can to the roof rack. Toivo's bare arms resemble those of a drying mud-wrestler but his face is largely clean. I wipe two fingers across my right cheek and, finding the tips already smudged with powder, begin to suspect that his wide brimmed headgear might not just be an affectation.

The Land Rover is fully provisioned, ready for some other guest's bush camping excursion. Other guests... Heck, we're probably messing with their holidays of a lifetime. Part of the lodge's luxury is keeping you in your own private bubble, but we have seen them: the young honeymoon couple who nudge and point as I pass; the retired Germans – he was something big in cranes, supposedly.

"You take number four Jeep," says Kaura, swapping to English as we approach. "The Schloermans will just have to go tomorrow. I will tell them." Toivo nods, tugs at the final strap to make sure everything is secure and climbs down. "The phone is still off, but you might be able to reach Moses on the radio when you are close to the escarpment." Kaura turns towards us. "Toivo will go straight away to search along the Gemsbok trail. It is possible that they went that way, especially with the storm."

"Mr Kaura, are they in danger?" I ask, through a lump in my throat.

"Not if they stay with their vehicle."

"And Moses only told us that about half a million times," Will chips in. "Why isn't the mobile phone working?"

"Dust gets everywhere," says Kaura, brushing at each shoulder in turn with the back of his hand. "The power supply for the mast is... troublesome. But you can use the land lines or the broadband if you wish." His face pinches into a pained smile. "Now, I must organise a helicopter and then go back to Moses."

"We're coming with you?" I say: half question, half demand.

"Mrs Woodlove..."

"Or can we go with Toivo?"

"I am sorry..."

I don't wait for his excuse. "Oh, come on, you can't just leave us here to stew. Ben and Anna are out there somewhere. I..." My eyes slide towards Will who is nodding in agreement. "We need to be helping, we need to be searching. Surely extra pairs of eyes are a good thing?"

"Mr Mason, Mrs Woodlove, I realise it must be worrying and frustrating, but you must let us do our job."

"If you were doing your job properly, you'd have found them by now."

Kaura stares and then transfers his gaze to Will. "Mr Mason, if you..."

"Don't give me the 'ignore the mad woman and talk to the reasonable man' bullshit," I shout.

Behind Kaura, Toivo's head jerks up, eyebrows raised. The reserve manager takes a deep breath, stretches out his fingers and re-clenches them. His irises smoulder – fire spat embers adrift in curdling milk – but he continues in a steady voice. "We try to meet the wishes of all our guests. But we value their safety above all things. If you helped with the search someone would have to look after you. To say it bluntly, you would be in the way." Fury keeps our eyes locked, but I can feel my bottom lip beginning to tremble. "I am sure it will all be okay," he says, applying his most sympathetic smile. He doesn't really have the face for it.

"Tchuh." Breath hisses out of me in disgust as I turn and stomp away, eyes beginning to well. After a few yards, I hear Will's loping stride beside me. "The next person who says 'It'll be okay' gets decked," I spit without turning my head.

"I'll make sure that isn't me, then." There's an odd tone in his voice. We walk alongside each other, past browned lawns and a murky pool before he verbalises that tone: "I've never seen you really angry before."

"I'm sorry, did the mad woman embarrass you?" I say, still facing straight forward. A hand grips my upper arm, persuading, if not quite forcing me, to turn towards him.

"Holly, why do you do that?"

"What?" I say, talking to Will's chest.

"You always think that people are going to say something bad about you."

"Bitter experience, I suppose." My gaze lifts as far as his stubbly chin.

"I wasn't going to say anything bad. I was going to say something about 'a force of nature'."

"Oh."

Hazel eyes mirror my fear and confusion, but just for a moment there seems a hint of humour in the corners. "Kaura doesn't look like the sort of man who's been sworn at very often."

"I guess not." I manage to haul the corners of my mouth into some sort of half-hearted grin. It collapses. "I'm... I'm just... so scared."

"Me too."

We fold into a desolate, soggy hug, both clinging to the one firm ground amongst the mudslide of the last few days. When eventually I unbury my head from Will's shoulder, I notice Mr Kaura, staring, motionless on the steps of the lodge. As my eyes meet his, he turns and enters.

CHAPTER 10

Scared

Scared for you. Stomach is churning.
Scared for you. Fear is burning
all sorts of hell on the back of my mind...
Everyone says, "It'll be okay," but those are just words:
meaningless things that thoughtless people say.

Only yesterday, you were just there.
Things that I took for granted,
they've vanished into thin air.
Only yesterday, I didn't care
much about what you were doing,
now you're my every prayer.

Scared for you. Stomach is churning.
Scared for you. Fear is burning
all sorts of hell on the back of my mind...
Scared for you. Fingers are shaking.
Scared for you. Worries are taking
all that is normal and making it mad.
Everyone says, "It'll be okay," but those are just words:
meaningless things that thoughtless people say.

Come back to me... come back to me...
why can't you come back to me, love of mine? (x2)

In my sweet fantasy you're walking back to me
and from your lips you are calling my name.
But what's the reason? It stings like a lesion:
the thought that somehow things will not be the same.

Scared for you. Stomach is churning.
Scared for you. Fear is burning
all sorts of hell on the back of my mind...
Scared for you. Fingers are shaking.
Scared for you. Worries are taking
all that is normal and making it mad.
Everyone says, "It'll be okay," but those are just words:
meaningless things that thoughtless people say.

Come back to me... come back to me...
why can't you come back to me, love of mine? (x4- crescendo)
Co-me ba-ck...

I can't stop the wobble in my voice as the final note fades. From the other side of the laptop there's a long exhale of breath. "It feels like you've just ripped open my head and sucked the thoughts straight out." For the second time today there are tears in Will's eyes.

"Maybe it's just too personal?"

"You'd have to ask your Henry fella about that."

"Somehow it's easier to write about it than to sit still and have to think it."

There's a hesitant rap on the door.

"Come in."

It swings open just far enough for Prudence to peer round. Today's headscarf is a vivid aqua-marine. "Excusing me. There is phone call for you miss."

"I'm coming." I throw down my guitar and virtually sprint across the room. Prudence takes a step back as I barge through the door and race down the corridor.

"Hello?" I gasp into the receiver, praying that it will Ben.

"Holly, darling, where have you been? I must have tried your mobile a hundred times. We just..."

"David, whoa, hang on a minute..." Will is following down the corridor but his pace falters at the name. "David Henry," I stage whisper.

"Talk of the devil," says Will, his anxious expression fading to rueful.

I take a deep breath. "David, I'm sorry, it's a bit mad here. Ben and..." I break off: my voice is echoing slightly. "David, have you put me on speaker?"

"Yes, darling. I'm here with Rory, Christian and Stella and we'd..."

"David, take me off speaker right now."

"But sweetie..."

"Now, David, I need to explain." There's a couple of thuds and then the fizzing on the line reduces.

"It's just me. What's the matter?" David is unable to keep a petulant tone from his voice.

"Ben and Anna are missing and..."

"That's terrible, sweetie," he interrupts, "but I've got..."

"David, you're not listening."

"I am darling, but..."

I raise my heels off the ground and stamp down in frustration. "You're not! Just shut up and actually listen. My husband Ben and my best friend Anna went off on a self-drive safari yesterday and they haven't come back. No one has seen them for..." I glance towards the ornate carriage clock at the far end of the reception counter. The time is quarter to one. "...more than twenty-four hours."

"Holly, darling, how awful..." There's a longish silence where for a moment I can almost imagine empathy, but no: "...and you're worried that the hussy has made a play for him? Darling, this is show business, everyone..."

"No David, I'm worried that they've been kidnapped by poachers or had a car crash. I'm worried because they've been out all night in a sand storm in one of the most inhospitable places on the planet. I'm worried that they might be dead." Will gulps. His Adam's apple is quite sticky out. I've never noticed that before. He turns away and saunters towards the main door.

"So it's serious?" At bloody last. I flop onto a bok-skinned sofa.

"Yes. The guides have been out all night searching. The manager has called for a helicopter, but he won't let us help: says we'd be in the way. The storm knocked out the mobile phone mast so we're going nuts here with nothing to do and no information."

"That's why we couldn't get through?"

"Yes."

"You poor darling. Can I fill everyone in?" He doesn't wait for my response. I glance towards Will and catch him staring. He rolls his eyes, mouths 'I'm going outside', and yanks open the main door. "Holly, Rory asks if I can put you on speaker for a moment."

"I suppose so." The volume of hiss on the line increases.

"Holly? It's Rory here."

"Hi."

"Holly, we're all really sorry to hear about this... this situation. Are you okay?"

"Well, no, not really, I don't know what to think. I mean, they could have found them by now, or... I keep imagining dreadful things."

"Of course... The authorities, they're doing all they can?"

"I... I think so. It's difficult to know. Kaura, the manager here, he's driving us mad not letting us help, but he does seem pretty organised."

"I'm sure he's just thinking of your safety."

"Maybe, but that doesn't make it any easier."

"'ang in there, love," says Stella in her ridiculously broad Manchester accent.

"Are the police involved yet?" Rory is relentlessly professional as ever.

"I don't think so. Kaura said that the national park helicopter would be more use for now."

"Do you want any help from the label? Perhaps we could phone the embassy? Find out how things are done over there?"

I don't know why, but this causes me to well up. It must be obvious in my voice. "Please... Thanks. Yes. If you think that's best." I finish with a sniff. Heck, I must sound all over the place.

"Okay, we'll fix that." There's conferring in low voices before he continues. "Holly, I understand it won't be the first thing on your mind at the moment, but we'd just like to say that David has played us your demos and we're very happy that you're writing again."

"Err, good... I mean, that's great." Any other time I'd be bouncing off the ceiling at an actual near-compliment from Rory.

"The Der-dup thing, it's catchy..." I can hear the 'but' coming... "but it's not really where we see you. You might think about passing it to someone... someone with a larger teenage fanbase."

"I were thinking Carley might be interested," Stella chips in.

"Mm... maybe," comes out of my mouth but all I can think is 'That's it then: they're already consigning me to Radio 2.'

"Now, the rhino song, that's... interesting. Do you feel you're moving to a more mature sound?"

"I suppose..." He interrupts before I have time to think of more.

"It's very rough and I'm not sure it would even make it as an album track, but this kind of thing definitely seems to suit your style. If you can build in that direction... then when you get back, we'll see where we are..."

"Thanks.... great... I..." Whatever I was going to say flits out of reach. "I'm sorry, my head's all over the place."

"I'm sure everything'll be okay, love," says Stella in the nearest she can get to a motherly tone. I roll my eyes at the platitude but it reminds me...

"Oh, I was going to say, I've been writing to keep my mind off things. I've..."

Will bursts through the door, followed by a cloud of brown dust. "There's a chopper coming."

I gabble into the phone. "I've done another song. I'll email it. Sorry, need to go, there's a helicopter. Bye." I press disconnect and rush after Will.

As soon as I'm outside I can hear the low-pitched whirring. Will points and I follow his arm to where a dot is approaching. The chopper passes almost overhead at a couple of hundred feet up, circles round once and then flies out westward.

"Joining the search," shouts Will above the throbbing. "Should've realised from the direction."

"Why's it taken so long?"

Will shrugs. "Maybe they had to wait till all the dust had settled. It's not falling anymore." I run fingers across one shoulder and inspecting them, see that he's right. "A white Land Rover should stand out for miles from up there," he says with just a little more confidence. But in my mind, as we watch the chopper dwindle, *Ben whispers in the pitch black, "It should be light by now, I'm going to try to get out." His arm fumbles along the now vertical roof of the toppled-over Defender, and flicks on the courtesy light.*

"I'll help," says Anna, raising her head. Even in the low yellow glow she visibly greens. "Maybe not." Her bandaged head slowly lowers back to the blanket with a groan.

"Deep breaths." Ben's eyes are full of concern. "That's it. In and out. Just keep still and you won't feel sick." Once his patient seems slightly more comfortable Ben rises to a hunched standing position under the passenger side rear door. Sand starts to trickle down as soon as he moves the winder. By the time the window is open far enough, the trickle is a flood. He sucks in a long breath and thrusts an arm upwards. Pushing, scrabbling, twisting, his hand forces through the sand until his shoulder is jammed between glass and metal. Still no sign of the surface. It's like reaching up through the neck of an hour glass: time slipping past.

"Ben, stop. Ben, you're burying me," shouts Anna from the bottom of the vehicle.

"I must be nearly..."

"Ben!"

He withdraws his arm and pushes on the winder. No movement. He leans on it with as much weight as he can, but the angle's awkward and it's still stuck fast.

"Let me help," says Anna, lurching to her feet, clambering through the torrent of sand to the front area, reaching a skinny arm between passenger seat and door frame. "You push and I'll pull on your hands. One, two three, now!" The lever starts to turn under their combined strength. "Now pull... push... pull... that's it." Once moving, the window closes much more easily, the flow of sand reduces to a trickle and with one last tug, stops.

"Phew..." says Ben, flopping sideways so he can see round the front passenger seat. "Thanks."

"You're welc..." starts Anna. "Oh..." Her hand rushes to cover her mouth but it can't hold back the flood of vomit.

"Just let it all out..." Ben waits for the retching to subside. "Sorry. I can't believe there's so much sand over us."

High overhead, the spotter scans his binoculars across the rugged terrain. A small dune passes across his field of view but doesn't even give pause.

"Northward circle?" asks the pilot through the intercom.

"Yes, and..."

"I am sure they vill find zem soon." A heavily accented voice wrenches me back to the real. The crane man is standing behind us, slim and wiry in an Adidas track suit. Beside him, his wife wears long shorts, vest top and a sympathetic expression. "We are sorry to hear about your difficulty," he continues.

"We're sorry if it's messing up your holiday," says Will.

"No matter. We come here many times before." His wife nods throughout in that way people do when they understand the sentiment but not all the words.

"Danke für Ihre Besorgnis," I say, surprising them both.

"Sie sprechen Deutsch!" she says, raising her eyebrows.

"Ich habe ein großen Teil meiner Kindheit in Österreich verbracht."

"Ach, wo haben Sie...?" she starts, but her husband tugs an arm, catching my eye with an understanding expression as he does so. I guess as a company owner, he probably had to spend more than a few times shaking hands and smiling when he'd rather have been left in peace.

"We walk," he says, tipping his head slightly before they stride off towards the perimeter trail. It's supposed to be two miles round the inside of the fence. I can't say from personal experience.

"I hope I'm still that fit at their age," says Will when they're out of earshot. I suspect he will be. "It's weird hearing you speak German. I hardly notice your accent these days."

"I was just thanking them and explaining about growing up in Austria."

"It's easy to forget you spent so much time over there."

"Not for me it isn't."

The helicopter seems to have brought everyone out: Prudence is standing on the main steps; three other brightly scarfed domestics are peering round the side of the kitchen block watching it recede; the honeymoon couple are sidling towards us from the direction of their safari tent. Their complimentary dressing gowns are still pristine white, but the matching slippers are decidedly rusty.

"We, err... heard about your partners. It must be terrible for you." The bride slips an arm round her husband's waist.

I force my lips into a pained smile, not quite sure how to respond. There's an awkward pause. The woman seems like she's bursting to continue. It all comes out in a gabble.

"And can I just say I love your music, err, Holly. Always playing your album, aren't I Tom?" Tom nods, although from his expression it's not clear if he thinks this is a good thing.

"Thanks. You're very kind," I say, entering PR automatic pilot mode.

"I'm sure that helicopter will find them straight away," she continues.

"We hope so. I'm sorry if it's messing up any of your outings."

"Gosh, no, don't worry, if Tom went missing I'd be wetting myself. We're keeping ourselves busy, aren't we..." She glances towards Tom who winks playfully, causing her to blush deeply. "Tom, you've made me go pink." She casts me a knowing look. "He doesn't say much, but then conversation's not everything is it?" It's tempting to respond with, 'shame you don't follow his example' but I've had 'smile, polite, smile, polite' drilled into me by David so many times it's second nature now.

"Holly, there's something coming down the approach road." Will's right. A vehicle is throwing up a cloud of dust as it races towards the lodge. Like the helicopter, it's coming from the east so it can't be part of the search and it's too soon for anything from the embassy, isn't it? We stand, eyes straining to resolve the shape of a Defender through the shimmering haze.

"It does look white," says Will.

"But it's a delivery bakkie, not a Land Rover," I sigh, as the front heavy shape becomes apparent. Almost every day a pickup truck arrives to top up stocks of fresh produce. It slows to cross the cattle grid where the road intersects the lodge fence. The metallic ringing reaches us noticeably later than we see it.

"Didn't you say you had an email to send?" says Will sliding his eyes towards my 'fans' who are still loitering awkwardly beside us.

"You're right – excuse us."

Once we are far enough away, I whisper "thanks" loud enough for Will's ears only.

"She was a bit annoying," he says, shoving open the reception door. "Do you get much of that?"

"Not really. I can't complain. It's great she's enthusiastic. People like her pay my bills. But there's a time and a place..."

"And that was neither."

Will fidgets with the map whilst I tap the laptop keyboard. Five minutes work and I'm back to fiddling with things in my bag, trying to prevent Ben and Anna from discussing suffocation inside my head. "Do you want coffee?"

He takes zero persuasion. I suspect he knows the local geography off by heart. "I'll come too."

We wend our way to the kitchen door where Prudence is directing the unloading of the bakkie.

"Could we have coffees, please?" I say.

"Of course, yes," says Prudence. She motions the man holding a crate of melons through the door, and gabbles an instruction.

"Any chance of a snack, too?" says Will. Prudence's eyes narrow in thought and possibly a little consternation: we've obviously caught her at a bad time. They widen again as a solution presents itself.

"Yes, I have whole hamper now not needed." She peers round the door, "Nangolo? Bring basket. Mr Schloerman prefer hot food when at the lodge," she adds, by way of explanation and disappears in search of cups.

Moments later, Nangolo appears having swapped the crate for a large coolbox embossed with imitation wicker patterns. Judging from the grunts as he heaves it down beside Will, it must be stuffed with buffet-style treats. He grins, and clearly totally unaware of our situation, says, "You very lucky people." Enjoying our confusion, he raises his voice loud enough to be heard inside and continues, "I hear Prudence say, 'yes' to you twice just now. I ask and I ask but she never say 'yes' to me."

"That because you never ask the right question," calls Prudence from the depths of the kitchen.

"Is coffee for me too?" shouts Nangolo, throwing us a broad wink.

"No, there is not. Does he bother you, Miss Holly?"

"See," says Nangolo throwing up his hands. "Prudence think I am not re-spon-sible." He stretches out the final word as if it is something very distasteful.

"I know you are not responsible," says Prudence, returning with a tray. The half smile on her lips betrays this as long running banter. "Where would like to sit?" she asks us. Despite the dust it would be nice to be outside.

"Maybe by the pool?"

"I come and clean chairs," says Prudence. "Nangolo, you carry food?"

He squints up at the sun. "Sorry, I have two more delivery today. I stay too long. I need fly."

"Like Bateleur?" says Prudence with a touch of disgust in her voice.

"No like falcon. Goodbye," he says nodding to us before making for his bakkie.

"Don't worry, I've got it," says Will lifting the hamper with considerably greater ease than Nangolo. "Bateleur?" he asks Prudence.

"Fly like drunk, always wobble," she says, but not in an unkind tone.

Despite Nangolo's supposed hurry, he still finds time to swing the bakkie round in a wide arc and pull alongside us. He has a brief exchange with Prudence in their own language. I'm pretty sure he says 'Toivo' and, a moment later, something that might be 'Defender'. Prudence repeats the same word and takes a quick glance towards me. Will has picked up on it too.

"Prudence, what is he saying?"

"Nangolo," she says, but his window is already rising as he pulls away. "Nangolo!" The window is closed and already the dust is rising as he accelerates away.

"Prudence, what did he say?" She stays silent and continues towards the pool. "Prudence, it sounded like he said something about a Defender."

"It is nothing. It can be nothing."

"Prudence, please," I plead.

Prudence dithers, lips pursed. She relents: "He ask if Toivo was taking a tour up north. He say that he saw a Defender that look like one of ours up at the C51 gas station."

"Did he see who was in it?"

"I ask, he say he sees a white man standing near the car."

"No woman?" says Ben.

"He only drive past," shrugs Prudence. "I ask him how he knew it is one of our Defender but he drive away." She flicks her head towards the receding cloud of dust.

"But it could be them, couldn't it? We need to tell someone. We need to go up there. All this searching could be in the wrong place!"

Prudence ignores my excitability and hands me the tray. "Please hold for one moment." She turns the low table sideways and bangs it against the ground, then begins to wipe with a duster. "You cannot believe what Nangolo say. I know this."

"But he might have seen them. Just because he's a bit vague, doesn't mean it's not possible."

She takes the tray, places it on the table and turns her attention to the deck chairs. "The cell phone still not work. I will tell Toivo when he is come back."

"But that could be hours. Maybe we should call the police or..."

"Wait for Toivo or Mr Kaura. They know what best. There," she says indicating that the seating is ready.

"Prudence..."

"I just housekeeper," she says backing away.

Will and I hover in indecision: to sit down would be to give up, to chase after Prudence seems futile.

"Grrr. This is driving me nuts," I explode. "We get a hint – maybe it is rubbish – but it's worth looking into and there's nobody here to do anything. Somebody should go and find out."

"Somebody should," says Will in an oddly flat voice. I follow his eyes to where the back end of a fully prepared and fuelled Defender is protruding beyond the workshop, then to the hamper of supplies on the ground beside us. We hold each other's gaze for a moment, the unspoken thought hanging between us.

"I bet the keys are in the ignition."

Our coffee cups are left to lounge in the poolside shade untouched.

CHAPTER 11

Africanised Defenders are not built for speed. The pedal is to the metal, the body work is vibrating like an annoyed wasp, but still we're a way short of the 120km/hr limit. About half an hour north of the lodge the highway leaves behind the undulating, thorn bush strewn landscape and enters what can only be described as featureless desert: flat grey-brown sand, dotted with beds of loose grey-brown rocks stretching away in all directions. Only a dark massif shimmering through the haze of the north western skyline hints at anything beyond this desolation.

"What's coming up on the left?" asks Will from behind large lensed driving shades. I reach into the glove compartment for binoculars.

"Bizarre. It's benches, tables and a rubbish bin." As we approach, the dune and baobab logo of the Namibian Tourist Board becomes discernible on the picnic furniture.

"Lovely place for a spot of lunch," says Will, not easing off the accelerator even marginally. "I wonder how they chose that particular spot – and not a mile further on or five miles back."

"Maybe we're exactly halfway across or something?"

"Officially the middle of nowhere..." muses Will. It would be a pretty good candidate for that accolade.

"I reckon they sent out a work party and they were meant to put that stuff somewhere else, but they got so bored driving across this plain, they just went 'sod it' and left them there."

Will makes a noise in his throat which I suppose is the nearest he can get to a laugh. This chit chat is fooling neither of us. The real question is what were Ben and Anna doing at a petrol station a hundred miles north of where they should be? If Anna was even there – and if she wasn't, then what the hell has happened to her? The sands of my buried alive day-mare have been blown away by increasing unlikelihood only to be replaced by a disturbing twist on the unfaithful husband strand.

Once the gas station and its attendant row of shacks have slipped out of the rear view mirror, Ben pulls the Defender off the road. He lifts a bottle of water from the passenger seat and climbs into the back. On the floor, staring up with fearful eyes is Anna – hands tied with the tow rope, legs bound with gaffer tape from the emergency repairs box. With gentleness seemingly incompatible with the circumstances, he lifts her to a sitting position and prizes the tape from her mouth.

"Here," he holds the bottle to her mouth. Anna gulps until she chokes. "Slow down, don't breathe it... Would you like patting on the back?" Anna shakes her head – keeps on shaking it until the coughing subsides.

"Ben, where are we going?" With enormous willpower, Anna's voice is small and calm.

"I don't know." His eyes meet hers, flick down to her chest, then back to some irrelevant point on the horizon.

"Ben, I've been thinking. I'm sorry for what I said before, about... it. You're right, I was being flirty. I was wearing this," she glances down at the ripped sarong, "so you'd notice me... And I was doing that because I fancy you. There's no need for this..." she raises her tied hands ever so slightly, "I'm bored with Superfan. I want someone cleverer, funnier. I want you, Ben... You just surprised me, that's all. So let's forget about what happened and start over, shall we? Ben?"

He continues to stare into the distance.

"Ben, let's go back to the lodge. We can meet up in the middle of the night or work out another birdwatching trip. Then when we're home..." There's still no response from the starer. "Ben, how about it?" Her voice is low and seductive.

Like the sudden reanimation of a human statue busker at the end of their act, Ben slips off the seat, crouches in front of Anna and kisses her full on the mouth. Her lips move with his in what might be desperate passion. He pulls back slightly, "Sounds wonderful..." She leans, seemingly eager to continue the kiss, but as a hand touches her bikini top, she flinches and despite all her willpower it amplifies into a full blown shudder. "It's a shame you're not telling the truth." Ben stands abruptly, reaches behind for the half used roll of tape, starts to rip off a length.

Anna's shoulders begin to quake. "Ben, no, I want you. I do. I'm not lying. Ben, no... Ben, I'll do anything th..." Her pleading is cut short by the re-applied tape.

"I disgust you, don't I?" Anna shakes her head frantically, tears streaming down her face. Ben places his fingers on either side of her jaw and rubs away the tears with his thumbs. "Oh Anna, you're such a bad liar." His hands move to her shoulders and push just hard enough so that she loses her balance and rolls backwards.

"You're just telling me what I want to hear because you're scared of what I might do to you... to us..." he finishes quietly.

"Hm hmmmmm."

Ben ignores the pleading, climbs back into the driver's seat and fires up the engine.

"Holly, you're shivering."

"Am I? Sorry."

Will stares sidelong from the driver's seat. Every few seconds his eyes flick to the road and then back to me. "You been imagining bad stuff again?" I nod. "Tell me."

"You really, really don't want to know." I breathe out slowly to halt the shaking.

"It can't be any worse than the stuff knocking around my head. Try me."

"It's not playing in your head like a bloody horror movie, though is it?" His eyebrows rise ever so slightly, but he ignores my snappiness.

"No, I s'pose not. I just get a thought and I worry round all the 'ifs' and 'whys' and 'hows' until the next one comes." He glances forward, although it's barely necessary on the runway-straight road. "It's really like a film for you?"

"Like a vivid dream. A day-mare, I call it."

"And you use them to write songs?"

"Kind of. I start to imagine a story and if it works, whoosh, I'm there seeing, feeling, hearing how the song should go."

"So it's a gift and a curse at the same time? Like the Midas touch?"

"Maybe. Not too many gold discs from it yet though."

"There will be." From anyone else that would seem like a meaningless platitude, but Will says it like it's an obvious fact.

"Now you're just massaging my artistic ego."

"I think we could all do with some mass..." Will breaks off as music erupts from the bag at my feet.

"Come on, where is it?" I scrabble past purse, tissues, bottles, then yank the bag up onto the dashboard. "Will! Road!" We've veered completely onto the opposite side and are approaching the far edge. I try the outside pocket... of course – idiot. Will corrects with a swooping curve. My hands are shaking so much I can hardly keep hold of the phone to see... bloody David Henry again.

"Wonderful, the phones are working at last."

"Seems like it." I'm not about to tell him that we probably just drove into the range of someone else's mast – in a 'borrowed' car.

"Holly, darling, I just had to tell you. Your email arrived whilst we were still wrapping up a few details, so..." The sound is suddenly muffled, "No, I'll pop out here. Keep the change." And back to normal volume: "...so I played it on speaker and..." I think he's off talking to London again but it's actually a results show length dramatic pause.

"David, are you still there?"

"It caught their attention, darling."

"What?"

"Scared – Sweetie, I kid you not, once you'd finished there must have been ten seconds of silence and then Christian raised his eyebrows and said, "Wow."

"Christian spoke?" The label's VP has a reputation for being a man of, well... no words.

"Yes, you clever, clever girl – he's normally the hardest to get on side. Rory and Stella are worried that it's a step too far away from your base, but if we have one ear it's so much easier to work on the others. Christian said 'passionate and honest.'"

"I was worried that it was too personal, too depressing."

"Depressing can sell better than happy: look at Adele, darling."

"I s'pose."

"Anyway, I thought you'd want to know. I have to go... and do a thing. Keep it up. Ciao."

I stare incredulously as the screen shows the call has been ended. Tears start to well and, despite rapid blinking, one runs down the edge of my nose. As I dab it with a tissue, I sense Will studying me, but he remains silent.

"Not once did he ask about Ben," I burst out. "I really think he doesn't care. All he's bothered about is that the label likes my bloody song."

"He does seem a bit of a knob."

"He is... but he's a knob who knows everyone in the business."

"A useful knob – they're the worst." He moves one hand to the gearstick and absently taps out a rhythm that might accompany Scared. "It's good that they like the song, though?"

I don't answer, but stare out of the side window at mile upon mile of nothing. Inside my head there's a writhing, seething mass of vipers all ready to strike: at David for being so soulless, at Will for being so reasonable, at the desert for just bloody being there. Every so often, as I fight off the torture of another Ben and Anna daymare, I let out a sigh which must be audible even over the engine.

"You ought to turn that into another song."

"What?" I only register Will's words after the automatic response.

"All that anger you're holding in, use it."

"Am I that transparent?" I say, in a tone which Ben calls my 'picking a fight' voice.

"You're boiling so much I can hear the steam coming out," says Will, widening his eyes. It's as disarming as ever. "Instead of fighting it, turn it into one of your daydreams... but make it a useful one, a song one."

Will and his straightforwardness – I want to scream, I want to chuck rocks... but... "Alright," I say, grudgingly.

"So what's it going to be? Pushing him out of a speeding taxi or drowning him in the Thames?"

"Nothing like that. I..." The snakes fade into an almost monochrome scene. "I'm in one of those big cemeteries, Highgate maybe, at the head of an open grave, surrounded by mourners. The pale robed vicar is staring, as if he's waiting for me. *There's a rose in my hand. I lean forward but someone taps my shoulder and I smell David Henry's alcohol laden breath as he whispers, 'Hurry it up, sweetie, we're due at the O2 in an hour.' I turn and scream, "*I'm hurting, hurting, but you don't care.*"* "
Whoosh...

I'm hurting but you don't care

If my eyes are the windows of my soul, are they so dirty,
that you can't see the torture lying there?
If my hands are the ends of all my nerves, are they so steady,
that you can't feel the tremble of despair?

What are you thinking? Is it just me?
Your little world isn't all there can be.

I'm hurting, hurting but you don't care.
I'm hurting, hurting but you don't care.

If my words are the insights of my mind, are they so pointless,
that you seem so completely unaware?
If my sighs are the outlets of a heart starting to fracture,
is that inconsequential to repair?

Okay, just ignore it. It might go away.
Nothing really matters 'slong as they still pay.

I'm hurting, hurting but you don't care.
Help me break through to dawn from this darkness.
Help me rip through to dawn from this darkness.
Help me smash through to dawn from this darkness.
I'm hurting, hurting... but you don't care.

"Is that the petrol station?" I say, glancing up from my phone where I've been tapping notes on a possible echo pedal intro.

"Whoa, Holly Woodlove has re-entered the building..."

I wrinkle my nose at Will's sarcasm. It's not like I'm totally unaware of the world when I'm in the zone – just concentrating elsewhere – like an athlete is not unaware of cheering crowds as they power down the straight.

"Successful?"

"Hopefully," I say, but don't elaborate as it's clear that the group of buildings rapidly approaching is a petrol station and Will begins to ease off. Rather than the ramshackle colonial building of my imagination, a modern canopy, if slightly wanting of some new paint, rises above the pumps, displaying a large 'Engen' logo. Beside it is a sand coloured building with a low pitched roof. Tourists expecting something more Namibian quirky are probably satisfied by the fine display of cacti protruding from an ancient bathtub.

"We may as well fill up," says Will turning onto the forecourt.

"Is this definitely the place?"

"It's the only petrol station on the C51 – according to this map anyway."

An attendant in a one piece overall shuffles from the building, grinning through wizened features. A short but unruly beard, almost totally white, contrasts sharply with his deep skin tone. "Fill up?" he says to Will as we climb out. The reason for his amusement is immediately clear as he pulls the hose round the back of the vehicle and starts to undo the fuel cap which is on the opposite side to the pump.

"My car at home has it the other way round," says Will. The man just continues to smile. He leaves the nozzle pumping diesel into the tank and begins to wash the windscreen.

"Have you seen another car like this today?" I ask. The man's brow furrows but his only reply is a still wider grin revealing several missing teeth.

"Some friends of ours are in a car like this one," I try again.

"Speak, shop." He touches his mouth and shakes his head, then inclines his head towards the building. The meaning is obvious. I leave Will with the car and go in search of someone with better English.

'Disen,' as it says on her name badge, has much better English but seemingly no memory for people at all. Every question I ask is answered with 'I do not remember' from beneath fluffy dark curls. She also seems fascinated by my handbag. Every time I catch her black coffee eyes, they drop to my bag. I mean, it's okay, but it's not a Mulberry. After about the fourth time I finally catch on. Turning away, I reach into my bag for my purse. I ask the question again, this time proffering a one hundred Namibian dollar note.

"Wow, amazing how memory just become well," says Disen, grinning shamelessly. "I have three customer this morning: a white man with red face and yellow hair, a white man with brown hair and a black man who smelled of the desert. He was..."

"The white man with brown hair," I interrupt, "was he tall?

"Not tall like your man," she says, her eyes indicating through the window to where Will is towering over the pump attendant as he works. At least in my imagination, her eyes linger for a fraction longer than is strictly necessary. I dismiss a ridiculous pang of protectiveness by searching through recent snaps and thrusting my phone under Disen's nose.

"Was this the man?"

"Maybe." I roll my eyes, but she's actually genuinely unsure and explains, slightly huffily, "He wears sun shades."

"Was there a woman with him?"

"Not in here. Maybe in car."

"They were driving a Land Rover Defender like that one – with the same logo on it. Do you remember?"

Disen shakes her head. "I put these on the shelves this morning. I not look. Nice present for child?" She holds up a hand carved and painted Springbok. "Or cheetah?"

"I don't have any children."

She regards me with an expression of incredulity. "That man and no baby?" The childlike question makes her seem even younger. Her eyes flick towards the window and then back to me. I really can't be bothered to explain, so I ignore it.

"Will the man out there remember? Please will you come outside and ask him for us?"

"I am not meant to leave the desk..." She leaves the comment hanging expectantly. "...but I am also to be helpful for customer," she finishes, as I thrust another note towards her.

"Good afternoon," she says to Will with strange formality before turning towards the petrol attendant. He's finished the windows and has just started to check the tyres. They converse in the language with strange clicked consonants which Moses demonstrated on our first day. None of us managed to pronounce a word to his satisfaction.

"He says, there was another car like this here today..." The attendant interrupts her with a comment, pulls a sponge out of the bucket next to his feet and waves it. "...but much dirty than this," she continues. "He says there was a woman with the brown haired man but they drive a Toyota. It was the black man with the Land Rover."

"Is he sure? Could he be forgetting?" asks Will.

Disen smiles weakly, "I ask him, sir." Car company names are incongruously recognisable amongst the clicks.

The attendant answers for himself: He points two fingers towards his eyes, says "Rover," and then touches his cheek, he follows this with "Toyota," and reaches to touch Will's. Will and I exchange confused glances.

Disen adds, "That what he say, but Hage is sometime strange." She lays a hand flat against her temple and says, "Old head."

I reach for my phone again and hold the picture of Ben for the attendant to see.

"He says, he is not sure."

I scroll down to find a picture of Anna. Surely no man would forget her? He pulls the phone closer and squints at it. When he's finished, Disen translates. "He says, he is not sure. He says, you from Europe are so difficult to tell apart."

Will purses his lips. I know how he feels. It's not the definite news we were hoping for, it's more maybes and confusion.

"I am sorry, sir," says Disen, staring up at Will, back to her most formal. "Can I help with anything else?"

Will seems unsure of what to make of Disen. "Well, um, we need to pay for the diesel... and, um, which way did they go?"

"Toyota go south."

"And the Land Rover?"

Disen seems to have to raise her voice to force a second response from the old man. "It turned onto the desert road."

"Desert road? Where's that?" asks Will.

"Please, come stand here, sir," she says, gently pulling him by the elbow to the roadside. Will throws me a puzzled expression but allows himself to be guided. She jerks her head to indicate up the road. "If you go straight, after many kilometre comes Angola but see there is a sign board? That way you go north of Etosha towards Oshakati. Instead, you take left you drive on the desert road."

I join the two of them staring up the highway. "Where does this desert road go?"

"Nowhere... there is old diamond mine. People go look and come back."

Despite the oppressive mid-afternoon sun, a shiver runs up my spine – this is too similar to my imagination. "Come on Will, let's pay and get going."

"Three hundred and twenty two dollars, please sir."

Once we've paid up, Will starts the engine and we idle across the forecourt. "North, I suppose?" he queries.

"What are the chances of a Lodge Defender being here and it not being Ben and Anna," I say.

He pulls onto the road and begins to accelerate.

"Very helpful young woman," he says.

"Oh she was fine once I'd given her an 'aide memoire.'" I rub my thumb across my fingers to make sure he understands.

"Really? And scarily polite."

"Only to you. You know, I do believe she was flirting." The car judders as Will's foot twitches on the accelerator.

CHAPTER 12

The desert 'road' is more like one of the game reserve tracks: gravel surfaced, winding, and frequently bumpy. We even pass a jackal lazing in the shade of a boulder. The landscape, initially dotted with hardy bushes, becomes starker as we push west until the whole world is rock, gravel and sand. It could have an otherworldly beauty, but right now it seems harsh and forbidding.

"Do you really think they would come this way?" says Will, changing down a gear as the track winds over another bare ridge.

"No... but I never thought they would drive further than Moses told them to in the first place. Something weird must have happened so they're not thinking straight."

"You've got an idea, haven't you? Something that you keep imagining? Tell me." Will sounds like he's going through a bad patch. I'll have to say something.

"It's just crazy, daft stuff that bounces round my head, it's not an idea."

He slams on the brakes so he can turn towards me properly. "Holly, stop protecting me like I'm a little kid. I'm feeling all the same stuff as you. If you think they've flipped and are on some mad how-many-different-bits-of-desert-can-we-do-it-in adventure just talk to me about it. You think I've not wondered about that too?"

"I'm not trying to protect you, I'm... I suppose I'm just embarrassed about how weird my imagination is." I take a deep breath. "It's not one thing. Every time we find some sort of clue it changes. To start with I was imagining them being kidnapped, or having been bitten by a snake. Then I was thinking about the shagging thing. That was why I... that was why we... But then back at the lodge I kept imagining that they'd had a crash and their car was buried by the storm and they were inside suffocating."

Will puts one of his big hands on top of mine. "I've thought about all those things too – well, maybe not the suffocating, but everything else. I don't get caught in some vivid gore movie like you do, but that doesn't mean I'm not thinking it. So what is it now?"

I swallow before starting. It probably sounds like a gulp to Will. "Now I'm worried that Ben has done something to Anna, something so awful that he can't bear it, and he's just going to drive off into the desert and never come back."

"Okay, you got me. I hadn't thought of anything like that." Will lifts the clutch and we continue along the track slightly faster than before. "And you think that's why they've come this way?"

"Will, it's just my imagination." There's no answer. I suspect he's now wishing he hadn't asked and concentrating on the driving is a distraction.

It's late afternoon and we seem to be racing the sun to the horizon. Dry river bed follows low hillside, follows gravel valley, the road's gradient never too steep or corners too sharp as befits a route once taken by heavy machinery and supply lorries. I'm beginning to wonder quite how far this mine can be when we crest another ridge and find ourselves overlooking a wide plain. The scene is dominated by a huge terraced hole which disappears into the ground who knows how deep like some petrified whirlpool. Rows of rectangular buildings cover the ground to one side of the hole. Will draws the car to a halt next to a couple of low bushes with unusual circular leaves.

"I think those must be what they call 'dollar bushes'," I say dropping down from the Defender.

"Mmm." Will is engrossed in scanning with the binoculars. The heat haze is beginning to subside and the view goes on for miles.

"Holly, look!"

"Where?"

"Over to the right, where I'm facing. There's something moving... it's..." I shade my eyes from the low sun with an outstretched hand, but without binoculars all I can see is distant dunes. "...It's gone. But, Holly, I'm pretty sure it was a white car." He stares at me with slightly wild eyes. That direction is way beyond the mine and towards the deep desert of the Skeleton Coast.

"Let me see." I grab the binoculars and sweep the horizon. There's nothing moving, but... "Was it where the dunes start beyond that dark boulder?"

"Yes."

"There might be tracks but it's so far away." I slide the view back towards the mine. There does seem to be a dark line – or is it my imagination? What I thought were buildings are actually just low foundation walls where structures have been removed. Just like the diamonds, the whole operation has been scooped up and taken elsewhere.

"Come on," says Will climbing back into the Land Rover.

"We're not going to make it before the light goes, you know." The sun is dipping almost visibly – so much quicker in the tropics than at home.

"We'd better hurry up then."

Even though we career along, almost taking off at times, it's twilight once we're onto the plain and Will has to fire up the headlights before we reach the mine. On the outskirts of what's left of the buildings the track spreads out and loses definition. Will slows to a crawl as we scour the illuminated arc for clues.

"That one," he says, speeding forward again. I agree the path chosen seems slightly wider than the others. It's eerie passing between rows of what must have been offices, workshops, accommodation. Our headlamps highlight the low walls: clean on one side, supporting a ramp of sand on the other – beyond them, nothing but blackness. Will takes a fork to the left; again it seems like the main route. We leave the skeleton town behind and the track rises to a low crest.

"Stop!" I scream, but Will's foot is already on the brakes. All four wheels lock and the Land Rover skids towards a gap between two heavy posts. Beyond them, the track gapes into nothingness. Beside the left hand post, I just have time to see the remains of a gate lying twisted in the sand as we career past. Fixed to the gate is a sign with one word, 'Danger.' The view through the windscreen goes dark as the ground disappears and the Defender tips forward.

"No..." shouts Will. I spin my head round to make eye contact with him one last time, but the dashboard light is too dim...

Miraculously, after a fraction of a second his terror frozen face is lit up again, the tyres are still scraping against something, the vehicle is still slowing. Realisation comes in about the same time it takes us to slide to a halt. We are on a steeply sloping ramp about two vehicles wide which curves gradually at the limit of our lights. To the right, sheer rock, to the left a gaping void. We've driven onto an access way that leads down into the mine. Huge wheeled lorries carrying tonnes of rock used to struggle up this slope on the way to sifting plants.

"Holy shit, I thought we were going over the edge," says Will bursting into relieved laughter. He stretches out a hand – it's shaking wildly. I hold mine beside his – it's just as bad. I take a deep breath, hold it for a couple of seconds and then push calmness along my limbs as the air flows out through my nose. "Bloody hell, how d'you do that? You're as steady as a rock," says Will. That's a bit of an exaggeration, but the contrast is now so sharp it makes me giggle – which in turn causes my trembling to return. "Ha, pride comes before a fall," he grins.

"It's just something I learnt. My hands used to shake so much I couldn't play the guitar properly if I was nervous."

"Which isn't much good in your line of work."

"No."

"Maybe you'd better reverse us out of here, then."

Will climbs out to allow me to slide across to the driver's seat. To my alarm, he doesn't just round the front of the car, but walks to the edge and peers into the blackness.

"You can just see the next terrace down," he says, sliding back into the passenger seat. It's not that far."

"Far enough." A brief vision of my little brother flinging toy cars end over end down the stairwell of our childhood apartment is enough to ensure that I double check reverse is engaged before lifting the clutch. Once back through the gateway, I turn the car away from the mine and pull off the track. "I don't think we should carry on in the dark. If we break the car out here we really will be screwed."

"I agree." I was expecting – perhaps even wanting – Will to argue and this catches me by surprise. Maybe he spots the ghost of a frown on my forehead because he adds, "If they were going to drive off the end of the world they'd have done it here... Not gone past."

He's right, of course, but then why drive out here in the first place? I mean, a little undisturbed privacy is one thing, but this? The thought of privacy seems to have a bloating effect on my bladder. "Umm. I need to get out and pee." I glance through the side window into the darkness. "I don't suppose you could, err, be look out for me?" My cheeks are burning. "I mean, so I'm not bitten on the bum by a jackal or something."

"Only if you do the same for me," smiles Will.

Squatting by starlight, concentrating on not wetting my sandals, the ridiculousness of all this hits me. "What the hell are we doing, Will?"

"Umm, I'm guessing you don't mean watering the desert?" His voice is faint like he's still facing away. I finish and pull everything back up.

"Chasing round the desert like some single-handed rescue mission – Kaura is right, we're a liability." I risk a glance towards Will, who does have his back turned and from his shoulder movements I'm guessing he's engaged in what Ben would term 'giving it a good finishing off shake.'

"Apart from nearly driving off the edge of a cliff, I think we're doing okay." He finishes up and turns. "We've managed to work out how to go to the loo without having our private parts savaged by wild animals and without flashing each other. How difficult can this survival stuff be?"

"Idiot." I chuck him the packet of wet wipes. Oddly, our brush with death seems to have lightened the mood.

"Seriously, though," he says, running each finger through a wipe, "we've got to follow now we're here. I mean, if there was a phone signal, I'd call, but there isn't..."

"We only have limited food and diesel."

"I know... Why don't we give it until mid-morning and then if we can't find anything we'll go back to the petrol station and phone for the helicopter?"

"Seems like a plan." I reach into the Land Rover and turn off the headlights. Now that the north-western glow has completely disappeared the stars are amazing.

"Let's picnic on the bonnet," he says, following my gaze. "It'll be warm for ages and we don't want to be cooped up in there all night. I'll get the hamper."

It's a lovely idea. The bonnet is warm and, with a blanket, not too uncomfortable. I lie back and take in the vista. Every so often the world shakes as Will moves about in the back. He's obviously searching for more than food. When he does reappear he has a torch in one hand, the hamper in the other and a long canvas bag slung over one shoulder.

"What's in the bag?"

"Look." He pulls open studs and draws the end back. The smooth black muzzle of a hunting rifle glints in the torchlight.

"Gosh... Is it loaded?"

"No, but there's a box of bullets in here too."

Any sort of gun gives me the creeps. I hate it when you walk through airport security and the police have sub-machine guns slung over their shoulders. It's a British thing, I suppose: guns are for the army, full stop. "They make me uncomfortable too," says Will, disconcertingly reading my thoughts. "I'll put it back." He hoists the hamper up next to me and retreats.

Once he returns with the torch, we explore our meal options. It's quite different from what has been prepared for our excursions and clearly has a more Germanic palette in mind – which is just fine by me. There is bread, cheese, cooked meat and several types of sliced sausage, fruit and, best of all, cake and sweet pastries. Everything is in separate sealed containers and still cool to the touch. In the layer below: more of the same, plus uncooked steaks for the barbeque. No doubt packed somewhere in the roof boxes is a portable brai.

"Those T-bones Moses cooked were gorgeous, but let's stick to the cold stuff for now shall we?" Will nods. I don't imagine he fancies cooking any more than I do. I open a side compartment and find drinks. The juices will make a pleasant change from the warm water we have been sipping all day from plastic bottles. There's also beer and, surprisingly, a bottle of Talisker whisky.

"Mr Schloerman obviously likes his single malts."

"Maybe it's Mrs Schloerman?"

"Maybe..." says Will in a tone that says, 'Okay I know that was mildly sexist, but the balance of probability is...'

For the next few minutes there's the near silence of two people whose adrenalin levels have dropped to the point where they've realised that they haven't eaten since breakfast and are determined to make up for it. Once stomachs are beginning to fill, the pace slows, allowing conversation to flow.

"This sausage isn't bad. I wonder if they import it specially?"

"Spicy, isn't it?" says Will, reaching for an apple. The movement of his hand draws my eyes to the bottle in the next compartment.

"I think I'm going to have a finger of the whisky to help me sleep. Are you up for that?"

"Never really been into spirits, but it sounds better than those tablets of yours."

Conveniently, there are two tumblers. I twist out the cork and pour. "It's a good one, if I remember rightly." Will takes a swig and promptly splutters half of it back into the glass. "You've never drunk neat whisky before, have you?" Will shakes his head, still coughing. "That was way too much. Take a sip; roll it round your mouth; savour it; swallow and then blow out gently; appreciate the heat and the after-taste. Watch..." I follow my own instructions. It's heavenly. Will follows suit. His throat almost catches, but he manages to blow and the pained expression mutates into a smile.

"Oh, I see what you mean. Earthy and salty?"

"They say it's meant to taste like seaweed. The distillery's right by the shore."

"I didn't take you for a whisky girl."

"It's not me, really. Ben dragged me on a crawl of Scotland's finest distilleries one June. Actually, 'dragged' is a bit harsh. It was a lovely holiday – those parts of it I can remember..."

Will takes a more confident sip this time without a hint of a cough. His expression is pensive.

"Do you really think that about Ben?"

"What?"

"That he would do something to Anna."

"Will, it's just my weird imagination."

"But why would you imagine it if you didn't think... He hasn't ever...?"

I roll my eyes. "Now who's getting over-dramatic?" I let out a long suffering sigh. "For the record, I'm not secretly putting up with a drug riddled wife beater or ashamed of admitting his date rape tendencies."

"Sorry."

"It's not very rock and roll, but we're pretty much a normal couple. David Henry finds it completely incomprehensible."

Will remains silent, probably realising what's good for him. He rests the tumbler on the metal and tilts his face towards the sky. After a minute or so I join him, staring up into the vastness.

"What's the one shaped like an upside down teapot?"

"Sagittarius." I just knew he'd know about stars. "If you go up and round to the left from there you come to the Southern Cross." He waves a hand unhelpfully towards a patch of sky but I think I see which ones he means. "From there you can find all the interesting stuff."

I sip a little more liquid Western Isles. "Go on."

"You see how the cross is made from four stars? If you follow the two which are furthest apart, they point towards the Magellanic clouds – the fuzzy patches."

"Maybe."

"One bigger and one smaller?"

"Oh yes, yes."

"They're outside our galaxy. They're small galaxies which are tagging along with the Milky Way."

"Like a couple of Maltesers?"

"Yeah, maybe." My feeble humour is ignored as there's clearly more lesson to come. "If you go back to the cross and follow the other two stars, they point towards a really bright star. That's Alpha Centauri: our nearest neighbour."

"How far?"

"4.4 light years, I think."

"You think? Not 4.3 or 4.5?"

Will snorts. "Okay, geek alert!"

"How do you know all that stuff?"

"Loved my 'Spotter's Guide to the Night Sky' when I was twelve."

We lapse into silence again. My thoughts slip back to Ben and Anna. Anna was my nearest neighbour at uni: the girl in the room down the corridor; the girl who had all the guys' heads turning.

"It's not exactly Ben, as such, it's Anna." My thoughts burst out through my lips. "She just has that 'thing' – whatever it is that guys can't resist. It's not beauty exactly, although she's pretty enough, it's... it's...

"Sexiness." Unsurprisingly, I suppose, Will has put his finger right on it.

"Yeah, and I suppose I'm worried that maybe being alone with her, if she... I don't know... he might..."

"You make it sound like her fault."

"Heck, no, of course it's always the guy's fault. I'm just saying what I see. If we're in a pub, all those little sideways glances; if we're out shopping, all those eyes following her as she walks past, all the mental undressing... and more. I mean, I suffer from a bit of that nowadays but she's always had it – and I know with me they're just thinking, 'is she that singer?'"

"Yeah, of course, they're never thinking, 'that Holly Woodlove I'd love to take her home and...' How could they possibly be thinking that about a tall blonde pop star with a touch of a foreign accent?" Will's voice is thick with sarcasm.

"Okay, I know you say I do myself down, but Anna's on a different level. You must know what I mean."

"Not really." I can't tell if he's serious or not. The torchlight throws shadows, hiding his expression.

"Come on, I mean, in our first term at uni she was asked out twelve times. Twelve! And she was the one with the boyfriend. I wasn't asked once."

"Ha, she's never told me about that. I bet it drove her nuts."

"That's how we got to know each other – she used to hide in my room to avoid overly keen guys."

"The more they pester, the less interested she is," he says, shaking his head. "It was exactly the same at college."

"What did you do then? If you don't mind me asking?"

"Hasn't she ever told you?"

"No, she never said much about you at uni. You were her private secret. And since we've got to know you, I suppose it's never come up. I bet you were really direct, weren't you – James Bond style?"

Will shuffles into a more upright position and drains the dregs of his tumbler. "Nothing like that. I didn't do anything. It was a complete accident. She was just this ultra-choosy girl with the fancy hair. She wasn't even on my list."

"You had a list?"

"Oh yeah, with marks out of ten for everything." He rolls his eyes. "No, I just mean the girls I liked and thought might like me back. I went through quite a few."

"Did you?" I raise my eyebrows.

"Not like that. I was always the one being dumped. I... I suppose I was a bit blunt back then."

Even more than he is now? That's hard to believe. "What sort of things did you say?"

His face puckers with the memories. "You can't win. I remember one girl asked if I thought one of those tube dresses fitted her nicely and I said, maybe if she tried the next size up."

My hand goes up to my mouth. "You didn't..."

"Wham, slap round the face, dumped. She asked. What was I supposed to say?"

"Lie," I say, a fit of giggles starting.

"Then straight after I went out with Lucy who was smiley and slim, but absolutely sure that all other girls had larger breasts. It wasn't even true. I told her I liked them just as they were, but she kept on and on. In the end I said maybe if she ate more, she'd get a few more curves. Wham, dumped. I was only..."

"...trying to be helpful." I interrupt in a gasp.

"Exactly. And there were several others until I went out with Eva-Marie. She was really funny. We had a blast. So when she asked me if she was the sexiest girl in college, I thought she was joking."

"You... said... someone... else... didn't you...?" He pauses to regard my guffaws with mock contempt.

"I do realise now that saying 'No, that would be Anna,' was probably asking for another slap."

"Did you get one?"

"Finger marks on my face for a week... But it was worth it cos that's how I got together with Anna."

"Eh?" My laughter pauses against a wall of confusion.

"At the next party... It was Halloween. I was pissed off with Eva-Marie and with girls in general. I didn't even bother dressing up. I had four cans of Caffrey's and that was all the company I needed. And then a vampire sat down on the sofa beside me and said something like, 'So I hear you think I'm the sexiest girl in college...'

"I thought she'd just come to take the piss, so I said, 'E-M been telling everyone has she?' and went back to my beer. But Anna's not one for being brushed off, so she says, 'if you think that about me, why haven't you asked me out?' I mean, it sounds pretty obvious now, but I had no idea she was even aware of me, so I said, 'What would be the point? You turn everyone down. Why would I put myself through that?' Her fake blood stained mouth opened but she didn't have any words. She just sat there like I'd completely floored her."

He pauses for a moment, wistful eyes glinting with African starlight, but I'm watching eagerly from behind the sofa in that messy, alcohol scented lounge, so I don't interrupt his tale.

"She'd pasted her face white, black eye shadow, lipstick bite marks, the works and she had on this purposely ripped black dress and from my angle I could see, well, a lot of everything. I didn't want to seem like I was checking her out, so I just followed her eyes round the room. Leaning against the door to the hall, two Draculas were eying her up really obviously. One whispered to the other and they both laughed in that 'way' you were talking about earlier. Anna flicked me a rueful smile before focussing on a couple of 'damsels in distress' who were hanging about close to the lechers. One was shaking her head and rolling her eyes, the other was stabbing poisonous glares towards our sofa. Anna took in a deep breath and held my gaze for slightly longer that time. It was weird... like she'd told me a secret without saying a word. That got to me more than all the ripped dresses in the world. I broke our silence with something like, 'Wow that's all a bit shitty, isn't it?' She gave a little shrug as if to say 'I'm not starving to death or anything...' And then the bluntness thing should have killed it. I said, 'You're too good looking, aren't you? The guys can't see past the ripped dress and your girlfriends are beginning to get jealous. If you want to be liked a bit more, take yourself off the market. Actually say 'yes' to the next poor guy who dares to ask you.' Honestly, I wasn't even thinking about myself, but she slid closer and whispered, 'So ask me.'"

"And you leaned forward to kiss her?"

"What else could I do?" he shrugs.

"Oh wow, romance central! I wish Ben and I had a story like that." I begin to put the leftovers back in the hamper. Will passes over a couple of empty tubs.

"You wouldn't say that if you knew what she said straight after our first kiss."

"Go on."

"She said, 'If we're going to keep doing this completely honest thing then you'd look a lot better with a six pack than a four pack.'"

"I see you took that advice to heart," I smile, ripping off a piece from a handy roll of foil which has been provided to wrap up part opened cheeses. The lodge really have this luxury lunching down to a fine art. Thinking of the lodge pops our old-friends-reminiscing bubble. "Oh Will, what the hell are they doing?"

"I wish I knew, but I can't think that Ben would do something to her... I mean we've been friends for years."

"You know those twelve guys who asked Anna out in her first term? Ben was one of those."

"Really?" Will seems taken aback. "But he ended up with you." He rolls off the bonnet to stand upright on the sand. "And you two are happy."

"Yes," I say automatically, "well... mostly." I slide down the other side far less athletically. "I know it's silly but what was Anna wearing when they left?"

Will frowns. "I don't remember. I was pretty much glued to the toilet seat."

"I just keep imagining her in that emerald bikini with the sarong she wears by the pool. She looks so effortlessly gorgeous I feel totally inadequate."

"It's not really birdwatching wear is it?" Will lifts down the hamper and smiles ruefully, "It's funny you use that phrase. Anna often says you make her feel totally inadequate." He raises his voice into an impression: "I'm just a boring sales rep for a boring soap company and she's a fucking pop star."

"I didn't know she felt like that... I'm not diva-ish, am I?"

"Course not – but you are a pop star, just like, in your opinion, Anna has that 'thing'."

CHAPTER 13

Ben concentrates on the route ahead with the intensity of someone who only has this one thing left to cling to. So undivided is his attention that he doesn't notice Anna squirming against one of the rear seat supports. Allowing the rattles and crashes of the Land Rover's bounding progress to cover any sounds, she rubs the rope against the jagged edge of a protruding bolt head. Gradually the strands are fraying. Half an hour more and it gives way. At sloth speed and without changing position she unwinds her hands and lies, still hunched, contemplating her next move. The tape on her face itches like mad but she can't risk moving it. One glance over his shoulder and all advantage would be lost. Tentatively, she stretches out arms and legs, freeing them from pain and stiffness, ready to snap back into position should his head start to turn.

What to do? He's shown you no mercy. He's lied to you, violated you and is going to kill you. Why hesitate? It's self defence... But how could you ever look Holly in the eye again. Could Will live with a killer? If you don't do something now, you'll never see him again anyway.

She springs up, rope twisted round each hand, slips a loop over Ben's head and yanks back sharply. He's caught completely off guard and struggles to loosen the noose from his partially crushed throat with both hands. But Anna's pull is too strong, too panic driven. He reaches behind trying to grab... anything... but she squirms away from his grasp, still pulling, pulling. Consciousness is seeping away, how to stop the crushing? How to breathe? How? He stamps on the brake.

The tension ceases instantly as Anna's off balance body hurtles forward over the front seats. But the rope is wound round her hands and doesn't come free from his neck which becomes the pivot point for her movement. As her back slams into the windscreen, pain sears down one leg, but the rope pulls again in the opposite direction, its force amplified by her moving bodyweight. She just has time to register a sickening crack before the Land Rover's unguided front wheels dig into a slope, start to twist and the vehicle tumbles onto its side.

I wake with such a start the whole vehicle rocks. My back is sore from hunching along a bench seat. Somewhere under the blanket, a seat belt clip is digging into my leg. I didn't think I would ever sleep, but sometime in the early hours daymares gave way to nightmares.

"Are you awake?" whispers Will from the front seats.

"Mmmm."

"I think it's just beginning to lighten through the windscreen." I shuffle into a crouched position and peer forward. The distant ridges are now visible: a black mass against the darkest of navy blues. "By the time we've had some breakfast it'll be light enough."

"Before that, can we do the toilet thing again? And, err..." I reach over the rear seat for one of the shovels and a roll of tissue. "...you might want to stand further away this time."

Breakfast is a hastily consumed banana and apple.

"There'll be sand, so you'd better drive," says Will, taking the core from my fingers and stowing it in a plastic box with his own.

As I pull away, I purposely deviate slightly to flatten the small area I disturbed earlier. The headlights are on but we won't need them for much longer. We retrace our route to the previous junction and take a track which seems to head north. After a few hundred metres it also starts to curve towards the mine.

"This is wrong too." The ground either side of the track is largely flat and bare. "What if we just drive east across this stuff? We're bound to cross their tracks sooner or later."

Will nods his agreement. "Slowly though. No more driving off cliffs."

I keep it in first gear and pick our way across open ground. After perhaps half a 'k' we reach some faint tyre marks. I glance a silent question to Will who nods almost imperceptibly. The Land Rover arcs round to follow the trail and picks up speed. This time we do seem to be heading for where the sea of dunes, now emerging from the twilight, meets the outlying slopes of the escarpment ridge. As we approach, the sand deepens and steering becomes tricky.

"I think we should let some air out of the tyres."

"You're the boss," mutters Will automatically. He probably says that at work when he's only half listening to a customer. As I coast to a halt the world seems suddenly lighter. The sun isn't visible yet but maybe it just broke the horizon beyond the hills.

Will locates the pressure gauge easily enough amongst the tools and as he sets to work, I take a glance at his map, lying on the dashboard. The road to the mine is marked, but beyond, only blank space: miles of wilderness, right up to the arbitrary line of the Angolan border and beyond. What the hell are they doing? Please let me be wrong.

"All done." Will climbs back in. "Other people have come this way. It's not just one set of tracks. It must go somewhere." Marginally comforted, I set off again with markedly improved control. The tracks weave around the edges of outlying dunes and approach the foot of the ridge. We begin to climb to a saddle where a dune protrudes from the slope like a flashgun frozen wave against a sea wall. This is the place where Will saw the car yesterday. Both of us hold our breath as we crest the brow.

Nothing. Nothing except the forbidding beauty of an ocean of dunes now caught in the sharp relief of the newly risen sun. At another time, the view of this testament to the elemental power of air over earth would alone be worth the drive, but today it just looks like a haystack.

"The ruts go that way." Will points down the slope into the gap between this ridge and the next.

"And we carry on until ten-thirty, yes?"

"If we want to be back to the main road before it gets dark."

"Let's not worry about that yet."

Our way leads a roundabout route: skirting the base of one hump, traversing the low end of the next, back down a valley, then circling round again – never more than two dunes away from the rock strewn hillside. It seems inconceivable to me that Ben could find this route from scratch. After a couple of hours the dunes thin out and we cross what must be a dry river. This almost flat area appears to stretch for miles to the west. Water must occasionally flow in vast quantities to drive this huge wedge through the sand, but right now it's as dry as the moon. Our trail passes straight across and continues to weave on the northern side. To begin with, we craned our necks round every bend, over every crest, but now the monotony of it has sunk in which is probably why we're already halfway along a valley heading back towards the escarpment before I notice it: a white vehicle stationary on the next saddle.

"Will, look!"

"It's a Land Rover." A few more yards and we can see the lodge's logo on the side, but also that it seems to be empty.

"Shall I drive up and park beside it?" I say, lifting my foot off the power.

Will must be feeling the same sense of concern. "Maybe it would be better to stop here and walk up?" he says and, nodding, I halt at the base of the slope.

It's nearly ten o'clock. The dune shadows are dwindling fast and the sky is a colour chart of blues from pale in the east right across to deeper in the west. Not a single wisp of cloud breaks the graduation. The heat is already building. Fairly soon it will be unpleasant to be beyond air-conditioning. We trudge up the slope. Will throws me a worried glance. Heck, I hope they're sunbathing over the ridge, going at it, even. Right now that would seem like a minor point.

Their Land Rover seems in good condition. The rear windows are caked in dust but the driver's side is wide open so I peer in. Stuffed in the well between dashboard and radio is the end of a packet of wipes that appear to be the ones out of Anna's bag, but across the passenger seat lies an unfamiliar dun combat jacket.

"Holly," whispers Will urgently. I follow his eyes over the bonnet, down the slope of the dune to where...

"Oh, shit."

"Down." Will starts to duck, but it's too late. We turn and pelt down the slope, the image of what I've just seen seared into my brain: fifty metres away, two dun Defenders stopped, one behind the other; a man in desert combats lying half under the front car; two more in similar attire standing over him; a few yards to the right a fourth wearing a maroon beret, cigarette in hand, staring straight at us with an open mouth. Of course, Will's version of 'pelting' and mine vary by about ten miles an hour. He reaches our Land Rover well before me and automatically makes for the driver's side. As he rips open the door he glances back towards me questioningly.

"Just drive!" I gasp. He's already turned the key and begins to reverse hard as I jump in. My door swings back open almost pulling me out with it. My head clouts the frame but I save myself with a grab for the seatbelt and an almighty tug on the door handle.

"Are you okay?" says Will, concentrating on his side mirror.

"Don't worry about me," I say, slightly dazed. I blink furiously, trying to clear my head. Will swings the car round as the beret man reaches Ben and Anna's car. He takes aim with a hand gun. Will floors the accelerator, yanks on the wheel and hopes. I don't hear or feel a shot but sand sprays up from a slope beside us. How could he miss? A few seconds later we're belting back along our own tracks at twice the speed we came.

"Are they following?" Will's eyes are wide and bloodshot.

"Can't see... too dusty..." As we circle the end of the dune, I arch my neck out of the side window for a rearward view.

"Fuck, one of the army Land Rovers." Will tries to up the speed but we're beginning to weave and the wheel is going to wrench from his grip any moment. "No quicker than that or we'll crash. They won't be able to go any faster." Will nods.

A thought occurs, I undo my seatbelt and clamber into the back.

"Where you going?"

"To get the gun."

"Shit."

I unzip the bag and pull out the rifle. There's a telescope thing on the top and under it is the bit where the bullets go. I know this from films I've watched with Ben under sufferance. Right now I wish I'd paid more attention. The Land Rover tips to climb to a saddle and slows right down. Our dust cloud reduces and the chasing vehicle looms large in the rear window.

"Will, they're gaining."

"It's just because of the slope." He's right, as they start to climb, they don't move any closer but in the distance I think I see the blurry whiteness of a second vehicle. Focus. Get back to the job in hand.

"How do you open it to put the bullets in? I'm sure I need to pull something back but nothing's budging."

"I think you lift a lever on the side and then pull back." That was it. I lift, pull and a hole opens in the side of the gun.

"Done it."

"It probably fits three bullets in the chamber. Then you push the bolt back and flip the lever down again to load it. Every time you fire you have to pull it back to let the old round out and then push it forward to load the next one."

"I thought you didn't like guns."

"I don't. My mate Paul was in the cadets. He had a wooden one to practise with that he kept shoving in my face every time I... hold on." We lurch over the crest and accelerate down the slope. Two of the three bullets slip from my hand as I make a grab for the seat-back to steady myself. They scatter across the floor. I shove the remaining one into the rifle and reach into the box for replacements. A few seconds more and it's loaded. I glance up to see we're almost at the end of the slope.

"Ease off and then floor it again just before you reach the bottom." Will does as bidden and the Land Rover hits the horizontal sand with a couple of big bounds, a larger cloud of dust, but nothing more. Keeping my hand well away from the trigger, I thread the rifle over the passenger seat, rest it metal end down on the floor and reach into my bag for the sleeping pills.

"Can you see them?" says Will, all of his concentration facing forward.

As the track begins to curve, the shadowy form of a vehicle appears as if through the clearing fog... but it's further behind, at the base of the slope. "Yes! They're stuck. One of them's getting out. Get down!"

There's a loud clang from the spare wheel hanging on the rear door as I lie across the seats. Will tries to shrink low as he begins to skirt the end of the next dune. Another thud: this time from somewhere on the rear nearside, followed by an odd whistling.

"We're round," he sighs. I raise my head to see that the path of any more bullets is now blocked by sloping sand.

"Just keep going. You're doing great." I squeeze Will's nearest shoulder. "I'll have a scan of the damage."

Moving around the bouncing vehicle is not easy. I clamber over the bench seat and slide to the back row. The whistling is due to some new ventilation we've acquired. The grey trim under the rear window is hanging loose and behind it a neat oval hole has been punched through the bodywork. What if that had hit flesh? I shudder and shove the trim back into place. The clips are mangled but after a thump it stays on and the wind noise lessens.

"What are you doing back there?"

"Plan B." David Henry always says you should have a plan B: a second plectrum held with Blu-tac to the side of your guitar; a second microphone on a second stand; a pre-prepared joke ready for if you go hideously wrong. This just seems like a time when a plan B – any straw to clutch – might be a good idea. Our hamper sits wedged between the two rear seats. I scramble inside for the whisky bottle, grip it between my thighs and pull out the stopper. Inevitably, just as the arrival of drinks on a plane signals the start of turbulence, the car bounds and a little of the whisky spills onto my trousers. Somewhere a detached part of brain thinks, 'what a waste'. I shock it further by pouring the whole bottle of sleeping tablets into the neck, slamming back the stopper, and shaking vigorously. Once my dubious cocktail has been returned to the hamper, I clamber back into the front seat and fasten the belt like a good girl.

We're approaching the hillside again. If we can just keep a steady pace and they're stuck for a while we should gain a good lead. Will risks a glance towards me. "What about Ben and Anna? You didn't see any sign of them, did you?"

Oh heck, no. In the adrenalin fuzz of self preservation, I hadn't thought. Now the implications of the lodge Land Rover, those men, and their guns hit home. Oh shit, oh fuck, oh shit...

"You didn't see them?" Will repeats.

"No. Only maybe Anna's tissues in their Defender."

"So..."

I'm not going to let him verbalise anything and interrupt: "...we need to get back to where we can call for the bloody army."

Will nods and changes down a gear as we start to rise out of the valley between two dunes. His eyes slip back my way, "What's your plan B?"

"I put..."

To the left of us, the lodge Defender bursts into view, hurtles down a slope that seems far too steep to climb; skids to a stop across the tracks ahead of us with a jolt. The driver, beret clearly visible through the open window, seems stunned for a moment by the jerk, but then turns and trains his revolver. He fires, aiming low.

"Go round the back of him," I scream. Another shot and this time a thud somewhere below us. It's clear from Will's fighting with the wheel and our slowing speed that one of our tyres has blown. It might not matter in deep sand. We round the back of his vehicle and continue up the slope. He's out on the sand now, still firing. More thuds. Our momentum really starts to fade and it's clear we're not going to reach the top.

Hands shaking violently I pick up the rifle, open the door, and jump to the sand just before we grind to a halt. I slide along the side of the Land Rover, shove the rifle against what I hope is the right place on my shoulder and peer through the telescope thing – just sand. Through my other eye I can see the beret man speaking into something like an old style walkie-talkie, but I can't keep the rifle from shaking. I point in the general direction, close my eyes and yank on the trigger. It won't move. Safety catch. They always talk about that in the films. On the other side of the gun there does seem to be a small lever. The man has started up the slope now. I yank the lever down, raise the rifle back to my eye and pull. The noise is so loud and the thing jerks back at me so hard I almost drop it. Somewhere, surprisingly close to the man, a puff of sand leaps into the air. He flattens himself to the ground. What now? Oh, yes, the bolt thingy. I lift and pull: a cylinder of metal falls out and I push back in and twist. I try to steady the rifle against the corner of the vehicle and use the telescope again. It's a small improvement. Beret man raises his head. I pull. There's a noise somewhere between a thud and a pop. Behind and to the right of the beret, which is once more tight to the sand, the other lodge Defender rocks as one of its rear tyres suddenly goes flat.

"Good shot," whispers Will into my left ear. He's holding the box of bullets and a shovel.

"I wasn't even aiming at the car," I murmur, pulling and pushing to reload.

"Hit it again and I'll put three more in." There's a puff of sand just in front of the Land Rover followed by something that sounds like a curse from the pinned down man. I retreat behind the corner of our car, Will jams in three more bullets and I reload. The man is sliding round to the left keeping flat to the floor. We can't have that. This time I purposely aim the little cross below and to the left of the other car. The passenger window shatters. To my complete shock, this causes the beret man to stand up, shouting. His hands go above his head, hand gun dangling from one index finger.

"Stop it, you crazy, crazy people," he says in deep accented English. I reload, put the rifle back to my eye and move it until the upper right part of the view is filled with combats.

"Why should we? You were shooting at us," Will shouts.

"I shoot your tyres with small bore. I only want to stop you. Do you not know where you are? You put a bullet in my radiator, you put a bullet in my head. Only lizard walk here."

"Your friends shot at us with a rifle." Good point, Will.

"They damage their car. They are angry. Better if we talk."

"Throw your gun away," I shout, watching carefully through the lens. For a second he makes no move, then the hand containing the pistol lowers. My trigger finger twitches but he doesn't aim; he underarms the gun onto the ground a few feet to the side.

I take my eye from the lens but keep the gun raised as I step clear of our vehicle. Will follows beside me, holding the spade like a weapon. We halt at what feels like a safe couldn't-leap-before-I-shoot distance in front of Beret man. His skin is a shade darker than your average Namibian, but a jagged pink scar splits one cheek from chin to ear. It hints at former combat and adds an air of menace not really warranted by his unexpectedly slight frame. His eyes – exactly the same tone as the surrounding face – seem to register surprise. Why – because the woman's holding the gun? Yeah, and she might pull the trigger by accident.

"Why are you driving a Damara Lodge Land Rover?"

The man's brow furrows. He glances over his shoulder and then towards our Defender. A brief dawn of partial understanding rises across his face, only to be covered by immediate clouds of further confusion.

"Where are Anna and Ben?" Will's voice is as icy as I've ever heard it.

"What is Annanben?" He's a good liar.

"Anna <u>and</u> Ben: the people who were driving that Defender, last time we saw them."

"I have never seen any Anna or any Ben."

"Why are you driving their car then?"

"Mother provide it for us."

"What?"

"We had to change plans, we had a difficult journey ahead and Mother sent us another car."

This guy isn't making much sense. "What have you done with them? Are they here somewhere, or have you..."

"I do not understand..." He's a very good liar. He genuinely looks confused. Will clearly decides that there's no point pussyfooting around.

"You're a poacher aren't you?" The man stays silent. "We saw the rhino you killed. What did you do with Anna and Ben when you stole their car?"

"You think I have taken your friends?" A cautious glance passes between Will and me.

"I think you might have killed my husband and his girlfriend," I say bringing the gun closer to my face. For a second I imagine fear in his eyes but then he seems to stare through me and an incongruous laugh explodes from his chest.

"You are the one with gun. You can believe me or no. We took the horn – yes, we are poachers – my men will feed their families for two years off this trip." He raises his eyebrows, perhaps even inviting the condemnation. He gets no reaction and after a couple of seconds, continues: "We drive south to take a different loop back, but there was a rockslide. We had to come back the same way. We fear we may have to fight, but no, instead, Mother provide us with a new Rover."

"What do you mean: mother?" say Will.

He spreads his arms wide. "She is all around you..." He indicates the dunes either side with a swish of each hand and raises a scar bent smile. "We are here between her breasts."

"You mean the desert? How did the desert give you a car?"

Again he spreads his arms so exaggeratedly wide it almost seems fake. "She is harsh parent. She provides for all life but she can take it," he makes a snatch movement with his right hand, "just like that." I take half a step back at the sudden movement. "But if you respect her, sometimes she gives you a gift – like a Defender, sitting alone with wide open doors, asking for you to take it.

Wide open doors. That's how it was. Oh, hell – is this the truth? I meet Will's eyes. Are we still searching in the wrong... Movement in the periphery of my vision causes my head to snap back forward, my finger to automatically yank on the trigger. The poacher chief is charging at me, bent low to the ground. I barely have time to register that the shot has fired harmlessly over his head before he springs upwards, ripping the rifle from my hands, knocking me sprawling backwards across the sand. The shovel comes whirling round at head height only to be blocked with a clang by the rifle. I roll onto my front, but as I start to rise there are two new pairs of dun legs bearing down on us from the direction of our own Land Rover. I raise a hand for protection, but a heavy boot smashes it into my face. A second kick connects with my stomach and I collapse again, gagging for breath against the sand. With a final rush of adrenalin I turn my head sideways and force open one eye. Will is tugging furiously at the shovel which has been grabbed by one of the poachers. Behind him Beret man is swinging the butt of the rifle. I scrunch shut my eye, but I can't keep the end-of-all-hope thud from my ears.

CHAPTER 14

A minute or an hour later, I'm being pulled upright by my pony tail. I kick out with one leg and it connects with something bony. There's a curse followed by a laugh and the beret man's scornful voice. The grip on my hair tightens and something hard and warm is shoved against my temple. Blinking, I open my eyes to see it's a pistol held by a very young looking poacher who's also yanking my hair. A few feet away another, more my age, is sat on his backside, rubbing his knee, glaring at me with unconcealed hate. Standing beside him, the beret man's lopsided smile has returned.

"Stay still, you crazy cow." My head is spinning, face throbbing, and every breath is a struggle. I just try to focus on what he's saying. "I tell my friend, if you stand near giraffe you get kicked, but he is not a happy lion. If you make too much trouble you will not be worth it." What's he talking about? Where's Will? Will, oh, no... My eyes search frantically for the familiar amongst boots and legs – a trainer in the extreme left of my vision. I strain against the pull to see more: leg, body, face half-turned into the sand, blood in his hair.

"No..." I attempt to struggle to my feet but a blow to the back of the head puts me down again.

"I said, stay still."

"What's the point when you've killed him... you fucking bastard."

"Giraffe that talk like a hyena." He chuckles like a wet engine turning over. "Your big friend is not dead. Not unless he has a very weak head." He gives an order in some African language and I'm dragged over to Will who I now see has his arms taped together at the wrist behind his back. As mine are similarly bound, a low groan escapes from Will's mouth. Yes! I mentally fist pump. He's pulled to a sitting position and we're arranged back to back, more tape wrapping our hands together. Will can't yet be properly conscious. His head is lolling and he's leaning on me heavily. I brace against the sand with my feet. When did it get so hot? The sun is glaring down unsympathetically. If they leave us like this for long we'll be barbecued like a pair of chickens.

The two 'soldier' poachers have already raised up our Defender onto a board and jack and are swapping over the first flat for the spare on the rear door. I can't quite turn far enough to see Ben and Anna's but it sounds like the 'captain' poacher is doing the same.

"Will," I whisper, jiggling my shoulder blades. There's another groan. "Will, wake up."

A splutter's followed by "Uh?" and the pressure against me eases.

"Will!" I'm pushed again by his body weight and his breathing deepens. All that athleticism and no use at all. "Will!" I'm worried he's more than just knocked out. "Will..."

Beret man must have heard me. He approaches, retrieved pistol in hand. His head inclines towards our Defender. "Mother keeps on giving." His lopsided smile fills me with a mixture of hate, fear and regret; regret that I made that basic Bond villain mistake: should've pulled the trigger when I had the chance. "I wonder how you followed us." The word 'you' is full of scorn and dismissiveness.

I remain silent.

"Has the hyena forgotten how to howl?" He pulls something back on the pistol and steps beside me. I wait for the gun at my temple but it doesn't come. Instead, a whisper in my ear: "I wonder how many more hits his head takes before..?" His arm swings up.

"No!" His arm stays frozen at the top of its travel. "Someone saw the Defender at the petrol station: a delivery man. He drove to the lodge and told us."

"And you arrive here in two days?"

"We drove fast."

"How you know we came through the dunes?"

"We guessed you went along the mine road, then yesterday evening we saw you from the top of the ridge above the mine."

"You catch up with us from there?" His voice is slightly disbelieving.

"He drives fast," I say, indicating Will with a flick of the head. I think the poacher captain suspects I'm lying, but he's not sure about what.

"Why are you alone? Where are your guide?"

"Right behind us," I say, a little bolshy madness returning. "They're probably just about to come over that dune and shoot you dead." Wham. Not the gun down onto Will thankfully, but the back of his other hand across my face. The bruises already present make it feel like a sledgehammer. A yelp escapes from my lips and by the time the pain begins to dull to an ache, I find my cheeks are wet with tears. Beret man is squinting down at me, pensively.

"Ah, hyena is giraffe after all." His voice is soft with an almost sympathetic tone. "Why would two tourist chase after poachers?"

"We weren't..." I stop, realising I've given too much away.

"You were not expecting us?" I say nothing, but he can see the truth in my expression. "You thought you were chasing this Ben and Ann. Your husband, his wi... ah.." I can see two and two being added. "You think you were chasing lovers... instead you find poachers and run."

He raises his eyes heavenward, shaking his head. "Mother, you are cruel, but thank you." Turning away, he claps at the other two, presumably to hurry them up. Despite not falling for my bluff, maybe he is worried that others are following. I wonder if Toivo or even Moses is on our trail by now? But how would they know where to go after the mine?

Now that beret man has lost interest, I suddenly notice that I'm not holding any of Will's weight, in fact, not since... "Will?" I breathe.

"Holly," comes the almost inaudible response. My heart skips and I have to swallow down a cry of joy. I move my head so his is resting on my right shoulder, ear to ear.

"Are you okay?" I whisper.

"Sore head, feel sick, but alive. You?"

"Same."

"I'm going to pretend to still be knocked out. It might give me a chance..."

"He's coming back." The captain and the other two are leaving our Defender, heading towards us. I nuzzle Will's head and moan "Will, wake up... Will..." They pass by without comment.

After a minute or two, Will, continues: "They're changing the wheel on his car now. Maybe when they move us we'll get a chance."

"If they were going to kill us they'd have done it by now. Maybe we should just go along with it. I suppose they want a ransom."

"Maybe." He doesn't sound very convinced.

SWEAT HAS BEGUN TO DRIP into my eyes and my forehead is definitely burning before the other Defender is ready.

"They're co'ing," breathes Will through stationary lips. The young poacher pulls me forward while the other cuts the tape holding us together. Will slumps sideways onto the ground.

"Soft head man still asleep?" The captain prods the prone body with a foot. Then without warning he kicks hard at a kidney. Will can't help but grunt. "No. I think not."

I am lifted to my feet and find myself peering down on beret man from a good three inches extra height.

"Come, giraffe," he says, guiding me towards Ben and Anna's Defender. I have little choice but to comply. I suppose Will will ride in the other car. Splitting us up. Clever.

He opens the passenger door, waits for me to get in, and then carefully does up the seat belt.

"I can't sit with my hands like this."

"You will live, giraffe." Well, it was worth a try.

I glance across the sand towards Will. The poacher I kicked has his rifle pointed to where Will is still lying on his side.

"Hey," I scream. Beret man seems almost as indignant and rattles off a tirade in his own language. Much to my relief the rifle is slung back over a reluctant shoulder. As Beret man climbs in the driver's side, I ask, "What did you say?"

He regards me with an almost mournful expression. "I tell him not to waste more bullet. Mother will do our work. It is respectful to let her finish what she started."

My head snaps back towards Will and beyond him, through the heat shimmer, to the two poachers climbing into the other Land Rover. No... they can't...

Panic words tumble from my mouth: "You can't leave him. I'm... he's a popstar, he's famous, in England he's important. People will pay you a lot of money to have him back. That's what you want isn't it: money?"

"I already get money from the horn. What do I know about hostage and ransom? I seen it on TV but it looks like a good way of getting a bullet in head."

"But I can find ten times what you'll get for a rhino horn. You can't leave him... please."

"Rich giraffe?"

"Yes, millions of pounds." Maybe I've overdone it. He stares at me, screws his eyes up and shakes his head.

"No. He too big, too strong, too much trouble. Not worth bullet in head."

"Noooo...." I try to struggle but I'm held in by the belt and can only flail and lean. He turns the key and pulls away as the other Defender passes. I stop struggling to fix Will in the rear view mirror for as long as I can. As we round the base of the first dune I still haven't seen him move. In desperation I slam my weight towards the captain but the belt holds, he fends me off easily and I slump against the door, whimpering.

"Why... take me... if you don't want money?"

"I try not kill women..." My eyes flick towards his face. In profile, I only see his ugly side. What has happened to him to cause this twisted morality? He continues to keep his eyes on the tracks ahead, "...and I always want a pink skin wife."

CHAPTER 15

He's going to rape me. I need to accept that. My whole body trembles in aversion to the incompatible thoughts. Even my nerve-calming technique takes three attempts before the shaking subsides. I need to focus on living: nothing else matters. I need to live so I can go back and find Will. Whatever happens, whatever it takes, they all need to drink the whisky.

Across the sand, they've almost finished stripping anything useful from the broken army Defender. It seems like the suspension collapsed or something similarly terminal during the chase, so they're removing its wheels, siphoning off the diesel, scavenging useful parts and loading it all onto the three remaining vehicles.

The chief poacher smiles as he passes the window carrying a jerry can. It's an oddly cheery smile despite the scar: like one you'd give as you pass a friend... or lover. The vehicle rocks as he clambers onto the roof. That's all it is. I'm not trembling again... I'm not.

The scrapes and judders stop, he slides off the driver's side of the roof and climbs in beside me. A couple of toots of the horn and we're off again, leaving behind a steel carcass. That's all these people do: leave behind carcasses. The conscious side of my mind means the rhino, but in that other part, which I simultaneously love and loath, a picture starts to form:

Will sprawls across the sand labouring for every breath. He tries to move an arm, to force his body onto its side. It quivers like a weightlifter on a world record attempt but gives way leaving him down and fading. A shadow passes across the sand next to his head. He wrenches his eyes skyward in hope but there's no spotter plane, no rescue chopper, just a pair of vultures signalling their intentions in ever lower circles. A third bird joins them from the direction of the highlands...

"We spend a lot of time in this car in the next days. The way is long and boring so it is better if we talk." The last thing I want to do is chit chat with this murderer. I turn my face towards the window. We're already almost to the place we first saw Ben and Anna's car.

"Better we talk. If not, I start to sing and you do not want to hear me sing. Sounds like a farting elephant." He chuckles at his own joke. Does this guy seriously expect me to laugh? When Will's out there dying? I'm about to tell him to go forth and multiply but the thought of Will reminds me of 'whatever it takes'. Doesn't the hostage police officer always try to make friends with the mad gunman in the movies?

"I'm a singer... The... man back there, Will, he's the main singer and I sing the backing vocals."

"What is backing vocals?"

"He sings the tune, I sing harmony – another tune to go with it."

"I know harmony. Harmony is hippo farting alongside elephant." I force myself to look at his face where a 'small victory' smile is playing on his lips. Without the scar he would have a surprisingly smooth complexion.

I stare into his eyes and plead: "Please go back for Will. I can see you're a good man underneath. He doesn't deserve to die. We haven't done anything to you. Leave us a car and we'll not tell anyone we saw you. You'd be long gone before we could even get back anyway... please..."

He fixes his bloodshot eyes on me for a moment and then lets out a sigh. "Giraffe always has big eyelashes and this one know how to flutter them." He turns back to the track ahead. "I am a little sorry about your friend. It was unlucky for him... but I am a practical man. He was too strong, too big, too much trouble. He almost killed me with spade."

I resist the temptation to say, 'I wish he had.' "Wouldn't it be more practical to let us go and avoid being hunted as a murderer?" His knuckles turn paler, strangling the steering wheel. Shouldn't have said that. He concentrates on the driving in a brooding, menace-filled silence. He doesn't do or say anything – I just have the feeling he's debating whether to kick me out of the door. It's a relief when he speaks again.

"You think it my fault that your friend dies, Giraffe? I was driving north. We were not looking for you, you appear... by magic. Mother wanted to give me two gifts and she used him. But she only use stupid people. Was he mad, this... Will? Driving you into the deep desert? One car on own, here! Stupid. He should blame his-self."

Wrong. This is all my fault. I should have listened to Kaura and let the people who know what they're doing get on with it. I close my eyes and attempt to reverse time. It's as effective as you'd expect. No, going forward is the only way out. "My name's Holly."

His eyes slide towards me in surprise. Maybe he was expecting another insult. "Holly. What is this?"

"It's a small tree. Its leaves stay green all winter and it has pretty red berries."

"Small tree... Giraffe is better. You call me Soba and I call you Giraffe." It doesn't sound like I have any choice in the matter.

"Soba, is Mother your god? Do you worship the desert?"

His mechanical chuckle sounds once more. "No. I respect the desert and she is kind to me. The others," he flicks his head towards the two following vehicles, "they will not say, but I know they think their captain has... what is the word... bolt come loose."

They may be right. It isn't a comforting thought.

And so it continues throughout the afternoon. A convoy of two white and one dun Land Rovers weaving a monotonous dance through ridge and furrow, furrow and ridge. Beside me, almost constant not-a-care-in-the-world chit-chat punctuated by weirdly out of place self-depreciating humour. I play along as best I can but my thoughts are elsewhere. The afternoon heat has built to the point where everything is a blur of shimmer and haze and the air-con is losing its battle with the heat pouring through the smashed passenger window. I dread to think of the temperature out on the sand. God, if you're there, Mother desert, or whatever, please keep him safe, just for a few more hours until I can get back to him.

The sun is low on the horizon when we reach a second, smaller area where historic water flow has ironed out a wedge of dunes. Our convoy makes for the far edge where a few strange green humps protrude from the ground. We pull up beside the largest. I know what these are, we've seen them in all the guidebooks: a bad hair day of dusty green ribbons, all twisted, tangled and ending in dry brown split ends.

"Our guide tour of the desert stops today at Welwitschia Forest. This plant has live here for one thousand years so give some respect." He jumps down from the vehicle, unbuttons the front of his trousers and pees at the plant. To start with I think it's more of his odd humour but from the expression on his face and the way he's edging round the plant I see he's taking irrigation duties seriously. Anyone's guess if it's actually good for the plant.

Somehow I expected that we'd sleep in the cars, but I can see tents, bedding rolls, crates being unloaded. I'm left to stew whilst they work. My eyes see the beginnings of another spectacular African sunset, but all my mind sees are bones: *a scatter of rough grey bones over a dark stain on the dune. All that remains of a sky burial sacrifice for Mother.* Stop it! I shake the image out of my head. This girl never had much respect for her mother anyway.

Eventually, when poles have been slotted into canvas, they lift down the gas brai. As the others heave it towards the tents, Soba opens my door and clicks off the belt. It's great to be able to stand, but the second I do, I'm dying for the toilet. I don't really want to think about it, but I'm going to wet myself if I don't do something.

"Soba, I need the toilet." I jiggle my arms and shoulders to highlight the obvious problem.

"Ah, Giraffe wants to pay respects." He nods towards the Welwitschia, turns me with a gentle hand on my right shoulder, and begins to cut the tape. Free hands feels even better than standing. I rotate my shoulders and reach out my arms. For one short moment there is nothing except the physical bliss of the stretch. When I look down, Soba's holding his pistol. "If you make any trouble, I will need shoot you." Then he adds in a kindlier tone: "Please do not make trouble."

"There's not really anywhere to run off to, is there?"

"Giraffe is learning. Mother only kills the stupid." He looks genuinely pleased. Somehow I need to use this 'pink skin wife' stuff that's going on in his head. "Go," he says, indicating the far side of the mound of leaves with a head movement. I will be hidden from the rest of the camp but Soba is clearly not going to let me out of his sight. I decide that I'd rather know exactly where he is than not, so I stand by the bush facing him, undo my shorts, then bend and pull down in one quick, modesty-keeping movement. Squatting, staring at uncomfortably close male boots brings home the likely futility of trying to keep my modesty when I'm alone in a poacher's desert camp. I'm bursting for the loo but it just won't come out. I suppose this is an extreme case of 'urinal stage fright' as Ben calls it. 'You whip it out, all ready to go and then someone walks up to your shoulder and suddenly you're about as effective as a bath tap in a Swedish ice hotel.' Aaah. The sudden intrusion of a stupid Ben joke relaxes muscles just enough.

When Soba guides me back into the heart of the camp, the other three are still fiddling with the brai. The gas is connected up but it's still unlit. Beside the brai is the hamper. My heart leaps to my throat and I try not to stare. It might as well have a flashing neon arrow and blaring siren. The whisky is here! At least, I hope it's still there. Please let it be there...

"Sit down," says the captain, indicating the sand rather than one of the packing cases. He gives a couple of orders in his own tongue and hands his pistol to the one who I kicked. The fourth poacher, older, with a few grey hairs, heads over to the army Defender followed by his boss.

The expression of the man holding the pistol is similar to the looks Anna receives, but worse... much worse. Relax. Think. Stay calm. I force the 'c' word along my limbs and avoid his eyes. I'm actually glad to see Soba and his companion return. That is, until I see what they're carrying. Before they reach me, the older poacher veers off with some rope, but it's the clamp-like object the captain is holding that concerns me. It could be part of an animal trap.

"Move out one leg, Giraffe," he says, confirming my fears. Whatever it is, it will make an effective shackle.

"But there's nowhere I can run to," I say, desperately trying to stay calm. I claw at the ground, my chances of escape seemingly slipping like the sand through my fingers.

"Yes, but I am practical man. I like insurance." Someone else with plan Bs – just my luck. He uses a spanner to tighten the nut, which closes the metal loop around my ankle. "Does that hurt?"

"No." He has been gentle, but there's definitely no way it would slip over my foot. The older poacher returns with one end of the rope. They loop it through a hole in the side of the ankle clamp and then use a similar smaller clamp to lock it fast. In the fading light I can just make out the other end, tied in an elaborate knot around the tow bar of Will's and my Defender.

"There. Now some dinner," says Soba, plucking the pistol from slightly reluctant fingers.

The young poacher still hasn't managed to light the gas. By now, Moses would have had the steaks half cooked and a glass of wine in each of our hands. That gives me a very interesting thought.

"You have to turn the lever and hold down the button at the same time," I say. The man turns as if he understands enough English to realise that I was speaking to him, but not to follow the instruction.

Soba chuckles. "You do it for him, Giraffe."

I push myself to my feet and take a step forward. The clamp slips so it's resting on top of my sandal and rubs skin as I move. Wish I'd worn trainers.

Having watched Moses do it several times, the brai lights with no problem at all. Soba laughs and makes some comment to the man I have displaced. The young poacher's eyes flick towards me and there's a hint of a scowl on his forehead. Please don't make them all hate me. Not yet.

"I've done it lots of times before," I say, trying a sort of embarrassed half smile. My lips wobble which maybe helps. His expression softens. Yes, that's right, I am bloody petrified. I set the brai to a good cooking heat for the steaks which I know are nestling at the bottom of the hamper. Come on Holly, you can do this – Will needs you. I turn questioning eyes towards Soba, my expression this time going for scared-but-eager-to-please. He smiles. Do the chauvinistic maths, you bastard...

"Giraffe cook for us." That's right, the good little pink skinned wife will cook for the nice poachers. Knob-head! I nod obediently.

Someone has clearly been rummaging through the hamper. Everything is higgledy-piggledy and every so often there's a loose cherry tomato from goodness knows where. One of the vacuum packed steaks has been pulled to the top, but I still have to dig for the other five. Much more importantly, the internal pocket still contains a near full bottle of slightly cloudy Talisker and two tumblers. If only there had been four, that would have made it all so much easier.

"Soba, how do you like your steak cooked?"

"Soba?" The poacher with the nasty stare is clearly bantering with the captain. They all stare at me and laugh.

"Soba like his meat pink in the middle..."

"Yes, Soba – and the others?" Again laughter at the word Soba. I suppose it isn't really his name. Probably means 'well hung' or something else terribly amusing.

"All like pink meat," adds Nasty Stare, fixing me with a prime example of the nickname I've just given him. This tips me over the edge and I begin to panic about being the after dinner entertainment. I can't open the vacuum packs, my fingers are shaking too much. A half smile lingers on Nasty Stare's lips. I kneel at the hamper, avoiding the leers, and try to calm myself. There are steak knives in here somewhere. They'll work. I prick the plastic with the point and then work the blade along. There: first one open. As I start with the second I'm aware of legs beside me.

"Giraffe will cut herself with the sharp knife. Give to me." The captain has the pistol pointed at my head. There's a weapon in my hand and I didn't even realise it. Now who's stupid. I have no choice but to hand it over. I hold the blade and pass the handle. I don't want this to muck everything up.

"Give," he says, indicating the meat. He slits open three more packets. As I pass him a fifth, he pushes my hand back. "Giraffes not eat meat."

"But..." If he's not going to let me eat does that mean...

"You have fruit." I let out a breath I didn't even realise I was holding, but the trembling continues as I lay the steaks across the griddle. Soba, or whatever his name is, picks through the hamper and pulls out three more steak knives, some standard table knives and a few forks. He also finds the whisky. It takes all my willpower to seem unconcerned as he holds up the bottle. The time is now...

"Would you like me to pour you all some, Soba?" He examines the label in the flame light.

"Whisky from Scotland... after dinner is normal, yes?"

"Yes, I believe so."

"You like?"

"I... I don't know, I've never tried it." He hands me a pair of barbeque tongs from the hamper. I suppose I can be trusted with those. He wanders over to the other white Defender and returns a couple of minutes later with three enamelled tin mugs.

"After dinner, whisky for all," he says, passing them over. I glance round at the other poachers, the mugs clanking together from my trembling. Soba follows my gaze. Luckily, fear mixed with a little hopeful anticipation must appear similar to terror.

He leans forward and whispers in a kindly voice, "Cook for a long time. They not allowed pink meat." My mind isn't quite ready to look upon one rapist rather than four as a blessing quite yet, but I nod and attempt something like a grateful expression.

The steaks sizzle and spit like they're furious with their current predicament. 'I hear you,' I silently affirm. I'm over-attending to them, fussing over them, but I'd rather not turn round and the last thing I want is poachers unhappy with the food. Despite Soba's double-entendred instructions, I have no intention of serving overcooked steak. When they're almost done I turn down the heat and find bread rolls and plates. There are four plates, although two are still dirty from when Will and I used them. I rub the crumbs off with the back of my fingers and hope it will do.

The four men sit squashed together on two packing cases tucking in with their fingers while I linger between the brai and the hamper. I collect up some of the tomatoes and begin to munch. Between every bite the captain seems to study me. He stands, leaves his half-finished plate on the case, and approaches the brai. He turns the flames yellow and then reaches for the gas bottle case. He plonks this next to me and inclines his head towards it. I sit. In the flame-light, I can only see his good side, the rest hidden by shadow. It's quite a baby-face. I bet he wouldn't be captain without his scars. I must have been staring too long.

"Ah, you look at Soba's beautiful side. Very handsome they once say." He peers down into the hamper and pulls out a bottle of beer. "Ai," he calls and slings it at the nearest of his men. Two more fly across – all are caught. He lifts one for himself and then hands me a bottle of orange juice. It's like having a bloody personal trainer. As he walks back to his place I slip a couple of salami slices behind a tomato and pop them all in at once.

Normally the smell of forbidden steak would drive me nuts, but for at least four obvious reasons my appetite's not that great. I'm still picking at an apple when the captain slips out of the light and returns moments later with a pale kit bag. There's an odd sense of anticipatory stillness in the other poachers. For a second I'm worried it's more clamps, but all eyes are fixed on the bag like it's a holy relic not a plaything. He unzips and pulls out two scythe-like rhino horns, one much longer than the other, both simultaneously things of beauty and disgust. Raising them above his head, he spouts a cry which in any language is clearly exultant. The other poachers cheer. He glances over his shoulder towards me, "Stars, desert, friends, and wealth..." He wiggles the horns at the final word. "We are blessed my brothers. We are all blessed."

Personally, I don't feel particularly blessed. But then I'm not his brother and I doubt if he really thinks of me as human. In fact, come to think of it, all the supposed little kindnesses have been no more than you'd do for a favourite pet. If my heart needed hardening any more, that just did the trick. I squat and line up the three tin mugs on the case where I've been sitting, then reach for one of the tumblers. My hand is half out of the hamper when I reconsider. No. I can't say I won't drink any: that would be too suspicious. But I can't actually drink much – any if I can help it. What would be believable? What would the stupid, weak, sub-human woman do? I place both tumblers beside the mugs and call out "Scotch whisky now, Soba?"

He stares quizzically, one horn still in each hand, and I begin to panic I've been too pushy. I form the eager-to-please smile in desperation.

"Yes. Mother bring many gifts this time. We raise glasses to Mother. Pour."

Phew... I pour. With the greatest of pleasure, I pour.

"And for me too?" I ask, easily feigning a fluster. "I've never tried it, but you said earlier..."

"Yes," he says, replacing the horns in the kit-bag. "It is better." Nasty Stare makes some comment, but receives a poisonous put down for his trouble. The words may be strange but the body language is quite clear – stay away from the boss's shag.

Every last drop of sedative-laden alcohol is precious and I make sure it's all carefully distributed: Soba with the most generous portion and my own as empty as I dare. The words 'last chance saloon' bat around my brain as I hand out liquid salvation. The captain takes a sniff. "Like in the movies, we drink to Mother." He raises his tumbler and they all follow.

I take a huge quaff and it's almost completely realistic that I splutter, cough and next to all of it comes flying back out. My hand shakes enough to spill a little for good measure. The men roar with laughter although Nasty Stare's laugh seems to have a little cough blended with it. As I recover my breath, I note that the pills haven't altered the taste too much – a metallic twang in with the seaweed. I doubt if any of them have had it before...

Soba lifts the tumbler towards the flames and peers at the liquid. He takes another sip. "Scot men like their drink strange... but strong." He smiles and glances round at his comrades. "We drink to the fine Giraffe." They all snigger and take another mouthful. I squint towards my glass and then to Soba.

"Drink," he says.

I take another quaff with the same results, only this time I really do choke and a few drops are swallowed whilst I'm gasping. But I'm more than halfway down the glass and a bit of discomfort and ridicule is just fine by me.

Still chuckling, Soba places a hand on my shoulder and says, like he's speaking to a child, "Maybe Giraffe should drink less at one time."

"I can't..." I say, "Please don't make me... It's just so..." I trail off aiming to sound as pathetic as possible.

"Try... Please." I peer up at him with wide eyes and then obediently take a smaller mouthful. I hold it for a second as if I'm really trying and then spray. His crotch is right in front of me. It's tempting to aim straight for it, but I don't want him mad, so I turn my head at the last moment.

"I'm sorry..." I gasp, "I can't... It burns..."

"Never mind, Giraffe. You leave the drink to the men." He takes my glass, pours a little into his own and then distributes the rest round the tin mugs. You're more than welcome, knob-head.

For the next half hour or so they're consumed by alcohol fuelled man banter, the volume level gradually increasing. Every so often, the captain calls out some small translation like: "He say he will buy a motorbike with his money. How will fit his seven children on that?!" As if I give a flying giraffe's turd... What's far more important is how long the drug will take to work. I'm a little worried about Nasty Stare. I'm not sure he's going to finish it all. You can see the captain and the others are enjoying it, but him, well... One awake poacher is one too many. I'm going to have to do something.

Once it seems like everyone else has finished, I wander slowly towards them wearing my if-I'm-helpful-they-might-be-nice smile. "Shall I take your cups and plates?"

"Ah, my Giraffe." Soba catches me by the waist and pulls me

beside him. He continues his conversation as if I'm not there and I can do nothing except wait and hope his hand doesn't move lower. It occurs to me that a big hole in my plan is that before they go to sleep – if they go to sleep – I now have four tipsy poachers to deal with. Oh hell... Eventually there's a pause in the talking.

"Have you finished your drinks? Shall I clear up?"

Soba sniggers and unwraps his arm, "Go on Giraffe, do your kitchen work." He slaps me on the backside as I move away.

I collect the plates, Soba's empty tumbler and two empty tin mugs. When I reach Nasty Stare's mug, it is, as I feared, still part full. "Oh, I'm sorry you haven't finished," I say, putting it back on the case beside him. He scowls at me.

"Do you drink like Giraffe?" Soba asks from behind me. He changes to his own tongue and the other two join him in some rhythmic chant. In the UK they would be singing 'down in one, down in one...'

Nasty Stare throws me a glance of pure malice and waves me away. "Go. I will bring."

I turn my back and in the darkness allow myself a small triumphant smile. Three and a half steps later, my right leg jerks to a halt and I sprawl forward shedding plates. "Pardon," says Nasty Stare, lifting his foot off my tether. He raises the mug to his lips. Bastard, I hope you OD.

I wipe crockery and glasses slowly and carefully with a serviette watching the men for signs of tiredness. How long did it take to work on me? I only took one tablet, they must have drunk three or four each, but it's much earlier and they're men and there's the alcohol. Maybe it won't work at all. Maybe I'll still have to... I almost gag as I lean to push the tumblers back into their pocket.

As if a switch has been thrown, it's lighter – tents, vehicles, welwitschia suddenly highlighted. For a split-second I imagine the lights of a helicopter with paratroopers abseiling to my rescue, but it's a paler, colder light which I would recognise immediately if I was at all rational. The moon has broken the horizon. The increased illumination seems to spur the captain into action. He stands, claps hands against thighs and barks out several orders. I'm please to see a couple of yawns as the others go about their tasks. Soba brings over the remaining mug, lifts the pile of plates from my knee, and shoves them all into the hamper. "I put in Defender, then sleep."

I remain on the crate praying he really means sleep – petrified that he doesn't. It feels like only a couple of seconds before he's standing beside me again, reaching for an arm.

"Come." I let him pull me into a standing position.

"Wh... where am I sleeping?" I stammer.

"With me."

CHAPTER 16

My skin crawls – his grip an infection my body is desperate to purge. "No, please. You know I'm married."

"And your husband is with other woman, yes?"

"No... I don't know where they are, I..."

"Come, Giraffe."

"But you've been so kind. I thought you weren't like them..." Panic plants my feet in the sand. He pulls at my arm but I probably weigh more than him and stand firm. The scary, calculating demeanour returns. He doesn't engage in a tug of war – he doesn't have to.

"Giraffe, you know I am practical man. You can fight me and I can hurt you." He inclines his head towards Nasty Stare's legs which are disappearing through a canvas flap. "I can let others hurt you... or you can be quiet and I can be kind." He scoops the horn bag from the sand and strolls to his tent.

My legs are jelly. My insides are a scrunched up paper bag. I can't do this. I can't just let him... But what's the alternative? And Will, I need... I need him to sleep. And men have no problem with that... after...

Soba turns towards me as he leans to open the tent. "Come." A wide yawn breaks across his face. He shakes it away, almost with embarrassment. Maybe... just maybe.

"Okay," I say and transfer my weight from one leg to the other as if plucking up courage to step forward. Then I shuffle forward, as slowly as possible. That's realistic. There's no scenario where he could imagine I'd be keen for this. As I approach, I make no effort to hide my quivering.

"Giraffe be good, I be kind," he says, stretching out a hand. I pause and then take it.

"Soba, what about this?" I glance down at the rope, snaking its way across to the Land Rover.

"You keep on," he says, guiding me past him through the doorway. It's a slightly larger version of a tourist type dome tent – not enough height for me to stand but fortunately not too cosy. A gauze window flap is open, allowing moonlight to filter inside. My toe stubs against a bedding roll causing a shudder to ripple up my back. It might as well be a rack or an iron maiden. Behind me, the captain makes a couple of coils and closes the flap until the rope is jammed between the zipper and the end stop. There's enough slack for my tether to lie on the floor whilst I'm anywhere in the tent. Bollocks, I had hoped he would take it off. I sit on the ground sheet as far away from the bed as possible and cross my legs. Soba slings the horn bag down on the opposite side, pulls off his beret, and collapses backwards onto the bedding. Hope springs to my throat, but after a couple of seconds he reaches under himself and slips his pistol from the back of his belt. He glances towards me with half narrowed eyes as if remembering that he has also seen this feeble scared Giraffe shooting a rifle. Using his body as a shield he attempts to hide it, but this is a tent, he's obviously shoved it under the head end of the sleeping roll – there is nowhere else. As he flips onto his side to face me, I make a conscious effort to keep my eyes on him – away from that direction. Without his headgear he looks even younger.

"Here, closer, Giraffe." Sit! Stay! Do you want your tummy tickled? I have a strong urge to loop my lead round his neck and pull hard – perhaps I could? But what if he makes too much noise? What if I'm not quick enough, strong enough? Your best hope is sleep – whatever it takes...

"Giraffe." His voice goes up at the end in warning. Don't annoy him. I need him calm, relaxed, sleepy.

"Sorry, I..." He undoes the top button of his shirt whilst stifling another yawn. "Let me do that..." I hear myself say. Take control – if you want it slow, make it slow. I shuffle closer and reach out. He lifts himself into a sitting position, facing me. I place both hands on his chest and hold them there – take a deep breath, as if submitting to the inevitable – reach for the next button. I undo each one with trembling fingers. His odour is an oppressive mixture of sweat and dust – perhaps what the petrol attendant meant by 'smells like the desert'. He reaches forward, runs a finger along my cheek, down my neck, to my top button. I place one hand inside his shirt, onto bare stomach, hoping to distract him. It does, momentarily, but by the time his shirt front is fully open three of my buttons are undone and my bra is beginning to show. That's not the only thing either: there's a very clear bulge forming in the groin of his combats. I need to slow him down, to distract. I run a finger up his chest to his chin, along his jaw, then, as if I find it fascinating, along the line of his scar. "How did you get this? In a war?" It's a risk, but it seems like he's proud of this scar and, anyway, how much worse can it get?

"Giraffe like scar?" Does the idiot really think I give a shit?

"It gives you character."

"What is character?"

"Something that makes you look interesting or important."

"Like a hero?" Like a murdering, rapist hero...

"Yes."

"I was hero, but they still kill my mother..."

"Who were they?"

"When I am thirteen, soldiers came to my village – MPLA." He spits out the initials with venom. I've absolutely no idea what they stand for. "My father was UNITA captain. He was clever, always killing MPLA, then disappear into desert. They not catch him. So they find out where family live and kill them instead. I stand in front of my mother but Kalashnikov..." His finger swipes across his cheek.

I suppose that explains a few things but I'm not about to feel any sympathy. His trouser bulge has begun to subside but I'm not sure this is making him sleepy. Keep him talking...

"But you survived..."

"MPLA careless."

"And your father?"

"Never came back from the desert. Now..." He stifles another yawn, but before I can think of anything else he's undone the last of my buttons and is pulling my shirt from my shoulders. "Take it off," he says. I know he means my bra. There's nothing I can do. Think... Think... Don't panic, think! As I reach behind to undo the clasp, I think of Ben - what would I do if this was a horny Ben and I didn't fancy it? There are hands on the breasts, pulling at the bra. Not my breasts; not my bra; they belong to the woman who is going to save Will's life. They're not mine. How would she put a man off, gently? The woman shudders as a thumb rubs across a nipple. How?

The woman places a hand on his cheek, runs a finger along his jaw, across to one shoulder, caresses the muscle, says, "Come, Soba, how tight you feel." Her other hand follows and they start to kneed the muscles. "Let me relax you." She ignores the hands on her breasts. "Is that good?" He nods. "If you turn, I can reach more easily," she says, placing one hand on his buttock and pulling slightly. She's good this woman, she's been married for long enough to know how to manipulate a man. She allows her breasts to slide across his side as she turns him, pulls him towards her, lets them rest against his back. His shoulders really are squirming knots of tension – so much the better. She works gently but firmly, keeping a steady rhythm, gradually kneading through the tension. A massage as perfect as if your life depended on it.

"This is good, Giraffe, where you learn..." The last word is interrupted by another yawn. The woman continues. Even when she hears his breathing start to change she dares not stop. Even when his head lolls forward and his weight presses back, still she kneads on. How long? How long? His breathing deepens further: now let's see. She leans forward and sideways, guiding them both onto the sleeping mat. One knee is part under him but she slides that out, one knead at a time, gently, gently, until they're side by side. Gradually her fingers slow until they're just lying on his shoulders. No change in the breathing. Her hands lift off and she lies, staring at them in the semi-darkness, not quite believing they're hers.

Fuck, fuck, fuck. I stare at the hands quivering in front of my face, scarcely believing they've done it. Ben says my shoulder massages are special, but I always thought he was just being kind. Calm now, calm. My hands still. What next? Think... plan... do... Gun... shirt... wait... Then we can have another plan. I slide back off the mat. Still no change in the breathing. His head isn't quite at the top of the bedding roll so slipping my hand under and retrieving the pistol is simple. I inspect it in the moonlight. I've seen how he pulls off the safety catch, but I know that makes a click. I point the gun at the back of his head and mentally rehearse clicking off the catch and pulling the trigger. I could do it now. Maybe the others are already in a drug-induced sleep? Maybe I can shoot them all? But what if they're not? Better to wait half an hour and if there's no noise, go quietly.

I retrieve my shirt but my bra is somewhere underneath him. It's not worth it. The first minute is spent stealthily slipping arms into sleeves and doing up buttons. The rest of the time is taken up listening to breathing; panicking at every slight grunt and swallow; wondering how long half an hour actually is; deciding to wait until the moon's shadow falls onto the door; watching a shadow.

It's almost there when I remember I need to plan what to do once I'm out of the tent. I begin to panic that I haven't left myself enough time before I remember that this is a purely self-imposed deadline. When I took my tablet I was out from, when, one a.m. until six? And then it was Will who woke me. No need to rush, but maximum head start would be good. Starting a car will be noisy. Maybe I need to slow them down if they do wake up?

I begin to unzip the tent flap, ever so slowly, and feed out the loop of rope. The pistol is stowed half protruding down the front of my shorts. Once the zip is about half way down I pull open the gap and step through. Even though I'm in slow motion, my clothes rub against the canvas with a hiss like all the world's snakes are telling on me: 'ssshe'sss essscaping'. I hold an ear to the gap, but the captain's breathing remains long and slow. Inside my head I gloat, 'Two things I didn't tell you about the holly tree: its leaves have thorns and the berries are poison.'

There's quite a lot of slack in the rope but I need to be careful I don't tangle myself up. Fortunately I'm well used to being tethered, it's just usually by a guitar cable from an amp stack. I run through my list as I creep across the camp: check car keys, water, diesel, food; get rid of shackle; disable other cars and collect guns if possible. Just past the brai, a snort stops my heart. I freeze, but the snort repeats and elongates into light snores. I creep towards the sound. Sprawled half hidden beside one of the packing cases is the Young One. He's so sound asleep he's fallen off his lookout perch. Beside him, not even touching him and there for the taking, is a rifle. I take it.

I reach my Land Rover to find the driver's window fully open and keys in the ignition. Desert habits die hard even when you have a prisoner. Moses would have done exactly the same. Tied to the roof are two jerry cans. Between the rear seats, I can see the lodge's rifle, the water barrel, the hamper and the extra water bottle we bought from the garage. I'm coming for you Will. Hold on. I just need... I can't see anything obvious for cutting rope. Slipping the poacher's rifle through the window, I move to inspecting the knot. It's been pulled extremely tightly round the tow bar and no amount of clawing at it with my fingers is going to undo it without some kind of tool. Bollocks. Come on, there must be something round here. Maybe in one of the other vehicles?

I gather the rope into a loose bundle and pay it out as I go, leaving plenty of slack. The army Land Rover is not locked but the doors and windows are all shut. Through the passenger side window I can see another rifle. I really want a knife but I decide to risk opening the door. Usually they're not too loud. I listen for the lookout's snoring as I pull the catch slowly. There's a quiet click and a small squeak from the hinge. My ears strain. No, the snoring is just the same. I climb past the gun and peer into the back. There are snares and other poaching gear, some metal water containers and basic provisions: boxes of dry breads and the like. Nothing worth hanging around for. As with my Land Rover, the keys are in the ignition. I slip them into my pocket and for pure devilment flick the diff lock lever. Sleeping beauty is still snoring loudly as I take the rifle and slide out of the door.

How can I cut this rope? A steak knife would be handy for slashing tyres too. Where were they hidden? Maybe I could let the tyres down anyway? It'll only take a minute. There's a hiss as I press the valve with my nail, but it's not as loud as the snoring. I work my way round and soon they're all doing pancake impressions. Once I've finished I wonder why I bothered. They can pump them up again in ten minutes and this is not getting me untied.

Ben and Anna's Land Rover is more of a problem. It's further away and I'll have to pass between tents. I unwind the rope from round the army Defender, gather it up, and creep forward. As I pass Nasty Stare's tent I hear a small stirring and freeze. I swing the rifle off my shoulder, but, no, it's okay, I can hear heavy breathing. I wait a couple of minutes just to be sure and then continue. The rope does reach... barely. Again the Land Rover's doors are closed, but this time the front windows are open. I retrieve another rifle and rest both of them against the front wheel. You could start a small war with all this stuff. Leaning in from the duckboards, I see there are keys in the ignition here too. I pull myself along the seat, retrieve them, and once again mess with the diff lock lever for good measure. In the gloom of the rear something is glinting on the floor. It might be a knife. I lean forward between the front seats, stretching, sliding, arms supporting my weight. The shackle is beginning to pull at my ankle. I need to be careful – just a little further. As my right hand edges forward, something sharp digs into the palm and my elbow gives way. I pitch forward, momentarily held back by the ankle clamp. Then the rope slackens and off in the camp there's a low clang. Shit. I fumble forwards for the knife, grab it and scramble back over the front seats. In my haste to slither out of the window my feet miss the sill, pitching me face first into the sand. Spitting and shaking my head furiously I crawl to snatch up the nearest rifle.

With heartbeats hammering in my ears, it's difficult to tell if the camp is still silent, but nothing stirs amongst the monochrome shadows. As I concentrate on slowing my breathing and wiping my eyes, I realise that the object in my left hand is a tyre lever, not a knife. Great. Nearly blew everything over a sodding tyre lever. I'm just about to chuck it when I realise it might help undo the knot. So it's shoved in my back pocket, I pick up the second rifle and retrace my steps. There aren't enough hands to gather up the rope, so I have to leave it trailing behind.

As I creep between tents I can hear the soft snoring once more. Ahead the rope is almost rubbing against the canvas. What did it touch? Better not risk it catching behind me. I rest the rifle butts on the sand and gather in my tether. Once I've created a loose coil at my feet I shove it under an armpit and continue towards the brai. As I approach, it's obvious what has happened: the gas cylinder is lying on its side, rope running across it. Idiot! Should've checked if there was some slack before climbing into that van. But the Young One is still prone beside his packing case – breaths heavy and regular. I silently thank Toivo for the strength of his pills, wind another coil, and head back towards my personal Gordian knot.

What am I going to do if I can't untie it? A flood of pessimism shivers down my back. I shake the despair from my head, let the bundle of rope fall and grind it into the sand with one foot. This stupid leash is not going to defeat me. Not now.

I shove the rifles in through the driver's window and get to work.

The tyre lever is a help. I manage to jam it between cords and pull upwards. A small loop is beginning to form. I lean forward to add more weight...

"Aaa..." My right foot flies out from under me, tipping me forward. The knot meets me on the jaw and grazes up across my face. I make a grab for the towbar, but the pull is too strong and my head ploughs into the ground. "Uhhh..." A knee, driven down with bodyweight, lands in my back, forcing out breath. I can't move. I can't breathe. I shake my head frantically searching for air. I lift one shoulder, twist my head sideways, and spit sand. The tyre lever is beside me, inches from my nose. I make a grab for it, but a brown hand gets there first and my hand receives a stinging metallic thwack.

"You want this?" The lever presses hard against my nose; Nasty Stare's slurred whisper at my ear. "You want?" His other hand grips hair, twisting my head so I can watch as he flings it into the darkness. Heavy, searing breath flows across my neck. "What you done me, bitch? What you done to boss? Is poison?" I frantically shake my head. "Boss think you giraffe but I know you clever bitch. Who clever now, bitch?" he says, pressing the knee down harder. "I know what do to bitchs." He releases my hair and tugs hard on the back of my shorts. Feeling them slipping, I instinctively reach with both hands to clutch the front of the waistband... and find the pistol. "Stop, bitch." My fingers are on the safety and as he rips my right hand from under me, it clicks back. The sound is muffled by my body. He seems too intent on his tug of war to notice. The button gives way and he gets his view of ugly pink ass. It's going to be the last thing he ever sees. He really shouldn't keep using the 'B' word. If there's one thing that really pisses me off... If there's one word that makes my blood boil... If he'd been in that radio station green room with that pea-brained US rapper who kept telling me how he 'dug English bitches'. Like I was meant to take it as a compliment... The pressure on my back eases as he shifts his position. I shut my eyes and twist with all my might. My face scrapes through sand, left shoulder rises, arm flings out and the pistol, guided by one half opened eye, crashes into male chest. The impact alone is enough to move my finger...

The weight is gone, the pull is gone. I struggle to my feet, blinking through eyes of sand. My head is a whirl. There's no time. That shot would have wakened the dead. I try to step forward but my shorts are half way to my knees. I yank them up. I need to leave now. But the rope... the rope... the rope is tied to the same vehicle I want to leave in. Idiot! Complete idiot! I lurch to the driver's door, wrench it open, and tug on my leash. My eyes are still so full of sand I can hardly keep them open. Cry, damn it. That'll work. I pull frantically at the rope shoving lengths of it onto the seat. No lights in the camp, no shouts, but surely soon. Come on... It snags, but a panic filled heave brings a tangled sandy lump into my hands. Once that's inside, the rope goes tight and through clearing vision I see it lift along the side of the vehicle. Pulling hard, I wrap it twice round the wing mirror, jump in and slam the door on it. The engine fires up first time. I press the accelerator, lift the clutch and automatically check the mirror. Behind on the sand, the moonlight highlights a still, dark shape.

CHAPTER 17

I've almost reached the far side of the flat area before I calm down enough to realise I'm still clutching a live pistol between my hand and the wheel. That's going to be really stupid when it gets bumpy. I coast to a halt and use both hands to make it safe. Whilst stopped I stick my head out of the window and scan back towards the camp, maybe half a mile distant. Was that a dim light or just something reflecting the moonlight? Doesn't matter, just keep going.

So far I've been following the tracks by moonlight alone, but once I'm into the dunes there are long shadows and I need the headlights. It's not like they don't know where I'm going if they do follow. I just need to arrive first. My right foot presses down a little harder. No, don't overdo it, crashing won't save Will. Every so often, when I near the crest of a high saddle I kill the lights and look back. There's never any sign of pursuit.

In the day time it feels almost oppressively vast amongst the dunes: like you're a dust mite on a Buckingham Palace carpet. At night, driving with lights, the reverse is true. The dunes loom either side, squeezing the small illuminated arc with the pressure of their darkness. It's easy to imagine shapes flitting in and out of the edge of vision, especially when your mind keeps slipping back to a dark shape lying motionless on the sand. I try to suppress everything by concentrating on the driving: smooth, careful, fast. To begin with I have the windows up, but I can feel the warmth lulling me, so I wind them down until I'm purposefully cold.

We must have been going for five or six hours yesterday

afternoon, but the captain wasn't rushing, he was route finding. We had to turn round half a dozen times. I've already passed a couple of these dead ends, easily given away by the curve of the tracks in and out. I can just blast straight on, safe in the knowledge that what came north must go south.

Even so, it's well into tomorrow, and I've sung through my entire back catalogue almost three times, before I'm descending a particularly steep slope, reminding myself to be careful at the base, when the abandoned hulk of those-who-weren't looms into the lights. I'm really close to where they left Will now. No more than a mile. I stop before I reach the scavenged Land Rover, leaving it bathed in light, and lower myself gingerly onto the sand. Maybe they left something sharp behind.

I stand to my full height, arms above head and stretch the hours of driving stiffness from my back whilst turning my head from side to side. Just about the whole of me aches but I'll live. I pull enough rope from the passenger seat to comfortably reach the other vehicle and shuffle forward. I'm barely half way when a mad eyed, pale faced ogre bursts from behind it, bellowing out a war cry and swinging what looks to be part of a bumper high in the air.

"WILL, STOP, IT'S ME!"

The weapon falls from his fingers, landing with a heavy thump on the sand behind as he stands frozen in disbelief. A second later I'm enveloped in a huge hug.

"Holly, oh shit, Holly... I thought you were... I thought I was..." He's shaking as he holds me. I don't know how long we remain locked together in blissful relief. It seems an age before his voice croaks, "How the hell?"

"Plan B worked... well, mostly." He pulls back to leave a hand on each shoulder and stares questioningly. There are tears in the corners of his eyes. "Sleeping pills and whisky don't mix well." His mouth drops open. "So they were all snoring like babies..." my grin falters, "until I knocked something over because of this." For the first time he notices the shackle and the rope. His expression darkens. "And one of them woke, and he pulled me over and... oh Will, I had to shoot him." My bottom lip starts to curl and I can feel a sob building.

I expect him to hold me again, but he doesn't, he squeezes the hands on my shoulders and says, "Dead?"

"I think so."

"Good. Was it the cocky little fucker with the beret?"

"No, one of the others."

"Pity..." He glances north. "Are they following?"

"I don't know. Not close behind." Will's matter-of-factness is exactly what I need to jolt me out of misplaced sorrow. The bastard was trying to rape me. I would have been killed... eventually. I wouldn't be here saving Will. Think on that. "They will have had a bit of trouble getting started without these." I slide two pairs of keys painfully out of my shorts pocket. Will shakes his head in open admiration. On my upper thigh, a tender patch will, I suspect, develop into key shaped bruises before long. "And if they do..." I lead him to the passenger door and pull it open to reveal a tangle of four rifles in the footwell and a pistol on the seat.

"Holly Woodlove, you're a living legend."

"Tell that to my label."

He steps up and peers over the seat into the back. "Have you got water?"

"Gosh, yes, you must be parched. There's still food in the hamper too, although I'm afraid my guests last night had the steak with their whisky."

"They're welcome."

"How did you get here?"

Will answers through sips from the garage plastic bottle. "It's only literally a couple of hundred yards over that dune from where they left me... I don't know how long it was until I came to properly. I'm a bit sunburnt though..." His nose certainly looks raw. "I'd just managed to roll onto my feet when I heard engine noise coming over the dune. I ran... I kept falling... rolling... running... I don't know what I thought I was going to do. I got up high, just in time to see you all disappear again."

"Aw, Will."

He screws the lid back onto the bottle having drunk surprisingly little. "Then I saw the army Land Rover and at least it was some shade."

"And here we are..." I stretch out, as if to ruffle his hair, but realise that I'll probably be disturbing scabs. It's a tangle of blood and sand. "Are you okay? Nothing broken or anything?"

"My head's still sore. I feel seasick every time I move it. Is that what concussion feels like?"

"I don't know... You are a quite pale apart from the nose." That's understating it. When he leapt out into the headlights I thought I was being attacked by an undead clown. Don't think that will be helpful to share though... "Have something to eat... just a little so you don't puke it up again."

He raises one eyebrow. "Yes, miss... but not until we get this rope off you." His eyes scrutinise my face. I must look a picture. "They didn't drag you behind did they."

"Heck, no, nothing like that. This was just so I couldn't run off. S... the little bastard with the beret, was quite careful."

"Not careful enough."

"I played the stupid, frightened, weak woman quite well."

Will manages a half grin, starts to shake his head, but immediately regrets it.

"The frightened part was easy," I say. "You don't know if there's a tool kit in here somewhere, do you?"

The torch seems to be missing, so the search is more by feel than sight. After I waste time with a little foray onto the roof, we eventually find a long bag strapped under one of the rear seats, right where we started. Inside there's a jack, wheel brace, spark plug spanner and various other specific tools, but nothing small enough for the nuts on my clamp.

"Why wouldn't you throw in a shifter?"

I shrug. "I suppose they're never normally that far from the lodge... At least we should be able to undo the knot with these." I brandish the three tyre levers from the puncture repair kit.

With Will's help the knot gives in surprisingly easily. As much as it's a relief to be disconnected from my trusty vehicle, I could do with loosing the fifty foot tail too. While Will nibbles tentatively on the one remaining stick of French bread, I set to work rubbing the rope up and down the edge of the bumper he was using as a weapon. There are a few sharp, jagged sections without which I'm not sure I'd be making any impression at all.

"Unlucky it's such good quality rope," says Will, noting my slow progress.

"I think most of their stuff is left over military, from the Angolan war. Soba... the beret man, said his father was a captain or something."

"He told you his name?"

"I don't think it was his real name – they laughed every time I said it. I... I tried to talk to him. I think he wanted a trophy wife, so I... err... played along a bit." I rub the rope extra hard along the roughest section. After a minute or so, I raise my eyes to find Will staring at me. It's difficult to tell his expression through the various cuts and bruises but I suspect it's concern.

"Let me have a turn," he says, squatting in front of me. He sets to with some vigour, sawing through another strand in half the time it took me to part the first. His exertions release wafts of stale sweat odour. Once upon a time, before yesterday, I might have wrinkled my nose. But what the hell does it matter? This is Will: alive and smelling like a man who's had seven bells pummelled out of him should smell. I take a deep breath and let it out as a sigh.

"I don't know how you did it. You must have nerves of steel," he whispers, his head remaining down on the task.

"I just kept telling myself I had to stay alive to come back for you. If I was dead, you were dead too. Whatever it took, I was coming back for you."

His eyes flick momentarily towards me and his jaw lowers as if he's about to speak. Instead, the sawing gains renewed fervour and before long I'm left with no more than a rather heavy ankle adornment.

"Thanks."

"No, bloody hell, it's me should be thanking you. You've..." He stumbles over his words. "You..." His hand still holding the rope is shaking. "You're the one who's been through... through shit to save me."

"I'm sure you would have done the same if it had been the other way round," I say squeezing his shoulder.

"But it wasn't..." He trails off weirdly. I thought Will was the one without the male pride? Maybe it's just the bang on the head. He makes a visible effort to gather himself and adds in a more normal voice. "I'll have a think about how to get that off, but maybe we should be making tracks?"

Although dawn can't be far off it's actually getting darker as the moon begins to set. We've dallied too long. It will be so good to get back to real roads. Will fills the plastic water bottle from the barrel in the rear as I stow the rope under the middle row of seats. In a couple of minutes we're off.

I'm not pushing it now. Will is beside me, the car seems to be running just fine and there's no sign of pursuit. There's no need to take any risks. As dawn breaks, our mood lightens with it.

"You know, I bet Anna and Ben are sitting at the lodge wondering where the hell we are."

"How do you work that out?"

"They must have been somewhere near the dead rhino all along – if that poacher was telling the truth."

"Can you pull down your visor, please?" The low sun has started to bother my left eye. "I think he must have been. If he'd done something to them he would've just told us. There would have been some cold hearted justification, but he wouldn't have denied it."

"So they must have just walked so far looking for that bloody bird that they didn't hear us either time. Moses will have found them."

He seems to have forgotten about the sandstorm... but the animals survive them... there must be lots of shelter behind all the rocks and bushes. "I hope you're right."

The tracks sweep us away from the ridge on one of the longer loops. After tracing the edge of a particularly impressive dune, it angles back towards the hillside in an unusually straight valley. With the low morning sunlight the desert is once more a thing of awe-filling beauty. Every dune crest is a razor line between red-gold and black, every curve picked out in super-contrast. Closer up, ripples cover wind-blown faces like finger-prints on plasticine, whilst near vertical cornices hang awaiting that one-grain-too-many on the leeward sides. We toil up to another saddle where the dunes meet the outlying slope of the escarpment. As we reach the summit, I ease off, peer out of the side window to gain an overall view... and immediately slam my foot back on the gas. Only a couple of hundred yards behind, steaming up to the bottom of the slope is the other white Land Rover. Worse still, way back down the valley, the army vehicle is just appearing round the dune.

"Will, they're behind us," I gasp, but he's already followed my gaze and is now reaching over his seat.

"Just drive as fast as you can. I'll shoot – if I have to." He pulls up the first rifle, examines the curved thing underneath and gives the whole thing a shake. "Is there any more ammunition?"

Bullets. Hell, I didn't think of bullets. "Sorry, I only brought the guns. Maybe our box is still in the back?"

"They wouldn't fit in here. Not to worry, if there's some in each, there should be plenty." How did we become so matter-of-fact about bullets? We shouldn't have dilly dallied getting my rope undone. Stupid. I thought I had more time. I didn't think they'd bother to follow us. Stupid, stupid. Why didn't I check if I had some slack in my leash before climbing into that Land Rover? Stupid, stupid, stupid!

"I suppose Defenders must be easy to hot wire," says Will mostly to himself.

Ahead, I can see the desert starting to open up. We've reached the large dry river plain. Maybe I can speed up and leave them behind? Unfortunately, the reverse is true. No matter how hard I dare press my right foot, Ben and Anna's Land Rover seems to gain. Dust is billowing behind us, but once we're properly out on the plain he really starts to close the gap.

Will has climbed through to the middle seats and wound down the window behind me, but before he can take aim the following car sweeps through our wake to the clear air on the other side. Will slides along the seat to the near side. The ear splitting report of a shot reverberates around the cabin. "Missed," he yells, above the roar of the open windows. The poacher's rover swerves back to the driver's side. "It looks a lot easier in the movies."

There's no return fire. Maybe I did find all the guns? What's their plan? Are we going to be rammed or are they waiting for the perfect shot? I don't want to wait to find out.

"How many are there in it?"

"Just one, I think. Can't see a beret."

"Younger or older?"

"Can't see."

What can I do to help Will? "Set up behind me and I'll make a wide turn. Unless he's very sharp, you'll get a sight." I veer right off the tracks, downstream, towards the deep desert. I hear two shots.

"I think I hit something with that second one but he's not slowing down."

"Let's go back the other way." I wait for Will to slide across and then veer left. More shots.

"Shit, I'm useless with this thing."

Despite the dust, the other vehicle accelerates until it's looming directly behind us. "Shoot him through the back window," I scream.

But before Will can set up, we're bumped, sending him and the rifle sprawling. I floor the accelerator, weave and curve right. Ahead, further downstream, perhaps a quarter of a mile away, the ground seems lighter. I wonder if that's harder sand or rock? I wonder...

"Will? Are you okay?"

"Ye..." We're rammed again, but the other Land Rover can't really get any umph behind it.

"Set up behind me. I'm going to try something. Be ready for a sharp left." The lighter area approaches fast and I can see it's one of those salt pan things and is perhaps a hundred metres across.

"Why am I behind you if you're going to curve left?"

There isn't time to explain. Our Defender kangaroos as it hits the new surface. "Trust me," I cry, "Wait... Now." About halfway across I turn the wheel hard. My shoulder slams against the door frame as we veer left. The whole car tips alarmingly before I straighten up and ease off. A shot; a second, followed by the sound of shattering glass. The other Land Rover careers past our off-side, windscreen half shattered, the Young One wrestling with the wheel. Will is out of bullets, scrambling for another rifle, as we reach the edge of the harder stuff. "Hold on." I dip the throttle and we transition back to deep sand with another manageable bound.

"What the..? Look!" Ben and Anna's car is already halfway through an ungainly sideways somersault, smashing its cab roof in the process. Like an under-practised gymnast it lands back the right way up, but has too much rotation and ends with its face in the mat, or in this case, its side on the sand.

A hand squeezes my shoulder. "Well driven. How did you know?"

"The steering can act really weird if someone happens to leave your diff lock lever engaged... remember?"

"You..?"

I nod. "I thought if I led him onto firmer ground he might not be able to turn so you'd have a better shot. I didn't expect him to still be yanking the wheel so hard when he hit the soft stuff that he flipped it... I also let the tyres down on the army Land Rover. I suppose that's why they're further behind... Where are they?"

We scan our respective horizons. No obvious sign. I loop round and head back towards the escarpment. The moment I'm pointing towards our exit route, the captain's plan is obvious. Whilst we've been weaving round the valley with Ben and Anna's Land Rover, he has blocked our exit. What are we going to do?

There's a pop and shards of glass sprinkle up over the bonnet. The scathing tones of my brother's voice spring into my mind from years ago. I'm holding a game controller, white streaks flash past, the view from my cockpit goes red. 'Got you, brainless... Never fly straight and level in the combat zone.'

I throw the Defender into as tight a curve as I dare. There's a thud from somewhere down the near side. We retreat out of range, partially hidden by our cloud of dust.

"They've still got one rifle, then, and he's a much better shot."

"Are they following?"

"Can't see for the dust." I turn and slow. "They're moving but not fast... Maybe if we lead them out into the middle we can drive round them?"

It sounds like a good plan but half an hour, three more bodywork holes, and a shattered side window later it seems like there's no way past. Like an expert keeper, the army Land Rover always seems to take up just the right position to prevent us from reaching our goal. And each time we retreat under fire, we seem to be a little further down the plain...

"The more this river bed narrows, the easier it is for him to block us. We need to do something different."

I nod. This is getting us nowhere. Any hope that they'd rush to the aid of his friend in Ben and Anna's car has faded. No doubt that is not the 'practical' thing to do. We're playing to their tune. We need to take back the initiative before one of these shots hits something vital.

"We could try to make it through the dunes?" I've considered that too but...

"We don't know if there's a way through and if we have to turn round we'll be sitting ducks." Will nods as if I'm only confirming his unspoken thoughts. "At the moment he's staying virtually still and we're doing all the running. It's easier to aim when the car isn't jumping about, yeah?" Will nods. "What if we stay still and make him move?"

"How do we do that?"

"What if we blast down this valley and then just wait. We can both set up with rifles. He'll have to come to us or leave us."

"A last stand?" I think I can hear a concerning fatalism creeping into Will's voice.

"No, more like taking the high ground."

"Okay, what the hell, go for it."

I swing round due west and speed up as fast as I dare – faster than I dare, really. The ground starts to become less even and more than once it feels like we take flight. I silently thank the old time suspension engineers who knew what built-to-last actually meant. The dunes either side begin to close in on us and ahead a few low bushes and hardy thorn trees mark the point where I suppose any water remains for the longest. That doesn't appear to have been any time recently.

"How about here? Can you see them?"

"Too much dust." I swing round in a tight loop. No sign of our pursuers. Will pulls my rather crumpled shoulder bag from the glove box, behind which are a pair of binoculars. He scrambles out onto the bonnet.

"They're coming, but not fast." I reach into the back for our rifle and its box of bullets. As I slide to the ground, the pistol is stuffed into the front of my shorts. It's served me well there. Will raises his eyebrows slightly, but doesn't comment. There are way more important things than innuendo at the moment.

"How many shots are left in those?" My eyes slip to the poacher rifles slung over each Will's shoulders and then to the empty one laid across the passenger seat. The curved bullet holders must take quite a few.

"I'm not sure. It looks like the magazines must take about twenty when they're full but I don't know how to take them off to check what's left."

We set up using the window ledge of the open doors as a rest. Through my sight I can see the brown dot of the Land Rover. It's dawdling along so slowly there's barely a wisp of dust curling behind it. I suppose it was too much to hope that Soba would come charging in. He's going to be ultra cautious. We need to do something else he isn't expecting. Will has obviously been thinking along similar lines.

"What if we hide behind that mound instead of waiting here?" Ahead, perhaps thirty yards away, is a small mound: a baby dune just a couple of metres tall. "We'd be a much smaller target lying down and they might think we've run off and drive right up." I doubt if the captain would be so stupid, but it's still a good idea.

"Okay, I'll bring the water bottle." I lift it from between the seats but find myself short of a hand for the bullets. My bag, that'll do. I shove in the ammo box, sling it over my shoulder, and hurry after Will. He's stooping low, scuttling along like an overgrown beetle. I follow suit and flop down next to him on the shaded side of the slope. We catch each other's eyes, an expression of shared fear and not a little anger passing between us. Then we peer over the top.

The army Land Rover is still trundling along at Sunday afternoon driver pace. "How close before we try a shot?"

"I don't know. Let them come right up – they'll be the sitting ducks."

I rest my rifle on the crest of the mound and peer along it. Last time this thing shot to the right and above of where I was aiming. "Do I adjust the telescope thing with these knobs?"

"Yes, I think, one does elevation and the other does right/left." I turn both a couple of clicks in what seems like the sensible direction. There's nothing for it but to see what happens...

They're still approaching, the dot in the sight growing all the time. "Come on," says Will, as if encouraging a dog to leave behind an interesting smell. They do. It can't be more than half a kilometre now. Another few seconds... Oh... Just as I'm thinking 'only a little closer and then I can definitely hit you,' they stop. Will scans through the binoculars.

"What are they doing?"

"I can't see... oh... the beret guy is getting out. He's got a rifle with a big sight on it. He's walking towards us. I think it's now or never before he sets that up..."

Will and I let off shots almost simultaneously. Soba is tiny in the sight compared to his vehicle, but I watch carefully to see if I can see where my shot hits. There's a puff of sand in front and to the right. I make another adjustment but Soba has hit the floor, leaving us with virtually no target. I hear a return shot but don't see or hear it hit anywhere near us. The poacher captain is crawling forward. Will fires a couple more causing him to flop down. Another return shot but again I don't even hear it whizz by. What is he doing?

My next shot is much closer. So close, that I see Soba start and then roll sideways over and over. I fire my third before he stops but it's worse than the second. I slip down the slope to reload. As I'm stuffing three more bullets into the rifle, there's a hollow thud from the top of our Land Rover, shortly followed by a second. The Defender suddenly looks odd, catching the sunlight like it's part way through a wash... Oh no...

"Will he's not aiming at us, he's hitting the car. Stop him!" Will fires until I'm back in position, then I continue, each round as quick as I can reload them. For a few seconds there's no return fire. Have we hit him? Is he reloading? I'm answered by a bright red streak leaping from the captain's rifle like something out of Star Wars. Our windscreen goes white. A second beam disappears through the radiator grill. I'm transfixed with horror as the third of these sci-fi nightmares hits the roof rack – there's an audible 'whump' even from thirty yards, and our transport bursts into flames.

"Clever bastard," yells Will, emptying his rifle after a retreating Soba. "Come on, just one... tsssk... Holly, see if you can hit them before they come to finish us off."

I'm not looking that way. I'm staring at the flames pouring down the sides of the Land Rover, leaping out of the open side windows, licking round the edges of the bonnet. Even the sand seems to be alight...

"Oh, Will, they won't stay," I say, in a small voice, turning back towards him. "He'd say it wasn't practical. He knows he's killed us anyway." As if to rub our faces in it, Soba reaches his vehicle, which leaps forward and accelerates off in a cloud of dust. My eyes meet Will's. "I'm so sorry, I didn't know he had a laser gun... I didn't even know they existed..."

"A what?"

"A laser gun – he set the Land Rover on fire with it."

Will snorts into a cackle of laughter. "Oh, bless you, Holly Woodlove. He shot holes in our jerry cans and then lit the diesel with tracer bullets..." Any trace of mirth vanishes from his face as quickly as it arrived. "...but we're just as screwed anyway... unless we can put it out really fast."

He sprints towards the flames, throws the rifles to one side, and starts shovelling sand with his bare hands. "Come on," he calls over his shoulder. The heat is intense and thick black smoke is beginning to billow into the sky as I reach his side.

"Aren't you worried it will explode?"

"They only do that on TV. Diesel isn't anywhere near as bad as petrol anyway... Try to stop it running under the bonnet." We launch handfuls of sand towards the shattered windscreen in an effort to divert the flow of liquid flame. After a couple of minutes, we do seem to be having some effect – at least on the outside. The jerry cans are running dry and we're only fighting existing fire, not new. Will works round the passenger side while I take on the rear off-side tyre which is well alight. Fortunately, there's no lack of raw materials for smothering.

"We need to stop it inside." I shout. Burning diesel has gushed through broken glass and open windows and the air is full of the acrid smell of burning plastic trim and seat covers.

"I'm going to open the back and get the spades." Will taps the handle with a couple of fingers to test the temperature. It's obviously not too hot yet and he yanks it open. If I'd remembered anything from my chemistry A-level I would have known not to add ventilation to a fire. It's always easy to be smart after the fact. It's not so easy to close a door again when an inferno of oxygen fanned flames burst out of it. We both fling ourselves backwards and land in a tangle. Will still seems to have his eyebrows. I suppose that means mine must have survived too.

"Maybe someone will see that..." I follow Will's eyes to the plume of smoke now drifting high above us. Maybe, but that's our transport, our food, our life in that smoke. I crawl to my feet and fling sand into the rear of the Land Rover. It hardly makes a difference against the wall of flame but once Will is beside me and we concentrate on the left side, we begin to damp down a small area. Will rips off his T-shirt and wraps it round his right hand and fore-arm. He approaches from where the metal of the open door blocks some of the heat, reaches under it and makes a blind grab for a smouldering shovel. It brings a burning mat with it. I frantically kick sand as Will rolls away, coughing.

"Are you okay?"

"Yeah, yeah..." he says, regaining his breath. He spins over onto his feet and reaches for his prize with his wrapped up hand. The spade is blackened but still sturdy. He raises it for a thrust into the ground, moving his left hand under the shaft to balance the weight. "Ahh, hot..." he gasps, letting it fall; blowing on his unprotected fingers. He needs something else to cover the other hand. I'm about to offer my shirt when I remember that's all I'm wearing on my top. Then rationality steps in. This is an emergency, what does my embarrassment matter?

"Do you want..." I start. His long shorts are already half way down his legs. Will clearly had no internal debate about showing off his black boxers.

With properly insulated hands the shovel makes a huge difference. Great clods of sand rain into the rear of the Defender, quickly snuffing out everything behind the rear seats. He hooks out the second spade and passes me the first. "It'll've cooled enough by now. I'll use the other one at the front." I shovel away at the rear whilst Will fills the driver's side with half a dune. "We're winning..." His almost cheery yell is drowned out by hissing. The black smoke is greying fast. "Shit, that's the water barrel." Before my mind fully registers Will's words, I see water dribbling from every corner, under every door, disappearing into the sand. "Catch some, drink it..." I cup my hands beneath a flow of warm drips. It tastes foul – burnt plastic with a bouquet of diesel. I almost spit it back out.

The water, or, more likely, the cloud of steam, has put out the last of the flames. I peer round the side of the vehicle to find Will lying on his back letting water from the door sill drip into his mouth. The expression on his face is TV advert chocolate bar bliss. He must be a lot thirstier than I realised.

"It's all out." I flop into the shade beside him – head on the sand, panting at the sky. The plume of smoke is dissipating fast. Was there anyone to see it? It must be forty miles back to the mine – a hundred or more back to the garage.

"It's like an upside down sandcastle, Daddy."

"It certainly is a big hole. The lorries carrying the diamonds would have driven round those terraces."

"Lorries full of diamonds?" Felicity's eyes are dinner plate wide with wonder.

"No. Lorries full of rocks with just a couple of diamonds somewhere in each load."

"How do they find them then?"

"You see all those patterns next to the big hole?" Felicity struggles to point her binoculars along the path of Daddy's outstretched arm to the plain below. "They're the left over bases of the machines and buildings where they used to crush the rock and sort out the diamonds."

"But how do they find them?"

Beaten by childish curiosity, Daddy shrugs, "I don't know, you'll have to search for it on the Net when we get home."

"Something's burning out in the desert."

"Will you come away from that edge, Sam?" Although Felicity's older brother is a good ten feet from the cliff-top, that is more than close enough for Mummy.

Sam takes a grudging half-step back. "Can you see the smoke?"

"What smoke?"

"Over there in the dunes."

Mummy squints in the bright morning light but to be honest she's not really sure where her son means. "Andy, Sam says he can see smoke."

"Where are you looking?" Daddy lays an arm round Sam's shoulder.

"Above the dunes, miles and miles away."

A quick scan with the larger binoculars reveals nothing obvious. "Where exactly do you mean?"

"It... it's nearly stopped but if you go right from the mine there's one dune that really looks like a triangle..."

"Yup, got it."

"Then up a bit and to the right of that. It was much blacker a minute ago."

"Mmm... I don't know... I can't really see anything. It was probably just a dust devil or something."

"It was smoke." The rest of the family recognise the tone in his voice immediately. Mummy intervenes.

"Darling, I'm sure you saw something, but that's the deep desert over there. No one goes there."

"It was smoke!" Sam's voice is becoming louder and more agitated. He starts to rub the back of his hair with one hand.

"I didn't see nothing," Felicity butts in unhelpfully.

"Anything... You didn't see anything," says Mummy, unable to help herself.

"It was smoke and those ranger men said to tell if we saw anything strange, didn't they?"

"But Sam..." The rubbing on the back of the head intensifies.

"It was smoke." Sam stomps off to the car, slamming the door shut. Daddy starts towards the Toyota but Mummy lays a hand on his arm.

"Let me." She opens the door and squeezes half a cheek onto the seat. Sam is glaring through water filled eyes. "Darling, none of the rest of us saw anything, but if you say you saw smoke then we believe you. When we get a mobile signal, Daddy will ring them. Won't you?" Mummy glances up to Daddy with her face hidden from Sam.

"Of course I will," say his lips, but from his wife's expression he knows that later he will be using all his amateur acting skills, performing a one sided conversation into a dead phone.

"Holly... *come and get in," shouts Mummy.*

"Holly... are you daymaring?" My mind wrenches back to the sky, the sand, the smell of burnt vehicle. Will prods my side with a foot.

"More of a dream, really... I was... oh never mind. What now then?"

"Now we clean this out, see what we can salvage, and, if by some miracle we can get it started..." He doesn't sound very hopeful and his expression is as grim as his cheeks are pale. I keep forgetting he's probably still partly concussed. He's re-dressed and his clothes are comically dirty for anyone who isn't an extra in a disaster movie.

"All the girls love a fireman." For a second he stares with 'how the hell can you laugh' petulance. Then his eyes drop to his T-shirt and I see the tension flow out.

"How about chimney sweeps?"

"Oh, yeah, definitely."

CHAPTER 18

Two charred spades; one rifle with seventeen bullets; one pistol with three; one pair of binoculars; one water bottle with about a litre and a half remaining; one shoulder bag with sun-cream, wipes, lip balm, and useless mobile phone; half a stick of French bread – now rather overdone French toast; an unopened bottle of semi-boiled prune juice; five charred slices of salami; various metal tools. This is everything in the 'useful pile'. I stare at it and pray that the Land Rover will start this time. Will's head appears from under the bonnet. His hands are now as grubby as his clothes.

Amazingly the battery has survived, but all electrics inside the cab are beyond repair: the steering wheel a metal skeleton; the dashboard a melted lump. Still, the only part that really matters is the ignition wire. We've traced where that comes through from the engine compartment and Will is about to twist the two ends together for the third time. He holds up a pair of crossed fingers and I return the salute.

The starter motor turns the engine over, but just like last time, nothing catches. Will separates the wires and sinks to the sand.

"I'm sorry, we're obviously getting no diesel but there's just too many things melted to know what might be wrong. It could be that there's no juice getting to the fuel pump but I don't even know where that is, let alone which wires go to it. I'm no mechanic, I only know a few things from helping Paul mess with his Astra when we were teenagers."

"You don't have to apologise. I'm not much help am I? I mean, I can change a wheel or a bulb but that's not much good right now, is it?" I sit beside him and nudge my shoulder against his. "The moment I saw it catch fire I never expected it to drive again. It's amazing you came so close."

"Close isn't saving us, though." Again his voice seems laden with guilt as much as hopelessness. Did he not listen?

"They must be searching for us by now. They knew we were coming to the petrol station. The station people knew we took the road to the mine. If they're anywhere close they will have seen the smoke. We probably just need to wait." I force my lips into an encouraging smile. Our eyes hold for a second before Will twists away with a rueful grimace and a sigh. I stare at the back of his head with puzzlement. Did I really just see that? As he turned, his eyes flicked towards my shirt. I peer downwards. With the second button missing I am gaping a little, but, flipping heck Will, this is hardly the time... Men! "I'm going to walk up to the top of that dune – see what I can see – before it gets too hot."

"Wha... Okay," comes the mumbled reply. I retrieve the binoculars from the pile and leave him to contemplate his navel.

It seems easiest to climb straight up the ridge, one foot in the light, one in shadow, but it's heavy going and I'm panting by the time I reach the crest. Squinting to the east, the dry river stretches into the sunlight. Although I know the plain gets wider and wider there's an odd effect with perspective that makes it appear almost the same width all the way back to the escarpment. I'm standing at the tail end of a huge red-brown desert snake. There's no sign of any movement. The little bereted captain has left us for dead. If we have to walk for it, I can't see how he's wrong.

I lie on the shaded slope, steadying the binoculars on the crest, straining to make sense of the small white dot near the limit of visibility. It's Ben and Anna's Land Rover still on its side, but what is..? Even as bubbles of hopeful possibilities rise, they're popped by the realisation that the odd glint above the dot is an open door on the upper side. This is Soba – it must also be beyond repair and anything useful will already have been stripped... Before leaving the summit, I scan right round: the view north is mostly blocked by an even larger dune, but to the west and south it's just ridge after ridge after ridge...

Will hasn't moved by the time I return. "See anything?" he says to my feet.

"Dunes, dunes and more dunes..." I reply, returning to my previous sand moulded bum print. "Nothing – except for the other crashed Land Rover, and that looks like it's been stripped."

Will's eyes slide again in that same breast-high direction. "Bastards..." he says with vehemence and flings himself flat against the sand. I roll my eyes. I can feel annoyance building. This guy is the king of blunt – prepare for some of your own medicine.

"Will, what is up with you? Of course this is all a bloody nightmare, but lying around sulking because I've hurt your male pride doesn't help, does it?" His face tilts up, frowning. "And stop the furtive peeking down my shirt. Aren't Anna's tits perfect enough for you?" His mouth drops open. "You've always seemed like one of the least sexist men I've met. Don't spoil it now things are tough."

Will brings his knees up to his chest and then flings his legs forward, rolling into a sitting position in one smooth movement. "You think... you... you wonder why I'm feeling guilty? What have I done? I got myself knocked out, I can't shoot straight to save my life – literally – and I'm a useless mechanic. Whereas you..." he pauses, the corners of his mouth pulling downwards as if he daren't "... you let yourself be raped to save me."

"Raped?" Oh...

"You... you were held captive by four men; you said you had to play along... every so often you wince and put your hand... then I noticed you don't seem to be wearing a bra anymore... I'm sorry, I wasn't ogling, I was just... I'm so, so sorry." His big hands cover his face and he peers though his fingers. Bless him.

"Will, you're adding two and two and making twenty-three. It wasn't so bad. I had to get partly undressed and I couldn't find the bra." Will's hands come away from his face and his expression begins to perk up. Keep it going... "I have a corker of a bruise from landing on the car keys in my pocket. Do I keep prodding it?"

Will nods. "Not raped?" he stutters.

"Definitely not raped." Absolutely no point telling him quite how close it was – twice. I hide a shudder by shifting position. "And if we're talking about being useless: I did all the hard work, I had the chance of sneaking off and leaving them all asleep and I blew it, woke one up and had to shoot. If I'd been less of a complete imbecile, they'd still be sleeping it off and we'd be at the mine by now. If this is anyone's fault, it's mine."

"Rubbish. You've been amazing. I don't know how you can think so clearly... It's not like you've ever been in the army or anything..."

"Exactly. Neither have you. We've no idea what we're doing, we're just muddling on through somehow... So don't beat yourself up about it."

The ghost of a cheeky grin crosses his lips. "No sir, cap'n Woodlove, sir."

"Muppet." I roll my eyes, but it's good to see a flash of the old Will. "So... how do we muddle our way out of this one?"

"Let's move into the shade and have a ponder."

The pondering continues for the rest of the morning and most of the afternoon, punctuated only by one bite of bread, one sip of water, and several repositionings round the car to keep out of the sun. The gist of our dilemma goes like this:

First: how long to wait? They always say 'stay with your vehicle' but there's only any point in that if the searchers have any idea where your vehicle might be. We're agreed that no one is going to look here unless they saw the smoke – and if they did see the smoke then they'll arrive today. So there's no point waiting beyond this evening.

Second: if no one comes, what then? The only other option is to walk out of here. Moving at night and sleeping during the day makes most sense.

Third: which way to go? This might seem equally obvious and impossible. Forty miles across dunes to the mine followed by the same or more back to the garage – on half a bottle of water and a stick of toast. If we meet someone part way, we might just make it – if not... But now Will's back thinking a little straighter, he's remembering that map he pored over for days. It's ash now, but much of it is burnt into his mind and he's sure that there's a road which follows the sea, deep into the desert, ending in a small village and a tourist campsite. We've come so far west the coast can only be twenty or thirty miles. Do we risk Will's memory or hope on searchers or tourist families visiting the mine?

Fourth: what to take with us? We agree on pretty much everything from the 'useful' pile minus the tools – except for one spade for 'digging our own shade if we can't find any'. The only point of disagreement is something that I didn't even rate as worthy of 'useful': the roll of foil. Of everything in the hamper that seems to have come out least affected – merely a little blackened on its outer wrap.

"I just think it might come in handy."

"For what?"

"I don't know."

"There's a box under your bed at home full of things that 'might come in handy', isn't there?" I raise my eyebrows. "Come on admit it."

"There might be..."

"And how often do you actually use anything from it?"

"Occasionally... Look, it doesn't weigh much. I'll carry it." One corner of his mouth rises. "I'll shove it down the front of my shorts... being as you'll want the pistol."

"I hear it'll be the first long hard thing they've ever encountered."

Will rolls his eyes. "Are there no secrets between girlfriends?"

As I shake my head, the chuckle turns into a sigh. "How the hell did we end up here, Will? This was meant to be a relaxing holiday."

"You've got sun, you've got sand – a bit too much sand, maybe, but what more do you want?"

"A swimming pool. I wouldn't be worrying about swallowing the water right now."

The edge of the shadow has reached us again and sunlight is tickling Will's toes. The afternoon is definitely wearing on. "We're going to have to walk, aren't we?" I say.

"Seems like it..."

We prepare to leave with reluctant sluggishness, nagging doubts making every action seem like swimming through treacle. We decide to leave a message wiped into the soot on the side of the Land Rover, just in case.

HOLLY WOODLOVE AND WILLIAM MASON WALKED...

There's no putting off the decision any longer...

"I just don't know which way would be better..." Will mumbles. Neither do I, from a geographical point of view, but someone needs his confidence restoring and right now that seems more important than choosing between lethal injection or firing squad. I press my finger beneath the 'H' and continue:

...WEST TO THE COAST ROAD – 23RD JUNE

Will nods his agreement. "Right then... one last look from your dune?"

We leave everything except the binoculars and the food in a pile at the foot and retrace my steps to the crest. We just need to be sure. The time of heat haze is passed, and with the low sun on our backs, anything moving would be obvious. I scan the horizon whilst Will breaks off two small portions of bread and divides a salami slice in two. It should take no more than five minutes to nibble these meagre pickings and wash them down with a gulp of prune juice but we make it last half an hour. Any vehicle would have turned on its driving lights by now. They've no idea where we are...

As the sun sets, the dunes to the east, the dry valley, and the escarpment merge into one dark, forbidding lump and part of me is glad to turn west and chase the light.

"May as well get going," says Will, lifting his arms into a long stretch.

The first couple of miles are simple. Although a vehicle would struggle, the network of low humps and dry pans marking the very end of the valley is easy going. There's even a few crickets to chirrup us on our way. Once we're amongst the dunes proper, it's a different story: every few hundred yards there's a ridge running more or less north-west to south-east. As we are heading west and maybe a little south, we have to climb every single one. We waste a lot of time with the first few, blundering around trying to make out the shallowest slope in the starlight.

"This is ridiculous," says Will. "One of us will trip and break something – we'll have to wait for the moon."

A chilly and frustrating hour later the silvery light does improve things. Spotting the lowest part of the next ridge from the top of the previous one is now possible and the Southern Cross hanging in the sky to our left is a constant compass for our overall route. The exertion of each climb keeps the cold at bay but I can feel the heavy going sapping at my energy. We mean to carry on until the sun melts the chill of dawn but even as the horizon behind us begins to pale, I know I'm exhausted.

"Will, I'm going to have to stop."

"Me too." I'm not sure if Will is just being kind or if his injuries have offset his superior fitness. I shed my shoulder bag and pass the water bottle. Despite our seemingly tiny sips, it's alarmingly lighter than when we left the Land Rover. I forego a drink this time and settle back on the sand. If only we still had the barrel...

"What are tracer bullets?" I don't know why I'm bothered, but it suddenly popped into my head.

"Sorry, I didn't mean to laugh... before."

"Don't worry, I'll get you back... sometime."

In the dim light I can see Will wiggling his shoulders, working out a more comfortable hollow in the slope. "They put a sort of firework thing in the tip of the bullet so that it glows as it flies. Makes it easier to see where you're aiming. They mostly use them for anti-aircraft guns but I suppose the army can get them for normal rifles... Is that rubbing blisters?" Will has noticed me prodding my ankle under the clamp. It is beginning to chafe. I nod. "Maybe if you wrap a wipe round that might be softer and stop it sliding around?"

"How would I do that without it falling off?"

"Shall I?"

"Okay."

I remain in a prone position whilst Will sits cross-legged at my feet, tearing the wipes into strips and applying them with careful firmness.

"How many miles do you think we've come?"

"I'm not sure. The dunes are slowing us down but we must be past half way."

My legs certainly feel like I've done fifteen miles or more. "So we should reach the sea tomorrow?"

"Yeah. There, let's see..." An involuntary shudder passes through my whole body as Will places a hand on my calf. He removes it like it's been stung. "Shit, sorry, did I hurt you?"

"No, no, I'm fine..."

"Holly, you're still shaking."

He's right, I am. Pull yourself together woman. He only touched your leg. "It's nothing you did," I mumble. "It felt... a bit like when they put it on."

Will opens his mouth as if to speak but decides against it. He regards me with concern as I breathe the shakes away. I know he'd be a sympathetic ear, but I really don't want to remember anything... at all... ever. I reach for the shackle, now neatly wrapped like a racquet handle, and give it a tug. It's tighter but softer. "It feels much better, thanks."

"No probs."

I turn onto my side, curl into a ball, wriggle a little to make the sand more comfortable, and close my eyes. Just as I'm dozing there's a short chirruping sound. Must be a trick of my ear on the sand. A few seconds later I hear it again – clearer this time. I open one eye and find with some surprise that it's full daylight, and, now that I'm a little more awake, recognise the pleasant warmth of sunlight on my back. Must have been asleep for a couple of hours. My gaze follows the red-brown sand to the top of the dune where a small red-brown bird is framed against piercing blue sky.

"Will," I whisper to an expanse of leg, T-shirt and tousled hair lying near my feet. No response. "Will, we have a little visitor." I prod shoulder with foot. "Will." This time there's a grunt and he twists to peer through squinting eyes. I point with my hand held close to my body. The gaze of two humans is too much and with a final chirrup the bird launches itself into the sky westwards.

"Wings would be very handy. Do you know what it was?" I ask.

"No, but it's just the sort of little brown job that Anna would be in raptures about." As he says her name Will's expression turns rueful. "Maybe Anna and Ben are drinking coffee in Kaura's office right now, wondering where we've got to?"

"I hope they're as worried as we were."

"It would be kind of ironic... We'll need to find some shade soon."

We climb to the top of the nearest ridge, hoping for a glimpse of sea but apart from the distant escarpment there's only sand and sky. We find a steep south-west facing slope, dig shallow hollows and settle into the shade for more sleep. Some time past midday it becomes unpleasantly hot and our shade shrinks fast. Will attempts more digging but there's only so much of an overhang he can make before it collapses – completely dry sand is useless for kid's sandcastles. The Mark One Improvised Parasol works better: the spade and rifle each shoved into the sand at an angle above us, Will's T-shirt threaded over them. But even though Will takes an XL it's not nearly large enough for both of us.

With Mark Two Improvised Parasol, I have to eat my words. The spade and rifle placed further apart and three lengths of foil sheet wrapped over them and held by knotted strips of wet wipe. Not total shade, but a lot better. He can't resist an I-told-you-so grin as he hands me a foil 'folded-paper' fan to waft.

Exhausted sleep must have snuck up sometime between wafts

because it's obviously late afternoon when a flapping noise wakes us. One foil sheet has come unattached at the rifle end and is slapping the spade, another has completely disappeared. My lower legs are in full sun and even though we put cream on earlier, they feel a little sore. That's the only downside of the breeze, though, otherwise the moving air feels wonderfully cooling after the earlier oppressive stillness.

"We may as well have a bite and a sip now and then set off."

CHAPTER 19

Our second night and day adrift in the petrified ocean passes pretty much as the first, but the time we gain through knowledge – to wait for the moon, how to cross ridges, setting up a parasol – is offset by fatigue. The empty ache in my stomach is growing and my throat seems constantly dry. The prune juice and salami are gone, just half a pint of water and ten centimetres of bread remain.

As we leave for our third night march, we take a small diversion up a dune which seems a little higher than the rest.

"I thought we'd at least be able to see the sea by now," says Will staring at wall-to-wall sand. Even the escarpment has disappeared. There's nothing but shadowed ridges to the west and dimly pale ones to the east.

"We must be close," I say with an encouraging tone that I don't honestly feel. "It's like being in a forest where you can't see the wood for the trees. We can't see the desert, or the edge of it, for the dunes. We'll probably go over one crest and there it'll be."

"Mmm." He doesn't sound convinced. "Bloody hell, I'm hungry." Me too.

"We could eat now rather than at the moon stop?"

"No, let's stick to the plan – see how it goes."

An hour and a half later we halt in the lee of another dune just before we lose all twilight. I feel a little light headed and as I bend to put my bag down, the world spins and I find myself on my knees.

"Are you alright?"

"Just a bit dizzy."

"That'll be walking without eating or drinking." He plonks himself beside me and offers a steadying hand. "I've been thinking. It's all very well rationing, but we need the energy now. It's no good collapsing one mile short of the coast road because we were saving some for later. I say we each eat and drink a third of what we've got left now."

"Okay." I can't fault his logic and I'm so hungry, I'm not about to put much effort into trying.

As we're consuming our five star meal of 'pain brûlé' and 'eau naturel', increasing moans mark the stiffening of the breeze. It isn't until moonrise that we realise what a pain real wind can be out here. Every crest has a silvery wisp of sand smoke – princess pretty... until you try to walk head on through it. Our trek becomes not only a fight against fatigue and heavy going underfoot but also a battle of sight versus grit. Will tries pulling his top over his face but it's too dark to see through. We end up taking turns as leader and follower: the follower gaining the benefit of a body to shelter behind, but carrying more, allowing the leader a free hand to cover their eyes. It's slow, slow going. We take to pausing in the lee just before the pull up the next slope. Each time it seems a little harder to force our limbs back into action.

"One, two, three... off we go." It's my turn as leader; I take five steps up the slope before I look back. Will hasn't moved. "Come on." Nothing. He's staring at the ground vacantly. "Come on, we need to keep on moving." I retrace my steps and place a comforting hand on his shoulder. He raises his head and fixes me with slightly wild eyes.

"We're going to die, aren't we?"

A little nagging voice at the back of my mind has been saying the same thing, but I'm not giving in to it yet. "Well, we will if we stop here. But we already outwitted four armed poachers, so I'm not going to let this arse wipe of a desert beat me."

"Arse wipe?" He almost grins. "Would that be more unnecessary bad language from Holly Woodlove?"

"It was completely necessary..."

"Can't say I disagree with the description..." He hoists the spade to his shoulder which I take as a good sign.

"See, if we keep on talking, it won't drag so much and we'll be okay... In fact..." Whoosh. Instant cliff dive into Ideas Ocean. The two sides of my brain wrestle between creativity and practicality. How to combine... Of course! Mind re-engages with body like it's been slammed into gear.

"Imagining things again?" Will asks, furrowing his brow. I must've paused longer than I thought.

"No, I... You know how American soldiers sing to stop the marching becoming too boring?"

"I suppose..."

"What if we try it?"

"Okay, but I don't think I know any..."

"Let's make one up. Come on." I already have the first two lines as I turn to climb the slope: "*Keep on walking, we'll be okay. Keep on talking, we'll be okay.* Now you think of something. *Keep on...* something else."

"*Keep on going?*"

"Okay, and the rhyme?"

"*Glowing... throwing...*"

"*Blowing...*" I add, shaking my head. "Another one? What about *keep on moving?*"

"*Grooving,*" comes the reply from behind me. We're over the ridge and down the slope.

"Good one. Let's sing those four lines." I start on my own and when I reach *grooving* I wiggle my bum. It's stupid... energy wasting... but so what! After a few repeats, each time we reach that word Will is waggling his booty in synchro. "Are you alright to keep on singing that while I try something else over the top?"

"Yes, ma'am."

A simple bluesy melody comes to me almost instantly and I experiment with lyrics and harmony. I've no idea how many ridges we cross before I home in on the final version:

Keep on

Keep on walking, we'll be okay.
Keep on talking, we'll be okay.
Keep on moving, we'll be okay.
Keep on grooving, we'll be okay.

When the worries of this world bear down upon me,
when my heart feels like it's ready to burst,
when it seems like everybody's out to get me,
music keeps me going through the worst.

Keep, keep, keep on walking.
Keep, keep, keep on talking.
Keep, keep, keep on moving, we'll be OK.
Keep, keep, keep on walking.
Keep, keep, keep on talking, ke-ep on moving...

When this life seems like a desert around me
When it feels like I am dying of thirst
When every little footstep just exhausts me,
Music keeps me going through the worst

Keep on walking, keep on talking,
Keep on moving, keep on grooving.

When the worries of this world bear down upon me,
When my heart feels like it's ready to burst,
When it seems like everybody's out to get me,
Music keeps me going through the worst.

Keep, keep, keep on walking.
Keep, keep, keep on talking.
Keep, keep, keep on moving, we'll be OK.
Keep, keep, keep on walking.
Keep, keep, keep on talking.
Ke-ep on moving and we'll be OK.

Will seems perfectly happy to repeat his four lines over and over whilst I do all the fancy stuff. The only downside of this distraction is an occasional gritty mouth. There's a pause in the singing as we plough through the near blindness of another crest. Once we're over, most of the airborne sand is below head height.

"If you use it, will I get a song writing credit?" Will sounds like a kid asking about a trip to the beach."

"Of course."

"Uber cool."

"I wouldn't get too excited. The amount I'm selling at the moment you might earn enough royalties for a pint of beer at the end of the y...ahh." The slope under my left foot gives way, turning my ankle over, pitching me onto my front. The pistol butt digs into my gut, the water bottle rolls away, but I manage to keep hold of my shoulder bag.

"All in one piece?" Will is down by my side in a trice.

"I... I'm not sure."

"Don't open your eyes." He helps me into a sitting position, turns me so my back is to the wind and wipes sand from my face with something soft. His touch is so gentle for a big guy. "Okay."

I open them to find it's the hem of his charred T-shirt. He lets it fall back over a stomach made piebald by the moonlight. From the aches, my own torso must be similarly bruise dappled. Bloody hell we're a mess.

"Ankle?" I nod. "Bad?" It's sore but pain isn't screaming up my leg like the time I put a foot down a rabbit hole at Ben's parents.

"Can't tell until I try it."

He pulls me upright, all the weight on my right side. I tentatively transfer some to my left foot.

"F...iddlesticks." The ache becomes a burn, "A... Ah... Ahhh," which gradually fades from white to dull red hot. I must manage somehow. "I think I can walk if I don't put too much weight on it... If I put an arm round your shoulder?"

Will is wearing a brave face, but I can see some of the song-pumped strength wilting in the droop of his shoulders. "Let's work out how we're going to do this, then," he says, fetching the water bottle.

"I can still carry that." But it and the pistol turn out to be the only things I can manage.

A few minutes later we set off with Will additionally draped with the shoulder bag and my left arm. Whilst we're on relatively flat ground it's workable, but fighting over the crest with three legs and no sheltered eyes is madness. We start to slither and in an effort not to pitch forward Will over-compensates and we end up on our backsides.

"Keep your eyes shut and bum scoot to the bottom." I do as bidden and when the slope reduces so that pushing with one leg no longer moves me forward, a strong arm pulls me into clear air again.

Will shakes his head. "We'll have to wait for the light... or the wind to drop.

"I'm really sorry. Maybe my ankle will improve with couple of hours rest."

"I'm not blaming you: it's not your fault. It's just... fucking hell, could anything else go wrong?"

We hobble into the shelter of the next dune, Will digs a shallow depression, and dispirited limbs crawl into it. I lie on my back, facing the stars. They haven't lost any of their beauty, I've just lost the capacity to appreciate it.

"We should've gone the other way," says Will in a breathy, sigh-laden tone. "I'm sorry, I thought it was twenty, thirty miles at the most. I must have misremembered."

"How many miles do you think we've come?"

There's a pause whilst Will considers. "Slow walking pace is about two miles an hour. We must have done more than twenty hours' walking by now."

"Forty miles?" My legs certainly feel like it's been that far.

"At least..." says Will, "I don't understand it."

I reach out a hand, find his and grip tightly. We lie, side by side, with only the moan of the wind and the occasional hiss of moving sand breaking the quiet. After a few minutes I begin to shiver. We may be in the tropics but it's mid-winter, the sky is crystal clear and I'm wearing nothing but shorts and a linen shirt.

"Are you cold?" asks Will.

"And scared."

"Me too." We lapse into silence again. I'm not sure how to phrase what I want to say. In the end I just let it tumble out.

"I don't mean this to sound like a come on, but could we snuggle together... for warmth."

Will exhales loudly. "I was thinking the same but I was a bit afraid to ask after peeping-shirt-gate."

"Sorry... It's become a 'gate' now has it?"

"All the big scandals become a 'gate' these days... anyway, how is this going to work?"

I roll so I'm facing him, he turns away and we squirm together. It's all fine until my breasts touch his back. *I'm in the tent massaging for my life. Everything smells of desert-worn poacher. His breathing is slow, but any second he could twist round and... And his back, his bare back is pushing against my nipples...* A huge shudder passes through me. If I was a cat my tail would be like a bottle brush.

"Did I do something?"

"No, it's me." Idiot. There are two layers of cloth and this is not Soba, this is Will. I force myself forward again, but it's no good, my breasts just don't feel like they belong to me anymore. "Will, would you mind if we swap the other way round, I... I just can't get comfortable."

"No probs." We wriggle round until Will is pressing his chest against my back, the front of his legs against the back of mine and with some relief I note a discrete lack of contact between crotch and bottom.

"Is it alright if I put my arm across your stomach?"

"I'll let you know if it isn't." I ought to feel more vulnerable, more dominated, like this, but I don't. I feel like a child, enveloped by tenderness, and caring... and love. Despite everything, it's nice.

CHAPTER 20

There's an odd feeling to the air when I wake: not a smell exactly, more a texture. I open my eyes to see... nothing. Well, not strictly nothing. I can see the edge of our hollow, but beyond that blankness: no stars, no moon, no sand, just pale grey. It takes a moment to realise what I'm staring at.

"Will, you won't believe this. On top of everything else it's now foggy."

"Wha?"

"Thick, almost-can't-see-your-hand-in-front-of-your-face fog."

"Really?" He pushes himself into a sitting position, blinking. "This... this could be good."

"How?" I'm confused. I thought this was a disaster.

"The wind's gone and we can walk in the daytime."

"But how will we see which way to go?"

"Easy. The wind comes from the sea and the dunes are a different shape on the windward and leeward sides, so every dune is a signpost..." His little spurt of regained animation lapses into thought and he continues in a half-absent mumble. "I didn't realise it got misty in deserts."

"It does here. The guidebook is full of stuff about these mists being the life of the desert – that the plants and animals take water out of the air." I glance towards Will but I can still see the cogs whirring so I just burble on. "I wish we could do that. My hair's a bit damp but we don't have specially shaped leaves or whatever it said."

"What's that?"

"What?"

"About the leaves..." Suddenly he's fully alert, hanging on my every word. The pressure of unknown expectation causes me to stumble.

"Er, some plants have, I think it said, er, specially shaped leaves that... catch the mist drops and collect the water."

"Genius!" he says, kissing me on the forehead before striding up the face of the dune beside us until he fades from view. I sit open mouthed in bemusement as he reappears ploughing a small depression down the slope with his backside. Once at the bottom, he fetches his trusty roll of baking foil and waves it at me, calling, "This is our leaf."

He unwinds a metre or so and places it at the foot of his furrow. "Can you hold this?" I think I'm beginning to understand, but my left foot still feels very sore. "Shall I come and get you?"

"No. I'll crawl." Hands and knees are no problem on soft sand and I'm there in seconds. Once I have a grip on the end of the foil he starts up the hill, unwinding and fitting it to the shape of the depression as he goes. Every metre or so he pushes a little sand onto the edges to weigh it down, although in truth there is barely a breath of wind. It's only seconds before the miracle begins to manifest itself before my eyes. Droplets are forming on the cold metal and, just like a gulley on the side of a mountain, the curve of the furrow is causing them to run together.

"Can you dig a hole at the bottom and put the bottle under the end?" I place two large lumps of sand on either corner of the free end and scuttle off. By the time Will has finished up top my hand-excavated hole is deep enough. Even as he folds a small spout at the base of the foil, his fingers are wet with the start of the flow.

We sit back and grin stupidly at each other as a steady drip falls into the bottle. "Our very own condenser," says Will grandly, "courtesy of Holly Woodlove and her passion for guidebooks... plus a little bit of inspiration from Frank Herbert."

"Frank Herbert?"

"The Dune sci-fi book. It's set on a desert world and the locals have big condensers to take moisture out of the air."

"There, and I thought it was all down to William Mason's technical guru-ness." I glance up the silver chute and snigger.

"Okay, I admit it. Sometimes those things that might-come-in-handy actually do turn out to be useful."

"Thank you," says Will in an oddly earnest tone. "I'm sure it must have taken a lot of courage for you to admit that." His face splits into a grin.

"Idiot." He receives a playful bat on the shoulder for his cheek.

After half an hour we're wishing it was a larger bottle. We take turns lying on our backs, head in the hole, letting the gorgeous cool liquid drip into our mouths. For the first time in days, the empty gnawing in my stomach recedes. It may have no calories, but it'll do for now.

A pale watery disk of sun is beginning to peep through by the time we've drunk our fill. "I think we should try to get going," says Will. "Let's roll this back up again." Easier said than done and the resulting cylinder has rather crinkled edges from which water is still seeping. He shrugs and tucks it into the side of his shorts. "No comments about wetting myself."

"I can't remember the last time I went for a pee, anyway."

"I think that'll be coming soon."

Will's right. Several traversed ridges later, we're finding our three legged rhythm, messing with the lyrics of yesterday's song to pass the time. One person starts and the other has to finish the line with a suitable rhyme.

Keep on hobbling, we'll be okay. Keep on... wobbling, we'll be okay,

Keep on hopping, we'll be okay. Keep on... shopping, we'll be okay,

Keep on hiking, we'll be okay. Keep on... biking, we'll be okay,

Keep on driving, we'll be okay. Keep on... jiving, we'll be okay,

Keep on trucking, we'll be okay. Keep on...

It was Will's first line and the reddening of his face makes it clear he hadn't thought through possible rhymes.

"I think I'll pass on that one..." I smile and carry on...

Keep on skiing, we'll be okay. Keep on... weeing, we'll be okay...

"You too?" I ask.

"Yeah. I'll leave you here and just nip behind the edge of that dune."

"I think we're past the point of bothering about that."

"You're probably right..."

"Can you leave me the spade to rest on?" I unwind my arm from his neck and take support on that side from the spade instead. I shove it into the sand and carry out a precarious balancing act whilst Will walks a few yards away to deal with what I imagine to be a much simpler issue. When I do finally manage to go it's only a few painful drops. There's a sucked in hiss from Will's direction.

"Stings like a pig, doesn't it?" I call.

"Aha."

As I'm finishing a faint whiff reaches my nose. Weird. The acrid, almost fishy smell isn't what I'd expect even from super-concentrated pee. I haul myself up the spade into a standing position and the odour disappears. No. There it is again. The faintest of breezes tickles my face, carrying more scent with it. I glance towards Will – no he's downwind. This breeze is coming from the west.

"Can you smell that?" Will nods. "What is it?"

"No idea, but it doesn't smell like desert."

We hurriedly gather our things and hobble onward. The fog is fading fast now and from the top of the next dune we notice that the horizon seems closer than usual. From the next crest, and the next, still no more new dunes appear. It could just be a particularly tall ridge or it could be...

The stench continues to strengthen. "It couldn't be a rubbish dump, could it?" I say, wrinkling my nose.

"I was thinking more like a dead whale," says Will.

"Did you hear that?"

"What?"

"Sounded a bit like a distant flock of sheep... There." A waft brings sound in addition to scent.

"Weird."

We don't pause as we cross the remaining four ridges and begin to struggle up what seems like it must be the final slope. I don't know what I'm expecting to see as we reach the crest: a huge seaside sheep farm, a whale carcass covered in braying seabirds? What I see first is the ocean. Not this fake semi-solid one we've been crossing but the genuine constantly-fluid article. A white-capped breaker rolls into a gently curving beach smothered in a dark seething mass. At the edges of the mass, brown dots sit or lumber awkwardly. In the water, more dots bob like a scattering of charred corks.

"Seals," says Will.

CHAPTER 21

Our initial euphoria on reaching the coast quickly wears off once we discover the lack of a road or any other sign of habitation. Sure, we now have the company of several thousand fellow smelly mammals, but that wasn't quite what we were hoping for.

"We must have come further north than I thought," says Will, staring along several miles of windswept beach as far as a low rocky point jutting out into the South Atlantic. "I'm sure the road must be pretty close." He sounds like he's trying to convince himself more than me.

We're sitting at the crest of the dune that marks the southern boundary of 'Seal Bay'; 'Who-knows-how-far' beach stretches teasingly south; immediately to the west there's a blunt point capped by slabs of chocolate brown rock, to the north the teeming colony. I stare ruefully at this chaos of well-fed life. All they have to do for their spot of lunch is hop into the sea and catch a fish, but that's no good to us. As if to accentuate the point, my stomach gurgles as the water fullness subsides.

"I think we should stay here for a couple of days until your ankle improves."

Puzzlement plays across my face: "We may have some water now but we're starving. We can't just go fishing like them." I thumb towards the seals.

"No, but I see plenty of meat."

My head flicks from Will's face to the seals and back again, outrage building. "We can't..."

"I don't think we've got the luxury of worrying about animal rights," Will interrupts. "We're two hungry animals and there's a whole load of prey... It's not like one or two will make much difference." He's right. Why should I worry about eating a seal to survive when I've already killed at least one person?

Leaving everything with me but the rifle, pistol and spade, Will heads down towards the edge of the colony.

"Man go hunt..." he grunts in his best 10,000BC accent. If he has a plan, he hasn't shared it, but it's pretty obvious that Hopalong here was going to be zero use in the sneaking or pouncing departments. And anyway, the last time I did any hunting was along the grassy slopes of Donaupark and the prey my brother and I were stalking was grasshoppers. Not for any good reason. Just to catch them and then experience the funny little push as they spring away from your open hands. Carefree Saturday afternoon strolls along the Danube with Dad – how long ago was that?

I watch through the binoculars as Will edges forward. One step and the seals are all carrying on their business as normal, the next and a Mexican wave of lifting heads ripples through the mass until it seems like every pair of eyes is fixed on him. He takes a couple of quick paces back. I don't blame him. I felt intimidated from here. For a few seconds all mammalian eyes remain on Will, then another wave, this time of head turns, radiates out from a point a couple of hundred yards further down the bay. There's clearly something else to fear.

Scanning along the edge of the throng I find the source. An unfortunate teenage pup is being dragged up the beach and away from safety by a pair of jackals working as a team. Rather than lurching to its aid where their size would surely tell, the nearest adults are squirming over each other in their haste to retreat seawards. Once the pup is a few yards clear of the main colony the jackals stop dragging and start biting and ripping. It's not a pleasant watch.

"Will!" I shout. Second time my voice carries and he glances back. "Jackals up the beach." I'm not sure if he can make out the words but he gets the idea from a wave and a point. By the time he reaches the pup it must already be dead. Either that or they're eating it alive. The jackals don't seem to recognise Will as a rival until he's almost on them. I see him clap and bellow. They dodge away. He runs a few steps, first at one and then the other. They back off a little further. They're so small next to him – barely bigger than foxes. Grabbing a flipper, Will starts to drag his loot towards me leaving a dull red trail in his wake. The jackals continue to follow, every so often nipping in close and spinning away.

As he approaches I begin to hear Will's bellows: "It's mine. Mine!" Knowing full well the inaccuracy of this claim, one of the jackals dives in for a bite at the carcass. Will swings a foot but only connects with air. He stops dragging, swaps the flipper to his left hand and the spade to his right. I know exactly what he's doing as he faces partly away from the seal, spade held at arm's length, seemingly staring intently at something on the ground. I suppose this kind of deviousness is why humans get to make a mess of the planet rather than any of the other species. Certainly, jackals are no match. The braver one edges forward again. Maybe this strange animal has forgotten about the seal?

Wham. The flat back of the spade knocks the jackal sideways, whimpering. Picking itself up, it takes one glance at the advancing Will and scampers away down the beach followed by its comrade – easier to find an alternative lunch.

"I feel like a lion on one of those TV safaris where it steals the kill from the cheetahs," says Will struggling up the last few yards of slope. He drops the flipper and sinks to the sand. "I'm knackered."

"Good job." I stare at the body. The sharp teeth of the jackals have cut through the fur and skin, particularly towards the back end. A few strings of what must be intestines hang from one of the wounds. I fight down a momentary sensation of nausea. Come on, this is just like a pig before it's butchered. What we really need is something to cut with... The edge of the spade might help but it's not a knife.

"I'm going to hop down to the beach to see if I can find anything sharp."

"Sure you'll be okay?" Will must be exhausted. I thought he might insist he went.

"I can use the spade as a sort of crutch and I'll crawl if I have to. You get your breath back and I'll find us a knife."

"Take the pistol."

Bum skiing to the bottom of the dune is the quick part but there's no urgency and with a mixture of hobbling and crawling I reach the shore soon enough. The beach is tropical-island-soft right into the surf. Not a pebble in sight. Along the tide line smoothed lumps of drift wood are interspersed with scraps of plastic bag and tangles of fraying nylon rope. So much for pristine wilderness...

My next find has possibilities. A part squished can – from its faded red colour, it probably once held the Coke of a Cape Town tourist. Having cut myself at least once on a ring pull, I know these can be sharp. Crawling another fifty metres of natural and human detritus yields two more possibilities: an empty oyster shell and, best of all, a lager bottle. Its glass has been frosted by sand and time but once smashed... well, I'll need to be careful I don't cut myself.

With my three prizes, I abandon any attempts to hobble and just crawl back up the slope. Will waves the tube of sunscreen as I reach him. "You can hardly feel it with the breeze, but the sun's pretty high up now." I stare at Will's bruised and weather beaten face, now somewhat paler with a layer of cream.

"Aren't we brown enough not to bother?"

"That's not what your nose is telling me," he grins. My finger goes to the tip. Hmm. It does feel a bit sore. I take the tube. "I see you've had a good scavenge. Is there really that much litter down there?"

"Along the tide line – I think the whole ocean is a rubbish dump these days."

Whilst I protect from the yellow peril, Will sets about making butchery tools. The spade is perfect for smashing and hammering and before long we have a sharp but flaky shell edge, a ripped can and three shards of glass.

"Where should I start?" asks Will, weapons poised.

"I don't know. Let's just open it right up and see. Steak is muscle, so I suppose near the flippers."

By far the most useful tool turns out to be one of the bottle shards. The neck end has stayed fully intact, giving somewhere safe to grip, whilst what remains of the body tapers to a wicked point. We soon give up using anything else. It's messy, smelly work, but hunger cuts right through civilised thought and my mouth starts to water in anticipation as the first chunk is separated from fat and bone.

"Imagine you're in a fancy French restaurant and you've ordered blue steak," says Will. It's so chewy that it's almost impossible to bite. I end up gripping with my side teeth and tugging hard to rip off morsels. It's jaw aching and a little salty, but the feeling of something solid sliding down to my stomach is glorious.

"What do we look like?" A meal of very fresh meat with no cutlery is not a white tablecloth affair. Our hands and most of our forearms are stained red. It's the same story round our mouths and there are numerous dark spots down the front of my shirt.

"Vampires," says Will, lifting his top lip to bare his canines.

"Or lions on a kill. Grraarr." I wave a pretend set of claws in his direction. We're both giggling like school children. I suppose it's the relief – death cheated, one more time.

Will sniffs the back of his hand. "I could really do with a wash. This is going to start stinking big time." He glances towards the sea. "Fancy a dip?"

"I guess so."

He offers me a shoulder and we shamble down to the shore on the 'who-knows-how-far' side of the point. We leave trainers and sandals above the tide line and test the water with our toes.

"Bloody hell that's cold," says Will. He glances towards me, then the water, grimaces, blinks twice, opens his mouth, then closes it again.

"What?" I ask.

"I think we're going to have to be very un-British about this... but the most sensible thing would be to give our clothes a wash and then leave them to dry whilst we wash ourselves."

He's right... and I suppose if I was Swedish I wouldn't give it a second thought. It's not like I've never been skinny dipping before. It's just previously it was always with Ben... "Okay," I answer. There's no way my bad leg will take much weight, so the only way to reach the water for washing is to lower myself into the edge of the surf. Almost immediately a slightly larger wave rolls in and slaps up my front, taking my breath and stinging my scraped forehead. "Wahow," I gasp as it flows away. I wriggle my shorts from under my bum and start to wring them and scrape them along the sand. Will is doing the same with his T-shirt from a standing position.

"I don't know how you can sit in it."

"It's fine once you get used to it."

"You must have very warm blood... Shall I take those?" I hand over my shorts and slip off my knickers as he lays the first batch next to our sandals. Uggh. How many days have I been wearing these?

They receive an extra hard scrubbing. When I've finished, I put them by my side, slip the shirt over my head and continue washing.

"Whenever you're ready..." I pass the two items into waiting hands without turning. I'm conscious of the probable face full of male crotch awaiting if I do. Once I hear retreating footsteps, I push off into the sea with my good leg, swim-hop into chest deep water, and let myself sink up to my neck as I turn. Will is still laying out the wet clothes. You know how some people just shouldn't be seen naked? It's not about shape or size necessarily – it just doesn't suit them? Will is not amongst that number. He's still covered in dark bruises from the seven bells he had kicked out of him but if anything that kind of adds to the effect.

I test my ankle with a few strokes parallel to the beach – feels fine without any weight on it. In fact, if anything, the other ankle seems worse, weighed down by the clamp and stinging with the sores beneath it. I twist round to see that Will is back at the waterline, edging forwards like a reluctant toddler. We'll see about that. I dolphin under a wave, surface a couple of yards away, and slap a volley of water towards him. "Come on, don't be feeble."

"Ahh, you little bugger," he screams, returning fire by throwing his body forward, creating a face-drenching wave. I push off and backstroke out of range. "You can swim like a fish," calls Will as he progresses in a jerky head-up front crawl towards me.

"I usually go twice a week – more often if I'm in a hotel."

"I'm more of a gym person."

"I can see that." He swims past, then stands and starts to wash. I follow suit. It's weird. I thought I would be more inhibited in front of Will, but as soon as I got into the water I don't seem to care. I'm not even bothering to keep the waterline above chest height as I scrape the dried blood off my forearms. We've been through so much. What does it matter?

It's easy enough to see what I'm doing for my arms but I've no idea about my face. I hop-swim over to Will. One of his feet is almost at the surface and he's giving it a good rub.

"Is my face clean?" I push up a little more out of surf so he has a closer view. He seems slightly surprised – I suppose he was in full concentration washing mode.

"Er, yeah... well, actually you missed a bit on your cheek... no the other one... higher... further back... further..."

"Will, that's my ear."

"Oh, is that what that thing is?"

I roll my eyes. "Seriously, though, have I missed anywhere?"

"No, you're fine." His eyes flick from my face to the foot still in both of his hands. "My ankles were almost black."

"Good point, I'd forgotten about feet." I copy Will's leg up move for my left leg but for the right I'll have to float on my back to save my ankle. I manage as best I can. I'm a lot cleaner than when I started... and colder. I right myself to find Will has drifted so he's facing away from me. Foolishly complacent move, Mason. I bend and slip under the water. It's just clear enough to make out legs. I swim forward, reach down to ankles and give them a yank. The mighty falls, flailing, but as I stroke away one of those outstretched hands grabs my good foot and grips tightly.

"Got you, you pest," he laughs, making me stroke my arms to keep my head above water.

"Unfair, I have a bad ankle," I gasp.

"It's the other one... and you started it." I bend round and scoop water towards him.

"That's enough of that." He releases my foot but immediately slides arms behind my knees and shoulders and I'm lifted to his chest, half clear of the water, giggling. He grins down at me, hair slicked back, drips clinging to increasingly beardish stubble. There's slight bemusement in his expression, like he can't quite decide what to do next. Our eyes lock and I feel myself start to rise again.

"Aaaiiiee." I'm launched into the air and land with a thumping splash back into the waves.

"Ok, truce," I gasp, snorting water from my nose. I allow a wave to glide me into shallower water and push up, attempting to balance all my weight on the good side. "Can you give me a hand up to my clothes?"

"Err, I was going to stay in a little longer."

"Well, okay, you help me up and then go back in." There's a pause. He looks distinctly uncomfortable and makes no attempt to move.

"It'd be better, just now, if you managed on your own." He accentuates the words 'just now' as if I should know what's going on.

"I don't understand."

He rolls his eyes. "Do I have to spell it out? All this frolicking around with naked popstars... I've got a bloody erection, okay?" My hand goes over my mouth. "And I'm not coming out until I've thought deeply about senior Tory politicians for a few minutes."

"Oh gosh, I'm sorry." It feels like every drop of blood in my body is rushing to my face. "Ben says doing a long multiplication sum in his head works pretty well in, err, similar circumstances."

"Holly, you're not helping."

"Wha..? My eyes follow his downwards. I'm balancing knee high in the surf. "Oh... right." I hop forward to the waterline and scuttle up the beach on all threes.

LATER, WHEN WE'RE RE-CLOTHED and everything is, presumably, back to normal size, Will broaches the subject.

"I'm sorry about that... it... it wasn't anything I could control."

I catch his eye and hold it. "You don't have to apologise. You already know that I can find you attractive in that way. We just have to ignore it, yes?"

"Yeah... of course."

"With all this..." I wave vaguely at the desert. "...I wasn't thinking about anything like that, but I can see how..."

"Neither was I," he interrupts, "Not until I grabbed you and then..."

"Whoosh?"

"Yeah, whoosh," he says sheepishly. There's a long pause as we both stare towards the sun dipping into the ocean. Why did Anna have to meet this man first? What if it had been me at that Halloween party? Would everything be different? Better? Worse?

"You've told me that Ben asked Anna out first, but you've never told me how you two actually got together." A little shiver runs down my spine as I realise that Will must have been thinking along very similar lines. Is it regret or pleasure? Probably both. He's right, talking about Ben probably is a good idea.

"Anna and I were on the same corridor in hall, but we also had some of the same lectures in the first year."

"I thought you did chemistry?"

"I did, but biology was my subsid and chemistry was Anna's so we overlapped quite a lot. I was aware that there was this dark haired girl who sometimes walked the same way, but I was a bit intimidated. She looked like she must be part of the in-crowd and I definitely wasn't – and she always seemed to have some different boy tagging along.

"One time, after a few weeks, fast footsteps came up from behind and Anna breathes in my ear, 'Can you help? There's a guy following me. Don't...' But it was too late because I was already turning round. The guy didn't seem dangerous, so I said that to Anna. She said, 'I'm just worried he'll ask me out and I don't want him to.' I can't see the guy's face now, but I remember thinking that I'd have been quite happy for him to ask me out."

"So that wasn't Ben?"

"No, I don't think that one ever actually managed to ask but he would have been number three or four, I think. Ben was nearer Christmas – ten or eleven. Anyway, rather than going straight into the front door of our block, we went down the side and then ran for the back door before he came round the corner. Anna asked if she could sit with me for a while, just in case. And that was the start of my room being her bolt hole."

"Were you alright with that?"

"I didn't mind. It was nice to have a close friend. It did bug me a little when we started going to bars and parties together and gorgeous looking guys would strut round her like peacocks... and I would be completely ignored. But it used to genuinely upset her. She'd say, 'You're gorgeous Holly and if they can't see that, they're not good enough for you.'

"She was right." We both continue staring out to sea.

"Mm, well... anyway, I think she met Ben at some joint biology-vet thing and it was dark by the time it finished and he insisted on walking her back. Next day he knocked on the door of her room. She was in the middle of washing her hair or something so she opened the door in just a towel. I remember her telling me, 'He probably thinks I did that on purpose as part of some big seduction thing.' After that she became a touch paranoid and started watching out for him. One lunchtime she comes scampering down the corridor: 'Let me in quick, he's coming.' We stood with our ears to the door as he knocked on hers. He tried three or four times and then there was silence. 'See if he's gone,' she said, so I opened my door a crack. The notepad Anna had hanging on her door was in his hand and he seemed to be writing an essay."

"Notepad on a door?"

"Yeah, it was something students used to do before mobile phones. You left a message on it if you went visiting and they weren't in. Anna enjoyed the retro-ness of it. She bought me one too, even though hardly anyone used it – except Ben. He always used to write the most embarrassing things: 'Where are you, Venus? I'm yearning for worship' and stuff like that. My Dad saw it once. I was totally mortified."

"And Ben spotted you peeking round the door?" Will brings me back on track.

"Yes, so he waved and said, 'Hi.' I started to close the door but he said something like hang on a minute and it seemed rude to shut it in his face. He walked over and said, 'You haven't seen Anna – the dark haired girl who lives at the end, have you?' 'No' I said, but I blushed like anything and he must've guessed straight away 'cos he raised his voice and said, 'That's too bad because I really like her and I wondered if she fancied going to see a film.' I said I'd tell her if I saw her. 'She's in there isn't she?' he said. 'I only want to speak to her.' 'She's not.' 'I don't bite.' He must've noticed my expression darken because he stopped his pleading abruptly and changed tack. 'I'm sorry, I don't mean to bug you. If I'm being a tit and she's not at all interested she can tell me to fuck off.' A voice bellowed next to my ear, 'You're being a tit. I'm not interested... so fuck off.' I remember shrugging at his bless little crestfallen face as I slammed the wood back in the hole. He must have heard us collapse in giggles."

A few snorts, not quite enough to class as a chuckle, emanate from Will's direction. "I'm surprised he had anything to do with you after that."

"So was I. I saw him in the Student Union canteen one day in the new year. I was sat at a table on my own and he was walking past with a tray. He did a double take and asked if the seat opposite was taken and I thought, 'oh, here we go', but actually he just teased me in a funny way and I was used to that from Dad and Toby."

"What did he say? Do you remember?"

"Yeah, he asked me if I recognised him so I said, 'yes, you're the guy who wanted to go out with Anna.' He said he wasn't sure if I'd be able to see him - being as I didn't always know who was in the same room as me. I said that at least I knew when I was flogging a dead horse and he said that was a pretty rude description of Anna and on we went from there, laughing our way through lunch break and half the next lecture I should have gone to. Eventually, he went all serious and said, 'So are you and Anna a couple?' I burst out laughing, 'No, nothing like that... she just has this boyfriend back home that she's mega dedicated to and you were about the twenty zillionth guy to hit on her last term. It was getting a bit wearing.'

'And you?'

'Me? Oh gosh, no, no one ever asks me.'

'Really? Are they all stupid?'

'Crazy. Obviously.'

'So what would you do if someone did ask you?'

'I don't know, depends who it was.'

'Okay, so, just for example, what if someone like me asked you?"

'Someone like you?'

'Yes, someone who is slightly funny, doesn't look like the total back end of a bus, but is lacking a bit of confidence because the previous girl he asked turned out not to be a girl at all, but actually a dead horse.'

My heart was pounding and my hands had gone clammy. Don't mess it up, I remember thinking. 'If someone like that asked me then I think I might say yes.'

'Great. How about if we went out for a meal this evening?'

'Yes, okay,' I said, knees trembling."

"I'm not sure why you think that isn't as romantic as Anna and me..." says Will. "I knew Ben would come up with some fancy line: 'someone like me'." He shakes his head; then lapses into silence. "Mega dedicated..." he mutters after a while.

My mind catches on to his thought: "You're right, I'm totally wrong about her and Ben. I mean, if she'd wanted to... at uni... she could've had her pick of much better catches than Ben."

"That just makes me feel like even more of a shit."

CHAPTER 22

The surf has strengthened and it's a struggle not to become the next piece of flotsam tossed onto the shore. I'm trying to keep out of the shallow water because that's where Will is, washing his shorts and... well, it would just be better if I wasn't too close. Every wave seems to slap me nearer and I have to scull with my arms just to stay still. Maybe if I swim off to the side, that would be better. The last thing I want to do... two waves combine to give a forward and sideways push ...is... I paddle frantically but the water has its arms under me ...land in a sprawling naked heap at Will's feet. Oh heck. I speak before I look up.

'I'm sorry, that's exactly what I was trying <u>not</u> to do." There's no response. Double heck. I stare at his feet wondering if he's angry or... worse. Something's not quite right about his toes but a cloudiness in the water obscures them. My gaze slips up his legs. The skin is dark brown. A syrupy liquid gushes down one of them. A shudder runs through me as I slam my hands down, pushing upwards, eyes following to the source of the flow: a neat round hole blasted in the left side of his chest. The putrid rotting smell that assaults my nose contrasts with a soft snuffling sound which seems to be coming straight from that circle of death. My knees wobble but I feel compelled to rise up further. Nasty Face stares back at me with a frozen expression of surprise and fear. His dead weight leans forward, his nose an inch from mine, and I feel warm breath on my lips.

My eyes flick open to find myself staring into my nightmare: a pair of dark eyes, inches from my head, glinting in the moonlight.

"Aaaaaaaaaa." The scream erupts before any conscious thought, causing the face to shrink abruptly. My hands scrabble down my front, connect with the pistol, rip it upwards and fire straight into the air. The hairy beast stumbles in its haste to twist away from the boom. Righting itself, it glances back, yelps as its face is slapped by some invisible force, leaps to the top of the dune and vanishes over the crest. Above me I see Will's hand release another volley of sand. We scramble forward to peer after it. An oddly shaggy shadow lopes towards the limit of our night vision. A few seconds later, the seals spot it too and fill the darkness with waves of urgent bleating.

"Hyena," says Will.

"Not like we've seen before?"

"No, a brown hyena – the ones that look like they're wearing an old rug."

"It sniffed me. I felt its breath on my face."

Will blows air through turned out lips. "We need to be more careful. Maybe we shouldn't sleep at the same time."

"I don't think there'll be much more of that with the colony making this racket."

"At least we buried the seal. We would have lost it otherwise. I suppose it could smell us anyway..." He drifts off into thought. "...I wasn't expecting anything bigger than jackals. You go back to sleep, I'll keep watch first."

Adrenalin and chilly air are not a soporific cocktail but eventually exhaustion kicks in and I do sleep. The eastern sky is postcard pink when I wake, shivering. Will has been busy in the twilight – a pale streak down the facing dune marks where he's already set up our home-made water factory, but now he's playing butcher. Three slabs of muscle are arranged on individual scraps of foil. He hears me stir and glances over his shoulder. "I wondered if some of this meat would slow cook when the sun gets hot. You know, 'you could fry an egg on this car bonnet' type of thing."

"Using the foil?"

"Maybe if I curve it, it will focus the light?"

"Maybe." He's so full of practical ideas. It's creativity, just like my song writing – less glamorous, but more useful. "Does the condenser work when it isn't foggy?"

"Nowhere near as well – but there's definitely a bit of dew. I noticed some on the rifle so I thought it was worth trying to top up the bottle. I put it on a steeper slope this time."

"Shall I go and check it?"

"Yeah, thanks."

I push myself up onto my right leg and gingerly transfer weight to my left foot. Nothing but a dull ache – that's more like it. I limp gingerly down the slope at an angle, keeping my bad foot on the high side. The pain doesn't increase until I'm almost there. Dew is forming on the metal, but the bottle is only receiving a few drips a minute. It'll be half an hour or more before it reaches the neck. I decide to crawl back so as not to overdo things. Before I reach the foot of our dune, sunlight hits its crest and the warmth seems to trickle down to meet me.

Will works away at creating his little oven in a north-east facing part of the slope while I just sit on the crest, drinking in the red-gold and black monochrome of the dawn-light dunes, the snow-flecked ultramarine of the sea, the line of foam and bubble dividing two opposite worlds. It's idyllic – idyllic and bladder-openingly scary at the same time.

"It's like being stranded on a desert island."

I'm not sure I realise that I've said it out loud until Will answers. "A few palm trees would come in handy."

"Or some buried treasure. What would you hope for?"

"A brai with a full gas bottle and a box of matches."

"Or maybe a Sat-phone with a charged battery?"

"Yeah, that would be much better," he sighs. "You know, if you count the Suez Canal, we are stranded on an island – a bloody big island, but you can sail a ship all round it."

Sun roasting the meat seems like a good idea, but by mid-morning we give up waiting for nothing to happen and set about chewing our way through half of it – warm but otherwise as rubber-like as before. Will hopefully creates new foil lined hollows further round the dune to catch the afternoon sun but by the time he takes his turn to nap there's no sign of any browning.

I'm quite content to sit guard whilst he sleeps. Talk of stranding and desert islands has set my creative juices flowing again – lyrics, melodies and rhythms surfing through my mind. There's no pen or paper, no way to play or record it, but it doesn't matter, I still have the two most powerful tools: imagination and memory.

Stranded

The water's ebbing slowly from under life's boat.
Soon there won't be quite enough to keep it all afloat.
I'm not sure how I came to be a shipwreck on this shore:
Chasing after fantasies, not thinking about it more.

And I'm stranded here with you (what can I do?)
I'm stranded here with you (what can I do?)
What can I do? What can I say?
I didn't mean it to work out this way,
But now I'm stranded here with you.

Ahs...

I'm stuck fast on this empty beach and I can only cope
by dreaming that the tide will turn before the end of hope.
A miracle is what I need: a knight upon a horse.
But that only happens in the fairytales, of course.

And I'm stranded here with you (what can I do?)
I'm stranded here with you (what can I do?)
What can I do? What can I say?
I didn't mean it to work out this way,
But now I'm stranded here with you.
Stranded here with you.

Ahs...

Where has my lover gone? Where have you taken him?
Where has my lover gone? Where have you taken him?
Where has my lover gone? Where's he been taken
And who's in his place?
Where has my lover gone? Where have you taken him?
Where has my lover gone? Where have you taken him?
Where has my lover gone? Where's he been taken
And what's in your face?

I'm stranded here with you (what can I do?)
I'm stranded here with you (what can I do?)
What can I do? What can I say?
I didn't mean it to work out this way,
But now I'm stranded here with you.
Stranded here with you.

Ahs…

By mid-afternoon there's a rough version rolling round my head to the rhythm of the breakers. Repeat, repeat, repeat – it's the only way to make sure I remember. I'm so immersed that at first my brain doesn't register a new low churning as anything other than imaginary backing music, but when a movement appears in the corner of my half-shut eyes, white hot reality sears through.

"Will, a ship!"

CHAPTER 23

They're not looking. "OVER HERE! HELP!!" The ship is much too far away for anyone to hear our cries. I wave one arm above my head frantically whilst keeping the binoculars to my eyes with the other. The 'African Explorer' sports a luminous orange hull and matching funnel. From the wide portholes and generous viewing decks it seems to be some sort of mini-cruise ship, but almost everyone is indoors. A couple lean against the rail about halfway along whilst at the stern three others all have binoculars trained towards the wake. The lone visible crew member appears hard at work completing some maintenance task at the base of the funnel. It'll be level with us soon, and no one's looking our way. "HELP! HEEELP! You'd've thought people would want to see the seals."

"I know," says Will, waving the spade in wide arcs over his head. "What we really need is... You keep waving, I'll be back in a sec." He hares off in exactly the opposite direction to what I'm expecting – down the far side of the dune, out of sight of the sea. The ship ploughs on, several hundred metres from the shore, heaving slightly in the gentle swell. Come on Will, what are you doing? I abandon the binoculars and wave with both arms.

He reappears with a rough square of foil that's obviously been ripped straight from the condenser. Holding diagonal corners, he attempts to pull it flat, but it just flops into a loose roll. "Help me." He swaps his hands to holding one edge. "You get the other side." I do as bidden, fingers trembling with the excitement of realisation. "Now let's see..." He takes a quick check towards the sun and I try to follow his tilt. A dazzling diamond of sunlight appears on the sand in front of us. "Now turn it... and right arm down..." The jewel arrows into the surf and I lose sight of it as our aim takes it over the sea towards the cruise ship. It's impossible to know if we have the correct angle so we wiggle it and then start again... and again...

The ship is definitely past us now. It's difficult to make out the figures without the binoculars, but the couple could be moving. We line up the reflection on the beach and resend our signal. I screw up my eyes. "I think they might be pointing..." I let go of the foil, wave with both arms and then snatch up the binoculars. The couple have moved to the stern and all five are peering in our direction. I wave with one arm above my head. Will continues with the foil, as best he can on his own. One of the people raises an arm and waves in reply. "They see us. They see us!" We both wave and beckon madly. Surely they'll realise we're in distress. When I refocus binoculars, there are only four people at the stern, but the ship powers on unchanged.

"Are they still looking?" gasps Will as much with fear and excitement as with physical exertion.

"Yes, but... oh..." If you'd asked me before to choose the best sound in the world I might have struggled to pick one thing from the daily bounty that fills our ears. Now, without doubt, the prize goes to the descending growl of a ship's engine throttling back. "It's turning, it's turning..."

"Yes!" Will hoists me off the ground in a triumphant hug. I wave my arms in euphoria, although I probably look more like a rugby player being lifted for a line-out. I'm half way down before either of us remembers.

"Ankle!" Will only partially manages to slow my descent.

"Sorry, did I hurt you?"

"Who cares?"

WE HAVE PLENTY OF TIME to decide which of our meagre possessions are worth keeping whilst the ship anchors and one of its landing boats is lowered into the water. Judging from the number of binoculars now bearing down on us, it must be some kind of nature cruise, so we consider it prudent to cover the remains of the seal. It's also doubtful if walking down the beach with a rifle and a pistol is likely to be viewed as friendly, so Will buries them on the far side of the dune whilst I wave and smile. The remainder fits in my shoulder bag.

When Will reappears he's carrying a very shoddily rolled up condenser and the water bottle, still three-quarters full. "You're just taking the piss with that foil now aren't you?" I laugh.

"If you think I'm leaving it behind after all this, you've got another thing coming."

"Yeah, cos you might need to make a life raft from it if the ship sinks."

"Good idea... I'm definitely taking it now." I might be teasing, but if he wants to frame it, I'd give it wall space. The grin on his face lapses into seriousness. "Holly, I've been thinking... Everyone's bound to ask us what happened... I think it might be a good idea if you didn't mention about shooting anyone. I don't know what it's like here, but at home, even if it's obviously self defence, there're inquests and inquiries and a whole load of stuff you really don't want to get involved with."

I purse my lips. Similar thoughts have been racing round my mind since the ship turned. "I know what you mean, but it doesn't seem... honest."

"He kicked the shit out of me and left me to die of thirst. I would've done if you hadn't..."

"He was horrible, but he probably had a family."

"They were all part of that little beret guy's private poaching army. It's up to him to put things right, if he cares at all about loyalty. It was his mistakes that got them killed or injured. He should've known better than to mess with a musician and a carpenter."

A couple of quiet snorts escape, but the corners of my mouth hardly rise. "You're right. I'll miss that part out... They would definitely have killed me... eventually." I know what I'm saying is true. I wish it made me feel better. A little voice in the back of my head whispers, 'killer.'

We sip from the water bottle whilst the inflatable casts off and motors towards us. It holds two men, both wearing a navy trouser and sweatshirt uniform. The engine cuts just before the beach and I notice the man who leaps into the surf has three stripes on what appear to be Velcroed epaulettes. We stand as he approaches.

"Ms Holly Woodlove, I presume?" he says, stretching out a heavily tanned hand.

My mouth drops open, "Err, yeah." I never imagined I'd be immediately recognised.

The second crewman notes my confusion as he drags the boat higher up the beach and holds it, rear end still bobbing in the shallows. White teeth shine against his deep brown face. "Don't worry about our Mate here – he doesn't have your poster on his cabin wall... but your face has been plastered across every screen for the last few days. Not sure there's been anything else on the news, has there... sir." It seems like the last word has a hint of sarcasm in it.

The Mate rolls his eyes. "As unAble-Seaman Phillips says, your disappearance is quite a big story." He stretches out his hand once more. "Miles Quigley, First Mate of the African Explorer. It seems like you might be in need of a lift." Miles is clearly a Brit and he blatantly shifts from a voice with definite West Midlands overtones to a plummier accent for the official sounding words. His expression is difficult to read behind a profusion of ginger beard, but it seems like everyone here is a joker.

I take his hand and put my other on top, Prime Minister style. "No, we were just waving for the fun of it. There's a 'copter on the other side of the dune." He hesitates for a second and then bursts into hearty laughter.

"We'll be seeing you then," he says and makes to turn.

Will steps forward. "Will Mason – not famous, in case you were wondering. You haven't heard if the other two who were missing have been found, have you? Anna Templeton and Ben Woodlove?"

"What? There are more of you here somewhere?" The Mate pulls out a walkie talkie from his rear trouser pocket.

Will raises a palm. "No, no, back at the lodge, but they went missing first. We followed a bad tip off and ended up lost."

"You don't remember anything from the news about that, do you Screwy?" Miles asks his colleague.

"No, I'm afraid it's been pretty much all about you, miss."

I wish the ground would swallow me up, right now. Ben and Anna – obviously that's the first thing I should have asked about. Instead, I'm joking around like a giddy schoolgirl. I daren't even catch Will's eye. There's a moment's stillness – the breaking waves and bleating from the colony suddenly seeming louder.

Will breaks it with a surprisingly cheery, "Well, Holly can do what she likes, but I'd very much like to take up that offer of a lift."

"Right you are... hop in then." He indicates towards the boat. "Is that everything you've got?"

"Yup." His eyes widen with incredulity as they survey my shoulder bag, the water bottle, and, of course, the roll of foil. Will offers me a shoulder for support and I limp forward.

Miles's face is a picture. "Oh bollocks, when I said, 'hop', I didn't..."

"Unintentional gaff Quigley strikes again," comments uAB Phillips as he holds out a hand to steady us into the boat.

"You know, I think they should bring back keel hauling for insubordination." The Mate pushes the landing craft until he is knee deep in water, then waits for the perfect time between waves. "Now." He shoves the front round hard, leaps in and, simultaneously, Phillips gives a surge of throttle, moving us on an arc away from the shore.

As we approach the side of the Explorer, Miles asks, "Can you manage a ladder or would you like us to haul you up?"

"I can manage as long as I take it slow."

"We'll put a harness and rope on you just to make sure." A minute or so later a tangle of straps is lowered from the main deck. Miles helps me into it and I begin the climb with the Mate following directly behind. Whoever is twenty feet above is not only keeping the rope tight, they're also supporting part of my weight, making it easier on the ankle, but one of the straps passes eye-wateringly over the bruise on my thigh. About half way up, I let out a small gasp as the pull increases. The voice from around my ankles, misinterpreting the cause of my pain, says, "Have a quick rest if you want." I peer down to find his eyes glued to the shackle still clamped to my right ankle. At some point Will's taping has fallen off and I haven't even noticed. Wearing a leg iron has become normal...

"If you have a spanner which will undo that, I'd be very grateful." His eyes are inevitably full of curiosity. I ignore it and continue to climb. Strong, friendly hands help me onto the deck and as I stand there's a small cheer and smattering of applause. Just about every passenger is peering down from the upper deck or craning necks from a crowd held behind the rope demarking the winching area.

A man in similar navy apparel but sporting a typical officer's hat steps forward. "Welcome on board the African Explorer, Ms Woodlove. We're glad to find you safe. I'm Captain Johnson."

Before he's finished speaking the Mate and Will have clambered up beside me. "And welcome also, Mr Woodlove."

"Mr Mason, actually, Will Mason... it's a long story."

After sparing Will the absolute minimum polite time of attention, the captain's gaze falls back upon me. He's a rather bulky man with unkempt hair poking out from under the hat and 'Buddy Holly' style glasses. Not at all how I'd expect a ship's captain to appear.

"We've had a politician and couple of minor TV celebrities on past cruises but I do believe you're our first star of the music business."

"Huh-hum." A fake cough emanates from a mousy haired man in the front rank behind the rope. A few titters flit through the throng surrounding him. He seems vaguely familiar, but oval dark glasses hide his eyes. Beside him a slim strawberry blonde woman with porcelain pale skin grins broadly.

"Don't worry, the Captain obviously doesn't count platinum albums," says Mate Miles.

A brief flush crosses Captain Johnson's face, "Sorry," he says to the man, "I tend to think of the book more than the music..."

"What can he expect if he does not sing them himself?" The woman's English is very good but there's an accent I can't quite place. The man replies to her with his tongue.

"As you'll have gathered," says the Captain, returning to the matter in hand, "it's all very informal here on the Af-Ex, but, please, I'm sure you'd like to wait somewhere more comfortable while we organise some accommodation. Follow me."

He leads us at my sedate limping pace along a corridor, through a dining area to a doorway labelled 'Layabouts Lounge', handwritten on a scrap of paper taped above the door.

"Somewhere under there the original sign says 'Officer's Mess'," comments the Captain as he passes beneath it.

"How come you're all Brits?" asks Will as the captain ushers us towards a sofa in the part of the room set out like a lounge. On the other side, a utilitarian dining table and fixed chairs contrast with the lounge's leather and rug opulence. Around the walls, dramatic photos of whales, seals, sharks and dunes emphasize the ship's purpose.

"We're not quite all Brits. A few of the crew are South African and we have a couple of Norwegians. Most of us have worked the usual wildlife cruise routes for years, but fancied trying something new, being our own bosses."

"You own the ship?" Will is in information gathering mode...

"Well, I have a stake in the travel company which owns the ship – all the crew do."

"I didn't realise anyone ran wildlife-themed cruises in Africa."

"We're one of the first... It beats the hell out of freezing your knackers off in South Georgia or crossing the Forties. Wildlife is great too." He points through the rounded rectangular porthole towards the brown horde of seals lining the shore.

After having let the conversation run for a while, my own curiosity is piqued. "We were wondering about why, if you were a wildlife tour, you didn't seem to be stopping to here?"

"Ah, we did that on the way up: anchored, put those-that-wanted ashore for a couple of hours – more or less where we picked you up. I suppose you weren't here four days ago?"

"No."

"Which brings me on to how the hell you came to be here? Where's your boat?"

"We walked."

"Walked? What, up from Mowe Bay? That must be nearly twenty miles." His eyes take in our scant clothing. "In just shorts and shirts with one bottle of water?" There's definitely an unvoiced, 'Are you nuts?' in his final sentence.

"Is Mowe Bay at the end of the coast road?"

"Yes."

Will shakes his head, "I'm sorry, Holly, my memory was right off."

"I don't know what you're apologising for, we're alive aren't we?" Alive – the word flickers at the edge of my brain, firing off idea sparks. Not now.

"So you didn't walk up from Mowe Bay?" We've obviously left the Captain way behind.

"No, we were inland somewhere, at the end of a dry river bed. Our car was burnt out so we decided to make for the coast. We thought it was quite close."

"But it wasn't," says Will, taking over. "We walked for three days and completely ran out of food and water."

"And then I twisted my ankle and I really thought that was it."

"But we saw you drinking from your bottle whilst we were lowering the boat?" He clearly hasn't quite bought into our story.

"We were saved by the fog. Genius Will here made a condenser out of that foil." Despite now reclining in a leather sofa, Will is clutching the tatty roll as if his life still depends on it. "We filled the bottle up twice with it."

"Is that what you used to flash at us, too?" Will nods in reply to the captain's query. "Resourceful... So did you crash your car?"

"No, a poacher shot one of our jerry cans with a tracer bullet." I can't resist dropping it like a paving slab into a duck pond.

The Captain's eyes bulge. "A poacher did what?"

Will catches my eye. I suppose he's warning me to be careful what we say. I don't actually need reminding... "It's a long story, but in a nutshell, two of our group went missing in a sandstorm from our Safari lodge. We were searching for them along the edge of the dunes when we ran into some poachers. They kidnapped us but we escaped, except they caught up, shot up our car, and left us in the middle of nowhere. I suppose they thought the desert would save them the trouble of finishing us off."

"It might have done if we hadn't seen your signal," says Mate Miles, entering with a shifter in one hand and can of WD40 in the other. "No wonder you both look like you've been kicked down a hill." He squats in front of me. "Poachers?" he queries.

"Angolan military types after rhino horns. They got some too."

"Would you like to put your foot up on the coffee table?" Captain Johnson's face pales as he notices the clamp for the first time.

"They put that on you?" he asks as the Mate sprays round the nut.

"Yes, with a rope to stop me getting away, but they tied the other end to our Land Rover so I drove off without having to undo the rope."

Miles shakes his head in disbelief as he adjusts the jaws of the shifter to match the nut. "This might be a bit stiff."

It is, but with the Captain holding the clamp whilst the Mate turns, it soon gives way. The sense of relief is almost overwhelming. My eyes well up as I express effusive thanks. I suppose it's the final physical connection back to Soba removed. Will's eyes are full of concern. I force the tears away with a weak smile.

"How long since you last ate properly?" asks Miles.

I let Will answer. "We scavenged some seal meat off some jackals, but apart from that, it's been about five days."

"Sounds delightful. You'd better take it easy for a day or two with the food. If you pig out straight away it'll probably all just come straight up again. How about soup and a roll?" We both nod to his advice.

"And whilst you're doing that, I'll contact shore to let the authorities know we've found you," says Captain Johnson.

"I've also arranged places for you to wash and rest," continues Miles. I'm afraid every cabin is in use, but some of the guests have spare beds in their rooms and they've offered to share – if that's okay?"

"Of course, we're just so grateful you found us. Sorry about all this trouble, Miles, Captain."

"Please call me, Rick... To be honest, it's no trouble at all. Rescuing you will get us more publicity than we could ever hope for."

CHAPTER 24

Warm water, shampoo, a soft towel taken straight from a heated rail – I almost feel human again... until I catch a glimpse in the full length mirror. Against a clean face, the graze across my forehead, nose and cheek is even more prominent. My skin seems stretched over my bones like shrink-wrap and everywhere there are bruises, scars and unflattering sunburn lines. It's anyone's guess what Will found to get excited about. I hide it all with the freshly laundered bathrobe provided.

This must be one of the largest cabins on the ship. As well as an enormous double bed, there's also a three-quarter size which I'm told is mine. I really hope I'm not crashing some over-generous couple's honeymoon suite. Beyond the foot of the master bed, his and hers wardrobe-drawer-dresser units are built in against the wall. I wonder if the mahogany craftsmanship would meet with Will's approval?

It's very good of them to let me borrow their room. I shouldn't repay their generosity with snooping, but another woman's wardrobe has always held a particular fascination... and it is already half open: practical safari clothes, mingled with a few pieces of beachwear and a couple of wrap-around cardigans for those cooler evenings, but it's the dress that gives me pause. Royal blue silk and taffeta, full length, off the shoulder – it's more than an evening gown – more like an Oscars outfit. And on the male side a sharp DJ with co-ordinating bow tie. Definitely for something special.

"None of your business," I mutter to myself and reach for a brochure lying on my bedside table.

The Benguela Cruise – Cape Town, Robben Island, Namibia and the Skeleton Coast – Enjoy the spectacular scenery of the Cape of Good Hope, visit the historic Robben Island, experience the thrill of close up encounters with whales, sharks and fur seals, identify numerous sea birds (including penguins!) with the help of our experts – all from the decks and landing craft of our luxurious liner – African Explorer. Many itineraries also include a unique access to the remotest areas of the world-renowned Skeleton Coast National Park. Spend a day exploring untouched desert where no rain has fallen in living...

My eyes flick up to the door. Someone is tapping very gently. "Come in."

"Hi, I thought I'd see how you get on." It's the pale woman from the deck. "Have you found everything you need?" Her strawberry blonde hair is held in an unshowy pony tail.

I sit up. "Hi, I'm Holly."

"Katri." Her smile immediately puts me at ease.

"Is this your cabin?"

"Yes. Mine and my partner...'s." Although very good, her English isn't quite natural and the possessive gets added as an afterthought.

"It's very kind of you to let me use the spare bed. I don't want to interrupt your special holiday."

"No matter. We are glad to help. You've had a difficult time, I think?"

I answer her with a nod. She's sensitive enough to realise that I don't want to go over it and moves on to more practical things. "They found these for you while your things are washed." She hands over spare crew uniform: trousers, shirt, and a pair of boxer shorts still in their cellophane wrapper . "I would lend to you something a little less..."

"Mannish?"

"Yes," she laughs, "but you are... quite tall." Katri isn't short but I must be almost five inches taller and I imagine that much of her wardrobe would remind me of those school summer terms when Dad was trying hard not to spend any more money on uniform until September and my forearms were increasingly on display. "I have some things if you'd rather not wear the man pants..." She pulls a pair of lemon yellow knickers from the back of a drawer in the unit. "I don't think I have ever worn them," she says, screwing up her nose slightly.

I grin. "Yellow not your colour? In my suitcase back at the lodge I have two pairs like that which I always bring along, in case of emergencies. One of them is lime green with grey spots."

"Lovely." She widens her eyes.

"Erm, you don't have a spare bra, as well, do you?"

Katri's brow furrows fleetingly. "Sorry, I thought maybe..."

Maybe what? My mind flashes back to crawling onto the deck from the ladder, the missing buttons. Blood rushes to my face. "Did you and everyone else assume 'the popstar's showing a lot of boob because that's what they do'? I... I... lost the bra, okay? And the buttons... I'm not like that." My bottom lip trembles, and tears start to form, but any indignation evaporates as Katri's face matches mine with the rouge of genuine mortification.

"Sorry, I did not know..." She opens her arms wide. I drop the clothes and accept the hug. She holds me gently until my sobbing stops then releases, leaving a hand on each of my shoulders. I blink at her kind but serious expression. "I don't know you, Holly, but I know this feeling. I don't know what happened to you... in the desert, but when you are ready you must find someone you trust and tell them. Tell them everything and tell them soon. Keeping all inside is bad... believe me!"

All I can manage is a nod. Part of me wants to deny... deny that anything happened... but it did. Another part wants to gush it all out right now to these understanding eyes, but... like she says, she's a stranger – I'll probably never see her again.

"Two questions..." her serious tone continues, "Do you need any medical kind of help?"

"No, no, it wasn't... I wasn't..."

"And is there anyone on this ship that you need protecting from?"

"What? Oh..." She leaves me to unravel her meaning. "You mean Will? You think Will?"

"When I was younger I learn that the monsters are often the people we know best."

"Oh, gosh, I'm sorry... No, Will's a star. We... we saved each other's lives several times in the last few days. There were others – poachers."

"Ah, okay," she says releasing my shoulders, obviously relieved that the need for further difficult action is avoided.

I feel I ought to reciprocate. "And everything's okay with you now? You were talking about the past, not the man here?"

"No, not Steven," Strangely, a tiny smile crosses her lips as if I've touched on a private joke, "although he has been accused of much worse... No, Steven is my redemption, and I am his." She makes this beautiful affirmation in such a matter-of-fact voice: we're right for each other – end of. I attempt to recall the face of the man who inspires such love.

"Your Steven, should I recognise him? He seemed vaguely familiar."

Katri wanders back to the unit and begins to rummage once again. "Steven Carter," she says, eyes in the drawer.

"The *Enough Rope* concept album?"

"And book, yes."

"Oh wow, everyone who's anyone is singing on that thing."

"Ah. Here." She tugs out a lemon yellow bra.

"Matching set, eh?"

Katri grins and shrugs simultaneously, "I'm so lucky... I think the size is not so different."

"Was I really flashing everything when I climbed on board?"

"Not quite everything... I'll leave you now," she adds, making for the door.

"I don't suppose you have a mini-USB type charger I could borrow? I want to see if this thing still works." I pull my phone from my somewhat battered bag. Apart from a couple of scratches on the flip open case and a flat battery it appears untouched by its adventure.

She veers towards one of the bedside units and pulls open the top drawer. "Is this right?" A lead wrapped tightly round the plug is proffered.

"Looks like it, thanks."

"But there is no signal on the ship. Not unless we're near a town."

"Oh." I had thought...

"I think the ship has a satellite phone. I'm sure they will let you use it if you ask." With one hand on the open door she parts with: "Dinner is at 7pm. We will come back at about six-thirty."

DESPITE NOT BOTHERING to dress or dry my hair properly Will has still beaten me to the ship's phone by a distance. He seems to be fighting a losing battle against some job's-worth receptionist and rolls his eyes for my benefit as he spots me slip into the chair opposite.

"I just want to know if Anna Templeton and Ben Woodlove have been found or not... No, I don't want to wait for the senior officer to come back. I don't need any details. Surely you must know... I'm not press, my name is Andrew Templeton, I'm Anna's father. The whole family is frantic with worry. Please, have all the missing British tourists been found? Please..." A broad smile bursts across his face and he raises a clenched fist towards me. "Great... that's great... thank you so much, bye." We both leap to our feet and share a hug of joy and relief. "I don't know any details," Will says over my shoulder, "but it's alright, everyone's been found. I tried their mobiles but got no answer, I tried the lodge, but that just went to answer-phone, so I found the number for the Windhoek police."

I let go and take a step back, "Why did you say you were Anna's dad?"

"The guy was quoting me all sorts of reasons why he couldn't tell me anything. Have you ever tried getting information when you're 'just' the boyfriend? Andrew won't mind."

"He didn't say if they were hurt or anything?"

"No, but there was nothing like that in his voice. You know, I bet they're all rushing to meet us – the Captain says he's been asked to drop us off at Swakopmund tomorrow morning." Will stretches his arms out wide, palms to the sky. "We're alive! We're all bloody alive!"

That word again... the song is virtually bursting out of me, but I need to call my Dad...

THE PHONE ONLY RINGS TWICE before it's snatched up. "Dad."

"Oh, Holly, thank God – Toby, it's your sister, she's okay – you are okay, aren't you love?"

"Yes, Dad. I'm a bit battered, bruised, and hungry, but I'm basically alright."

"That's great..." They're only two words but I can hear a whole load of pent up emotion being released. "I'm... I'm going to put you on speaker so your brother can hear."

"Hi Toby," I say after the click. "Sorry about all the worry."

"Worried? What's to worry about? Dad rings to say you've been reported missing on holiday. Then we get a detective asking questions about your state of mind, saying you were last seen driving off into the desert. You been doing a Bear Grills out there, Prickle?"

"Something like that."

"I told them you'd come back as soon as you broke a nail."

"Yeah, how could I play the guitar then, eh?"

"You call that playing?"

"Thousands of people do..."

"What, you mean all the ones who bought your record by accident thinking it was the return of Holly Valance?"

"Yeah, all of those disappointed souls..." I smile as I recite my lines in this well worn piece of banter, but I'm not up to retaliation quite yet. Surprisingly, Toby seems to pick up on that.

His voice softens. "You're alright now though, Prickle?"

"Yup."

"And Ben?"

"I think so."

"Holly?" There's a clear 'what haven't you told us' in my Dad's tone.

"I haven't actually seen Ben yet. It wasn't Ben, I... Look, I can't tell you everything now, but basically, Ben and Anna went missing first – their car was stolen whilst they were out birdwatching, although we didn't know that to start with – and then Will and I tried to find them when we should have left it to the professionals, and we got ourselves in a right mess and ended up walking for miles in the desert."

"Oh, Holly." Dad still sounds like he's going to burst into tears of relief any second. How am I ever going to tell him a less edited version? The second I mention poachers his Dad radar is going to be peering straight into areas I'd rather not go.

"Hasn't Ben been in contact, then?"

"No, we've only heard things through our liaison officer."

"Really? I thought... if he was found days ago... he would've... oh, well..."

"The little visits from the LO haven't been all bad, though have they Dad?" says Toby over my spoken thoughts. "He's a bit in love with her – aren't you Dad?"

"She's very kind – but that's their job."

"Notice he didn't deny it..." I did, and the tone in his voice. "...and she's not wearing a ring."

"So where are you now?" Dad moves on as if he hasn't even heard Toby's teasing.

"We were picked up by a cruise ship. They're going to drop us back to civilisation tomorrow."

Toby hoots with laughter. "You're on a cruise ship? Only my sister... If I got rescued, it would be by a smelly fishing boat, but no, Hol gets a cruise ship."

"Yeah, after we're done, there's some caviar to finish before my pedicure."

"Oo, don't let us keep you."

"Remind me how old you two are?" says Dad in his old 'telling off' voice. He's only messing, but half a lifetime of conditioning still brings us up short.

"Sowy Pwickle," says Toby in a little boy voice.

"Sorry Titch."

I HARDLY FEEL MY ANKLE as I return to the cabin, my mood is so buoyant. Everyone's okay. My daymares are all fiction and it's good to be alive. *Ali-i-ive.* I test out a melody with a quiet hum. It's a shame I don't have my guitar – the phone's voice recorder app will have to make do. I must check that everything's still on it, and record Keep On and Stranded before I forget them. At least David will be pleased with some more output. Maybe, just maybe, one or two of these will connect with the public – like Fusion did – and I'll not go down as just another one-hit-wonder. Idiot – it's only a few hours since you cheated death and already you're headlining Glastonbury.

Cheated death? As I reach for the door handle I notice my hand trembling. It really is like that feeling you get if you've nearly been run over. Mmm, now how would that work as a lyric?

Alive

Ever thought you looked left, thought you looked right,
then had to leap back on the pavement in fright?
And that unnoticed bus screams right past your ear
leaving your breath stolen by fear.

But after the shock and the trembles have passed,
adrenalin blows all the clouds from my head
and everything seems so straightforward
that my fears seem so dim.

I'm alive! Possibilities are endless...
Alive! Ready just to give one a try.
While blood is pump, pump, pump, pump, pumping,
nothing can be something.
Don't, don't, don't be scared to fly.
I'm alive! The world is so completely my oyster...
Alive! Ready to poke fate in the eye.
While blood is pump, pump, pump, pump, pumping,
nothing can be something.
Reach , reach, reach up to the sky.

Ever stood near the edge, took a careless step back,
seen your life pass your eyes in fast forward playback?
You wobble and rock, as you try not to fall,
till your best mate's strong arm pulls you back from it all.

But after the shock and the trembles have passed,
adrenalin blows all the clouds from my head
and everything seems so straightforward
that my fears seem so dim.

I'm alive! Possibilities are endless...
Alive! Ready just to give one a try.
While blood is pump, pump, pump, pump, pumping,
nothing can be something.
Don't, don't, don't be scared to fly.
I'm alive! The world is so completely my oyster...
Alive! Ready to poke fate in the eye.
While blood is pump, pump, pump, pump, pumping,
nothing can be something.
Reach , reach, reach up to the sky.

I'm alive, I'm alive,
I'm alive: my blood is pumping,
pump, pump, pump, pump, pump...
I'm alive, I'm alive,
I'm alive: my blood is pumping,
pump, pump, pump, pump, pumping... now!

I'm happily singing away, banging out the rhythm on the arms of the chair when there's another knock on the door. I glance towards the wall clock – six thirty already and I'm still in a bathrobe.

"Come in."

"That sounded good – through the door, at least," says the man who must be Steven Carter. Considering how much his name has been bandied about for the last couple of years, he has a surprisingly anonymous face: neither good looking or ugly, maybe what they would have called 'plain' in the old days. Short mousey hair accentuates the impression.

"Sorry, I should have dressed already. I've had pieces of a song in my head for half the day and I had to record it."

"Ah, I know this," smiles Katri, stepping into the room beside him. "The whole world stops for a song idea. I could dance round Steven naked and he would not notice whilst he's scribbling in his notebook."

"You should try that next time," he says, eyebrows dancing.

"Maybe I will..."

For about half a second I feel distinctly green and hairy as their eyes spark off one another. Then they're back in the room.

"Sorry, err, Holly. I guess you already know I'm Steven. Did we disturb you?"

"No I was pretty much finished. The rhythm of the chorus is something weird and I was trying to work it out."

"Time signatures are the worst for me," he says, nodding. "The first thing a producer wants to know is what time it's in, but it just comes out how it comes out. I haven't got a clue. Do you..."

"I'll leave you two talking shops while I have a shower," interrupts Katri.

"Okay... It's 'shop' by the way, 'talking shop', not 'shops'," he says.

"How does that make sense?"

"It doesn't, but that's what it is." He shrugs and turns his attention back to me. "I always have to correct her English..."

"I will never learn without it..." says Katri disappearing into the bathroom with a robe.

"... and she corrects my Finnish. It's a pig of a language."

THE EASY CONVERSATION CONTINUES once we've joined up with Will for dinner. I feel more than a little self conscious in this borrowed uniform. It is large enough, but everything is on the baggy side... and tatty sandals don't really go. The feeling is heightened as we enter the main dining area: the chatting stills and dozens of heads turn our way.

"Seals," whispers Will in my ear. I bite my bottom lip to keep a straight face. It is just like that – we're the jackals, they're the seals, and every head follows us in synchronisation. Unlike seals, the majority of the holiday-makers quickly remember their manners and a gradual hubbub resumes.

We're led between circular tables, each surrounded by eight guests. It's not a black tie affair like I've heard happens on some cruises, but it is a proper sit down meal and most people have changed into shirts and blouses or equivalent.

Captain Rick rises to welcome us to the end table. Like all the others it's largely glass but with a wide chrome rim and matching legs. Across it are laid all the necessary accoutrements for a three course dinner. It's a shame we're going to have to take it easy with the rich food. We're seated girl-boy-girl-boy so I'm between Steven and Will, then there's a female crew member before the Captain, and between him and Katri are a middle-aged couple who look like they can't quite believe their luck.

The Captain reaches for a nautical bell attached to the wall and gives a couple of sharp clangs. The room falls silent. "Hi everyone. I hope you enjoyed your day. Thanks to you all for your help and patience whilst we picked up these waifs and strays. Unfortunately, we haven't quite finished with the unscheduled stops just yet as the Namibian authorities have asked us to put our castaways ashore at Swakopmund in the morning. If you're wondering why the bow end of the ship seems to be a little higher than usual that's because Mate Miles currently has his foot to the floor on the bridge trying to make up for lost time."

"It's a lever..." mutters the crew-woman to his left.

"Seriously, though, part of the reason we have these last few days with no scheduled stops is to keep a little time in hand in case of emergencies. So, please, relax, enjoy the sun and the on-board activities and if you do happen to spot a whale or something, I'm sure there'll still be time to slow down for a gander. Although, Paul," the male half of the unknown couple on our table realises he's being addressed directly with a start, "if you spot any more people waving from the shore, just wave back and don't tell me..."

"Shut up and let them eat before it gets cold." The disembodied shout emanates from the doorway beside a short bar. Presumably it leads to the galley.

"A good point, well made by ship's cook there. Come on, start bringing it out. Anyway, joking aside, we're very happy to welcome Holly and Will on board and we're glad to have been part of their rescue. And no one should worry," he seems to take a quick glance towards Steven, "we'll be in plenty of time for the special event at Cape Town."

As the smattering of applause dies away, I catch the eye of 'Paul'. "Was it you then, the one who spotted us?"

Paul's cheeks colour. "I was just tracking a Giant Petrel trying to work out if it was a Southern or a Northern when one of your flashes caught me right in the bins. Was it baking foil?"

"Yeah, that foil," I flick a grin towards Will, "turned out to be very handy. Thank you so much, you probably saved our lives."

Paul smiles and shrugs. His partner nudges him with a less than subtle elbow and he throws her a glance which clearly says, 'I'm about to.' He begins with a pinched expression, "Err, I know it must be a real drag, people asking you this kind of thing, but our daughter is a fan of yours. I don't suppose you could sign something for her?"

"Of course, is she here?"

"No, she's at university... back in the UK."

"If you give me her details, I'll have a signed copy of the album sent to her... and a couple of VIP passes for the next gig she can get to."

"That would be wonderful." Paul glows with the prospect of major parental brownie points.

"No problem. It's the least I can do. Where's she at uni?" Smile, polite, smile, polite.

"Nottingham."

"Oh, nice. I remember looking round there – lots of grass and a lake by the student building?" Paul nods. "But then I fluffed my maths and had to go wherever would take me."

"What subject did you do?" asks Steven. Paul seems content with the amount of attention he's received, so I feel I can turn off PR mode.

"Chemistry – not that I've ever used any of it – I really caught the music bug in my final year, only just scraped a Desmond, and as my husband is fond of telling everyone, I've never really had a proper job."

"Women and science professions is a tough combination." The female crew member grins, her eyes slipping slyly towards the Captain. "It's not that we can't do the work. Of course we can. It's just that generally you're the only competent one amongst a group of useless blokes and then there's only so much you can do."

"For those of you who haven't already met," says Rick in the long-suffering tone which seems to be his trademark, "this is Amy. She seems to be under the impression that without her this whole cruise would come to a grinding halt. Unfortunately, being as she's our Chief Engineer that is actually a fair assessment."

"Richard, that almost sounded like a compliment."

"I'm always complimentary..." says Rick in a mock hurt tone. "Just for some reason everyone always assumes that they're meant as well-disguised insults."

As they begin to dish out the starter, Will asks the question that's been in my mind but I haven't dared ask. "How does it work with all this banter, then Rick?"

"How do you mean?" replies the captain.

"Well, normally on a ship everything's quite formal, almost military style, whereas you guys back-chat each other like you're on a building site. Don't get me wrong, I like a bit of banter, but how can you keep your authority?"

Captain Rick face's morphs from surprise into a wry smile. "Are you worried they'll mutiny and throw me overboard?"

"No..." Will shrugs. "I'm not judging. I can see you work differently so I'm curious... and Holly will tell you, I'm not one to avoid direct questions."

"It drives all his friends crazy."

"Fair enough," says Rick. "In which case, I'll give a direct answer. My crew have years of experience. We've all worked on ships where it's been stiff and 'siry' but this is an entertainment vessel. Everyone's here to have a good time and we think the passengers have more fun if they see the crew having a laugh too. But just because we have fun doesn't mean we don't know our jobs. If there's some issue with the engines I don't need to order Amy to look at it. It's her job. She'd stay up to her neck in oil until it was fixed."

"I would," says Amy, nodding with approval, "and Richard knows better than to tell me how to do my work."

"Heaven forbid, I've seen what you can do with a wrench."

"Mm, well, there're always more nuts need tightening." The women round the table snigger whilst the men's smiles are slightly more pained.

Miles, our self appointed dietician has obviously left instructions that Will and I should have something to eat with each course but plainer and in smaller portions than everyone else. It's a bit like being the vegan at a traditional Christmas dinner, but it's a small price to pay... and that first slice of chocolate cake is going to taste amazing when I'm allowed it.

Perhaps to distract from the lack of gateau with my scoop of ice-cream, Captain Rick asks, "Holly, I know it's something that you probably get asked a lot, but how did you get into the music business? What was your big break?"

He's right, it is a common question, but I don't mind. I ask other artists the same thing. Everyone loves to hear your story, even if it's as ordinary as mine. I glance round the table. Even Will, who must know most of it, is looking up with interest. I hope I don't disappoint. "I don't think it's ever just one moment – maybe there's more still to come... I was quite a late starter. I always loved singing but it only occurred to me that I could write when I was sixteen. We were still in Linz at that point when one of my school teachers arranged a write-and-perform-a-song-in-a-day workshop. It totally blew my mind that we could even attempt it – that a song wasn't just conjured out of the air by an impossibly talented pop-star, but something anyone could have a crack at.

"Making my own music became almost an obsession and my poor Dad was pestered unmercifully until an acoustic guitar turned up for my seventeenth birthday. I taught myself to play and sing from '90s Hits for Easy Guitar'."

"I think I've still got that somewhere," says Steven, spoon halfway to mouth. "Did you play a lot of covers to begin with, then?"

"A few and they were virtually all in English, but my life outside home was all in German, so if I was asked to play in public I always did something of my own with German lyrics. And everyone is so kind when you're a kid: you sound like an angel; your songs are 'wunderbar'; Beyoncé better watch out – when actually I'm spoiling a party or school fair with clichés and caterwauling. Some of my early songs were really quite awful." I regard my plate, where a yellow lake is beginning to form. "Sorry, I'm going to have to eat this ice-cream before it's totally melted. So, Steven, what does it feel like to have a platinum album?"

He smiles almost apologetically, "Weird. I mean I'm not sure if it even counts. That was the trouble to begin with: no one knew how to categorise it. Was it a crime novel with a soundtrack... or a musical autobiography... or a concept album with a very thick sleeve? I don't think it would've been taken very seriously if I hadn't been asked to 'write my story' in the first place. My publishers certainly didn't get what they were expecting. The whole thing was in limbo for a while... until Chris agreed to sing on the first track. Then it all went completely barmy and it's stayed that way ever since."

"It is such a good idea," I say, having swallowed the last mouthful. "The book advertises the music and vice versa."

"It's also really easy to put on the 'too difficult' pile. Some people say that the album is weak and only sold because of my story and then others say the book isn't well written and only sold because of the music. But that's the whole point! The sum is better than its parts." Steven's right hand accentuates his words with a swish of the pastry fork. My eyes slip towards Katri, who is smiling with quiet pride in his passion.

I can't resist. I raise my eyebrows and grin broadly. "Of course, some people weren't even asked to be on it."

He launches into a justification exactly as I'd hoped... "Well, there are only two songs for a female voice, and when it all snowballed we had some offers that..." He stops mid-sentence, his eyes sliding towards my face without the rest of his head turning. A rueful grin breaks, "Okay, I bit." He leans back in his chair and shrugs. "If you want to sing on one, you'll have to write your own."

CHAPTER 25

You never finished telling us your story last night," says Katri.

I shrug. "The conversation moved on. It's not that exciting anyway." Katri, Steven, Will and I are leaning against the deck rail squinting into the pleasant morning sunshine. Swakopmund beachfront stretches north to south and behind it holiday homes, apartment blocks, and hotels jostle amongst palm trees, elbowing each other for the best sea views. The old lighthouse pokes its sunburnt head above these newcomers, hinting at something more historic away from the shore.

We're anchored opposite a headland protecting a small bay where we'll be put ashore. The car park on the headland is steadily filling and through binoculars I can already see far too many telephoto lenses for my liking. And there are at least two of those TV vans with satellite dishes. I glance down at myself. At least I have my own clothes back... and, I suspect at Katri's insistence, someone has sewn a couple of buttons on my shirt. Will hasn't been so lucky. His long shorts are okay but the hot water Swiss-cheesed his scorched T-shirt, so it's navy or nothing. Actually, it almost suits him...

"Looks like you've attracted quite a welcoming committee," says Steven from behind his retro shades.

I stretch my cheeks into a false smile. "How's my PR face?"

"Like you just sat on a drawing pin."

"Perfect then." Gentle waves are slapping against our landing boat and 'Screwy' Phillips is busy detaching it from the winch with the help of the Mate. Just as the captain explained, their work is quietly efficient even if their mouths are far from it. "What's next for you after the end of the cruise?" I ask Steven.

"Funnily enough, we're coming back here... well, not Swakopmund, but Namibia. We're flying to Windhoek and then driving up to Ovamboland. Katri's grandfather was a missionary there. We're going to do the 'following in the ancestors' footsteps' thing and then finish off with a few days in Etosha."

"One of the guides at our lodge was telling me about the Finnish missionaries. He had an odd name, something beginning with 'T'..."

"Toivo," says Will.

Katri nods, "Yes, that is Finnish."

"I wonder if Anna and Ben are over there?" says Will, inclining his head towards the beach. I shrug. Despite resumption of a phone signal since breakfast, I haven't managed to get an answer out of either of them. I'm guessing they both lost their phones in whatever happened and I expect neither of them knows my number off by heart, but surely they'd have tried to find out? Rung someone back home, rung the network – explained the emergency? Instead I had to trawl through twenty-three messages from an increasingly agitated David Henry. Twenty-two messages of haranguing about new music and commitments. Then one quite different: 'Darling, I've just seen the news... What the hell is going on out there? Shit... If you pick this up then bloody buzz me to say you're okay... err... ciao.' That's the nearest David's ever been to sweet. I will phone him... later.

The landing boat pulls alongside the ladder. A shout issues from it. "The royal launch awaits." We shake the captain's hand and say our farewells. As my first foot feels for a rung, Katri calls, "Look us up next time you play in Helsinki." I nod. It's not just for show. I might well do that – assuming there is another tour. It's always good to escape from hotel culture for a while.

A careful hand guides my foot down the tricky last move into the swaying boat. "Is that your good ankle?"

"Yup."

"How's the other one?"

"Much improved for some rest." Just as my second foot lands a larger wave passes and I grab Miles's shoulder to steady myself.

"Careful," says Screwy. "You'll be messing up his hair. He's spent hours beautifying himself for all those cameras." The Mate is very well turned out this morning: trimmed beard, hair slicked back and an ironed-to-within-a-degree-of-melting white shirt rather than the usual navies.

I don't join the teasing. I'm not totally immune to such thoughts myself. It's difficult not to when you've seen some awful photos in gossip pages past. I know it shouldn't matter... but a little of Katri's foundation has helped my forehead look less like Harry Potter's and might prevent my nose from being mistaken for a stop light.

"At least I am aware that irons exist," retorts Miles. We all smile – AB Phillips's trousers have more lines than a crazy pavement.

As we round the headland and approach the sheltered beach, I scan the crowd. No sign of Ben or Anna. Maybe they've been advised to keep away from the press. Already the TV cameras are tracking us and microphones are being clutched in anticipation. I glance towards Will. "Smile, polite, smile, polite." He grins sheepishly. "I know David would want me to milk it, but he's not here. I'll just say the absolute minimum."

"This is your bag. I'll just follow your lead."

Barely have I put a foot ashore before I'm assailed with questions from all sides.

'Mrs Woodlove, how does it feel to be safe?'

'Holly, is it true you were rescued from the Skeleton coast?'

'Have you any message for your fans?'

I had hoped there would be someone official to keep order, but it's a mêlée.

'Mr Mason, what do you...' No, I need to take control here. What would David do?

I clap my hands together a couple of times and raise my voice, "Hey, if you all quieten down a minute, I'll say a couple of words. Come on, back up, let us get our feet out of the water." The reporters grudgingly give way and quieten. "We'd just like to say that we're okay and we're very grateful to the crew and passengers of the Cruise ship African Explorer for rescuing us and bringing us back." That's part of a debt paid.

"Shinovene Hamola from NBC. Can you tell us what happened to you?" asks one of the TV journalists, thrusting a microphone.

"It's a long story, far too long to tell now when we're tired and keen to be reunited with our loved ones. But basically we got lost in the desert, managed to walk to the coast and luckily the wildlife watchers on the African Explorer spotted us."

"Sir," says another reporter, thrusting her One-Africa emblazoned microphone towards Will. "How did you survive the Skeleton Coast for so many days?"

Will has a little of the air of a rabbit in headlights. His mouth opens, but no sound comes out. I step in. "What can I say, we never miss a Bear Grylls show." A few chuckles ripple around the journalists. A white reporter, clearly just off a plane from the lack of tan, raises his hand.

"Holly, your disappearance has been big news back in the UK as well as here in Namibia. I wonder if I can ask how you managed to be lost in the desert with a man who..." The last part of his question is drowned out by a loud revving from the boat's engine behind us. I catch Screwy's eye, and receive a broad wink in return. As the noise abates, the problem of what to say next is solved in the form of two official looking shirts and ties jostling their way towards us.

"Sorry, but I think our reception committee has arrived. I'm sure there will be a press release with more details soon. In the meantime, I expect that Miles, the Mate of the African Explorer, will be happy to give you details about his ship and the actual rescue." I see Miles nod in thanks before I have to turn my attention to the two men.

Will is handed an open leather wallet. Inside, a photo card sits beside a star-shaped badge denoting Namibian Police. "Mrs Holly Woodlove? Mr William Mason? Please will you come with us?"

"Detective Chief Inspector Visser," whispers Will as we slip into their wake. I had wondered if there might be someone from the embassy but we emerge from the journo-jetsam beside an empty white Mercedes.

"Where are Ben and Anna – our partners?"

The two police officers' heads flick towards me and then they exchange a glance. It's the kind of raised-eyebrow expression which professionals should learn to hide. Something is very wrong. This is not the joyous reunion we had expected.

The second police officer opens the rear door. We hang back.

"I was told by the Windhoek police that they had been found," says Will, "that they were..."

Will halts abruptly as he realises that although Miles has begun to speak, a number of the reporters have followed us and are listening. For a split second there seems to be a collective intake of breath. Then the Chief Inspector is bombarded with a volley of questions.

'Are there still some tourists missing?'

'Have the police given out bad information?'

'Chief Inspector, where are you taking them?'

"Please get in," says the second officer, motioning with his head. We clamber forward into what seems like the lesser of two evils.

"Where are you taking us?" asks Will as the Chief Inspector slams his door and the Mercedes inches forward, nudging journalists aside.

"First to Swakopmund police station. It..." He lets out a hiss of annoyance, "Mbuae, get out of the way." He leans on the horn but the main exit is snarled up with badly parked vans and new vehicles trying to squeeze past.

"Take the promenade," says his colleague, indicating to the right.

"Are Anna and Ben alright?" I can tell from Will's tone that it's not only my anxiety level which has skyrocketed.

"Please, even with this diversion, the police station is only five minutes away."

"But why can't you just tell us?"

"We need to speak to you as part of an investigation. We should wait until we are not driving."

"What investigation?"

"Please wait, Mr Mason, just a few minutes."

Now I'm really panicking. "Stop the car. Stop and tell us."

"Mrs Woodlove..."

"Stop the car." I reach for the handle even though we are moving. It's child locked.

The Chief Inspector raises his voice. "Mrs Woodlove, please. I am not going to stop until we reach the station and if either of you try to make us stop, we will arrest you."

"Arrest us?" says Will. "For what?"

"I will start with stealing a Land Rover..." I feel like I've been punched in the stomach. If his intention was to shut us up, it worked. Will and I gawp at each other with barely-holding-it-together eyes. I've never been in trouble with the police before... and here I am, abroad, facing a charge that will be difficult to deny. It's not like we can give the Defender back. And if they go looking for it, what else might they find? My hand slips into Will's and we grip tightly. Beyond the window beachfront villas, palm trees and glimpses of sandy shoreline pass by, but my mind is racing back to the lodge.

Why did we take that car?

The promenade is smattered with pedestrians and it's slow going as they make way. We're approaching a pier – not a pier like in the UK with amusements and a theatre, more like a large wooden jetty, but tourists are strolling along it, leaning over the sides, taking selfies.

We took the Land Rover because of Ben and Anna. No one else could check up on the sighting at the petrol station – and it kind of was real. It was the right car...

Every few metres we pass a lamp post, but these are odd even by old colonial standards. Each post is topped by a huge bird statue sitting above the light – quite out of proportion. Maybe it's some old town logo. As we turn inland, one of the statues opens its beak: pelicans, not statues; real pelicans; each of them staking claim to its post like gulls on Brighton seafront. Anna would be in heaven.

When will they let me see Ben?

A couple of streets inland we turn back towards the lighthouse, and shortly pull up in front of a large building. 'Police Station Swakopmund' is emblazoned across the white slab frontage.

As the car stops, the Chief Inspector's colleague turns in his seat. "Very short journey and away from the press." As he finishes speaking, his eyes lower to where my hand is still gripping Will's.

We're taken inside, signed in at reception, led down a side corridor to a small windowless room, seated on one side of a fixed table and provided with machine coffee in plastic cups. The Chief Inspector introduces his colleague as Detective Sergeant Tomo. Both men have the same ultra short, military style hair but the inspector carries a full moustache and considerably more weight. Perhaps these count as a badge of rank in the absence of the epaulettes we have seen on uniformed officers.

"So what's happened to Anna and Ben?" Will butts in before Inspector Visser has managed to form his first question.

"It is interesting that you ask that, because we would like to ask the same question."

"So they haven't been found?"

"No, they are still missing."

All the supposedly quashed fears cascade back into my mind. "But..." Both Will and I say the same word simultaneously. I let him continue: "...I phoned Windhoek Police station from the ship. We were told all the missing tourists had been found."

"I am sorry, but this is not true. Who told you this?"

"I didn't get a name. He seemed to be some kind of administrator. He said that the investigating officers were all out of the building and he didn't really want to say anything, but I pleaded, so he told me that everyone had been found."

"This person should have stayed with his first thought." Visser thrusts his top lip forward in an exaggerated frown. "I think he was confused because we had news about you."

"So there's been no word from Ben or Anna for..." I mentally count back days, "...gosh, it's a week now?" Ben's lack of contact with my Dad and their permanently unavailable phones now makes chilling sense.

"No. Your re-appearance is the first new lead we have had."

I slump in my chair. Seven days without a vehicle. Is it possible? We barely survived four. And they could have walked back to the lodge in little more than one. Thoughts swirl round my brain like smoke from a blazing tyre yard: black, acrid, choking.

"Are they still searching at the lodge?" Will's voice has the shrill note of near panic.

"Which lodge?" asks Visser, even though I'm sure he knows.

"Damara Gemsbok Lodge, the one where we were all staying – the one where Anna and Ben first went missing... because that's where you need to search. Right next to the dead rhino. Everyone was looking for a Land Rover but they didn't drive off in it, poachers stole it. You need to be searching for two people on foot – the hill sides, ravines, thickets – all the places no one would think of checking when you're trying to find a car."

"Poachers steal the Land Rover which Anna Templeton and Ben Woodlove borrowed?" Sergeant Tomo raises his eyebrows. "How do you know this?"

"Because we saw the car and spoke to them."

"You have a friendly talk with poachers, shake hands, and drive away?" His voice is laced with irony.

Will's frustration rises. "No, they kidnapped us and nearly killed us, but we escaped. That's how we ended up having to walk to the coast."

"Wait," says the Chief Inspector, holding one palm towards Will and the other at his sergeant. "Tell the whole story."

"But we're just wasting time... you could be searching."

"When I have all the facts, I can decide on the appropriate response. You can start from when you decided to steal a Land Rover." The Inspector's tone brooks no further argument.

"It wasn't like that," I say. "We had a tip-off from a delivery driver. He'd seen one of the lodge's Land Rovers up at the C51 petrol station. All the guides were out searching. There was no one else who could go and check it out. We had to do something; we were out of our minds with worry. I know we didn't ask to take it, but it just seemed like we were helping with the search. We'd driven the Lodge's cars before... We would've returned it."

"You cannot return it now?" asks Tomo.

I glance towards Will for an automotive opinion. He answers for me. "Err, unlikely, it's burnt out, most of the interior and electrics melted – probably a write off."

"How did it burn?"

I notice Visser's eyes slip towards his sidekick with a tinge of annoyance. "That is a very good question Sergeant Tomo, but I am sure we will come to that." He turns his attention back to us. "So you drove to the gas station..."

We recount our tale, each taking the lead as seems appropriate. Sergeant Tomo maintains a sullen but watchful silence. The Chief Inspector only interrupts to query our reasoning if we don't state it: 'Why did you not believe the garage attendants when they said the Land Rover only had one person in it?' 'Why did you not phone the police... or the lodge?' 'Why did you decide to follow the vehicle into the deep desert?' When I hear our replies out loud, we sound stupid and reckless. He's particularly interested when Will mentions our worry that they had gone off on a weird affair adventure.

"Were you having relationship problems?" he asks, pulling at one corner of his moustache.

"No," we answer simultaneously, then both dither, waiting for the other to continue. Will grunts, "You go."

I hold the Inspector's gaze. "There wasn't anything behind it. We were just trying to think of some reason... and when a man and a woman go missing together it's an obvious thought."

"Yes, it is," he replies.

Once we're beyond the mine, Tomo fetches a detailed map and more plastic coffee. I try ordering black, at least to remove the taste of UHT milk, but it's barely an improvement. Although the map only shows the dunes as plain orange shading, the escarpment and several dry river beds leading from it are clearly marked.

As we begin to describe our brush with the poachers, the two police officer's eyes bulge as our story becomes increasingly violent and desperate. Their expressions are not easy to read, but it seems they are sceptical – Tomo especially so – even when Will lifts his T-shirt to reveal an array of purple bruises. If they have doubts, they don't voice them and, again, the Chief Inspector only interrupts with pertinent questions: 'How did you know the Land Rover belonged to your lodge?' 'Why do you believe this poacher Captain when he says he stole an empty vehicle?' 'Why did you have sleeping tablets?'

When it gets to the part that only I can tell, I notice that Will is hanging on every word. Of course, it's the first time he's heard the detail. I make two omissions and tell one lie: Nasty Face's attack is deleted. He stays blissfully asleep in his tent whilst I suddenly realise I don't need to untie the knot and drive off. The lie, I don't actually 'tell', I point to the wrong place on the map in answer to, 'where do you think these poachers made their camp?' A dead poacher probably wouldn't raise too many questions, but like Will says, it isn't worth the potential aggro.

The other omission is more difficult to explain – even to myself. Katri would know why. In this version, Soba fell straight asleep in the tent. It's easier and makes no difference.

It's odd seeing our final chase marked out on the map – the huge expanse of dunes compressed to a few inches, the escarpment ridge to a set of close inked lines. Will marks in pencil our best guess for the positions of the scavenged army Land Rover; where the young poacher flipped Ben and Anna's car; where ours burnt out.

It turns out that Will's memory wasn't so far wide of the mark after all. Our walk to the coast was only about thirty miles, whilst it was more than forty back to the mine. We must have been travelling at tortoise pace, barely more than one mile every hour. I suppose trudging through soft sand and over countless ridges takes longer than you think. Sergeant Tomo marks the co-ordinates where the African Explorer says we were picked up. Somehow, our route took us almost due west. If we had gone slightly south as Will intended, it would have shortened the walk down the coast to Mowe Bay considerably. Still, we never had to do that, and there's no denying the seal colony was a lucky find.

"And you have this foil here?" says Visser, as we finish our tale making sun flashes at the ship. Will pulls the tatty roll from a 'last-a-lifetime' canvas shopping bag donated by the African Explorer. "Clever," Visser comments, prodding it with the end of his pen. Although, Tomo has been making notes, Visser now slips his own notebook from an inside pocket and jots a few points in a dashed list. I can't read it upside down and I suspect it isn't in English anyway. "Obviously, we have been to Damara Gemsbok Lodge and spoken to everyone there, but remind me how it was you first suspected that something had happened to Miss Templeton and Mr Woodlove."

Recalling everything from that day – the day when my stupid work ruined everything – proves more traumatic than I'm expecting. My waterworks begin to flow the minute we get to the dead rhino. Will doesn't do blubby and snotty, but his moistened eyes and cracked voice reveal an equal amount of emotion. The detectives seem immune to it, though. The further we carry on, the more I'm sensing coldness from the other side of the table. Visser's tugs at his moustache increase in frequency and every time I make eye contact he immediately breaks it. Their expressions are like setting concrete.

"So, in summary," he says to his notebook, "you found the empty car, carried out a small search, then you drove to find a phone signal, but in the meantime some poachers arrived, stole the car and drove off at speed throwing up a dust cloud. You drove back, found the Land Rover gone and returned towards the lodge. And now you say that, all this time, your partners were somewhere close by on foot, but somehow did not notice all this activity?"

"Yes." I can't help but sound defensive.

"I can understand how it might seem unlikely," adds Will, "but for them to go missing at all is unlikely. Normally they would have just gone out for the day and come back. Something unusual must have happened. They must have walked further than they thought or someone twisted an ankle or something..." His voice goes up a gear. "That area needs to be searched again, right now – before it's too late." The final four words come tumbling out without thought, and realisation hits Will like a knife in the belly. He seems to suck in all the oxygen from the room and then lets it trickle out in one lengthy floor-staring sigh. A week out there, with no hamper leftovers or lucky foil – it may already be too late... I shake horror images from my head, lift Will's chin with a bent finger, and meet his eyes.

"They're clever like us... They'll find a way." He manages a weak half smile. I swivel back towards the officers, just in time to catch the tail end of a look passing between them. What now?

"Please complete your story," says Visser.

Will shrugs. "There's not really anything more to add. We were taken back to the lodge and then had to kick our heels for almost a day. As we've said, it was frustrating."

"Before that," says the Chief Inspector, "Just so I have it correctly... You left the dead rhino and drove back to the bottom of the dry river bed. Why were you sure that your partners had driven back up to the plateau?"

"We'd seen the dust; the car wasn't there; where else would they be going?" I answer. "I remember saying that if Ben and Anna were playing a trick then it would serve them right to have to explain it to the search party. So it was a massive shock when the lodge vehicles came round the bend and they hadn't met anyone else."

"So you think the poachers must have gone a different way?"

"I suppose so. I think they would have steered well clear of the lodge."

Visser nods and flicks back a few pages in his notes. "The people from the lodge said you were stopped when they met you?"

"Yes," says Will, "We'd reached the edge of the deep sand and had to deal with the tyres. I was just about to start pumping when they arrived..." He seems completely oblivious to his choice of words. Surely he can't have forgotten the little extra he's missed out? My cheeks start to itch and it spreads to a slow burn. Hopefully scars and sunburn will hide the blush.

Visser settles back in his chair, arms folded, while his eyes pass over both of us. After a few seconds of this scrutiny, Will speaks again, frustration crackling his voice. "It seems like you don't believe us. If you need proof, send a helicopter into the desert – you'll find everything like we told you – but, please, get them searching at the lodge again."

The two detectives confer in their native tongue. It doesn't seem to be a disagreement, more an apportioning of tasks. After a few moments, the chief inspector waves an open hand of conciliation. "Please do not assume what we are thinking. The facts will speak for themselves – and with all the new information you have given us, Sergeant Tomo and I must go to find more facts. We have arranged for you to be driven to Windhoek. You have rooms booked at the Hotel Schwerinsburg."

"We're not going back to the lodge?"

"Please understand we were conducting a missing persons investigation for some days. Your luggage was transferred to our office for examination. It will be at the hotel when you arrive. I am sorry, but obviously it was searched and we took copies of files held on your electronic equipment. We will only keep them for as long as they stay relevant to the investigation."

"My laptop was encrypted," I say. Being ever more wary regarding rights issues, the record company insist on a level of security.

"Yes," says Tomo, for the first time with a half smile, "but you might think about higher security passwords." My mind clicks through various codes and numbers: 'Fusion3' – the title and track number of my hit – idiot!

"If there are any developments," says Visser, rising from his seat, "we will tell you immediately, but it is good that you stay in Windhoek – away from the temptation to go searching again."

For a second, anger rises within me: weren't we the only ones who've actually found out anything useful? But the opposing thought quenches it: how much time did they waste chasing after us which could have been better spent searching for Ben and Anna?

"Can we borrow this?" Visser indicates the roll of foil with a chubby index finger. "...and your bag, Mrs Woodlove – to help us check your story?" I can tell that Will is as reticent to part with his shiny talisman as I am with my few remaining possessions.

"What about my phone?"

"We will return it as soon as possible."

Will widens his eyes and pulls in one corner of his mouth: 'what choice do we have?' It can't possibly help, but it's also totally clear any refusal will be viewed with suspicion.

"Okay," I say. "But we're not under arrest for anything?"

"No," says the Chief Inspector. "You are not under arrest... but, how do they say in the American films? Do not leave town..."

CHAPTER 26

The temperature at the bottom of the ravine is at least ten degrees cooler than the searing hillside above. It's probably the only reason the man is still alive – that and the gruesome choice he had to make... The sheer walls of his rock prison rise perhaps forty feet. They may as well be a mile. On the first day he'd dragged himself to the upper end, then the lower, but there was no easy path, nothing that wouldn't require climbing skills greater than any he had possessed even when able-bodied.

It was as if the hillside had been rent by a blow from the mother of all battle-axes. If it had been a recent wound this never would have happened, but the earth had been healing for millennia. Perhaps attracted by moist air from the coolness below, lichens and other clinging plants began to grow. Generations of their bodies created soil for the thorn bushes which now cling to either side of the lip, in places meeting across the void like branches over a pitfall – a trap that he has not been the first to fall foul of. The thigh bones of some small antelope strapped to his fractured leg with strips of T-shirt are testament to that.

From somewhere amongst those unobtainable bushes comes a flutey warble. He has come to think of it as his taunting prison guard. It was the sound they had been hoping for, the end of their ridiculous, what-if-we-just-go-a-little-further search. 'If we squeeze through there I think we might be able to see it.' There hadn't been any melodramatic teetering on the edge, just a sudden gasp, a yank on his arm, then falling, scraping, bashing, nothing...

It had been difficult to know how long he had been out for. The pain from his leg screamed for his whole attention – until he realised why the base of this ravine seemed oddly soft and damp under his chin. The other one had saved him: her body taking the full impact, her skull crushing like a snail shell beneath a careless boot, whilst his was cushioned by compliant flesh. They had landed in a gruesome parody of the position in which he had often fantasized finding himself – when such things had seemed important.

In those first hours of pain and disorientation, his mind had played tricks: the distant sound of vehicles, his wife calling his name, the other one's partner calling her name – even though there was no way anyone would have missed them so soon. Maybe he was getting the days confused.

Once enough time had passed for his wits to gather, he'd set his leg as best he could and, despite the fruitless search for an escape, he had still been hopeful. Surely they'll find the Defender? Surely they'll search? He'd just need to keep up regular shouts. But after two more days with nothing more than the fleeting glimpse of a high-flying helicopter, his parched throat was hoarse and energy flagging. His training had told him there were only two choices. One was death – the other was almost as unpalatable... almost.

Five days on the man glances towards the body of the other one. Despite the lower temperature, it's beginning to smell. Soon even that resource will be beyond use. It makes sense to stock up now... to consume as much as possible while he can. He drags himself backwards with both arms towards the prone form and props himself beside the torso. "I'm sorry An..." His whisper stops abruptly. Mustn't think that. This is the 'Other One', the one who's keeping him alive. His hand trembles as the Swiss Army knife approaches a skinless buttock...

"Uggh..." It takes all my will power to hold down a wretch. "P...please can we stop, I think I'm going to be sick."

Will leans across to press the window button. "Take some deep breaths, you've gone green." The police driver swerves onto the hard shoulder and pulls up sharply. I stagger out to lean, hands on knees, drawing in long slow swigs of hot air and shuddering them back out. The nausea gradually subsides and after a couple of minutes, I stand straight... Rushing geometric patterns cloud my vision. One knee begins to buckle and I flail in the direction of the car. A firm grip catches my right forearm, supporting a hefty fraction of my weight for the second or so it takes my brain's blood supply to catch up.

"Stand up too quickly?" Will is supporting me, concern overcoming the tiredness in his eyes.

"Yeah..." I let him hold my arm until the wobbles have definitely passed.

"I didn't think you got travel sick?"

"I don't... I was... daymaring again... It was... It was stupid; it was something you really, really don't want to have in your head too."

He takes a step back, palms raised. "I'm not even going to ask, not if it was anything like the last one."

"Sorry." I'm slightly surprised by the strength of Will's reaction. Is my mind really that much of a pollutant? Oh come on, Holly, who are you kidding? Of course it is... Why should he spend the rest of the journey thinking about his girlfriend being eaten?

I try every distraction technique in the book as the remaining miles pass: cars versus bakkies up to ten, spotting weaver bird nests, mentally reciting song lyrics – old and new. It's a struggle, but eventually we turn south, the road spawns a second carriageway and the industrial outskirts of northern Windhoek flash past.

Hotel Schwerinsburg turns out to be a modern pretender, looked down upon literally and most likely metaphorically by its more historical neighbours up the hillside. A glance at the map on the inside cover of the guest information folder reveals the two sets of faux battlements breaking the skyline above my window to be the Hotel Heinitzburg and the Schwerinsburg castle itself. We were told at the front desk that our booking had been made by the British High Commission, not actually the police, and that the High Commissioner will be visiting at four.

It's only just after one, so there's plenty of time to settle in. Will was after something more substantial, and is probably tucking in to half a cow somewhere downstairs, but I opted for room-service soup. As I wipe the bowl clean with the last of the bread, I ponder the luggage. It was already in the room when I arrived. My battered guitar case and the oversize laptop bag are no problem; I'm used to those being messed with by roadies, techies and the like. It's the clothes that bother me. Opening the case does not improve the feeling that everything is somehow tainted. It's all folded neatly, smells freshly laundered, but it isn't arranged how I would do it. My skin crawls as I hang shirts and stuff underwear into a drawer. Someone has been through all this – searching, and worse, inevitably judging me by what they found.

"Oh..." Beneath a nightshirt lies a pair of Ben's boxer shorts. Tears trace lines of fear down my cheeks before dripping onto the cotton white duvet. Please be alright, Ben. Please by some miracle be okay. Please don't be anywhere near any ravines... I shake images from my head and scan the room for anything to distract. My eyes alight on the landline phone. I suppose I ought to call David...

"Darling, I've been trying your mobile all day... You won't believe how relieved we all were to hear that you're safe. Of course, we've all had acts go AWOL before, but a quick buzz round all the rehab clinics and Bob's your mother's brother. Rory says he can't remember anything quite like it. To be honest I think he was concerned you'd gone and done a Richey Edwards on us. Anyway, it's wonderful everything's okay and..."

"Everything's not okay. Ben and Anna are still missing." My voice cuts across David's cheerful tone: a birch rod onto an open palm.

"But we... I thought..."

"Yeah, even we were told they were safe at one point but no one knows where they are."

For a moment, there's nothing but the faint noise of passing traffic – he must be outside some office, probably sneaking a crafty fag. "Sweetie, I'm sure they'll be okay."

"It's been a week. It isn't like London here."

"You're in one piece aren't you? Ben always seems like a... competent chap." Hmm, I think that's the closest he's ever been to complementing my choice of husband. They've never got along, the two men in my life. Although my relationship with each is completely different, they've always acted like competing suitors – jealous of the time I spend with the other.

David clearly takes my silence as proof that he's convinced me: "Anyway, darling, you wouldn't believe the publicity you've been getting back here: 'Popstar missing in the desert' on the front of The Mirror; second item on the TV news two days running. The label is ultra keen to release something new asap. They've been discussing whether you should keep Der-dup and rush it out as a standalone single. And nothing official, but Nick at Abbey Road tells me they've been enquiring if any slots could be made available next month."

"Abbey Road, really?" That's like the stratosphere compared to where I thought I was. A jumble of excited thoughts tumble out of me: "I've kept on writing. There are three... no, four new ones... I haven't had time to record demos yet. They're a bit different, more like Scared – about the crazy stuff that's..." What am I thinking? How is any of this important? Ben and Anna are...

"Sweetie, are you still there?"

"David, I can't think about this stuff, not whilst... I can't..."

There's another silence, this time punctuated with my sniffs. "Holly, darling, I know the label has been speaking to the embassy over there. I'm sure everyone's doing all they can."

"The High Commissioner's coming to see us at four."

"Is he? Well, there you are. Just sit tight... and if you do get chance to ping over the new stuff that would be perfection... Ah, my twelve-thirty has just arrived. Ciao."

Stress counselling courtesy of David Henry. Wonderful.

DESPITE DAVID'S ASSUMPTION, the British High Commissioner to Namibia is actually female, although I have to admit that when a short woman in her fifties clicked across the hotel lobby in low heels and a tan trouser suit, I thought she might be the PA – particularly as her skin is quite Namibian in tone. Only her precise Home Counties accent saved me from making an embarrassing faux pas.

She introduces herself as Marjorie Halden and we agree on first names as the hotel manager shows us into the so called "Jazz bar". A laminated notice stating 'Privates function' has been tacked to one of the panelled doors.

"That's good to know," comments Marjorie with raised eyebrows but a deadpan voice. I see the corners of Will's mouth twitch in spite of the circumstances.

This is the first time I've ventured into any of the bars or restaurants the hotel has to offer. It's rather obviously decorated after the musical theme: black staves and notes on gold walls, black and white photos of jazz legends, a few old instruments hanging above the bar – interior design by numbers. The thing that does pique my interest, though, is a grand piano at the far end of the room. I wonder if guests are allowed to play it?

We seat ourselves at one of the several round tables. The manager beckons a barman and takes his leave.

"It's rather early," says Marjorie, "but under the circumstances, I think brandies could be in order, or whatever's your preference?"

"Scotch, ideally, if you have it," I say to the bow-tied waiter.

He glances towards Will. "Me too."

Marjorie leans forward in her chair. "Is the hotel alright? We were asked if we could arrange somewhere comfortable. My assistant tried for the Heinitzburg, but it was fully booked."

"It seems fine, doesn't it?" Will nods his agreement.

"I hear the pool is a decent size." I suspect this same assistant has briefed her on my Wikipedia stated hobbies.

"I haven't sampled the facilities yet."

Marjorie clearly hasn't been a diplomat for however many years without learning to recognise when people don't want the chit-chat. She brings the conversation straight round to relevant matters as the drinks arrive. "I'm very glad to see you two safe, but I understand your partners are still missing." We nod. "It must be a very worrying time for you..." She shifts her attention specifically towards me. "Holly, your record company contacted us just before all the press coverage broke. We're happy to provide advice and assistance where we can but please be aware that you have to work within the laws and systems of Namibia – a British passport is not a magic ticket these days." A wistful tone enters her voice – perhaps wishing for simpler times past.

"It's alright, we get it," I say.

"I know the police will have debriefed you quite thoroughly, but it might be helpful if you could give me an outline of what has happened so I can see where we might help."

Between us, Will and I recount a ten minute potted history of our adventures. She sits through it without comment, her politician's face automatically switching between appropriate expressions to match our words. There's a lot of horror and disgust, but it's not real. I'm sure she means to be sympathetic, but second hand horror seems fake now. True horror is standing over a brai, knowing that to the four pairs of eyes on your back, you're just another piece of meat to be grilled.

"...so you can see why whisky is a current favourite," I say, taking a swig to mark the full stop of our tale, "even if this is just a blend."

"The lodge you were staying at is the Damara Gemsbok?"

"Yes."

"And you're convinced Anna and Ben are still near there somewhere, lost in the bush?"

"It's the only thing that makes sense now we know that the poachers stole their car," says Will.

"Are you sure these poachers were telling you the truth?"

Will glances towards me for an answer. "There was no reason for them to lie. They didn't think we'd live to tell anyone. Besides, Soba wasn't like that. He would have boasted about killing them – said it was unfortunate, but the practical thing to do. He would have used it as another way of terrorising me." An involuntary shiver rushes up my spine, ending in a visible twitch of the shoulders. This, more than our story, seems to galvanise Marjorie into action.

"What did the police say they were going to do next?"

"They didn't really tell us," says Will, flinging both palms open in frustration. "That's the problem... They treated us more like criminals: threatened to arrest us for stealing the Land Rover..."

"I think they could only do that if the Lodge actually pressed charges," inserts Marjorie, "and I can't see them aggravating a well-known customer..."

"...and they seemed more interested in checking our story than doing any searching... The way they were acting, I think maybe you should recommend a good lawyer."

"Well, I can if it comes to it, but I expect it was just a misunderstanding... How can I put it? Like the sign on this door, not everything happens here quite as it does in the UK. Of course it would be procedure for the police to question family members – everyone knows how often they're involved. It sounds to me like they have just been a little over zealous. Your story, it is quite..."

"Unbelievable?" I finish off.

"I was going to say, 'unusual'," answers the High Commissioner. She leans forward and presses her hands to her knees as if to rise. "I will do what I can with what little influence I have to make sure that a search is resumed. Other than that, I'm afraid it's just more waiting."

"That's the worst part," I whisper.

Marjorie throws me her best sympathetic smile as she stands. "Unless there's anything else, I'll be getting along."

"No, thanks, you've been very kind," says Will for both of us.

THE REST OF THE EVENING is an exercise in 'keeping your mind off it'. Will reads a motor mag by the pool-side lights, whilst I stroke and turn, stroke and turn thoughts from my head with the hypnotic rhythm of exercise. At dinner we comment on the menu, the wine, the decor, the waiter – everything and anything, except... Afterwards, we drift round the 'sights' of the hotel: the 'Garden View' terrace bar beyond the pool – too cold; the small 'Dune' bar in the foyer beside reception – too much hubbub; the 'Cheetah' lounge – too quiet. Even the sight of a couple of single malts high on a shelf behind the 'Jazz' bar is not enough to cause us to linger long in the face of 'too jolly' music.

"How about seeing if there's a decent film on the telly?" suggests Will. We end up watching 'Stargate', sitting on my bed, sharing peanuts from the mini-bar. We've both seen it before: it's feel-good; it's mindless; it gets switched off for a few seconds during the sandstorm scene. The credits roll at close to eleven-thirty. Will stretches out his legs and slides off the bed. "I suppose I'd better try to get some sleep," he says in a far from convinced tone.

I don't want him to go. I want him to stay. Not for anything like that... I'm just not sure if I can sleep alone. I want to feel safe – protected. I want to be held... I... I want to snuggle for warmth like we did in the dunes... 'On a double bed, in a hotel?' says another part of my brain. All that comes out of my mouth is, "Okay."

I don't even attempt to sleep once Will has left. I open my laptop and ponder a change of password. Something I won't ever forget, that only I know – something to do with Ben: s*omeonelikeme*. Perfect. A watery smile forms as I remember that student canteen.

I have four songs to record. I daren't play or sing at this time of night, but there's plenty to do: setting up each file; adding blank tracks with the usual effects; creating beats to keep my strumming and singing in time... Sometime in the small hours I'm trawling through different recordings of waves crashing on beaches, head on one hand, clicking down a list. That one? Put it on repeat to check...

"Wha...?" I wake with a huge start, snapping my head upwards, terrified that the rescue has all been a dream and I'm still on a desert shore... But it's the same hotel room, now with the paleness of dawn tickling the edge of the curtains. Idiot! I yank the headphones from my ears and the sound of waves halts abruptly. The clock on the TV says seven twenty-three: time for another swim before breakfast. I pull on my swimsuit and slip a hotel gown over the top. Before making my way to the lift, I creep to Will's room – two doors down on the opposite side of the corridor – and place my ear to the door. The TV is on but I have to wait for quite a while before I hear a creak which might mean he is awake. I knock lightly. From the speed he answers, I can't have woken him. He peers round the edge of the door, hair sticking out at odd angles.

"Hi. Sleep well?"

"Not really."

"Me neither. I'm going for another swim. Do you fancy it this time?"

"Yeah, why not? Err. You go ahead, I just need to put my trunks on."

Three other guests have the same pre-breakfast idea. I wonder what they make of the scar across my face, the red ring around my ankle, the huge purple bruise on my inner thigh. I feel even more self-conscious than normal and slip into the water as quickly as possible. I think I have it bad, but when Will removes his robe, there's still more bruise than normal skin on his torso. He lowers himself beside me.

"Oh, that's not bad – the air's nippy, but the water's much warmer than the sea."

"How are the bruises?"

"Past their worst. Yours?"

"The same."

We only swim for a short time. I'm not sure about Will, but with both of us in the water I'm reminded of the skinny dipping and the last thing I need is another thing to avoid thinking about.

During breakfast, there are two topics of conversation. The first is in-laws or in Will's case, whatever you call the parents of your long-term partner – in-sins? Will has already spoken to Anna's. Ben's haven't even crossed my mind. Without realising it, he shames me every time I find out he's done something that I haven't. I only thought to ring Dad from the ship because Will said he was going to phone his parents. And now he's called Anna's family when the only person I've spoken to is bloody David Henry. I'm just not a family person – not like that anyway. What is wrong with me?

The second thing is how to occupy our time to prevent ourselves from going nuts. Given the lack of mobile phones, we decide we have to stay at the hotel in case anyone needs to contact us.

"We could record the songs I started whilst we were lost... maybe?" I suggest diffidently. Will's spoon stops half way to his mouth, he exhales a gentle snort and the corners of his mouth rise ever so slightly. "What?" I'm struggling to see how anything is funny.

"I knew you were going to say that."

"We don't have to, it was just a thought." I try not to sound too huffy.

"No, no... It's fine..." He raises apologetic eyes to meet mine. "I was just thinking how much better I know you. It's only been a few days, and, a minute ago, I could see you were uncomfortable and I thought, 'She wants to do music, but she's worried that I'll think she puts work before everything else.' And you were thinking that – at least, I suppose you were from what you said... Don't worry, I know you like to work. I haven't got any better ideas."

I don't know why, but my eyes are watering and his expression, which is now turning to concern, is making it worse. He lowers the spoon which still hasn't made its way to his mouth and nudges my shoulder gently with a fist. "Assuming all this shit somehow works out, it's been the one saving grace amongst all the pain: a week ago, you were just Anna's friend. Now I feel like you're my friend too."

I smile as the flood of tears bursts.

WILL KNOCKS ON MY DOOR at eleven: a time which seems late enough to avoid any complaints from neighbouring rooms. He's dressed properly, but I'm quite happy to stay in a bathrobe for as long as possible. I've left a message on Jill and Graham's answer machine. I expected them to be sitting next to the phone, but I'll try again later.

"Am I here?" Will says, taking the seat behind the laptop which I've set up on a small table beneath the window. I nod. "Your view's better than mine," he comments as I fuss with the guitar lead.

"Shall we start with 'I'm Hurting'?"

"Is that the one you were doing on the way to the petrol station?"

"Yeah."

"Isn't some of that on your phone?"

"U-huh, but they've all been going round in my head for days. I don't think I've forgotten anything."

It takes a couple of hours to lay down a version that captures the essence of the track, even if the production leaves something to be desired. But, hey, this is only a laptop in a hotel room and studio-craft was a complete mystery to me before the first album.

"Shall we have lunch brought up?" I say after feeling my stomach rumble for the second time. Will nods gratefully. I suspect he would have succumbed some time ago. "What do you fancy?"

"A burger and salad would hit the spot."

I dial 02 and order the food. "Drinks?" I query to Will. He shrugs unhelpfully. "Can I have a bottle of still water, please..." An idea strikes me. Why the hell not? "...and I noticed in the Jazz bar last night there was an almost full bottle of Laphroiag whisky. Could you bring that up with two tumblers?" I have to spell the name.

Will has one eyebrow raised as I replace the handset. "Too rock and roll for you?" I tease.

"Just so long as you don't smash the telly with your guitar."

With fuel on board and just a little lubrication, the afternoon is highly productive. Bless him, Will is quietly thrilled to be singing on 'Keep On'. He takes it so seriously – won't have any whisky until after he's done his part – and then sings eight repeats perfectly on the first take. More than enough to loop him right through. I kind of get why Ben calls him 'Superfan', but it isn't scary or creepy. He just seems to be genuinely enthusiastic. It's nice to be appreciated.

Once his moment of stardom is passed he does succumb to liquid temptation and his reaction to the Laphroiag is priceless.

"Bloody hell, it's a mouthful of smoke."

"Kind of puts a whole new light on the term 'fire water' doesn't it?" I watch, grinning, as he takes a second sip. "Good smokey or bad smokey?"

"Good... I think... It was a bit of a surprise after the others."

"It certainly is a distinctive one."

By six-thirty we've finished all the recording but I'm still fiddling with the arrangement for 'Stranded'. We've moved the table and chair next to the bed so Will can sit beside me and witness the process. We're sharing a pair of in-ears, his in the right, mine in the left.

"You've taken some very specific things that happened to us and then changed them slightly, haven't you?" he says, out of nowhere, "so they work for anyone." I twist sideways, but it's clear from his eyes that he isn't offended, just curious, as ever.

"I guess so."

"Were you ever a waitress who fancied one of your customers, like in the 'Der-dup'?"

"No, it's not like that every time. Sometimes they're just pure fiction, but it's easier if some of it comes from life. I suppose I did have a few daft crushes back in the day..." Will's eyes are lingering on mine as he listens – no, don't go there. "It's important that people relate to the lyrics, so it's no good writing, 'I'm stuck on a beach and I might die unless I eat enough seal meat to walk out of here.' Not too many people are going to relate to that. But nearly everyone has been in a relationship they felt wasn't going anywhere."

"Clever."

"Well, not really," I say, feeling a touch of colour in my cheeks, "pretty much everyone else does the same thing."

"Apart from all the rock songs with loads of cool sounding phrases that don't actually make any sense?" he says, a smile breaking.

"Yeah."

"And all the R&B that spends its whole time bumping and grinding in da club?"

"Yeah, apart from those."

"And all the dance music with only three lines?"

I can't help but laugh, "You know, David is always complaining that my songs are too wordy."

"Fuck David Henry," says Will shaking his head.

"A surprising number of attractive forty-somethings do just that."

"Really? I've only seen the guy once, but he didn't seem... What do I know? I suppose he has a good line in patter." Our laughter subsides and I squint along the screen for the source of the timing mis-match I heard a moment ago.

"There's definitely something wrong with my 'Ah's but I'm not sure..."

Will collapses on the bed in stitches. He stares upwards, takes a gasp of breath and says, "From what I remember your arse looked just fine."

I snort and roll my eyes, "Idi..."

There's a rap at the door. I suppose it must be room service come to collect the plates. I slide off the chair, wobble across the room and fling open the door, still grinning from the stupid pun. Chief Inspector Visser's serious face wipes it like I've been tazered. His eyes travel down my body. Although I'm wearing a fairly dowdy set of short pyjamas under this towelling robe, they are not actually visible. I see him take in my bare forearms and calves, Will still prone on the bed, the half-empty bottle... and make obvious but incorrect conclusions.

Heat streams into my face, "Will has just been helping me record some songs." The Inspector steps into the room flanked by three uniformed officers. "Mr William Mason and Mrs Holly Woodlove, you are under arrest for the murders of Anna Templeton and Benjamin Woodlove." My mouth drops open. "Mr Mason, go with these officers. Mrs Woodlove, please get dressed."

CHAPTER 27

"Tell me how the Land Rover driven by your husband came to be on its side?"

"I already told you about that."

"Tell me again, please." Inspector Visser's voice is polite but firm. It's been like this for more than an hour – going over the same ground that Will and I told him in Swakopmund. Except this time I'm on my own. Well, I have the Embassy recommended lawyer beside me, but what I mean is: Will isn't here. He's probably in a similarly intimidating cell-like room, answering Tomo's identical questions.

I glance towards my solicitor: a slim man with short tight curls, black on top, greying at the sides. He nods. I sigh and carry on. "The youngest poacher was chasing us in Ben and Anna's Defender. He kept ramming us from behind to force a crash. You could probably see the marks on the bull bars if you checked." Visser makes no comment. "Will tried to shoot at him but it's difficult with the car bouncing around. There was a hard patch of ground – one of those salt pan things – and I thought maybe I could get Will a better shot because I knew that the other Defender might still have its diff lock engaged – you know, the little lever which..."

"I know the differential lock," says Visser, his tone as if I'd just tried to explain what the steering wheel was for.

"Well then you'll know that if you use the diff lock on hard ground the steering doesn't work very well." He nods grudgingly. "So when we reached the solid stuff I swerved, but he couldn't, which gave Will an easier shot. I don't think Will hit him, but he did smash the windscreen. I don't know if that put him off or if he just didn't know what he was doing, but he was still yanking down on the wheel when he drove back onto the sand and that made him flip. I expect the diff lever is still engaged, if you've checked?"

Again Visser ignores my question and poses another of his own. "How did you know that the differential lock was engaged?"

"Because I engaged it... When I escaped from the poacher's camp, I messed with the other vehicles. I took the keys with me. Let down some of the tyres, and put the diff locks on."

"You crept around doing all this whilst these armed men were sleeping?"

"They were more than just asleep. Like I told you before, I really didn't want them to follow me."

"You must have nerves of steel, Mrs Woodlove."

Is that a trace of sarcasm? I take a deep breath and try to keep my voice level. "It was life or death. That concentrates the mind."

"But they did follow, and caught up with you easily."

"Yes, Will and I were stupid, we shouldn't have dawdled around when I found him, we should have just blasted straight on... I suppose Defenders must be easy to hot wire. You could check if they did that..."

"What I am far more interested in is why, if a poacher was driving this car, we found Anna Templeton's bag in the vehicle – and your finger prints on certain items." He fixes me with a cat-who's-cornered-a-mouse stare... but there's a gaping hole in the skirting board.

"That's easy," I say, shrugging. "Anna's bag was in the car when we originally found it next to the dead rhino. I remember checking her phone, but I don't know what her unlock pattern is. We left it when we went off to contact the lodge. So it was in the car when the poachers stole it and still in the car now."

"But why would Ms Templeton leave her bag behind in the car?"

It's not the first time I've considered this: nothing new springs to mind, so I trot out my best guess. "I don't know. Why did they leave the doors open, too? I suppose they thought they were alone on private land so there was no need to worry about security. After all, the guides leave the keys in the ignition overnight – you wouldn't do that in the UK."

"Okay," he says with a sigh. I can't tell whether it's real or for effect. "I will change over the tape." He pulls out the cassette and swaps it to side B. The recorder is a 1970s antique, pretty much identical to one which has been sitting at the back of my Dad's sideboard since I was old enough to yank open the door. I used to love pressing the fast forward and rewind buttons, purely to watch one reel grow and the other shrink.

"Tell me how your Defender caught fire." Visser brings me back to the present. He raises both hands, palms out. "I know you have already told me the story. I would like to hear again."

"The other Land Rover, the army type, blocked off our escape route towards the mine. Every time we came within a few hundred yards of them they shot at us. They were too good. They knew to stop and shoot so the aim was good. They were like the dog and we were like the sheep and they herded us gradually further away from where we wanted to go. In the end we decided to play them at their own game and we backed right off, stopped and waited for them."

"In this other Land Rover was the man called 'Soba'?"

"Yes, and the older one."

"There were two in this car and one in the vehicle that crashed?"

"Yes."

But did you not say there were four poachers? Where was the fourth?" His eyes widen and his eyebrows rise and stay up, waiting for my answer.

"I don't know. Maybe he stayed back at their camp. Er... maybe the sleeping pills affected him more than the others." Did I answer that too quickly? Does my voice sound different when I'm lying? The Chief Inspector's brow falls into a brief frown, but he doesn't pursue this further.

"You stopped to wait for the other Land Rover?"

"Yes, we walked back a few yards and hid behind the crest of a small dune. Our idea was that when they drove up they would be sitting ducks for our rifles."

"You were preparing to kill them?"

"It wasn't like that. You're making it sound like we were the aggressors. We just wanted to escape, but they kept shooting at us. Our only hope was to attack them back and hope they weren't expecting it... But Soba was too clever. They stopped a long way off and he walked up. We were aiming at him with rifles we barely knew how to use, whereas he concentrated on a much bigger target. He knew he only had to make our car undrivable and we were dead anyway – at least we should have been."

"And when they had set your vehicle alight these poachers just left you and disappeared into the desert?"

"Yes, they..."

"You see the problem I am having," interrupts Visser, "is that we have flown into the desert, we have searched where you told us, but what we have not found, anywhere, is any sign of these convenient poachers you keep mentioning."

"So I suppose the rhino cut off its own horn?" I know I'm being stroppy – maybe I should calm down – but for goodness sake, they're accusing us of killing Ben and Anna...

Visser purses his lips, "Okay. I will say again. Apart from the dead rhino at the Damara Gemsbok lodge, I have seen no evidence of poachers – in fact, there are questions even about the rhino."

"What questions?"

"The animal was killed very inexpertly: many shots. But the men you describe are military types who can shoot holes in jerry cans from long range and hate to waste ammunition."

That is a bit weird, but what is he saying? My mind races for other pieces of evidence. "Didn't you find the tracks of the other Defender?"

"No. There were no tracks."

"Do you mean there weren't any extra tracks or that the wind had covered all the tracks with sand."

"We found no tracks at all – just the vehicles."

"Well that doesn't prove it one way or the other, does it?" I glance towards my solicitor, who shakes his head ever so slightly. "But the stripped down army Land Rover where Will sheltered. That must still be there."

"We found no other vehicle."

"You followed the edge of the escarpment north, searching every hollow between dunes, and you didn't find it?"

For the first time, Visser looks a touch uncomfortable. "Searches in that area are not yet finished..."

"Well there you are. Carry on hunting and you'll find it."

"...but," says Visser, ignoring my interruption, "what we found were two damaged Land Rover Defenders which have been involved in a fight. The last known drivers of these vehicles were you, William Mason, and your partners. We compared bullets found in both cars to ones recovered from the remains of the rhino. Three rifles were used on each occasion, two are the same."

"Isn't that the evidence we want then – that links the poachers to both places?"

"...or that four tourists, or maybe I should say 'poachers posing as tourists', used the rifles in both places."

I stare at him for a moment, open-mouthed. My mind clicks round his statement and its implications. The very idea of Ben killing an animal in such a way is ridiculous. "So you think that we've come here for rhino horn? That we somehow smuggled rifles into your country..."

"...or bought them here..."

"...Okay, or bought them here, killed a rhino, and then... what? Argued over the spoils? Chased round the desert shooting at each other? Killed our partners over something made from the same stuff as my fingernails? Are you serious?" This is so ridiculous I'm struggling not to sound scornful. My lawyer obviously thinks so too.

"Chief Inspector, I have yet to hear any solid evidence which links my client to this crime. In fact, as no bodies have been found, it is difficult to understand how you can conclude that a crime has actually taken place. Unless there is more, I ask that you release my client immediately or I will complain to the Attorney's Office.

Visser sucks in a deep breath. He attempts to melt my lawyer with an acidic stare. "Your client has stated the basics of one line of inquiry. There is also another." His gaze returns to me, not loosing much of its venom. In contrast, his voice is honey smooth. "Mrs Woodlove, will you describe your marriage?"

"What do you mean?"

"Are you happy together?"

I glance towards the solicitor. "If you are willing to answer, then go ahead," he says. I have an idea where this might be heading, but they're wrong, so, yes, I will answer.

"Yes, our marriage is fine. I mean, that's not to say we don't have a few cross words now and again, but that's normal. I love Ben and I know he loves me."

"But Mr Mason told us in Swakopmund that you were worried your partners had disappeared on a 'Lovers' adventure'."

"That was one possibility. When two people just vanish, your mind plays tricks and you start to think of all sorts of things that you wouldn't normally. I've imagined them buried in sand drifts, fallen down cliffs and all sorts of horrible things. I'm worried sick and that messes with your brain."

"What about your relationship with Mr Mason?" There, I knew it!

"We're friends. Close friends now, but just friends."

"So you are not having sexual relations with Mr Mason?"

"No."

"Or a romantic affair of any kind?"

"No."

"In Britain, then, it is normal for a man to be in a hotel room with a woman who is married to another? The man lying on the bed and the woman only half dressed? And drinking and laughing when they say they are 'worried sick' about their missing partners?"

I hold Visser's eyes for as long as I can. He's right, it did look bad, but it was just one moment... "This nightmare is happening to both of us. He knows exactly how I feel because he's feeling it too. Who else can we talk to? If you'd arrived at a different time you might have found us both crying in our own rooms. We're not allowed to help search for Ben and Anna so we've got to do something. I write songs. It's not just what I do, it's who I am. In a situation like this they just fall out of me. Will was helping me with some recording. We weren't going anywhere, so I didn't see the point of getting properly dressed. If you had been at the pool before breakfast you'd have seen me... and Will, wearing considerably less, but you wouldn't be asking questions about that.

"We were drinking because we're scared. We were laughing because we're scared. The fear, it's like a vice squeezing your head. Any kind of temporary relief is welcome. Haven't you ever laughed at a funeral?" My eyes water at the word funeral and a solitary tear runs down the edge of my nose. I wipe it with a finger.

Visser appears unmoved. "That would be very touching, Mrs Woodlove, except that I have two witnesses who say they saw you sitting on Mr Mason's knees, kissing him – kissing him passionately on the lips – on the day your partners first were missing."

Oh, so they did see... My bottom lip trembles, I try to hold it together, but the guilt is too strong. "I know... and that makes me feel... so much worse," I sob. He waits in silence for my tissue to appear and the sniffs to subside. I decide the complete truth can't hurt. "When we went back to the dead rhino and found their Land Rover gone, I was convinced they were trying to avoid us – playing a trick on us. All the way back up the dry river bed I was more and more convinced they were having an affair. Anna is so gorgeous and I know Ben fancied her when we were younger. So when we stopped to inflate the tyres, I threw myself at Will. It was a stupid spur of the moment revenge thing. It only lasted a few seconds. I think even if the Lodge cars hadn't appeared we would have stopped before it went too far..."

I hear my words as if outside of my body and think, 'You were going to tell the truth and you just lied again. No, I didn't. Yes I did. How do you know what would have happened? You know...'

"And then we found out that they were still missing... and now I know that we'd left them behind somewhere near the rhino... and a storm was coming... and we should have been helping them but we were betraying them instead..."

Through renewed sobs I hear the lawyer's voice. "Chief Inspector, you are clearly distressing my client. She has been very open and honest and you seem determined to rub salt in all the wounds. I still haven't heard any evidence that would stand up in court. Where are you going with this?"

"I am trying to find the truth – something which your client seems to change as it suits her." He may as well have slapped me – it couldn't have stung more.

"No you're not... You're trying to take one mad moment and swell it into a motive for a fight between rival lovers. How many times do I have to say? I have not seen Ben or Anna since they drove off from the lodge on the morning they disappeared – no one has. They are lost in the bush and all the police effort should be spent on searching for them. Will and I followed the only possible sighting and that turned out..." Gears crunch together in my head. After a momentary confusion, my brain speeds up. "Yeah, what about that? You've interviewed the people at the C51 petrol station?"

Visser pulls at his moustache. "Yes?"

"So you'll have a statement that says the other lodge Land Rover was driven by a black man who 'smelled like the desert', not by Anna and Ben."

"Is this true?" chips in my lawyer.

The Chief Inspector is silent for a moment. "The statements from the gas station attendants and the delivery driver are contradictory."

"But you do in fact have statements which place a probable poacher in Northern Namibia with a stolen vehicle as my client has always maintained?" He lets Visser's non-committal silence extend for perhaps ten seconds before rising from his chair. "Right, Mrs Woodlove, please do not answer anything more. I am going to put an end to this farce."

WELL AFTER MIDNIGHT, our solicitors force a path through the scrum of journalists outside Windhoek Central Police Station. Harsh white camera lights illuminate the otherwise deserted street. "It is late and our clients are tired. There will be no questions or statements tonight."

'Mrs Woodlove, why were you arrested?'

'Mr Mason, where is your girlfriend?'

'Holly, what did the police want..." The hubbub ceases abruptly as the door to the Mercedes slams shut and we accelerate away. I scramble to find my belt although no one else seems to bother.

"Do they ever sleep?" comments my lawyer from the front seat.

"They crawl back to their coffins in the daytime," says the other from the far side of the backseat. Will's solicitor is considerably younger but wears an identical 'company' charcoal suit with royal blue tie. "The police ask that you stay in the country while investigations continue. I am not sure they can enforce that as there is so little evidence, but..."

"We're not going anywhere until Anna and Ben are found," says Will. I nod agreement.

"No, I imagine not," says his senior colleague, flicking his head forward as the car slows rather sharply for an unexpected red light. "Hopefully that will be all, but if the police contact you, call us immediately. It is clear that Visser is going for the easy option of blaming the partners and we need to counter that if he tries again... I will send you a text so you have my cell number," he adds, pulling a mobile phone from his jacket's inner pocket. For the first time since being reunited, my phone vibrates against my leg.

We hardly seem to have been in the car for more than a few

seconds but already we're drawing up in front of our hotel. They wait until the night receptionist buzzes us through the door before pulling away. We're handed our keys and head through the bar area towards the lifts. There's still one hardy guest keeping the bartender from his bed.

"They saw us in the Defender," I say to Will, unable to keep it in any longer. "Did they ask you about that?" In reply I receive a hard nudge with his left elbow. "Ow, what was..." I see what it was for. The late night drinker is the British journalist we saw in Swakopmund. He slips off his stool.

"Who saw you doing what in a Defender, Holly?" he asks, with the casualness of an old friend.

"How about you mind your own business," says Will, but I can feel my face reddening and of course he picks up on it straight away.

"Oh, it's like that is it? That's a nice thing to be doing while your partners are missing."

"I don't know what you're talking about," says Will, stabbing at the lift's call button. "Shouldn't members of the public have left the hotel by this time?"

"Yes, but I'm a paying guest," he says flashing his key card. "Why did the police arrest you, then?"

Before he's finished the question, there's a chime and the doors open. We rush inside but our unwanted tag along makes to follow. Will swings round just beyond the door's sweep. "You're not sharing our lift."

"I have just as much right as you." He steps forward, but Will stands his ground, looming a full head taller. The doors start to close and the journalist makes no attempt to stop them.

CHAPTER 28

For hours I toss, turn, and sweat: a human washing cycle of anxiety. Then, typically, just as dawn approaches, I drop off, only to be woken by my 'last possible breakfast' alarm.

As I enter the dining area, fully dressed, a noticeable hush flows across the smattering of tardy guests like a lull between gusts. The near silence gives way to a low murmuring as furtive glances are taken and whispers exchanged. It's quite clear that there's been something in the papers or on the telly. I've had some pretty uncomfortable meals in the past with curious starers, but never before have the peeking eyes been cold and the mutters disapproving. Maybe I should have ordered room service... I munch soggy croissant as quickly as possible and make my retreat.

I don't want to disturb Will in case he's sleeping in, so I take a deep breath and lift the lid of my laptop to survey the damage. It's everywhere: Woodlove arrested for murder; UK singer questioned over husband's disappearance; arrest twist in safari disappearances saga. And those are just the Namibian headlines. The British papers are worse and one headline really rankles: 'One hit Woodlove in arrest shock.' Why do they have to do that? Isn't the story enough without taking a sideswipe at my absence from the charts? Bastards.

I'm still picking holes in that particular journalist's writing style, grammar and pen name – I mean, 'Phil Boots', really? – when the hotel phone makes me jump so hard, the mouse falls off the table. Ben would be in stitches. I snatch up the receiver.

"Hello?" I say, with anti-press caution.

The matter-of-fact voice of the High Commissioner is simultaneously a relief and a concern. "Good morning Holly. Before you ask, I have no more news of your husband. I hear you had a difficult evening?"

"Yes, but the solicitors you recommended were very good, thanks. Do you know if they have started searching at the lodge again?"

"I have asked, but there's little I can do to influence things... The reason I'm calling is because we were contacted by a Steven Carter this morning. He says he's a friend of yours?"

"Err, yes..." I wouldn't go quite that far, but I'm curious.

"He's passing through Windhoek this afternoon and would like to see you. Is it alright if I let him know where you're staying?"

"Okay."

"Good..." The word tapers off, as if, for once, the diplomat is uncertain as to her next. When she does restart, there's a human chink in her professional armour: "I'm glad they released you. It didn't seem... likely. I'll let you get on. I expect you're exhausted from yesterday."

We exchange pleasantry goodbyes and I'm left staring diffidently at the receiver. I really ought to try Ben's parents again.

It's a prolonged conversation with Jill, in which she, totally out of character, swears, 'I knew they'd got it all bloody wrong' on numerous occasions. Between us, wife and mother, we veer between forlorn tears and reasoned hope. On one of the up-slopes, Jill, particularly heartened by our desert survival exploits, abruptly decides to end the call. Ben's cleverer than me, we decide; he'll be okay; end of... The spell is broken by the harsh note of the disconnect tone. Ben's cleverer than me – if he was only lost they'd have found him by now. I throw myself onto the duvet and surrender to an oblivion of sobs and snot.

THE CALL announcing the arrival of visitors comes after half a day spent drowning thought with cheesy multi-language soap operas. I knock on Will's door as arranged and for the first time today actually see him. His shoulders droop with the weight of unanswered fears. Uncombed hair straggles over his forehead like a storm-tattered flag. Part of me wants to enfold him in the sympathetic hug he surely needs, but that bloody journalist will appear round the corner with a camera... As if responding to my scrutiny, he runs a hand through his hair and straightens his back. "What do you think Steven wants then?" he says.

"I don't know. They did say they would be passing through. Maybe they just think it would be nice for us to see a friendly face. I'm sure Katri would think that anyway."

"You're expecting both of them?"

"Oh yes."

My certainty is well-founded as I'm enveloped in a strawberry blonde hug almost the second we emerge from the lift. "Oh Holly, it must be so worrying."

"Come on," I hear to my left, "we can't let the women call us emotionless lumps." Having disentangled themselves slightly after us, Steven steps back from Will rather sheepishly. "I took the liberty of asking if they had a private lounge. Hope that's okay?"

"No, that's perfect – I should've thought – there is a reporter lurking around here somewhere."

We are ushered to the Jazz bar once more where a now corrected notice indicates no admittance to general guests. From his sideways glances and visible relief as he closes the door behind us, it seems the hotel manager is more than happy to keep Will and me away from public areas. Maybe some of the guests have complained about sharing breakfast with a murderer. They're wrong. I'll show them.

"Nice piano," comments Steven, as we sit. "Have you?"

"No." A rueful smile plays on my lips. "I've had other things on my mind... like criminal charges."

Katri catches my eye and rolls hers. I'm sure I could be good friends with this woman if circumstances allowed. Now that I'm examining her more closely, I can see a certain tension in her concerned face – like she's trying to hold down a bubble of joy. In fact, if it wasn't for the frown, I'd say she was positively glowing. Steven is similar, except with him it's more like Toby's face used to be during Dad's 'Christmas-present-thought': 'Before you open them, let's think for a minute about what it might be like for the kids who won't be getting any.' Bless him, his forehead would tremble with the strain of maintaining a suitably serious face amid the excitement.

What's changed? My gaze searches over freshly shaved skin, freshly plucked eyebrows and finds its answer close to freshly manicured nails: on Katri's fourth finger, a stunningly elegant ring. Thin gold bands curve in two opposed hooks, seemingly joined only by a delicately rouge stone. The combination of metal and stone leads to a hue which matches Katri's hair perfectly.

"Oh, wow... Congratulations... Can I see?" Katri holds her hand forward with reticent pride. "Specially made?" She nods.

"Mine too," says Steven. His is similar but with a pale sapphire mounted in thicker platinum. It seems to bring out a blue in his eyes I hadn't noticed before. "Both had to be wearing the ownership bands if we had them at all..."

"So the big Cape Town party the captain mentioned was for your engagement?" says Will, smiling with their infectious happiness.

"Yes, it was outside on the rear deck with the sunset and views over Table Mountain, and..." He stops abruptly, smile vanishing like a lowered blind. He leans forward. "Look, we didn't come here to rub your faces in our good fortune, we came to help. When we saw the papers this morning... We couldn't pass by without seeing if we could do something."

"It's very kind of you, but..." starts Will.

"I know it might seem like we're just poking our noses in," Steven speaks over him, "but, really, I don't want anyone else to have to go through the same as I did, and some of it was beginning to sound horribly familiar." He glances between our sceptical faces. "Please, you can't trust it to the police. You can't trust it to lawyers. You've got to work it out for yourselves."

"We already tried to find Anna and Ben ourselves," says Will, shaking his head. "Look where that got us – lost in the desert for days, arrested and, worse, it probably stopped the authorities from searching in the right place. It's our fault they're still missing."

Steven slumps against the back of the chair, nodding his head ever so slightly. It's clear he is recalling similar feelings but knows better than to say it. I'm softening. He takes a deep breath, "I'm not saying you do anything, not yet, at least; what I'm saying is you should think. There's always something more. Something you don't realise you know. Something that might help."

"Don't you think we've been racking our brains – been through every likely scenario..." Will glances towards me, "and a few horrible ones that we'd rather not have in our heads."

Steven opens his palms, "Of course. All I'm saying is that I spent months sifting through memories trying to find relevant details... so maybe I've got a bit more experience and I could help you?"

"What do you have to lose?" adds Katri in a small voice. Her expression is anxious and uncomfortable, but she clearly believes he could help. That decides me.

"Okay." "Thanks, but..." Will and I speak simultaneously. He halts and raises questioning eyebrows.

"What harm can it do?"

His forehead creases. I counteract the frown with widened eyes. We stay joined in silent conflict. After a couple of seconds he turns away and mumbles, "Go on then."

"Great," says Steven, not attempting further persuasion. "So we'll talk through it to see if we can find the important moments and then we'll try the thing." I'm not quite sure what he means by 'the thing' but I nod anyway. I guess we'll find out. "On the ship it seemed like you thought your partners had been found? What happened?"

"I had bad info from a police clerk," says Will. "He must have confused them with us being found."

"That is really poor... So how come they arrested you?"

"The first time they questioned us we told them all about chasing round the desert after Anna and Ben's Land Rover, only to find that it had been stolen by poachers. I don't think they believed a word of our story about escaping from the poachers."

"So what are they saying?"

"They flew out to the desert, found the two wrecked Defenders and now think we had some massive row and shot at each other."

Steven snorts, "They seriously think that ordinary Brits have been in a gun fight? Do either of you even know how to shoot one?"

I exchange a glance with Will. Maybe he was right: however well meaning, Steven doesn't understand...

"That would be, kind of a good point," says Will, "except we hadn't ever shot a rifle before, but we still ended up in a gun battle with the poachers – you learn fast if you have to."

Katri's hand goes to her mouth, but Steven appears unmoved. "Okay... What do the police think you were arguing about?"

I roll my eyes. "Ben and Anna go missing together. Will and I are found together... Take a wild guess."

"That someone was having an affair." He doesn't even raise his tone to form it as a question.

"And every time Will has to suffer me bawling into his shoulder everyone takes it as confirmation that something's going on."

Steven's eyes linger on mine and my cheeks prickle with the uncomfortable feeling that with male-female friendships, he does understand... and perhaps more than I would wish. He drops his gaze. "But they haven't actually found any... trace of your partners?"

"No. They found Anna's bag in the crashed Land Rover, but we had already seen that she'd left that behind before they went missing."

There's a pause whilst Steven processes this. "So you're saying that the police are concentrating on completely the wrong place and time?"

"Yeah," says Will, getting in just before me. "The poachers stole Anna and Ben's car after they'd already left it. That was why everything got so confused. We were all searching for a Land Rover when we should have been searching for two people on foot. The poachers had nothing to do with it."

Steven says nothing but can't stop his eyebrows rising slightly. It does seem unlikely. I clarify: "We know that because the poachers told us... and it was... the sort of situation where if they had done something, they would have gloated about it... particularly with Anna being like she is." I notice Katri's alert eyes upon me – picking up on the 'unsaidness' in my pauses.

"What is Anna like?" Steven turns back to Will.

"Um, she means she's quite pretty."

I can't help but roll my eyes. "More like effortlessly sexy – fair?"

"Yeah, alright."

Steven nods, "So when should we be talking about? What was the very first thing that was odd?" Will and I stare at each other with matching pensive frowns. After a few seconds, Steven prompts: "Think back to before they went missing – at your Safari lodge, even before the holiday – did they or anyone else do or say anything that seemed unusual?"

Odd, in all my worry and daymare imaginings, I've never considered the involvement of the lodge employees or anyone else except the poachers. Will and I hold eye contact – his mind obviously whirring as hard as mine but nothing obvious springs forth. "Can you think of anything at all before the self-drive, before they weren't at the place Moses told them – that rocky ramp?"

Will shakes his head. "No, it was completely out of the blue – that was the first thing."

"Okay," says Steven, "Let's start there. This is going to sound weird and corny but think back to that exact moment. What did the place look like? How was the weather? Was the car uncomfortable? Anything that will transport you back. Then when you're ready, describe it in as much detail as you can. Don't leave nothing out."

Oddly, he slips into a poor US accent for the final sentence. I find myself wondering about that rather than Ben and Anna. Concentrate woman! What was that valley like?

"It was absolutely frying hot outside the car," says Will before I even form a picture. "I... I could feel sweat forming everywhere and there was no breeze at all."

"You kept flapping the bottom of your T-shirt."

"Did I?"

"Yeah, while I was on the phone – my manager called to say he liked the song. I thought it was going to be Ben – you tried to call Anna, but couldn't get through – just kept getting voicemail."

"We checked the tracks in the sand," says Will, "and the freshest ones seemed to lead down the valley. You were a bit mad with Ben for going further than they were meant to."

"I thought he must be showing off for Anna. 'I'm the petrol-head, I can drive through any conditions' – something like that."

"I remember thinking it was more likely that Anna didn't see that bird and persuaded Ben – 'there's just one more place we could try.'"

"You... you told me I should stand up straighter." I'm not sure where this appears from. Will's face jolts into an equally surprised frown.

"I did, didn't I... Sorry."

We're both silent for a moment. Again, my cheeks prickle slightly. We restart simultaneously, "The driving was..." "It was really bumpy..."

"You go on."

"No, you."

I shrug. "Okay... The sand was deeper and the driving was more tricky," I catch Will's eye, "and bumpier. We followed the freshest tracks to the bottom of the dry river bed and out onto the plain. The tracks weren't that obvious, but we guessed they would head south because that way looked more like the sort of place where the Rockjumper birds might be found. There was a ridge sticking out into the plain, wasn't there?"

"Yeah, and some bushes, so we were quite close when we first saw their car..."

"...and the rhino... I just slammed on the anchors... and I have to admit my first thought was poachers." I glance towards Steven, whose attention is fully engaged upon us. His lips twitch as if he considers an encouraging smile but decides against it. "There was a dead black rhino. Its horn had been cut off... and beside it was Ben and Anna's Defender, with both front doors wide open."

"We were wetting ourselves for the first few seconds," says Will. "You read these stories about tourist kidnaps and stuff, but as soon as we got out things didn't add up. The rhino stank – it wasn't freshly dead – and what poachers would wait around to get caught?"

"...or kidnap tourists but leave their Land Rover?" I add.

"Anna had left her bag, but both sets of binoculars were gone. After two minutes of panic we decided they must have gone for a walk. We shouted and thought we heard a reply... but later it seemed like it must have been an echo..." Will trails off, clearly wondering what we should have done differently.

"More detail... if you can," murmurs Steven.

Again Will and I share a thoughtful stare. "You searched through Anna's bag," he says after a few moments.

"Yeah. There wasn't anything unusual: phone, make-up bag, wipes..." I take a long blink. "There were vultures. They – or something else – had already been eating the rhino. There was blood on the sand and lots of tracks. Do you remember, we..."

Will's head jerks up. "I don't need to remember, I took photos."

"But your camera was smashed..."

"I know, but the memory card should be alright. The kit bag is upstairs. Your laptop has an SD slot, hasn't it?" I nod as we leap to our feet.

Five minutes later, I'm booting up with three expectant people literally breathing down my neck. My heart is pounding, mostly, but not entirely, from the dash to my room and back. The splash screen takes forever to fade. Will's hand moves towards the slot as the desktop appears but I nudge it away. "There's no point. Bitter experience – you need to wait until everything's loaded or weird stuff happens. The printer icon's the last thing – there, now." Will shoves the card home and almost immediately a window appears with thumbnail images gradually loading down it. The first few are gemsbok and zebras, followed by dozens of the cheetah we saw on our second day. "See what I mean?" I double click and a photo of a bikinied Anna grinning upwards from waist deep in the pool fills the screen.

"Yeah, I do see..." says Steven, hurriedly adding, "although dark-haired women aren't really my thing." From the corner of my eye I catch the end of a Katri head shake. I continue scrolling past more animals, more Anna, deep sand driving, bush camping, and finally the mutilated face of the rhino. Enlarged, the grisly portrait is even less pleasant. Katri mutters something unintelligible and a whispered 'horrible' emanates from Steven. The following dozen or so shots show lots of sand with glimpses of rhino as Will made his way methodically round the carcass. The second last also shows the bottom half of a Defender with its driver's door open.

"At least that backs up your story, if nothing else," says Steven, a trace of disappointment clear in his voice.

"I suppose the police must have already been through these. They told us they'd taken copies of everything," I add.

"Yeah, but who did they have look at them?" My eyes shoot up to Will's face, surprised by his urgent tone. "Go back a couple." He points towards a pair of furrows a little way from the rhino. "What made those, or those? What prints are they?"

"I don't know."

"Neither do I, neither will 99.9% of people, but I know a man who will: Moses. I took these photos so I could ask Moses what had been eating the Rhino but," his voice rises in pitch, "maybe, just maybe they might show something else. Steven," he says, taking a step back as we all turn towards him, "you've been very kind. I have to admit I thought you were just wasting our time, but this 'thinking about the details' thing of yours has thrown up something new. Will you help us follow it through? You're about to drive north. yes?"

"Yes."

"Would you take a detour to Damara Gemsbok Lodge, give this memory card to their guide called Moses, and tell him that Holly and Will are sure that Anna and Ben left the dead rhino on foot and could he check out these photos to see if there are any clues?" Steven glances questioningly towards Katri as Will continues, "I mean, we could try phoning or email but a personal visit would be..."

"Of course we will." Katri nods agreement. "It can't be far out of the way. What's the name of the place we are staying tonight?"

"Otjiwarongo. Where is it from there?"

We spend the next fifteen minutes giving directions and making plans for them to phone us when they've run the errand. As we're walking back through the foyer, Steven stops and turns to us. "I hope it won't come to it, but if you do have to deal with the police again, can I give you a piece of advice from a wise person I once ignored?"

"Yeah..." I say, perhaps not totally concealing the 'what now' that also passes through my head.

"Sorry, I know I'm sounding like a parent, but always admit everything. Even if there's one silly thing that you think doesn't really matter. It will matter. Admit it."

I avoid Will's eyes and answer, "Okay" to the floor. I already admitted the silly thing; it's the huge thing I've kept quiet. We wish each other luck and wave our goodbyes as their hired SUV pulls out of the car park.

"Have you read his book?" asks Will as we head back upstairs. "What happened to make him so paranoid?"

"Not sure. Something bad in Finland. Some of the song lyrics are quite dark but I don't know the story. Come to think of it, I must have the eBook on my laptop somewhere, it came with the music."

My phone springs to life as if awakened by the touch of the door handle. I wave to Will and answer it as I enter my room.

"Hi David."

"Sweetie, how are you doing?" This is odd: concern from DH...

"Not good really. There's still no news. You'll have heard about our arrest, I suppose?"

"But you're out now, aren't you?"

"Yeah, it was such a total waste of time when they could've been out searching."

"It must be nice to have a shoulder to cry on."

"What?" He's lost me.

"This man you're with, William Mason..."

"What do you mean?"

"Darling, you needn't be coy with me. It's totally understandable. I've almost done the same myself... It's only... as your manager, it's better if I hear these things from you rather than from the press."

A knot tightens in my stomach. "What have you read?"

"You haven't seen? Links to the article are trending everywhere." He sounds incredulous that this might have escaped my notice. Sorry for being more worried about my missing husband...

"No, I've had... other things on my mind. Tell me the gist of it."

"The gist is, sweetie, that someone over there has let slip that you were in bed with this Will when you were arrested."

My mouth drops open, "But I wasn't. He was in my hotel room but..."

"Darling, you don't need to justify yourself."

Petrol – match – whoompf. "I'm not justifying myself," I bawl, "I'm trying to tell you what actually happened. It would be nice if you waited to hear my side before you believed every lie printed by the gutter press. Just because some of your previous acts did that kind of thing all the time doesn't mean I'm the same, does it?" Silence. "Does it?"

"Holly, darling, sweetie, let's not fight." David's voice is laced with the conciliatory charm which has served him so well over the years. "If you say it's not true, of course I believe you. Cast your eyes over it and if there's anything that really rubs, ping me an email and I'll issue a denial. It'll just be more exposure – you know the saying, 'any press is good press'. Fusion has re-entered the download chart, you know?"

"Really?"

"Only number fifty-eight, but it's a petit reminder of your appeal – speaking of which, Christian is still on side with the new tracks you sent, I think Stella is wavering, but Rory just isn't getting this semi-autobiographical thing you're doing."

"He doesn't think it'll sell?"

"He's the money, darling."

It occurs to me that I have incontrovertible proof that he's wrong. "You tell Rory, I have two words for him about autobiographical music: 'Steven Carter'."

"Now that is a thought... that is a thought... Look, I know it's difficult, sweetie, but if you do get the chance to fizz me any more material, it just strengthens our hand."

"I'll see. But that was why Will was in my room: he was helping me to record those songs. It's him singing the backing on 'Keep On'.

"And the bottle of scotch?"

"Liquid nerve calmer. You should know all about that, David."

"Indeed I do, sweetie... indeed I do. Well, 'keep on moving' or whatever darling. Ciao for now."

He's already clicked off before I say, "bye". I open my laptop to survey the damage...

HOLLYWOOD-LOVER?

Murder Suspect Woodlove 'in bed with' Victim's Boyfriend

A source close to the Namibian police has revealed that pop diva Holly Woodlove was sharing a luxury hotel room with fellow murder suspect William Mason when they were arrested yesterday. 'She opened the door wearing just a bathrobe. I could see him lying on the bed behind her. You could smell the alcohol. I was shocked, what with their partners being missing.' A source at the hotel confirmed that Mrs Woodlove had ordered an expensive bottle of Scotch earlier in the day.

One-hit-wonder Woodlove was on an exclusive safari with her husband Ben, and another couple: stunning college friend Anna Templeton and her Neanderthal boyfriend Mason, when they all went missing. Mrs Woodlove and Mason were picked up by a cruise ship on the notorious Skeleton Coast after having apparently walked across the desert for several days. No trace has yet been found of Mr Woodlove or Miss Templeton.

On their arrest, the Namibian Police stated, 'We have reasons to believe that Mrs Woodlove and Mr Mason are involved with the disappearance of their partners.' This morning Woodlove and Mason were released without charge. The Namibian Police have declined to give further comment.

More to follow...

by Phil Boots

Beside the article is a photo of Anna, the one from her firm's website, but the thumbnail portrait of the author is of more interest. It's the hack who bothered us in the lobby. Smug little prick. It's not just what he's said, although I dread my Dad reading it; it's all the little insinuations: 'apparently', 'expensive', 'diva'... and calling Will a Neanderthal. Diva! I'll give him diva! I fling a pillow against the wall and stamp round the room shaking clenched fists. I know I must look like a tantrummy two-year-old, but it calms me enough to be able to compose a reply for David. My poor laptop keys have never been hammered so fiercely. I let rip knowing that David will edit it down to a brief, pained-but-polite paragraph.

Then I text Toby: 'Arrest was a farce. Still no real news. Don't believe the press. They've got it all wrong.' Thirty seconds later, I receive the reply: 'Knew the racy headlines couldn't be about you. Hang in there Prickle.'

The sibling sarcasm manages to raise a wry smile for a moment, but I soon return to pacing. Why does everyone always assume the worst? Not just people who don't know me, but even David laps it up. It's meant to be about trust – isn't it? And poor Will: all these lies and distortions are dragging his name through my mud. He never set himself up as a public figure; he's just an ordinary bloke... Actually that's dead wrong. He's not ordinary at all. He won't blame me; he'll be worried about me. He'd say I shouldn't stew, I should use this anger, channel it. Come on then...

Legs only partially hidden behind the oak panelled screen, the woman towers above the rest of the court room, shoulders back, sneering down her prominent nose. That sneer has always incensed me more than anything else in the world.

"Please can you describe your relationship to the accused?" asks a wigged attorney.

"I gave birth to her."

"But you are now estranged?"

"Yes, since she was ten – since her and her brother wouldn't come home with me."

"You are referring to your return to the UK from Linz, Austria?"

"It weren't reasonable, dragging me over there, away from my whole life, just because of his job. I put up with it for six months – but they always took the side of their perfect father."

"How did you react when you heard your daughter had been accused of murder?"

"Well, I weren't that surprised to be honest. She was always a sly little girl. Always pretending to be a goody-two-shoes. No one can be that good. Had her father wrapped round her little finger... and then she went and married him."

"She married her father?"

"Well, someone just like him. That vet: sensible and boring – it was no wonder in the end she went looking for a bit of muscle and a bigger cock..."

The anger seethes within me, but the python grip of the formal setting prevents it from exploding as a scream or a curse. Instead, when it's my turn, it flows out like a gentle spray of hydrofluoric acid:

Wrong about me

I thought it was about trust.
I thought you knew the person that I am?
I shouldn't have to prove that... my life is not a sham.

I thought it was about truth.
I thought you would believe me when I said,
'They've got it all wrong,' but... you can't see in my head.

Where is your... (x3) Where is your faith in me?
Where is your... (x3) Where is your love?

Can't believe you've thought it. How d'you even think like that?
Maybe they distort it, but how can you rely on that?
Can't believe you've thought it.
How are you so wrong about me? Wrong about me.

I thought it was about care.
I thought you would protect me from these stones.
But now it seems you've left me... to fight this on my own.

Where is your... (x3) Where is your faith in me?
Where is your... (x3) Where is your love?

Can't believe you've thought it. How d'you even think like that?
Maybe they distort it, but how can you rely on that?
Can't believe you've thought it.
How are you so wrong about me?

You're so wrong (x4) You're so wrong about me.

Wherever I go, the eyes are staring,
whatever I do, the sighs despairing,
whatever I say, the lies fly back at me.

You're wrong about me.

Sometime in the middle of the red-eyed night I finish it. I don't know if my neighbours are lying in bed, fingers in ears to block out my singing, or if they phone the management whilst I'm trialling guitar parts, but the only knock on the door is more room-service espresso. I'm past caring about the minor inconveniences of others. I render an mp3 file of the demo, attach it to an email, and 'ping' it off to David under the subject, 'Shove this up your pipe and smoke it, Mr Journalist.'

CHAPTER 29

Moses creeps along the hillside, now stooping to check a misplaced rock, now rising to his full height, squinting at the skyline. It's another cloudless morning but under his breath he mutters, "Darkness is coming, storm is coming, find shelter I must..." A few hundred metres ahead, to his practised eyes, there's more water. A broken and wavy line of verdancy – if you can use that term for thorn bushes with slightly reduced levels of water stress – implies an underground spring. Part way along this line, a large boulder nestles on other broken rocks. He quickens his pace.

On the eastern side several crevices reach into the darkness beneath the boulder. His tongue makes an audible click as his eyes alight on an out-of-place form beside the largest crevice: a pair of binoculars half covered in dust. He leans forward, peering into the opening. It's large enough for a person to crawl inside but Moses makes no attempt. Not having the nose of a mongoose, holes are no place to enter blind. From his top pocket he pulls a small shaving mirror and angles it to throw a beam of sunlight into the darkness. Just beyond the entrance, the cave opens into a larger chamber, but... he swings the mirror round just to make sure... it's empty. Part of the floor is out of sight – there must be a depression. He plays the light around the visible edge.

"Hello?" The voice is husky and weak but Moses twitches so hard the mirror slips from his fingers – landing, fortunately unbroken, with a clatter on the bare rock. "Hello, is someone there? Help!" The woman's voice sounds a surprising distance away but there's no missing the desperation in it.

"Anna is that you? This is Moses."

"Moses, thank God. Ben, wake up, it's Moses."

"Where are you?"

"Down a hole, the ground fell in. We can't climb out. Ben, it's Moses. Ben!" A low male groan answers.

"Are you injured?"

"Not really. There's water down here but we've had no food for days. Ben he's... it's difficult to wake him up."

Moses considers his options. It's no good crawling in and possibly falling himself. "I am here on my own. Go back to the Jeep, I must, to radio the lodge. Then I will fetch rope and torch."

"Moses, are you still there?"

"Yes, Anna."

"Please don't be long. Please come back." Obviously! But the fear in her voice echoes his own from those nights in that wrecked Toyota when he was...

"Miss?" he says, an idea forming. "Start counting: one and two and three and..." Her repeats filter up from below. "Yes, like that." He peers over his shoulder towards the Jeep a few hundred yards away. "I will be back before you reach five hundred." He turns and sets off at a jog: steadier than it used to be, but still distance munching. His feet seem to slap out a rhythm on the rock. Slap, slap slap, thump, thump, thump, bang, bang, bang...

"Awrrrh." The dream desert image slips from my mind like sand through outstretched fingers. Knock, Knock, KNOCK. It's my room door. I move my head to be greeted by the sharp pain of a stiff neck. My waking eyes find themselves uncomfortably close to an out of focus keyboard. Knock, KNOCK, KNOCK. My name is being called. KNOCK, KNO... "I'm coming. I was asleep," I shout, staggering to the door.

"Morning," says Will squinting at my face. "Been using your laptop as a pillow again?" There must be key impressions all across one cheek.

"I couldn't sleep... and then I woke up with my head on it and you hammering on the door."

"You haven't heard from Steven, then?"

"They wouldn't be there yet, would th..." I catch sight of the bedside clock – eleven forty. "Bloody hell where's the morning gone... Oh heck, I haven't slept through it have I?" A quick phone to reception confirms they have not put any calls though. Phew. "I dreamt about them being found – just as you were knocking on the door, Moses was radioing it in."

Will raises an eyebrow. "You actually had a pleasant dream, not a clip from a low budget horror film?"

"It does happen occasionally... They were alive. Not in good shape, but alive. I didn't want to wake up." I wander to the window and open the curtains. "You don't think... I mean, it's the first time I've had a positive dream about them. You don't think it could be..."

"What, a premonition? Who knows? After that miracle you pulled in the desert, I'll believe anything."

I stare upwards to where the white-washed faux battlements of the Heinitzberg gleam in the sun. A hornbill of some kind swoops across the intervening hillside. "I've been thinking about what Steven said... about admitting everything. Maybe I should tell the police about the one I shot. I mean, if they find the body..."

"...They'll just think they had a fight between themselves. It must happen all the time – arguments over the loot. Anyway are you sure you even killed him?"

"I shot him in the chest from point blank range – he was dead."

Will frowns, staring through his eyebrows. "However it happened, it was self-defence... It's your decision... but I think you could be making another problem for no good reason."

"I don't..." The phone interrupts my reply. "Hello?"

"Hi, Holly, it's Katri."

"Hi. How did it go?" I don't know why, but I was expecting Steven to make the call. Has he put her on to break bad news?

"We have stirred up a little of a wasp nest. The manager here..."

"Mr Kaura."

"Yes. He is mad that they were never shown these photos before. At first he was angry with you and Will. He shouted a lot about ruining his business and he... he said quite a lot of nasty things, but Steven just kept asking him to have Moses look at the photos."

"But Moses has seen them now?"

"Yes, eventually; I think Kaura called for Moses just to make us go away... but it all changed once the first photo was on the screen."

"Moses saw something?" I motion Will to press his ear to the other side of the receiver.

Katri pauses before continuing. "He would not say exactly what he saw, but he kept flicking between the photos. Steven said to him, 'Holly and Will know that the poachers only stole the Land Rover... so something else must have happened to Anna and Ben. What do you say to that?' And Moses said that he might believe you."

"So what's happening now?"

"Now Moses is already driven off with a print of each photo and Kaura is shouting down the phone at the Police. Steven is still in the office with him. Apparently the police visit here a couple of days ago to ask more questions about you but didn't say anything about the poachers and did not carry out any more searches. I... I am sorry."

"Bastards," I hear under Will's breath.

"So it's more waiting," I sigh.

"I am afraid so, Holly."

"Okay, thanks ever so much for helping us... So you're off for the rest of your holiday now?"

"Yes, but we will be thinking about you."

"Not too much, hey? Enjoy your special time."

"Okay. Good bye then." I think I hear a waver in her voice as she ends the call. I know what she's thinking. I've had those thoughts dozens of times, but just now I'm still in the bubble of this morning's dream. I slip the phone back in its cradle and turn to Will.

"In my dream, Moses finds them trapped in a cave under a boulder. Maybe that's what he'll find."

"Maybe," says Will, his eyes a little wild.

ANOTHER TWENTY-FOUR HOURS of anxious waiting, teary phone calls and sleepless fidgetry has strengthened my resolve. I must come clean about Nasty Face.

"Are you sure?" Will lifts his sunglasses so I can see the appeal in his eyes.

"Yes. It may not help, but it's the only thing I have left."

"Okay." I expect him to keep arguing like Ben would, but he doesn't, he accepts. I suppose it's different when you're married...

We turn the corner from where the taxi has dropped us at the side of the police station. Several journalists are still loitering beside the entrance, marshalled by a bored looking officer. I immediately recognise one as Phil Boots. My fingernails dig into the palms of my hands. Will glances at me and twitches an eyebrow. "Ug," he says loudly, frowning his deepest, most forehead-clenching frown at the surprised Mr Boots. "Ug, u, u, ug," continues Will pointing a finger in short jabs. "Ug, ook, errr," he concludes, hands now on hips.

"What is he doing?" says the journalist. Clearly it was a throw-away comment to him, but I get the reference to the article immediately.

"Well, being as you cleverly identified him as a Neanderthal, I guess he assumes you can speak their language. I'm a bit rusty myself, but I have a feeling it wasn't very complimentary."

"Ug," Will agrees.

There are several sniggers and we shove through the door before anyone thinks to ask a question.

"Nice one," I whisper as we cross to the reception desk.

"You too."

I remove my shades and ask to speak to Chief Inspector Visser. It's clear the officer on reception knows exactly who I am. "Someone will see you in a moment."

It really is only a moment before Sergeant Tomo appears.

"I need to speak to Inspector Visser about..."

"Yes, of course," he interrupts, seemingly a little flustered. His tone is full of caution. "The Chief Inspector has gone up to the Damara Gemsbok Lodge late last night. I do not know what you hear but..." He turns to the officer on the desk, "Call Officer Kugara and ask her to come to interview three with coffee."

Will and I exchange confused glances. This isn't playing out at all how we expected. Tomo leads us to the room and indicates we should take the pair of seats on the far side of the table. Less than a minute later, Officer Kugara appears bearing plastic cups in a wooden holder. She slips her thin frame into the fourth seat and hands out the drinks: milk and no sugar for all. "There you are..." she says, revealing quite a gap between her top front teeth.

Tomo takes a deep breath before he speaks. Oh, heck. "We were soon to come to see you at the hotel... to tell you... there has been a development." Come on, just spit it out. My hand instinctively grabs for Will's but misses as my brain is totally distracted by the next two words. "The remains of two people have been found at the Damara Gemsbok Lodge. There will have to be a DNA identification but from the location and items of clothing it seems certain that it is your husband and your partner."

"We are sorry to be giving you such news," says the steady quiet voice of Officer Kugara.

Everything slows to a drip. It feels nothing like my fears had imagined. That was heart-clenching pain, mind-numbing sorrow; this is... nothing... that's a good description: a hole, an absence, a lack of... everything. I'm not sure how long I stare at the blank wall behind the two heads opposite before I realise my hand has been enveloped in another. Trembles emanate from the connection but I can't tell if they're mine or his. My head turns slowly. I can see the same lack in his eyes. It's filling them, squeezing everything out down his cheeks. Vision blurs as my own bubble of nothing exerts its pressure.

"How?" It's more of a groan than a word but it pushes against the hole just enough for me to lift my head from his shoulder and realise it's Will's voice. I push away and slump back into my chair. A box of tissues has magically appeared on the table in front of us.

"Yes, how?" I agree, squinting at Tomo through stinging eyes.

"It is not confirm but it seems like it was animal related."

"What does that mean?" says Will in a rasping voice. "They were killed by an animal?"

"That is what we are told."

"No Ben wouldn't, he couldn't, he's a vet..." I hear myself say.

"Who is telling you?" says Will. "Is it Moses from the Lodge?"

"The... remains were found by one of the guides."

"You keep saying 'remains'. What does that mean?" asks my mouth, seemingly on autopilot. There's silence from across the table.

"It means there's not much of them left, doesn't it?" says Will.

"Not for a visual identification."

An image of the Springbok carcass we saw half a world ago crashes into my mind, rib bones still pink with blood as the vultures picked it clean. Those vultures we saw at the rhino, they could've been... Ugh. I swallow hard to hold down rising bile but choke on it. Will pats me firmly between the shoulder blades until the coughing subsides. "Sorry... I... I had the wrong sort of picture in my mind... Can we speak to Moses?" I have a sudden need to know. "Can we phone from here?"

The two Police officers glance at each other. Will speaks before they reply. "We're only going to imagine all sorts of awful stuff. It would be better just to know as soon as possible. Please."

"I am not sure we can..." starts Tomo.

"Look, you questioned us and clearly didn't believe us. You arrested us – wrongly – and we've been dragged down by the press ever since. Don't you think you owe us a couple of favours?" I nod in agreement.

Tomo's eyes pass between the pair of us. "I will phone the Chief Inspector." He stands and leaves the room.

After a minute or so of rigid silence Officer Kugara mutters, "Perhaps the coffee?"

I sip absently until Tomo's return, mobile in hand. He touches the screen and places it on the table in front of us. "Mr Mason and Mrs Woodlove can hear you now, sir."

I expect it to be Visser, but Moses' steady voice speaks, "Holly? William? Are you there?"

"Yes, we're here."

"So sorry I am to have found this – to have to tell you. They were good people."

"We know, Moses..." I answer. "Moses, I'm sure it won't be nice to hear but please can you tell us what you think happened. It can't be any worse than we are imagining."

"I cannot know all, some I guess."

"Moses, we trust your guesses more than what the police call facts," says Will.

There's a pause and I wonder if we've lost the connection but it seems like Moses is just deciding where to start. "When I see your photos, I fear. I go straight to the rhino. Sorry, I am, I did not use my eyes properly on the first day... There was sand in the air and we think to search for a Defender. I only check poacher shots. I assume jackal and vulture start to eat, I did not examine... Yesterday I find lion teeth marks on the bones, just like I see lion spoor in your photos."

"Lions?" The skin on my arms prickles.

"Yes, Holly, I know I say they do not come away from the herds. I am sorry, Moses not know all." There's another long pause before he continues. "So, I think myself lion and search for a place to shelter... to eat... After some hours I find cloth and the... bones in shelter under thorn bushes. Also I find fresh spoor. I follow the trail for some miles. It seem like I follow two lion then only one. Lucky for Moses he is cautious and look behind. One lion try to hunt me. He and his friend I soon put right."

"What do you mean?"

"Bang. I shoot. Old lions with bad teeth, thrown out of pride, not fast for hunting, live by scavenging or easy prey. The most dangerous a desperate animal is. One time before I hear about this at Etosha many years ago. A man sleeps on a bench by one of the lighted water holes you see from the rest camp. Old lion jumps low fence and takes him." I'm not sure if this revelation makes me feel better or not. It wasn't the lions' fault. He makes one of those tongue clicking noises and takes an audible breath. "I am sorry. Maybe my instructions were not good. I never mean them to drive so far."

Will glances towards me, but I let him answer. "No Moses, I heard you tell them. I'm sure they knew they were only meant to go as far as that sloping rock. Maybe they didn't see the Rockjumper bird so they went further. It's the only thing we can think of."

"Yes, maybe. There is always another place when you are searching."

"Moses..." My voice is low. I'm not sure I want to know the answer but I have to ask. "How do you think it happened – at the rhino – could you tell from the photos?"

Moses is slow to reply. "William, do you want to know this also?"

"Yes, Moses, please..."

"This is only my guess, but... I think Benjamin and Anna mean to get out of the car just for a moment. They leave wide the doors and walk round to where the rhino was open, where the lions had been feeding. The lions must have been close by, maybe resting in the shade. One lion attacks Benjamin. Probably he never sees it coming. It drags him, but then it lets go. There are footprints there. I think Anna hits the lion with binoculars – today policemen find with metal detector the binoculars close by. Benjamin stands up, moves towards Anna, but then second lion catches her and first lion knocks Benjamin back over. After that, there is no photo... I think brave they both are and fight for each other..."

"Thank you Moses," I croak, fighting back more tears, "but why would the lions bother to attack humans when there was a whole dead rhino to feed on?"

"Maybe they only attack because of the rhino. If hyena come, lions would chase to protect their meal – would kill if they catch. Maybe lions expect just to chase off, but people are slow. It was... a very unlucky thing."

"Moses," says Will in a voice which is hardly any clearer, "where was the place that the lions dragged them to? It wasn't up the hillside next to the second dry river bed, was it? Only that was the way we walked to look for them." I know what Will is thinking. He's wondering if we did hear them call.

"No, it was along the edge of the plain. Maybe lucky you went other way, not end up being hunted too..."

"But maybe they were..."

Moses interrupts before Will gets properly started, "No William, there was nothing you could do. Old cat does not carry live prey. You might have passed close in your car, but they were already gone. The persons were gone. Only meat remain."

I need to keep hold of that thought – the persons went quickly. Whatever may have happened to the 'meat', that was something else. "Thanks Moses for being brave enough to tell us everything," I say in between sniffs.

"It is nothing for me to tell a story. It is you now who brave has to be. But, Holly, this policeman tell me an amazing story, that you are taken by the poachers, but you trick them and escape to rescue William. Is it true?"

"It is true, but..."

"Then it is you who should teach me to be brave." There's a pause. We've nothing more to ask. Tomo reaches forward but before his hand touches the phone, Moses speaks again. "When my first wife die with birth, the nights, very long they were. Remember that you are not dead also..." Then further away we hear him say, "There, I have said all." And the line goes dead.

Tomo pockets the phone and sighs. I notice moisture in the corners of Officer Kugara's eyes. "Can we help you with more?" she asks. "You may stay here as long as you wish... or go now. We will take you back to the hotel..."

"We'd rather walk." I glance towards Will realising that I've spoken for him.

He nods. "Is there a back door we can go out of to avoid the press?"

"We can take you to the side fire exit. You are sure you do not want to go in the car?" says Kugara.

"Yes."

We're led round a corner and along a busy corridor. Several officers and other staff move to the side or duck into offices as we pass. No one makes eye contact.

"You know the way?" says Tomo. We nod, but I notice he is still watching as we turn right onto Robert Mugabe Avenue. Side-by-side we pace, faster and faster, as if speed will somehow leave the emptiness behind. By the time we pass the curved angularity of the Independence museum we're almost jogging and beginning to pant in the rising heat.

"Not the hotel – not yet," gasps Will. "How about the Botanical gardens?" We've peered at a corner of them from the hotel veranda but that's as far as we've got.

"Okay." We follow a sign to the left.

Namibia is a desert country and its botanical garden is no different. Released from the urge to get somewhere, we wander aimlessly through the vegetation displays until Will flops down onto a shaded bench beside a quiver tree. We're surrounded by a grove of these oddities, each resembling a sprig of oversized desiccated broccoli. Desiccated... something with all the life sucked out of it. I reach over to the stout trunk and place a flat hand against its knobbly bark in silent solidarity.

From inside a nearby thorn bush a bird begins a flutey warble. The song seems vaguely familiar. Will and I exchange a wild glance as the chestnut-sided form of a Damara Rockjumper hops to the uppermost branch.

"Little bastard," I yell, scooping up a handful of gravel, and launching it at the bush. Of course, I miss. The bird's head moves from side to side as if confused by this unusual reaction. I fall onto my knees and fire another salvo – no closer, but this time it takes the hint and flits out of sight. I continue to launch increasingly frantic volleys of grit into the bush. "Piss... off... haven't... you... done... enough?!"

"Does it make it feel better?" says Will thudding onto the path beside me.

"Yup."

We sling futile stones into an inoffensive bush after a long-gone bird until our immediate supply of ammunition runs out. Finger nails running through sandy soil rather than rough pebbles causes me to look down. Either side of me are two dark brown arcs – the same beside Will.

"What are we doing?"

Will's eyes follow mine. "Making a mess by the look of it."

"How can they just be... gone?" He lifts his shoulders in a slow desolate shrug. "Why didn't they stay where Moses told them?" I sob.

"I wish I knew," he says, rising to his feet. He stretches out a hand for me to pull myself up. "Maybe we should go back to the hotel... before the local wildlife suffers too much."

We scrape with our feet, attempting to spread the remaining stones over our stupidity, but a scar is a lot easier to create than it is to heal.

CHAPTER 30

Come on Hols, keep it together, you need to do this.' The voice inside my head is Ben's. I take a deep breath and press the final digit. Jill picks up almost instantly.

"Hello, Woodlove residence." Ben's Mum's posh telephone voice normally makes me crack up, but humour is in cryogenic storage, possibly never to awaken.

"Jill, it's Holly."

"...Graham, it's Holly." Her parent's sense has heard the tone in my voice, just like I hear the rising panic in hers. "We'll put you on speaker. Is there news?"

At least she's left me no room for procrastination. "There is... he's dead... I'm... I'm sorry, I don't know how else to say it." There's a low moan from the other end of the line. I plough on because... because I have no idea how to do this. "He was dead right from the start... it was a lion attack... before we even knew they were missing. They would have been found sooner but their car was stolen and there was the storm – everyone thought they had driven off somewhere..." At the other end of the line high and low pitched sobs restart my own tears. I don't say any more, I just wait for it to end.

Eventually there's a low sniff, "Holly, are you still there?"

"Yes."

"You said 'they', so the other girl is dead too?"

"Yes, Anna as well..." My husband... and my best friend... I try to explain what Moses said had happened, but I'm not sure I'm making any sense... and then Jill asks about the body. Her wail is still bouncing round my skull as I press disconnect.

I lie back on the bed, immediately roll off and stare out of the window, plonk down in the chair, switch the telly on and then off again; only one thing for it... I pick up my guitar... but even that seems wrong. A guitar is a sensual instrument – you hug it, you stroke the strings, you make musical love with it. I don't want sensual... and love – where is that now? I want something cold and aloof, something I can beat with rage or lean on to weep.

A thought occurs, and I pad barefoot along carpeted corridors and down polished wooden stairs. The door to the Jazz bar is closed, but not locked. I slip inside the empty room and onto the stool of the grand piano. Once upon a time I passed a grade five exam on this thing... but then the guitar took over... I place my fingers on the keys and hit a chord – nothing. Another – nothing. Of course there is sound – a beautiful tone from the instrument, I'm sure – but I feel nothing. Try a minor key – ahh. After a few minutes I have a chord. I force myself to play with it, running up and down with the right hand, experimenting with different bass notes. I start to hum and with it comes a tear, another chord, and a snatch of melody. Soon my fingers are weeping phrase after mournful phrase into the keyboard. I try to find words to my 'la's but they're not there. It's too soon. I have no idea how I feel. How do you describe absence? How do you define 'lack'? How can you put your finger on nothing?

A sniff from somewhere over by the door brings me to an abrupt halt. Will is slumped at one of the tables, his own grief pouring down his face.

"How long have you been there?"

"Long enough. What's it called?"

"I don't know. I'm just messing about. There's way more than could be in one song – unless it's fifteen minutes long."

"Why shouldn't it be?" He pulls a key card from his back pocket. "You might be wanting this. You left your door wide open and this still in the holder. Don't worry, I don't think anything's missing."

I take it from his outstretched hand. "Thanks. Have you rung the in-laws yet?" His wince answers my question.

"Me too. Oh Will, what are we going to do?"

CHAPTER 31

In the desolate hours of a pre-funeral dawn a few weeks later, the words finally come:

Working title – Death Suite?

Part 1 – Gone

How? Oh how? Oh how? How can you be gone?

I stretch out a hand in the darkness, but only find coldness
in the space where you used to lie.
I turn round to tell you a story about how my day went,
but only the wall can reply.

How? Oh how? Oh how? How can you be gone?

Sometimes in a crowd I will see you – I rush for a clear view:
it's always another someone.
I pull your shirt close, take a deep breath, it smells just as always.
How is it that you can be gone?
How can you be gone?

How can you... how can you be gone?

Part 2 – Guilty Secret

I've got a secret: you were not perfect.
And if I'm honest you could bug me a lot.
I've got a secret: you could be thoughtless.
Sometimes you didn't understand me at all.

Can I say all these things out loud? (Is it allowed?)
Or should I keep all my guilt down inside? (I'm down inside...)

I don't always think how everyone expects me to think.
I don't always say what everyone expects me to say.
And I don't always do what everyone expects me to do,
but that doesn't mean I didn't love you.
That doesn't mean I didn't love you.

I've got a secret: I was not perfect.
Sometimes I wondered about somebody else.
I've got a secret: I was too lazy.
Simpler to whinge than try to make it alright.

Can I say all these things out loud? (Is it allowed?)
Or should I keep all my guilt down inside? (I'm down inside)

I don't always think how everyone expects me to think.
I don't always say what everyone expects me to say.
And I don't always do what everyone expects me to do,
but that doesn't mean I didn't love you.
That doesn't mean I didn't love you.

Part 3 – Good Grief

I should celebrate your life,
but all I want to do is cry...

You'd say, "Don't be a dope.
Think of me fondly.
Good grief girl don't mope."

"Don't dwell on what you've lost.
Got to move forward.
Don't yearn for compost!"

Good grief, I want to celebrate...
Good grief, not just commemorate...
Good grief, but really celebrate
your life, your life, your life...
Good grief, I want to celebrate...
Good grief, not just commemorate...
Good grief, but really celebrate
the love and the times that we had.

I should celebrate,
I should celebrate your life,
I should celebrate your life,
but all I want to do is cry...

Three linked songs, with a running time of over eleven minutes. The label will probably have a fit or ask me to change my name to Holly Floyd. Still, maybe if it's dire, everyone will go easy on me, given the circumstances. They say that Ben's life insurance means I'll never have to sing again if I don't want to. Of course I want to... I'm just not sure how marketable the 'teary widow' look is these days. I suppose it's nice to have a safety net. It would be a lot nicer to have a husband...

Through the window I notice plant pots suddenly highlighted against the lawn by light from what must be the kitchen window. I remove the headphones, but in my music room I can hear nothing from the rest of the house. Ben had it specially insulated for exactly the opposite reason: 'I know you love your music, but I can't listen to the same four bars fifty times.'

The door swings open to reveal a tousled and boxer-shorted Toby. "You alright, Prickle?"

"Can't sleep."

"Fancy some toast?" He never seems to have grown out of the teenage munchies.

"Butter and runny honey?"

"What else... One slice or two?"

"Just one, please."

"Worried you won't fit into your dress?" He retreats under the double salvo of two fingers and an out-stuck tongue. I return to my laptop, attach the mp3 file to an email, and send it to David as 'unnamed suite of 3 songs about grief'. Normally the title of a song is obvious from the lyrics, but groups of songs I find much trickier. That's probably why the first album ended up being called Fusion – not very inspired.

It'll be the first time I've seen David since... since I came home. Everyone will be there, peering at me.

THE HEARSE ARRIVES at precisely ten-thirty. Dad and Toby ride with me in the attendant black limo. Dad is subdued, sneaking frequent concerned glances in my direction. Toby gabbles constantly on borderline inappropriate topics: 'What do you think the etiquette is for getting off with people at wakes?' 'I wonder if your favourite liaison officer will be there, Dad?' 'If that Phil Boots turns up, I might just push him into the grave first.' We ignore him, just as he ignores Dad's silence and my petulance – everyone has their own way of dealing with it all.

Even though it's a Tuesday, a small crowd has gathered on the opposite side of the road to the church. Press? I've vowed to myself that I'll stay calm, whatever, but I can feel a rant rising. They have been asked to give us some privacy!

It seems to have been wall-to-wall coverage since I arrived back in the UK. Dad has been trying to hide it from me – telly flicked off as

I walk into the room, his normal Times nowhere to be found – but in my bleaker moments I can't help surfing the news sites. Rather than drawing everything to a close, the Namibian Police's statement exonerating us merely sent the media frenzy to new heights. And when all the animal attack angles had been exhausted, someone hired a helicopter to check out the wrecked Defenders in the desert. 'Woodlove in poacher shootout?' restarted it all last week.

As we pull up alongside ornate railings, my dress is gaining fingernail marks just above the knees where I'm clinging onto calmness with both hands. My grip releases abruptly and the waterproofness of my mascara is tested earlier than expected. A hand-painted banner appears in front of the coats and umbrellas: 'We're thinking of you Holly.'

"That's nice," says Dad, handing over the first tissue from his suit pocket.

The Woodloves' limo has already arrived and side by side we follow the casket down the aisle. I keep my eyes steady on this ridiculous lump of polished oak and brass. Ben would have preferred recycled cardboard, although, in truth, a small packing box would probably have been sufficient. But if his mother needs this to force the image of that reality from her head, I'm happy to go along with it. Once the coffin is lowered onto trestles at the front, she stands a large photo upon it: Ben's graduation from Veterinary College. I guess that must be their proudest moment.

The vicar is as warm and caring as she seemed on her visit. You could almost believe she knew him. We open with a song of her suggestion – something I vaguely remember from school assemblies. Graham gives an emotional eulogy to his son, although I don't quite recognise the Ben he's talking about. We pray to a God who even if he does exist, I'm not sure I want anything to do with. As we process outside for the burial to the strains of Keane, I begin to wish I'd insisted on more of his favourites. But I've never done this before and you can't ask for a second go...

I stand at the head of Ben's grave with a handful of soil and decide I must... even if I offend his parents. "Ben was many things, but for me, above everything, he was funny. He used to make me laugh – even sometimes when I didn't want to." I hear murmurs of agreement. "He loved to mess about and tell a joke... Didn't he?" Many nods. "He wouldn't want us all standing around looking glum;

he'd be making a joke about it; saying something daft and inappropriate, like... 'When I said I wanted to see wild Africa up close and personal this wasn't... exactly..." I fight hard to keep the waterworks at bay, "...what I had in mind." There's a smattering of sniggers. "So if you want... when you say goodbye... think of your favourite joke of his... and say it out loud if you like." I step forward and gradually rotate my hand to let the earth fall. "What kind of motorbike does Santa ride? A Holly Davidson." In my mind his voice continues with the smutty follow-up line, but that's for my memories only. I step back and glance towards Jill. She doesn't raise her eyes, but steps resolutely towards the edge, scoops and lets the dust fall. Her bottom lip trembles and shoulders quiver. Her free hand clenches and somewhere in the pit of my stomach a vomit of panic starts to rise that she is about to turn and deck me.

Graham steps up, steadies her arm, and lets his own farewell fall. He pauses for a few seconds and then in an increasingly loud voice, says: "I tried to reset my password the other day to 'Arsenal defence' – the computer said it was too weak." The laughter is louder. Most of the guests know of the father and son football rivalry.

From then on they come thick and fast. Just about everyone remembers something and for a moment his spirit seems really close. Jill nudges my shoulder with hers and whispers through teary eyes, "Thank you – he was like this, wasn't he?"

I nod, and then seeing Toby step forward, whisper back, "I apologise in advance for whatever my brother says next."

He doesn't disappoint: "Two nuns were sitting in a bath..."

"HOLLY, DARLING. HOW AWFUL." I'm treated to a gin and aftershave kiss on both cheeks. "You... you seem even taller than usual," says David, taking a step backwards.

"I've been trying to keep my back straight... Someone," I glance to the corner of the room where Will is hemmed in by two veterinary nurses, "pointed out that I often slouch."

"Mm." David's eyes return from where he's followed mine. "It does give you a certain confidence. I like it." He takes my arm and steers me out of the squeeze of the function room, into the less oppressive hotel lobby. "Sweetie," he whispers, "I got your latest – very emotional. Burning the midnight oil?"

"It's hard to sleep at the moment."

"Of course." From his tone, it's clear his brain hasn't registered any of the implications that might have, and presses on regardless. "I did mention that book chap to Rory and I think he's melting; already talking about rushing 'Dur-dup' out as a single, so one chalk to you... but a personal visit would be..."

"David. It's my husband's funeral," I interrupt.

"I know darling, and I'm..." This time, the conciliatory tone is not going to work.

"Have you read the lyrics of 'I'm Hurting But You Don't Care'?"

"Sweetie..." His bottom lip protrudes like a disapproving costume drama aunt.

"So everything else can wait... At least for a little while. This music is welling up out of what's happening to me. I can't rush it; I have to live it..."

"Holly, there's... someone who wants a word." Will is framed by the heavy panelled doors. Behind him, the queue for the buffet winds round throngs of plate and drink balancers.

It's alright, David and I have just finished." I unwind my arm and retreat towards the door. As I reach Will, I glance back, "Don't worry David, when I get to the last song I'm sure it'll be obvious." He stares, slightly aghast, like a sports fisherman who's just realised the shark they hooked is pulling the boat.

Now, finally, I can speak to Will. It's been odd to be so close, so intense, and then nothing but a couple of texts for two weeks –we've both had our own horrible stuff to deal with. He's wearing a dark green tie. I'm glad it isn't black. There's something disconcertingly morbid about a piece of clothing worn only for funerals.

"The 'someone' is only me," says Will, once we are submerged back into camouflaging chatter. "Does that guy have any idea when to give it a rest?"

"He means well. I suppose it's better that he's too focused rather than uninterested." A tiny smile quivers at the corners of Will's mouth. "What?"

"You always look for the positives in people."

"I don't know about that; not everyone – Toby was saying that if Phil Boots turned up he was going to shove him into the grave and frankly, I couldn't fault the idea."

A waiter appears in front of us with a tray of glasses. I choose a 'with', Will a 'without'.

"Have you seen some of the wild theories they've been making up about what happened to us in the desert?" I continue between sips.

"And none of them are close to being as mad as what actually happened... Are they still pestering you for comments?"

"Daily."

"I won't say anything."

"I know." We lapse into silent solidarity. I don't really mind if some of what happened does come out... eventually. But right now the focus should be on the ones who didn't return. "I finally wrote some words for that piano thing... in the middle of last night."

"You do look like you've been missing some sleep." The concern in his eyes dissipates any annoyance I might have about the ineffectiveness of this morning's make-up.

I nod. "Maybe I should try some tablets?"

"Perhaps not with a small malt though."

"No, perhaps not." I almost smile. If anyone overhears, they won't understand.

Two of Ben's many cousins vacate a table to join the queue, mouthing the usual platitudes as they pass. We take their places. It's not until I sit that I realise how uncomfortable these shoes are. I slip them off and rub my feet together under the table.

"Are you happy with it, then?"

"What?"

"The piano song."

"I'm not sure 'happy' is the right word. I haven't been able to sing it through without my voice cracking yet... and it actually ended up being three songs linked together."

"Fifteen minutes?" Will raises an eyebrow remembering his suggestion.

"No, more like eleven and a half... but still not very 'pop'."

"Good. What's it called?"

I draw breath through my teeth. "Well, that's the problem – I don't know. The three parts are called 'Gone', 'Guilty Secret', and 'Good Grief' but I can't pin down an overall name. I've written 'Death Suite' at the top of the page, but that's a bit..."

"...Brutal," Will finishes. Sometimes he surprises me with an insightful word. I hope it doesn't show. I mentally kick myself for allowing what society would believe of a muscle-bound carpenter to seep into my own thoughts – that way leads to 'Neanderthal'."

"Any suggestions?" I add in a rush. He appears completely oblivious of my internal worries.

"Mmm. You've got three songs all beginning with 'G' making up your 'death suite'. Could you do something with that?"

As I take a pondering sip of white wine I realise that I'm talking shop, just like David wanted to. But it's different – it's on my terms. "Three piece suite... No, I'm not serious."

Will is obviously part way through a thought of his own and hardly registers my suggestion. "3G is a phone thing, isn't it?" I nod. Our eyes stray to one corner of the room where assorted sons and daughters of family and friends are glued to their smartphones. "How about 'Death by 3G'?" I can tell by his voice that he isn't totally serious.

"Sounds a bit Agatha Christie."

"Or like a techno-themed cake for that table."

As I turn back, I notice Jill sitting quietly with Graham a few yards away. Her head swivels away just before our eyes meet. Odd.

"If all else fails you could 'Google' it." Will wrenches my attention back to the conversation.

"Google what?"

"I don't know, something like, 'phrases with sweet in them'. Might give you some ideas."

"Go on then, do you have yours with you? Why should they be the only ones?" I say, inclining my head towards the teenagers.

A few seconds of tapping and Will pushes his phone across the table. The second one immediately catches my attention: whisper sweet nothings – 'suite nothing'? It clicks with me... but I'm not sure other people would understand what I meant... Sweetheart, short and sweet, sweet and sour. Oh. My eyes take in the next phrase and its origin. Perfect...

"Will, you're a genius – look."

"'Parting is such sweet sorrow' – from Romeo and Juliet," he reads. "Suite Sorrow, then?" I notice as he raises his head a slight wetness in his eyes.

"Got to be. We make a good team, eh?"

An almost embarrassed expression crosses his face. He gapes like a goldfish. "Holly, I need to ask you something... I'm not sure what you'll think... Next week, at Anna's funeral, I'd... I'd like you to sit on the front row with... the family if that's okay with you." He stumbles on without giving me a chance to answer. "My Mum isn't really well enough to travel... and they've been in Chicago so long they hardly ever met her... so I haven't really got... and I've already asked her Mum and Dad and they're fine with it – you were her best friend... and..."

"Stop." I put a comforting hand over his. "Of course I will."

CHAPTER 32

Will has learned from Ben's funeral. As I pull into the crematorium car park, I see that the majority of other mourners have noted the new instructions on the reissued invitations.

I tug at the bottom of my dress as I step from the car. It's shorter than I would have liked, and sleeveless, but it had to be this one. The sky is hazy blue and already the day promises to be one of the warmest of the year. I make sure all my straps are straight using the car window as a mirror. At least this thing is relatively cool. Anna would be giggling at my discomfort.

I join the edge of the crowd milling around the entrance and wait with everyone else, in the full heat of the sun, for the previous service to finish. Is there anyone I know? Craning my neck only seems to elicit a few 'look, she's here' nudges rather than smiles of greeting.

"Holly?" I'm touched on the shoulder and turn to see a stick-thin dark-bobbed woman staring diffidently. "Remember me: Paula?" she says.

"Of course," I say, although in truth I might have struggled with the name, "You did biology with Anna, didn't you?"

"I'm a teacher now."

"Cool. Primary kids?"

"Yes, year ones." I'm not surprised. Any bigger and they'd knock her over. Paula has gone for a purple trouser suit. She catches me inspecting it. "I think it's really nice the way her William asked us all not to wear black."

"And impressive that he managed to persuade Anna's parents.

Still, they've always treated him like a son-in-law rather than just a boyfriend."

"I... I was sorry to hear about your Ben. I knew him a little at uni. In fact, I sort of fancied him, but then he went out with you and..."

The hearse arrives with perfect timing to prevent any further awkward revelations. Will climbs out of the following limo and holds the door for Anna's mother, sister and father. Anna's sister, Ellen, has always been an object of curiosity. The family resemblance is obvious and yet, where in Anna all the features led to something that was visually breath-taking, with Ellen... it just doesn't – at least not to my eyes.

Will spots me immediately and I'm beckoned over. Somewhere he has found a kingfisher blue suit and an even louder tie.

"Are they birds of paradise?" I ask, taking in the silken magnificence.

"Yup. They were always her favourite – although we never did get to..." he trails off with a catch in his voice.

"It's amazing – you know she'd have loved it." He nods, blinks several times and takes a deep breath.

"And look at you. I wondered if you'd wear that one."

"Anna loved her florals." I surreptitiously tug at the dress again but it's as low as it will go.

After hugging each of the Templetons, it's time to follow another coffin. This is a much less ornate affair but no one is paying it any attention. Instead, as we enter the chapel, Anna smiles, grins, and pouts from a series of projected pictures, leaping randomly through her life: a bath-time baby, an advertising campaign launch, one of many brownies, a teenager dressed up for a Halloween party... Oh gosh, that must be from the night of their first kiss. Will completely forgets to walk for the five seconds the image is displayed. The queue behind him shuffles to an unexpected halt. When we reach the front row and he turns, I see wet lines down his cheeks. I mean to sit next to Ellen, on the far side of Anna's parents from Will, but they leave an empty seat next to him and I have to take it.

"Don't forget to breathe," I say as I sit. A long slow sigh escapes.

Anna's Dad, her sister and a work colleague all say tributes which have me reaching for the tissues, but when Will grips the lectern and spends what seems like minutes doing nothing except staring up at the changing images, I lose control of my shoulders too.

A photo of an evening-dressed Anna gripping his tuxedoed arm is his cue: "Everyone always told me that Anna was gorgeous. And look, she was... but I only ever saw that as a minor thing. I think that's part of what she liked about me... What I saw was a woman who hated to be judged by her looks, but always posed for a photograph; who was passionate about important things like conservation and equality and less important things like fashion and finding small brown birds she'd never seen before..." His voice cracks and I know exactly which bird he's thinking of. With some effort he restarts, "...a woman who loved and was so easy to love back; a woman who could drive me mad pestering to get her own way..." A recent picture of Anna appears, lying on grass with her magnificent mane spread over the ground like an advertising shot. "...a woman with the most incredible hair and, wow, did it moult everywhere... In other words, a totally real, non-perfect person with all the great things and little annoyances that we all have..." He pauses, eyes scanning the congregation as if for dissenters. Of course, all he sees are tears of agreement. "So, after... when we're at the hall, we're going to have a time of storytelling. Anything you like, good or bad, funny or sad – but it has to be about Anna. No pressure, say something or just listen." He glances towards the screen again. It's a picture of her sitting on his knee at a wedding reception or some other posh do. "Anna, I'm gonna miss you..." He dashes back to his seat, catching the minister slightly off-guard. During the pause, his hand falls into mine and we grip tightly as if it might squeeze out the emptiness.

THE COMMUNITY HALL has a much homelier feel than Ben's hotel. The food has been prepared mostly by the Templetons themselves and it's pour your own drink from the numerous bottles provided. I limit myself to a driver's small white wine at the start and then swap to juice. By the time the storytelling begins, the buffet has been stripped and tongues have been well lubricated. Will starts it off with the Halloween party and all manner of tales flood out: precocious Anna embarrassing her parents; fluffing her lines in her first school play; winning an unexpected order with an amazing sales pitch; tipping gravy down a councillor's front whilst waitressing and on and on... So much so, that I'm having trouble getting my word in. Will throws me a half smile the second time I'm interrupted after one word. Never mind, it's therapeutic just listening to all the love and letting the warmth seep in.

"Holly, did you have one?" Ellen's assistance catches me off-guard and I stumble over the first few words.

"Yeah... It was... in our second year at Uni, I think. It was blazing hot like today and we'd persuaded one of the guys we knew to take us to Skegness. We were sunbathing on the beach when Anna's phone pings and suddenly she's all excited and asks if we'd like to see something amazing. You know what she's like. We knew we'd be pestered to death if we didn't agree, so we drive down the coast into the middle of nowhere, turn a corner and there are cars everywhere and dozens of guys carrying telescopes and binoculars. Everyone is wearing green and even though there's not a cloud in the sky, half of them have waterproof coats and wellies. Anna drags us out of the car and asks the first complete stranger if 'it' is still showing and where we should go. We're pointed down a path between some sand dunes. As we walk, people coming the other way raise their eyebrows and make comments such as 'it's a beauty' and 'crippling views ten minutes ago'.

"We arrive to find a horseshoe of about fifty people – virtually all men, surrounding one side of a small group of bushes. The rest of us hang back, not quite sure what to do, but Anna creeps forward. Just as she reaches them someone shouts, 'Second sallow from the left, three feet up.' Every lens turns to that spot like iron filings to a magnet. With the naked eye I could just about make out some tiny bird flitting amongst the leaves, but that's not why I remember this. Imagine it: fifty twitchers with their scopes, cameras and camouflage jackets and Anna in fuchsia hot pants and a bikini top." There're sniggers from all around the hall. A smile plays on my lips. "And she's not just staring at it, she's discussing with the guys round her whether they think it's the same bird as somewhere else and if such and such a feather means it's less than a year old: using their lingo, like she was one of them – I suppose she was one of them." My smile turns rueful. "Of course that didn't stop them fawning over her dreadfully... but guys always did that. She shone so brightly the rest of us might as well have been invisible."

"But he can see you now, can he dear?"

My head twists towards the elderly woman who has just spoken. I'm not exactly sure who she is – a great aunt or something. My forehead furrows. I'm not sure that last bit came out exactly how I meant it but... "Sorry?" I ask.

"Sitting in her place, holding his hand, wearing your short skirt, before she's even cold in her grave – it's a disgrace."

"Wha..?" I feel heat rush into my cheeks and my bottom lip starts to tremble. I can't focus on anything except the woman's accusing eyes. "It... it's not that," I stammer, "It's just you... you don't know what we've been through." I struggle to my feet and rush for the toilets, fling open the door and lean heavily on the sink, tears dripping onto the porcelain. Is that what everyone thinks of me?

The walls must be cardboard thin because even above my own sniffs I hear Will's raised voice. "Bloody hell, Enid, Holly only sat on the front row because I asked her to, because she was Anna's best friend and because none of my family could make it and I needed some support." I hold in a sob so I can hear more easily. "And why is she wearing that dress – the one she's clearly uncomfortable in? She's wearing it because Anna bought it for her. Anna, bless her, wasn't always the best at buying presents people liked, but Holly wore it anyway... because that's what you do for your friends."

I'm caught between being upset at what was said and pleased by the way Will has defended me. I stare at the woman in the mirror and wonder what the hell is going on in her head. Sounds of chairs scraping across the wood block floor are soon followed by a tap at the door. "Holly, can I come in?" Will's voice sounds strained.

"Is that a good idea?" I say, wondering what Enid will say if we appear from the toilets together.

"Oh fuck them all," he says, pushing his way in anyway. "Like you said, they don't understand. How could they?" He slumps against the wall, accidentally starting a hand drier in the process. It runs for a few seconds before grinding to an oil-deprived halt.

"Will, I'm really sorry. I never meant to cause a fuss. I... I don't really know what I said wrong."

"Why the hell are you apologising? The woman is a deluded old troll who puts far too much stock in the tabloids."

"Careful, the walls are quite thin," I say in a lowered voice. "I could hear most of what you said out there."

"Really?" he says, raising his voice to a bellow "Deluded old troll!"

"Will, don't," I say, even as it almost forces a grin from me. "It'll only make more fuss."

He takes a deep breath, visibly forcing his frustration to subside. "Anyway, like you once said, she's put two and two together and made twenty-three."

Mmm, I did say that, didn't I? Except I seem to remember that sum was much closer to being accurate. "What have the tabloids been saying this time?"

"Ben's funeral report by you-know-who mentioned how much time we spent together at the wake."

"Daaah," I clench my fists and stretch my arms down as far as they will go. "Why can't they cut us some slack? Leave us to grieve in peace."

"Because everyone likes to gossip." Will's tone leaves no doubt as to what he thinks of that part of human nature.

I wipe my cheeks with my hands, "Which is exactly why I should go. Today is all about Anna – and it was really special – you made it special for everyone. It shouldn't be spoilt and the easiest thing is if I go."

Will eyes are moist again. "You shouldn't have to."

"Maybe, but it's the easiest thing. It's quite a drive anyway." He opens his mouth for further protest, but I put a finger to my lips, "I'm going to go, okay?"

"Okay. Come here then." We hug... for far too long. Well past the point where Enid would be tutting. But we both need a hug and who else is there? As we part, he stares down with concerned eyes. "I suppose you heard what I said about the dress too..."

I snort, "As usual, Mr Mason, it was a blunt but accurate assessment."

I squeeze past and as the door closes, he calls after me, "Don't be a stranger. Come and see me whenever you need a chat."

"You too."

THE DRIVE HOME just serves to simmer my frustrations like a stew gaining flavour. As I pull into our road my phone pings and when I'm stopped on the driveway, the contents of the text flashes them to boiling point: 'Studio booked for next week but Abbey Rd no longer available – call me. David.'

Why can't I catch a break? Slam – car door. Why are some people so mean? Stomp – driveway. Why can't they leave me alone? Rattle – letter box after the front door receives the same treatment.

Why can't they cut me some slack? Fling – handbag arcs through the open lounge door to explode on the sofa. I carry on through to my inner sanctum and reach out a hand to rip my acoustic from its stand. Now I understand what pole-axing a guitar through an amp stack is all about... Instead, I freeze, fingers on the neck and breathe calmness along my arm. Then, like the parent of a screaming baby, I lift it delicately and cradle it in my arms – it's not its fault.

Some Slack

Someone told me yesterday,
all the hurtful things you say.
Let me tell you right away:
It is not okay.
Come and stand here in my shoes,
let me hear you still abuse...
You might find that you would choose
a different way.

Never asked for this – no, not at all.
No instructions or the wherewithal.
But somehow I'm expected to be perfect,
when no one quite agrees on what that means,
but, naturally, they'd do so much better if it were them...

So cut me some slack, you don't know about the context.
Cut me some slack, you don't know – it might be you next.
Cut me some slack,
take it all back,
re-find the knack of thinking before you're speaking.
Cut me some slack (x4)

Making it up as I go along.
No idea what or for how long.
But somehow I'm expected to just know things
as if I was quite skilled at reading minds.
But, naturally, they'd have worked it out first if it were them...

So cut me some slack, you don't know about the context.
Cut me some slack, you don't know – it might be you next.
Cut me some slack,
take it all back,
re-find the knack of thinking before you're speaking.

Cut me some slack
Won't you cut me, cut me some slack.

CHAPTER 33

In fact, the studio downgrade makes it a lot easier for me to stay in contact with Will. Although much of his work is done at client properties, his lock-up-come-workshop base is only ten minutes' walk away.

Some people, particularly the technicians, seem able to live in the studio. They work through the night, constantly fiddling with this reverb effect or that snare sound, existing on fried chicken and curry – and, yup, in the end they make it sound great, but I can't sit for hours in front of screens and dials. Give me a guitar and an idea and I can lose myself composing until a week next Tuesday, but not recording. I'm not for a moment saying that there's not a skill or art in recording, I've experienced some great moments when that unexpected sound or new little riff makes all the difference, but for me it's the afterward. I suppose like with making cakes, I'm primarily a baker rather than an icer. So when it gets down to real minutiae, I tend to leave them to it and go for a wander – catch some sunlight, see some green, or, more often than not at the moment, wander over to Will's workshop.

He's not always there, but when he is, I enjoy just watching him work. Not the power tool stuff so much, but the hand finishing. The care that goes into each tap of the chisel, stroke of the plane, rub of the paper. I never realised he was an artist too.

Today, he's standing over a thick rough plank swinging what I'm told is an adze between outstretched legs. "It's what they used before someone invented planes. It's a bloody good way of chopping off your own feet if you're not careful." I had thought the rigger boots weren't his usual style... "But the scalloped effect you get is very 'in' if you want that historical look."

"What's it going to be?"

"The mother of all island units – only eight more of these to go."

The conversation lapses into brooding, as it often does, but the smell of freshly cut wood and the rhythmical scrape of tools has become a familiar comfort.

"Enjoying the view, Holly?" I haven't heard Will's business partner, Jack, arrive and his whisper in my ear makes me jump. Grinning broadly, he deposits supplies on top of a nearby rack and begins to sort them. Jack must be twenty years older than Will and stocky-strong in that way many older tradesmen become. He was the original 'master' to Will's apprentice but these days they're equals.

"Quit teasing," says Will without breaking rhythm.

"Oh, I wouldn't be blaming her – fine figure of a man you are young William. If I wasn't as straight as a plumb..."

"You'd do what?" laughs Will.

"Gaze at you during my lunch break." Jack's eyes dance with old school humour.

I try to remember how to do alluring and cast him a glance. "Jack, you've got it all wrong, I only keep visiting in the hope that one day you'll cast off that boiler suit and show me what you've got."

"Huh, huh, huh," his hearty laugh would work for an amateur Santa. "Now there is a woman with taste..." He turns back to the rack. "...Mind you, Sandra would break your neck."

BANTER OR NOT, Jack's comment has me prickling with uncomfortable thoughts as I sit down for afternoon tea with Jill. This seems to be turning into a weekly ritual: Jill takes the train into London, supposedly to shop, and I catch the tube, but she's rarely carrying anything when I meet her at some pre-arranged cafe. Today it's a tea-room she's been recommended on the main street in Stoke Newington.

"Isn't this lovely?" It is. All old-fashioned drawers, white table cloths and fancy china.

"Yes," I pant, still a little out of breath from my march through the park. I'm not sure she realises what a pain it is to get here on the tube. Still, at least it isn't an Arsenal match day.

Jill orders scones and a pot of tea whilst I go for carrot cake and a latté. Whilst we're waiting, we discuss the practice. The remaining two partners have decided to rename it 'Ben Woodlove Animal Care', which is about the only thing that I have seen cause Jill to smile these days.

"So you're definitely going to let them buy out Ben's quarter?"

I bite my bottom lip with trepidation. This is a tricky subject. "I know you and Graham have decided to keep your money in – and I can understand that – but they don't need me. They've already interviewed for a new partner and she wants a stake, so why not take mine? What do I know about running a vet's?" I reach across the table and squeeze her hand. "You know I loved to see him with the animals but it was very much his thing... I'll always be happy to be their 'rent-a-celebrity' when they need one – assuming that anyone buys the second album, that is."

"You always had very separate careers," Jill acknowledges. "How is the record?"

"It's going okay. I just wish I knew how to finish it. It feels like there's one or maybe two songs missing but I'm not sure what they need to say."

The waitress arrives with our order. As she retreats with an empty tray I see her peer at me over her shoulder. Rumbled.

"Writer's block?" asks Jill, pouring her tea.

"Not exactly. The new songs, they're a bit different from what I've done previously.... At least, not the first one – the single they're rushing out – I wrote that before... But the album, it's far more... personal. The songs have all come out of what happened... with Ben and Anna... and Will. The music sprung out of what I've been living through. Except now I'm..."

"...not really living?" Jill finishes my sentence with exactly the same words I was going to use and I realise I'm not the only one treading water.

ONLY EVER YOU gets its first radio play a few weeks later. The DJs make all the right noises but you can tell they're struggling to know how to pitch it. 'Here's the new one from Holly Woodlove, who was recently involved in that tragedy in Africa' – and then on comes this cheerful piece of girly pop. It jars. I did tell them...

David made a deal with me: no interviews as long as I record the video. I can't face those sorts of questions yet... and they're bound to ask, no matter what they promise is off-limits.

In fact, I barely have any screen time. They go pretty much with my waitress and diner suggestion, but bookend it with shots of me song-writing – misty-eyed and rememberful. It's the easiest bit of acting I've ever done. The actress who plays the 'younger me' is, of course, way prettier than I was at sixteen, but it's all fiction anyway. I comment sarcastically to the make-up artist that it's odd how the extra four inches I've grown since then all appear to have come out of my cup size.

All this means I haven't been to the workshop very often recently and mostly when I have, Will's been out on site, so it's a pleasant surprise when a text arrives during a rehearsal: 'R U in 2nite. Can I cum O? W' I'm getting used to his old school minimalist texting but even so it takes a couple of mildly embarrassed seconds to realise he means 'come round'. I extricate myself as soon as possible and rush home to tidy up and get ready. Of course I don't need to 'get ready' for Will, but my hair is greasy and this top is a bit smelly.

He arrives at eight fifteen with a bottle of white wine and a bag of posh popcorn. He's clearly been paying attention... As I take the offerings, he stuffs in-ear headphones into his jeans pocket.

"Guess what Radio One was playing on the way here?" He hums a little snatch of der-dups.

"Really, I thought it had stalled?"

"What, with over two million You-tube plays already?"

"But a couple of days ago it was only a few thousand."

"See for yourself."

"Do you mind if I do? Come in." He follows me to the lounge. "Park yourself where you like." I open the You-tube app on my tablet. Only Ever You is on the first page. Will's right, 2.4 million.

"I wonder what's happened to make it pick up like that?" I glance towards Will who has taken one end of the main sofa. I'm forgetting my manners. "But not now..." I sling the tablet back onto the coffee table. "Shall I find a couple of glasses for that bottle?" Will has visited several times before but it's mostly been during the day on his way past to jobs or suppliers. He's never brought alcohol before. I wonder if he's going through a bad patch.

"How's the kitchen coming along?" I ask, as I return with a now open bottle, and pour.

"Finished and paid for a couple of weeks ago. We're on with a secret book case now."

"Is it that long since I last visited?" I try to remember exactly which day. Surely it was last week or was that when they were out?

"It has been a little while," says Will. His mouth splits into a small grin. "Jack's been missing you."

I snigger. "You tell him I'm still waiting to see him in a T-shirt..." I take a sip of wine and prepare my excuses. "I've been busy with the video and now the rehearsals for this showcase gig are almost every day. I did call a couple of times, but you were out."

"Work's been really busy for us too. You get caught up in it, don't you? And then weeks have gone past and you find you haven't actually done anything else."

I nod sympathetically. Now is the time to ask. "Is everything okay, Will? I know it's... hard, but can you bear it? Are you swimming or sinking? Sometimes it feels like my head is barely above the water."

He sucks in a deep breath and sighs it out. "It's the evenings that are worst. I miss a night in, chatting, laughing at a rubbish film, sharing nibbles, just... sharing really. That's what I miss. Don't you?"

I nod again. He does totally understand. "It's like an emptiness inside that sucks at your mind and your strength, and if you don't keep busy, then... I call it my bubble of nothing."

"I knew you'd have a poetic way of describing it." His eyes flick to the wine and popcorn and he continues diffidently, "So I thought maybe we could do that stuff, cheer each other up... If you don't mind?"

"Sounds great. Any idea what's on?"

The second film channel we try has a brat pack era comedy literally rolling the opening titles. Neither of us have seen 'Mannequin' before so we decide to give it a whirl. How bad can it be?

After fifteen minutes, Will swallows his latest handful of popcorn and states his opinion, "This is total rubbish."

"Don't mince your words," I grin.

"But... strangely compelling rubbish."

"So you want to carry on?"

"Yeah, I suppose."

"That wouldn't have anything to do with a young Kim Cattrall would it?"

"Like I said, strangely compelling."

We've moved closer so we can both reach the corn bag, which means it's easy for me to bat his shoulder with the back of my hand.

Will's right, it was never going to win any awards, but it is wonderfully silly and more than anything, heart-warming. As the final credits roll, I find myself wishing for someone to break my curse and whisk me off on his motorbike. Perhaps someone a bit less drippy than Andrew McCarthy but... I glance slowly sideways and find myself staring into eyes which seem to exude the exact gender reversed thought.

It's so sudden, out of nowhere, but as my arms slip round his neck I realise I miss 'it' too. In our initial hasty grab, the popcorn bag upends onto the floor. "Leave it," I say, disconnecting my lips for a moment. We snog like teenagers for some while, until gradually our hands begin to explore. He turns me, nibbles my neck, his fingers on my hips, stomach. A thumb rubs one nipple through my bra...

"Aaaaa, aaaaiiiiiii..." I struggle against the arm, screaming, and find my head forced into the sleeping mat. The smell of desert and stale sweat fills my nostrils. "Get off me, get off me, get off," I bellow and squirm to peer upwards... except where I'm expecting canvas there's a ceiling rose and my head is squashed into the corner of the settee and there's no Soba, only Will standing six feet away, mortified, palms raised like a Fabergé egg just shattered from his slightest touch.

"Holly, I'm sorry. I didn't... I thought... I... I don't know what I did wrong, but I'm so sorry." My head spins and I find myself sobbing violently. Somewhere up a tunnel, Will's voice says, "Shit, Holly, have I hurt you? Should I call an ambulance?" It takes all my strength to shake my head and force out the words, "No, it's him, it's... it's Soba."

"Oh hell," Will mumbles. I hear him cross the room and mutter something else before he opens the door. It's probably 'goodbye'. He's had enough of this crazy damaged frump. The howling restarts as I topple into my inner vacuum.

I'm only conscious of the outside world when an odd scent forces its way into my snot-ridden nose. Chocolate? I realise I'm still wailing and stop abruptly. A groan escapes as I wipe my eyes with my fingers and open them. I'm on the floor, back to the sofa. Right in front of my nose on the coffee table are a bowl of water, tissues, and a steaming mug of hot chocolate. Behind it, Will is cross legged on the floor, a towel draped across one shoulder. The expression of concern on his face almost restarts my waterworks.

I reach forward and gulp warm brown heaven. "William Mason you're a star – a bloody supernova!" I croak. He remains silent as I clean myself up. The water in the bowl is pleasantly warm. "Is that towel for me?" I say with closed eyes. It appears in my hand and I dry my face. Another swig of chocolate provides the strength to slide back onto the settee. It has to be now.

"Will, I need to say something. I've been meaning to for ages but it never seemed right and I wasn't totally sure who I should tell, but it needs to be you and it needs to be now." My voice quavers over the last few words and several deep breaths are required. "Will you come and sit next to me... maybe don't touch... yet, but I need you close." He crawls across to the sofa and with extreme care slides up beside me without the slightest contact. I hold his eyes and begin: "When we were in the desert you asked me if I'd been raped. I told you I hadn't and that is true... but when I said you were putting two and two together and making twenty-three, that was a lie. You were making more like four and a quarter. I was very nearly raped twice and the second time I had to kill the man to stop him."

I recount the whole story of Soba and the tent, this time leaving nothing out. Will blanches when I talk about having to delay Soba, to let him touch me so the drug would have time to work. His head shakes constantly as I describe my struggle with Nasty Face and as I finish there are tears in the corners of his eyes. "I'm sorry I didn't tell the whole truth before – you were so down on yourself when the Land Rover wouldn't start, I just didn't want to add to your burden."

He dabs at one eye and then in a voice that almost makes me jump says, "I don't ever want to hear you apologise to me. You saved my life, Holly... by being clever, by being brave, by... by being fucking magnificent."

I'm not sure it's the response that a psychologist would recommend, but right now being called 'fucking magnificent' for the first time in your life feels... well, pretty close to fucking magnificent. A little fire returns to my chest and it tingles along my limbs.

"Can I hold your hands?" Will asks. We clasp fingers together. "You do know that absolutely none of it was your fault, don't you? I was totally sure before and what you've just told me makes me even more positive."

I try to remain serious, but the tingles are rising into playfulness. "So is that a hundred and ten percent sure?"

"Just let me finish," he says, a half grin forming. He wipes it. "I can't imagine how awful it was, but you beat them. There were four armed poachers and you beat them. It may take a while, but I'm sure you can beat their memory too."

I'm itching to say 'Would that be a hundred and twenty per cent sure?' but his expression is so earnest and he's been such a star and his touch is so gentle. I make a decision... a very surprising decision. And if it's surprising to me, you should see Will's face after I reply, "I totally agree, which is why, Mr Mason, I think you should follow me upstairs." I kiss his open mouth, hard, just to be sure that there's no room for misunderstanding.

"Are you sure this is a good idea?" he says as I tug him off the sofa, lead him through the hall and upwards.

"Shouldn't I be the judge of that?" I say, although for a split second I waver as we pass the door to the master bedroom. "Don't they say you should fly again straight after a crash?"

We stand at the foot of the guest bed staring at each other by the light falling through the open door. I break the moment of awkwardness by lifting his hand and pulling it firmly to my left breast. No, I'm still not ready for that. "Ok, new rules of engagement –" I say, shaking my head and laughing, "In a weird teenage reversal, it's bottom half only, alright?" I slip down my trousers and knickers in one movement and stand before him in just my top and bra.

"Bottom half only it is then," he says and debags. Despite his earlier protest, he's clearly up for the job.

A SWEATY, AT TIMES AWKWARD, but, overall, joyous hour later we're lying half under the duvet catching breath. It's odd, a different man smell... but I'm sure I'll get used to it. I lie with my head on his chest listening to a different heart beat, powered by different breathing and try not to compare.

"What's this showcase gig you mentioned earlier?" says Will out of nowhere. "Sorry, it just popped into my head." I guess he has been pondering about lying beside slightly famous singers.

"The label want to test the water with some of my new stuff – being as it's quite a change of direction. So I'm going to do a one-off live show. It'll only be a relatively small thing for some fans and industry people... Your invitation should be arriving in the next few days."

"Really?" His face briefly assumes a kid-who's-just-been-told-about–trip-to-Disneyland expression.

"Will, you have a writing credit. You'll automatically be invited to everything. Sorry, did I not tell you?"

"What did I say about not apologising to me?" he scolds and tickles just beneath one buttock. I squirm away but he follows. "So this time, what would you really like me to do?" I gawp. Luckily it's too dark for him to see me blush. "If you don't tell me I won't know," he pesters, pecking my shoulder. I think back to all those suppressed fantasies about rough tongues and whisper in his ear.

CHAPTER 34

Was it ever that good? My resolution not to compare has gone right out the window and off into the cool morning light. I peer at the sleeping form beside me – it's not exactly snoring, but the breathing is heavy. A feeling of naughtiness keeps my face prickling on the edge of a blush – like I'm sixteen and my Dad is in the room next door trying to be a modern parent and ignore any noises he may have heard. Rationally, I know it's actually the memory of the next door room, come on, name the name, of Ben, which is making me feel like this. I remind myself that it's only natural and that sooner or later I'd have to face this – unless I'm planning on doing a Queen Victoria. But... my heart feels what it feels.

I slide out of bed and pad along the landing to the main bathroom, even though it's further than the en-suite – that would mean walking through our room. There I am again: 'our' room. Quit it. And as I sit, pee stinging as if in punishment for last night, I realise that I'll have to go in there anyway for my dressing gown. I'm not prancing round the kitchen in just a top.

Rather than actually having to enter the room, I reach round the door and lift it off the hook. Fully covered, I immediately feel less wanton.

Whilst the coffee maker is gurgling away, I clear up the popcorn from the lounge floor. My tablet bleeps for low battery – must've left it on all night. As I'm attaching a charger, it occurs to me to check the video again: now over three million views. That's more than half a million last night alone. What is going on? I must ring David, but a glance at the kitchen clock shows seven forty-two – absolutely no point doing that for a couple of hours.

Just as I'm about to put it to sleep, I notice the first comment. It's not always wise to read them – people can be too cruel – but this is odd: 'OMG I couldn't stop crying.' That isn't the reaction I'd expect. I scroll down: 'Soooo sad.' 'What a heartbreaker...' 'So different when you know who it's about.' Who do they think it's about? It isn't about anyone, it's fiction.

I swap from 'most recent' to 'top' comments and there it is with 1413 thumbs ups: 'Daisy1990 – Do U thk this is how she met her dead hubby? See this...' A shiver runs up my back as I click the link. It connects to an old interview I did after Fusion: Twenty Quick-Fires for Today's Hottest Act:

Q#14 – Where did your husband first ask you out?
A – In a cafeteria.

"Nooo," I moan out loud. "That's not what I... It wasn't..." I swap to Twitter. #hollywoodlove is getting quite a lot of attention but it's a linked one that's going absolutely ballistic: #onlyeveryouben. The tablet slips from my fingers, pulls the lead from the charger and clatters onto the tiled floor. I don't bother to check if it's broken.

The whole world thinks this is about Ben, that this is our story... and they're all loving me for it – and what am I doing? I'm cheating on him... on his memory... on... Oh, no... Oh shit... I think back to the video and me moping about at the beginning and the end as if I'm remembering something tragic. That will just confirm it...

What have I done? How did I let this thing with Will get beyond friendship? What was I thinking? I force myself to rise and traipse into the hall. I glower at the pasty face in the full-length mirror. You even look shorter today – either that or this dressing gown is longer. My eyes squint down to the embroidery on the lower pocket: 'B'. It's Ben's. Mine must be hanging on the en-suite door... His and hers bathrobes, a first anniversary present from Jill and Graham. Jill... How exactly were you going to tell Jill that her son meant so little to you that only a few months later you're doing somebody else?

I open my gown to reveal my semi-nakedness and whisper, "Hussy, whore, slut... bitch." I punish myself with all those misogynistic words men have used to abuse women over the years. It's no more than I deserve.

Will is propped up against a pillow, eyes twinkling through tousled hair, still wearing the shirt he so considerately left on so as to match with me. The smile which had started to form as I entered wipes as he registers my expression. I keep my voice steady and cold. "I'm sorry, but this was a big mistake. I'm not blaming you, I know it was me, but you have to go. Please leave now."

Will sighs, "I was worried it was all too soon."

"I'm not just talking about too soon; I'm talking about at all. I can't do this. I was having enough trouble with all the pussyfooting around our mutual attraction – pretending we're just friends... Now we've... I just can't stand the guilt."

He's silent for a few moments, then very quietly, "I feel guilty too... but Anna would want me to move on. I know she would. And you know that there would be no one she'd be happier for me to move on with..."

For some reason his calmness grates. "Well, that's all very nice for you, but I don't want to feel like a cheating whore, okay?" I virtually shout the last word.

He looks a little shocked, but again ponders his reply, "I never wanted you to feel like that. I'll go. Maybe we can talk about it some more another day?"

"You mean when I'm calmer? When I'm more rational?" I scream. "It's never going to work, okay?" I pick up his trousers from the foot of the bed and chuck them at him. "I'm going to have a shower and I expect you to be gone when I come out."

I increase the temperature until it's virtually scalding, but I can't rid myself of the dirty feeling. I'm sorry Ben... I'm really, really sorry. My tears are washed down the plughole with all the rest of the dirty water.

WILL HAS GONE, but after I emerge from a frenzy of tidying and laundry I find a nasty sting in the tail on my mobile: an hour old text, saying, 'Just got papped leavin UR house, thought U should no, soz.' Perfect, let's just scream it out to the whole world, shall we? Maybe David can do some damage limitation?

"Darling, good morning, or should I call you Queen of the Net? Have you seen?"

"Twitter and You-tube going mad?"

"...and your download figures too, sweetie."

"They all think that Der-dup is about Ben."

"Isn't it, darling?"

"You know full well it isn't. I'm not happy about it. It feels like I'm... making light of his passing."

"Mmm, more toast would be perfect..." I hear, muffled, before he answers me. I guess he didn't sleep alone either. "That's not how others are seeing it. Sweetie, I can understand why you might worry, but they're loving you for it."

"They may not be loving me for much longer. David, I think I might need some of that damage control you're always talking about."

"No, no marmalade is tickety-boo... Damage control, darling?" He sounds slightly bemused.

"Yes... You know Will?"

"Keep on moving guy?"

"Yes, well, he... err... he stayed over last night and had his photo taken leaving the house this morning."

"Holly Woodlove you dark horse." David can't keep the glee from his voice. I knew he'd react like this. I hate him... but I need him.

"David, don't. It... it was a big mistake and I don't need you gloating."

"Sweetie, pardon me..." He actually sounds stunned. "You mean you aren't going to tell me that he actually slept on the sofa or you stayed up all night recording?"

"No."

"Okay." His voice gains a more business like air. "This Will, what about him, will he tell?"

"No."

"100% sure?"

"Absolutely." We saved each other's lives – everything else is small beer.

"And he'd give permission for his name to be used in an article?"

This, I'm not sure about. "You'd have to ask him."

"Will do. Should be no problemo. Leave it to me. Press manipulation is my middle name."

It's not a completely false boast, I've seen him do some masterful work in the past... A light bulb pings in my head. "David, you wouldn't happen to know anything about Daisy1990, would you?"

He chuckles, "Impersonating young girls on the internet – that's a nasty accusation even for you. But I could kiss the darling, whoever she is..." I hear a faint female titter in the background. "Must go, sweetie. I may get back to you over a few details later, tootle-pip."

Hmm. Was that actually a denial? I wouldn't put it past him.

CHAPTER 35

The press is managed, just like David promised: 'no problemo.' Whilst the gutter editors are still bidding for the photo, an article appears on my fan site. It's an update on the new album giving tasty little titbits not previously released: 'the songs are very personal and inevitably darker than my previous material'; 'although 'Only Ever You' might be included as a bonus track it won't form part of the main album, which will open with a song called Scared'; 'another of the songs is co-written by Will Mason whose partner was also lost in the African tragedy.' The article goes on to reveal a few insights into the recording process:

Although the final track is laid down in a top London studio, Holly prefers to do much of the demo work in her purpose-built home studio, either alone or with collaborators. 'Once I'm in the zone, we just keep on working until the rough cut of the song is finished. If it turns into an all-nighter, I keep myself going with coffee, popcorn and the occasional spritzer.'

No actual lies; no need for a statement; just enough information to imply a plausible alternative. With all the fuss about 'Der-dup', it's linked all over the Net in minutes – especially as it finishes with news of a special gig to be announced the following day. When the photo does appear, it's buried in the middle pages under the much diluted title 'Grievers reunited in all-nighter'. There's a little innuendo, but they also mention the co-written song, and, anyway, it's totally eclipsed by the chatter surrounding the promised preview show.

Having seen Der-dup take off, Rory appears to have jumped on board big time and rather than an intimate gig at some discrete venue, they now reckon I can fill the Apollo. They're opening up ticket sales to fans and giving away the first fifty across a number of radio stations. No pressure...

I spend most of my days practising – with the backing band and on my own. Otherwise I'm at the studio polishing the tracks already laid down. In the evenings, I'm trying to finish the last song. Actually that's rubbish. Trying to start the last song would be more accurate. It's called, 'I am who I am' and it's an uplifting track about making it on your own... Except it just won't come – no melody, no words that don't sound trite, no whoosh, nothing. I've tried forcing scenes into my head, but every time the internal cinema starts to roll, it transforms into a version of the same daymare:

I'm dawdling through Victoria Gardens on the Embankment – it's one of those still, warm, late autumn days that are wistful reminders of the summer passed. As I approach the cafe I notice a couple seated at one of the outside tables. They're laughing and as the man turns his head, I see that it's Will. I duck behind a tree and peer diffidently round the trunk. Beside half-eaten cake, their fingers are intertwined...

I'm struggling along the pavement of a crowded Oxford Street wishing I'd not left it so late. Highly unlikely snowflakes are falling, swirling in the wakes of black cabs. I pass a boutique – far too trendy for me. Between the near skeletal mannequins of the window display I spot a young woman lifting a halter neck dress from a rack, holding it in front of herself and posing for her companion with suggestive eyes. As I move, the angle changes and I see the companion is Will...

It's always the same young woman – the actress from the 'Der-dup' video, the younger me, with her dreamy smile and plastic tits.

Fruitless evenings drag into nights whiled away staring at my laptop rather than actually composing, sipping the occasional whisky to drown the daymares and the silent taunts of 'killer' and 'whore'. I can't remember the last time I slept through – well, I can, but I don't want to think about that night...

The only person outside the business that I'm seeing regularly is Jill – every week, always Thursday lunchtime. It's sacrosanct – even if you have the biggest gig of your life the following day.

"HOLLY, WHAT'S CHANGED?" Jill whispers as she leans forward in her navy trouser suit and takes a sip of tea. All round us are the low voices of others similarly intimidated by the rarefied atmosphere of the Ritz's Palm Court. I prod at my scone with the cream spoon and wonder how to answer. She continues, "I'm worried about you. I know professionally it's going well... but you don't seem the same as you did a month ago. I thought coming here might cheer you up... but I see it's made no difference."

I bite into the scone. Of course, it's delicious, but all I can think is: a month ago... how can I possibly tell her? I blink several times but fail to hold everything back and a single tear leaks down my left cheek. I dab at it with the corner of a stiff cream serviette. "I'm okay. I'm just busy and stressed about tomorrow. You know it's going to be live on Radio 1 now?"

"Really? That's great. Graham and I will listen."

"You don't have to. I know it's not really your type of music."

"Rubbish. We'd listen to... to Megadeth if you were in it." I'm moderately impressed that she's heard of Megadeth even if they are ancient. An immaculately dressed waiter appears; asks if everything is to our satisfaction. When he's retreated having received two affirmatives, Jill whispers, "Can you imagine complaining here?"

I shake my head, taking in the chandeliers, ornate ceiling and gold leaf fountain. "I'm sorry," I say, "this cake is just not quite as perfect as I was expecting." We manage tiny smiles.

Jill's smile continues. As she speaks, I realise it's to soften her words. "Nice try, but I don't believe you. I may be your fuddy-duddy old mother-in-law, but I'm still a woman... and I listen. And I'll tell you what I haven't heard for the last month. You were always very careful with it... very sensitive, but it was always there and now it isn't – the name: Will." She holds up one hand to stay my protest. "Just let me tell you a story – before you say anything." She takes a preparatory sip of tea. One of my legs starts to quiver. She knows... How does she know? "My mother's mother died in childbirth. They managed to save my aunt but not Grandma Jane. She was only twenty-two. Her husband, my Grandfather Donald, was, by all accounts, devastated. As was the way in those days, he hadn't much clue about cooking or housework and with a baby and toddler things were pretty desperate for a few weeks. Then in steps Margaret..."

"Ben's Granny Margaret?"

"Great grandmother actually, but, yes, she was a school friend of Jane's and she more or less just took over – they were married within a year. There was a lot of fuss and raised eyebrows for a while but it blew over soon enough."

"I didn't realise she wasn't Ben's... I mean your, real Gran."

"No one does... and she is my 'real' Gran in everything but DNA, even if she barely remembers it these days." She pauses, regarding me as if to fathom whether what she's saying has registered. It's beginning to, but before I can vocalise it she continues, "I asked my mother about it once. She said she was too young to remember, but she'd seen similar things and her opinion was that some people just can't stand to be alone – not for any time at all... and that's not a bad thing, it's just how they are." She reaches across the table and takes my hand. "Are you like that Holly? Because... that's alright." She squeezes my hand and fixes me with a concerned smile.

I expect myself to cry, but I don't. Instead, it feels as if part of me that had vanished into my bubble of nothing reappears like a loose connection being remade. Not a big part, but something significant nonetheless... like a kidney or a lung. I struggle for words, but eventually they come. "Maybe... I don't know... It's not quite the same... but..." I halt and go right back to the start, "In the desert, Will and I, we shared all the same fears together, we got lost together, we nearly died together and we saved each other's lives – literally. We've seen each other at rock bottom. It's like a bond – it's like family. And since the funerals we've seen each other quite often and a month ago we... we got a bit too close and I felt so guilty and pushed him away. I haven't seen him since." I pull my hand out from under Jill's and suck in a deep breath. "And if I'm totally honest, I feel like I've lost Ben and now I've lost the only person who really understands how I feel." There are tears in the corners of Jill's eyes. "I thought you'd feel betrayed."

She shakes her head with her eyes squeezed closed. When she opens them she keeps her head lowered but fixes me with plaintive eyes, "Holly, you're all we have left. We want you to be happy."

"Oh Jill, I'm such an idiot."

"Aren't we all when it comes to love... aren't we all..."

CHAPTER 36

"..like nuclear fusion..."

A final mad hammer on all the instruments simultaneously makes for a decent alternative to the explosion sound effect. Applause and cheers echo round the auditorium. Away at the sound desk I can see confusion. I'm early. I know. All the lights facing outwards from the stage come up revealing my crowd. I swing the guitar up my back and lift the mic from its stand. "Thanks very much. Thank you. Please can you give a big shout out for my super talented band. They bow to more applause, and I receive thumbs ups and a wink from my only accomplices as they move to the back of the stage.

"Umm. That was meant to be the last one, but I'm going to go off script." I glance to the wings where David is frantically waving a finger across his throat. "My wonderful manager is doing his nut over there but for once I'm going to ignore him. I think we still have a few minutes?" Cheers and a couple of shouts of 'go for it Holly'. "Would you like to hear a song I only wrote yesterday?" Louder cheers and yeses. "There've been a lot of things in the press. A lot of things about the death of my husband and what I've done since." The crowd quietens. "I've done a whole load of worrying about moving on – too much worrying – and I've pushed away the one person who's helped me through all of it. So, if you're listening, I'm really sorry and this one's for you." I re-fix the mic, force calmness along each arm and hope...

More than anyone

Sometimes, my words, I wish I could take back again.
Seems like I've been a complete utter pratt again.
Cos I told you I thought that we'd never work.
You were total calmness while I went berserk.

But you get me more than anyone,
and I trust you more than anyone.

Growing regrets make me ponder the where and when.
Tears in my eyes, take deep breaths, counting up to ten.
Cos I know that I've made a massive mistake
and how many more can you take?

Cos you get me more than anyone,
and I trust you more than anyone.
You lift me more than anyone,
and I value you more than anyone.

And I know that's rarer than pixie dust:
one twist too many and end up bust.
And now I can see that this mess is all me.
Such a numpty, is this all too late?

Staying up late at nights, setting the world to rights,
felt so natural.
My head on your shoulder, your arm round my waist
like we're tailored to fit.
Only you and I know what we've come through.
Only him upstairs knows the end.

Cos you get me more than anyone,
and I trust you more than anyone.
You lift me more than anyone,
I love you more than anyone...

I whisper the last line into a collectively held breath. As the final note fades, the murmurs of assent begin to grow, but above them a loud male voice shouts, "I love you, Holly." Almost as one, the crowd crane their necks. A gap near the front opens to spit out a medium-height, medium-build man who stares up at me rather sheepishly. I cover a gulp of disappointment with a broad smile. "I love you too, chuck... but I'm afraid you're not the one I was meaning..." There's a slightly awkward pause as the audience realises they've been robbed of their Rom Com ending. Just as I wonder if David is always right, two voices shout from the front row, "We all love you Holly." It's like a chain reaction: shouts of love and support bounce around the auditorium building with applause into the loudest ovation of the night. It gradually resolves into a chant of 'Holly, Holly, Holly, Holly...' I acknowledge the crowd with a two-armed wave, and shout into the mic, "I love you all, bye for now..."

At the side of the stage David has his arms wide, palms up, and eyebrows raised in what might be described as surprised respect. "That," I shout, above the continuing ovation, "is the final song." He nods and gives me the double thumbs up.

As I walk along bare narrow corridors, a small disappointed thought surfaces: he wasn't here. I shake it from my head. No, I told him to stay away. I straighten my back – you broke this, you need to fix it. Before I reach my dressing room door I'm determined that even if the building catches fire, I won't wait to make that call.

He's beaten me to it... With shaking hands I swipe the screen and read: 'Heard U on R1. I can take as many as U can make. Not 2 L8. I do 2. Call me when U R ready. W'

For the second time in two days my bubble of nothing relinquishes another organ. This time it's my heart.

The End

EXTRAS!

Visit: http://peterwindridgesmith.net for suggested reading group discussion questions, a Namibian tour and much more. If you enjoyed *Some Slack*, please recommend it to your friends, write an on-line review, tweet about it, or like it on my Facebook page.

ENOUGH ROPE

Curious to know what happened to Steven Carter in Finland? Find out in *Some Slack*'s 'twin' novel *Enough Rope* –

He's 1000 miles from home... He says it was only in his head... Can you believe him?

Engineer and songwriter Steven Carter is being assessed by psychologist Dr. Hiltunen, but why? As he recounts his journey through the temptations of Finnish nightlife, it becomes clear that this is not just a simple case of infidelity and regret. Who has caused Steven's downward spiral and how will it affect his marriage and his future?

Steven pours his conflicting feelings into words and music. Share the emotion by listening to his demo versions (available free on-line) as you read his lyrics on the page.

"*A blend of Nordic mystery, confession & music seen from the unusual perspective of a visitor to the region.*"

"Enough Rope *gently draws you in to its world of icy weather, welcoming bars, and misplaced attraction... and then hits you.*"

THE SINGER – TINA J

Holly's vocals were interpreted by Dorset based singer Tina J. She can be contacted on tinajthesinger@gmail.com.

Tina J also assists musicians, singers and artists with eliminating performance anxiety as well as increasing confidence and reaching new levels of success.

For more information visit www.freefromyourfears.com
or contact her via fb.me/freefromyourfears

Printed in Great Britain
by Amazon

73369087R00182